ROSE'S PLEDGE

DAUGHTERS OF HARDWOOD HOUSE
Book One

SALLY LAITY AND DIANNA CRAWFORD

BARBOUR
PUBLISHING

Acknowledgments

The authors gratefully acknowledge
the generous assistance provided by:

Abigail Andrews
Washington County Free Library
Hagerstown, Maryland

Sandy Weston
Grafton Library
Grafton, West Virginia

These individuals helped us gather necessary period data
and shared their extensive knowledge of various settings
used in this story. To you we express our sincere appreciation.

Special thanks to fellow writers and friends:

Delia Latham
Sue Rich

Your tireless critiquing of our work in progress,
together with suggestions and comments along the way,
were an immense help. May the Lord bless you both.

Dedication

This book is lovingly dedicated to our Lord and Savior, Jesus Christ,
who blessed this magnificent nation from its founding, and to our
families, whose love and support makes our writing possible.

Chapter 1

Bath, England, 1753

The *rat-tat-tat* of the brass door knocker echoed eerily through the spacious house.

Kneeling on the kitchen's stone floor, Rose Harwood started. *Oh no. Please, not now.* She dropped the scrub brush into the bucket and scrambled to her feet, wiping her hands on her long work apron. The pungent odor of lye soap clung stubbornly to them, but she could do nothing about that at the moment. Perhaps the caller would not notice the smell—or worse, her red hands. Never before had she undertaken such menial labor.

Even as she tore off the soiled apron, her frantic gaze searched worktables and shelves until it landed on the spice chest. Mexican vanilla beans could mask the scent. But no. . .she could not justify the ruination of something so costly to replace.

Especially now.

The knocker rapped several more times. Louder. More insistent.

"Do calm yourself, Rose." Clasping her hands together, she hiked her chin with new resolve. "I simply shan't go to the door."

But that wouldn't do either. Under normal circumstances, if none of the Harwood family happened to be in residence, the hired girl would answer a summons. But circumstances were no longer normal. Several weeks past, Rose had been forced to let Hildy go. Word must not get out, lest people begin to suspect.

Expense be hanged. She lifted the spice chest from a niche beside the hearth oven and opened it, releasing myriad exotic fragrances into the air. Without so much as a second to savor the sweet perfumes, she snatched the small pouch of vanilla beans, shook two brown stalks out, and rubbed them vigorously over her hands.

A third, more demanding, tapping resounded through the rooms.

Was this to be the day of the family's undoing? Inhaling a troubled breath, Rose hurried to the front door and opened it. "Constable Bradley." She swallowed her angst and bobbed a curtsy. "Good morning to you, sir."

"Good day to you, Miss Harwood. I trust you are in good health." He touched his hat in a polite gesture. "Is your father at home?"

Rose had never noticed how huge the local official was. In his great winter coat, he quite filled the entry. She shook off the wayward thought. "I am most sorry, sir, he is not. May I be of service?"

"'Tis gentlemen's business, miss." Clutching the edge of the warm fur hat he'd removed, the aging man turned to leave. "I'll fetch him down at his shop."

Fetch him? The constable had come to place Papa under arrest! Her worst fears realized, Rose caught hold of the man's arm. "My father keeps no secrets from me. Pray, do come inside. I'm sure there must be another answer."

His bushy eyebrows dipped as he frowned down at her. "Forgive me, miss. I have me duty."

"Please, sir. I ask but five minutes."

He hesitated then exhaled in a huff. "Very well. But not one minute more."

As she stepped aside for him to enter, she glanced up and down the lane. No one seemed to be about, but that didn't mean that some snoopy neighbor wasn't peeping out from behind lace curtains. Bath most certainly had its share of busybodies.

She closed the door and turned to the official, who dwarfed the small, tastefully furnished parlor. "Do warm yourself at the fire."

Moving to the marble hearth, the constable thrust forth his beefy hands toward the comforting glow. But despite his seeming compliance in giving ear to her request, the expression on his heavily jowled face remained dour.

Rose attempted a bit of light conversation, desperate to establish some measure of rapport. "I shall be exceedingly heartened when April brings a bit of spring weather, will you not?"

It was wasted effort, as her visitor did not deign to reply. Instead, he shot her a worried look. "Be assured, Miss Harwood, 'tis all legal and final. I've the papers right here in me pocket." He patted his coat. "I'm duty bound to take your father into custody."

"But if you please, sir, Papa is seeking a loan even as we speak. Tomorrow or the next day he's certain to have the money. See if he won't."

The constable shook his head. "Forgive me, miss, but Merchant Solomon, of Bristol, will wait no longer. I've been ordered to collect either the money owed by Henry Harwood or the man himself this day. So I'd best get meself down to his shop."

Rose twisted her hands together and bit down hard on her lip. She could not let such a thing happen. Not to Papa. Especially since none of this was his fault.

She stepped in front of the constable, blocking his path. "You said you were told to arrest him today. Yet the day has scarcely begun. I beg you, please give me until the last hour. I pledge most sincerely that I shall satisfy Papa's account with Supplier Solomon before the sun sets."

The officer absently brushed back strands of his graying hair and plunked his beaver hat atop his head once again.

Rose sensed the man was contemplating her proposal and therefore pressed her advantage. "Constable Bradley, you've known me my whole life. You know I am a responsible person. I've run this household since I was a mere thirteen years of age, taking care of my brothers and sisters, never once straying from my obligations. If I say I will do this, you can be most assured that I will."

His expression softened. "Ye've been a blessing to your pa, that's certain. A comely lass such as yourself, sacrificing your courting years to help your family. Nevertheless, if your father is unable—"

"I vow I shall see to the matter. I mean this most sincerely." She met his gaze squarely, despite the fact he'd as much as called her a spinster. She had to remain strong. Do what Papa could not bring himself to do.

The constable sighed. "Very well, Miss Harwood. Ye have 'til nightfall. Not a moment more."

Vastly relieved, Rose ushered the official out then returned to take mental inventory of the room. Each familiar article of furniture, every table decoration, and even the exquisite carpets had been carefully, lovingly, selected by her mother. The family had basked in its beauty over the years. But alas, sentiment no longer had a place here. All must be sold. Now. Today. But where? Market day wasn't until Friday.

In a rise of panic, she pressed her hands to her temples. "Where? Where?"

The Bristol docks.

"Of course!" Several ships were certain to be in port, with captains looking for quality merchandise to take abroad and sell for profit. Since she must journey there to deal with Mr. Solomon anyway. . .

She plucked a Chinese jade figurine from the mantel. So much to pack and load. So little time. La, why had Mariah and Lily chosen this day of all days to go visiting? She needed their assistance desperately. With no time to waste, she'd simply have to go and fetch them.

But reality stopped her in her tracks. Mariah was on a mission of her own, to gain a wedding proposal from Lawrence Wirkworth before their family's calamitous reversal of fortune became common knowledge. Rose shook her head. How typical of Mariah to think only of herself.

In truth, however, Rose had to concede it was essential for her sister to find swift success. Once the family's finest goods were loaded onto the cart and hauled out of town, all of Bath would see *and know* that something was amiss at Harwood House.

"May God help us all."

~

Chilled to the bone and exhausted from a day of dickering and bartering, Rose trudged up to the front entrance in the last faint light of eventide. The thirteen-mile distance from Bristol had seemed more like a hundred on the rutted, ice-crusted roads, despite the fact that, partway, a kind passerby had provided a ride in his wagon. The elements had been the ruination of her best shoes, and several spots on her feet burned as if a hot poker had tormented her heels and toes. But her return to Bath before nightfall had been imperative.

Thank Providence, the wax-sealed envelope from Mr. Solomon now lay in the hands of the constable. She'd obtained a reprieve for Papa. Gotten him another month to pay the remainder of his debt.

With a weary sigh, she reached for the door latch. The threat of this day had been conquered, albeit at great cost. Far greater than she would ever have foreseen.

She swallowed her trepidation and pushed the door open.

A cluster of relatives—her entire family—turned to face her, their grim faces snatching from her mind the fine speech she'd concocted along the way. Papa stood beside Mariah, a comforting arm about her, both looking as if they'd just returned from a funeral. In sweet contrast, her youngest sister, Lily, greeted Rose with a gentle smile. Next to Lily stood Tommy, the baby of the family. Only a scant spark of his usual mischief glowed in the twelve-year-old's eyes.

Even Charles, their married brother, was present. By this hour of the evening, he should have been in his own home with his wife and children. In the erratic light of an untrimmed lamp wick, his lean face seemed much older. Much harder.

Mariah broke from the group. "Just where, might I ask, have you been?" Anger contorted the family beauty's delicate features into an ugly accusation as she rushed toward Rose. Her deep blue eyes flashed fire, and her mass of black ringlets bobbed in disarray. "Look about you, Rose. We have been robbed. Our family home has been ransacked. Everything of value is gone—even the money Papa set aside for my dowry." She paused, and her expression became accusing. "Tell me this is not your doing. If it is, I demand you explain yourself." She planted a hand on either hip, her lips pressed into a grim line.

Rose had hoped for a moment or two to rest before facing her loved ones, but it was not to be. Somehow she would have to relate the sordid details of this trying day.

Henry Harwood, the kindest of fathers, now loomed before her, more agitated than she'd ever seen him. He grasped her by the shoulders. "I must ask what you know of this, daughter. Speak up. Tell us all."

Rose felt the bite of his fingers through the thickness of her woolen cloak. She lifted her gaze to the beloved face that had aged noticeably in the past few weeks since the financial trouble erupted—when the flamboyant Sir Gordon Ridgeway had met an untimely death in a duel mere days after taking possession of fifty signature brooches he was in the habit of passing out to his lady friends. The gentleman had begged off paying for the jewelry, promising to return in a fortnight with the money. Papa could not have refused the young bachelor, his best customer. But now Sir Ridgeway's uncle refused to honor the debt, refused even to acknowledge a debt existed, leaving her father, the finest goldsmith between Oxford and Bristol, in ruin.

Surely he would understand her actions of this day and forgive her desperate deeds. She fervently prayed it would be so. Hadn't she proved how much she cared for her family these past twelve years since her mother's death on the childbed? She'd taken charge of newborn babe Tommy, as well as the other children, run a well-ordered household. Putting the needs of her dear ones first, she'd unselfishly set aside even her own chances to wed.

Of course her father would understand. He knew her heart as she did his. She reached past the folds of her cloak to smooth a crease alongside his tight mouth. "I've aided the family in the one way I knew you could never bring yourself to do, Papa."

She looked past him to Charles, who bore a strong resemblance to their lank-boned father, down to an identical trim mustache. "I know you'll all see the wisdom in what I've done. I'll tell you everything. But first—" Rose shifted her attention to her youngest sister, who had yet to venture forward. "Lily, dearest, would you mind fetching me a cup of tea? I've had a most tiresome day."

The growing worry in Lily's dove-gray eyes melted away, replaced by a simple trusting goodness that never ceased to lift Rose's spirits. "I shan't be a minute," she said in her airy voice. "The kettle is already heating."

As the girl hastened out of the parlor, Rose noticed how tall the lass had grown this past year. The child had become a maiden last month, on her fourteenth birthday. She was now old enough, Rose fervently hoped, to do without her big sister. Older than she herself had been when their mother passed from this life.

"Rose." Her father pulled her attention back to him. "I must ask you to explain yourself. I came home from the shop to find the house stripped of everything we hold dear, and your sister Mariah in high dudgeon."

"Aye." Tommy nodded. "You'd have thought she was musket shot the way she wailed and clutched herself." With an exaggerated moan, the twelve-year-old grabbed at his shirtfront and staggered toward the nearest wing chair, where he collapsed into its confines. The merry scamp could always be counted upon to lighten the gloomiest of moments.

Despite herself, Rose's lips curled into a smile as she moved across the room and gratefully took a seat in the companion silk brocade chair. The larger pieces remained in the room only because the pony cart had been too full to fit any more items.

Obviously Mariah had derived no humor from their younger brother's imitation of her. She shot him a scathing glower before lighting on the settee and eyeing Rose with naked malice. "If you intended to rob me of my dowry, I must know why you waited until Lily and I had gone to the Wirkworths'. I wasted hours smiling and cooing over their horse-faced heir. Had you an ounce of common discretion, you should have allowed me this one last chance to make a successful match before people learned of Papa's huge debt. And I had Master Lawrence so close to pledging himself to me. So close," she grated through clamped teeth. Angrily she tossed her head, sending her midnight curls to bouncing like so many coiled springs. "I shan't be surprised were he to come here this very eve to ask Father for my hand. Can you imagine anything more dreadful? One look at this room bereft of so many fine furnishings and he'll surely draw the most shocking conclusions. That is, if one of our neighbors doesn't enlighten him first. Soon enough everyone will be aware of the shame that has befallen this family. We shall never be able to hold our heads up again."

Rose got up and stepped toward her sister with an outstretched hand. "Please, Mariah, you must trust that the Lord will see us through this valley of misfortune. Today I had no choice but to act immediately and choose the only open path to reverse our tragic circumstances. Surely you will all come to understand it was the prudent one."

"Daughter." From her father's tone and unyielding expression, Rose realized he had reached the end of his patience.

"Why don't we be seated?" She pulled loose her cloak ties and carefully lifted the hood from her head, tucking a loose strand of amber-colored hair into the heavy coil resting low at the base of her neck. "I'm afraid this day's sad happenings touch us all."

As her father and Charles settled in the hard-backed armchairs flanking the settee, Rose's gaze roved the room. This once cozy parlor of their neat quarried stone house now appeared stark and spartan, devoid of most of the lovely furnishings that had made it home. It was as if she saw it for the first time.

None of them had the slightest suspicion it would be her last.

But no tender memories would she take from this bare skeleton of a room, no comfort. Mariah had voiced the truth when Rose first stepped inside. Their home had indeed been robbed—of all its grace and charm.

Every wall hanging and crystal lamp, every porcelain piece, stitched tapestry, and doily had been stripped from the parlor. Even the prized Chippendale table. Rose had managed to find room in the pony cart for that one last elegant piece. And should Papa but open the music cabinet, he would discover the absence of Mariah's violin, Lily's flute, and her own mandolin. The windows stood bereft of their fine Belgian lace curtains; only the heavy velvet drapes remained for privacy's sake.

The room looked as utterly cold and dreary as her journey home had been.

Charles's voice interrupted her brief reverie, sounding every bit as overwrought as their father's. "You should be aware, sister, that we arrived here just in time to prevent Mariah from going after the constable."

A tremor coursed through Rose. She clasped her hands to steady them as she turned to her father. "'Twould not have been his first visit here this day."

Paling frightfully, Papa sat up rod straight and clutched his knees.

Rose's brothers and Mariah also stiffened as if frozen in place. Only their eyes moved as they looked from one to the other. They had not realized how desperate their situation truly was.

Lily returned at that moment, carrying a tea tray with cups for all. Her guileless expression gave no import to the everyday crockery used in place of the fancy china now missing from the kitchen. "I thought we all might enjoy tea." She placed the tray on the low table in front of the settee and began to pour from the pot.

Rose appreciated the few moments' reprieve while Lily served everyone. But before she managed even a second sip of the comforting brew, her father interrupted. "Rose. We've waited quite long enough. Enlighten us now, daughter."

Slowly, deliberately, Rose set her cup and saucer on the table beside her, placing the spoon just so along the side in vain effort to delay the telling. After inhaling deeply, she began. "'Tis most fortuitous that our house sits on the line between the jail and your shop, Papa. Constable Bradley stopped here first, on the chance you were still at home."

As she related their exchange and explained her promise to the official, Tommy broke in, wariness ringing in the boyish pitch of his voice. "I did not see the pony cart in its normal place. Where is it?"

"I'm most sorry to say I had to sell it, Tommy."

"Surely not!" He sprang to his feet, his fists knotted. "But Corky! Surely you did not sell Corky along with it!"

"Sit!" Papa commanded with uncharacteristic harshness.

Rose's chest tightened with pity for her father. This terrible trouble should not have befallen such a kind, gentle man, much less her baby brother. The pony had been the lad's pet, his bonny companion. She attempted a sympathetic smile.

"Not Corky." Tommy crumpled into his seat, his chin quivering.

Charles cleared his throat, looking as if his passion hovered on the verge of erupting. "Continue, Rose."

"As your eyes can attest, I loaded everything I could carry and drove down to the Bristol docks, hoping to sell it. This could not wait for market day."

"Or for Father's approval, I daresay." Charles's accusatory tone effectively placed the blame squarely on Rose's shoulders.

She ignored his comment. "Nonetheless, I was able to make more of a profit than I had even hoped. As Providence would have it, three ships were in port. They were loading cargo for the American colonies, and you know how eager the colonists are for some of our more civilized articles. Oh and Mariah, I'm very sorry to confess I also had to sell our few pieces of jewelry and our most fashionable gowns."

Her sister gasped so violently, Rose surmised that had a crystal lamp remained in the room, its dangling pendants would have been set to tinkling.

Notching her chin a touch higher, she continued. "Some healthy competition started between the captains, and by the time all the bartering and dealing ended, I walked away with forty-three pounds sterling, two shillings, and a sixpence for our possessions."

Papa let out a weary breath. "I say, my dear. You did exceedingly well to obtain such a goodly sum. However, I must avow 'tis barely a third of what I owe the gold supplier."

"So Mr. Solomon informed me. He refused to accept any less on account than seventy pounds. So Mariah's dowry of twenty pounds had to be sacrificed as well. He left me no other choice."

A low, mournful whimper issued from her sister.

Perhaps Mariah was at last beginning to comprehend the necessity, Rose decided as she tore her gaze from her middle sister and rested it on young Tom. "You do understand we couldn't allow the constable to take Papa to debtors' prison. Such a horrid fate would be punishment far beyond what should be imposed upon him." She then turned to Charles, whose stone-hard expression had yet to yield to the gravity of the situation. "Brother, even on the chance that you possessed enough of Papa's skills to fashion most of the pieces on order, no supplier would give you credit for gold bullion or for cut gems once they learned of Papa's imprisonment. And you know the only way to get someone out of that unspeakable place would be to pay off all creditors in full. No more bargaining, no more promises. We would be out on the street, forced to sell the very roof over our heads."

Charles turned to Papa. "See what comes of your relying so much on Rose." He wheeled back to her, his jaw set tighter than before. "Had you come to us before running off in typical female panic, we would have told you Father was in the midst of arranging a mortgage."

Papa raised a hand, effectively silencing any further outburst. "Son, I had hoped to spare you, now that you've your own family to be concerned about. I did obtain a loan, that much is true. But not nearly as much as I requested. And since the gem cutter was pressing harder at the moment, I had to use the funds to pay him."

Rose hurried to further her own defense. "So you see, there was no recourse left to me but to sell even the pony and cart, as well as. . .as. . ."

Every eye focused on her, waiting.

She took firm hold of the chair arms for support and met her father's stare as the remainder of the news poured from her lips like water over a precipice. "I suppose there is no easy way to tell you this, Papa. After I sold the cart and pony, I still lacked four pounds. And Mr. Solomon was not to be bargained with. He'd accept no less on account than the agreed upon sum. The constable was waiting. The afternoon was dwindling away. So I—" She swallowed. When she spoke again, she could barely manage a whisper. "I. . .sold myself."

Chapter 2

It took the huge vessel *Seaford Lady* six interminable weeks and four days to carve a passage through the vast, dark waters of the cold Atlantic Ocean. Rose doubted she would ever forget them. But once she'd recovered from the seasickness that laid her low for the first week, she found the voyage somewhat more enjoyable as she watched the crew dealing efficiently with monstrous sails, changing winds, and strong sea currents. Yesterday's first glimpse of land had thrilled her, and on this last night aboard ship, she wished she had more time to prepare herself for what lay ahead. . .four years of servitude as an indentured servant.

At least the crossing had been without mishap. Surely that was a good sign. She had to trust that this voyage to the American colonies was God's will, not merely her own rash choice. She could hardly bear to look back on the pain and sorrow in her father's eyes when he bade her a last farewell. Even now she blinked away stinging tears and suppressed the lingering doubts that had plagued her during the entire trip.

The fragile promise of dawn began to show through the porthole of the overcrowded ship's cabin. In the faint light, Rose slipped from the bottom bunk and onto the narrow wooden floor between two sets of cots stacked three high. The thought of a few moments of solitude on deck, breathing air she did not have to share with five other travelers, left her almost giddy. She plucked her cloak from the foot of her narrow bed and snugged it around her, then pulled on her slippers and tiptoed out the door, careful to close it without waking her cabinmates.

She padded along the lantern-lit passageway then out onto the wide deck of the three-masted merchant ship. A chilly breeze billowed the huge sails, which swelled and flapped, their gentle motion causing little stress to the scores of ropes and spars. The vessel plowed slowly north into the deepest reaches of Chesapeake Bay, heading toward the tobacco port of Baltimore.

When the *Seaford Lady* first entered the bay yesterday, one of the seamen had informed Rose that the inlet cut between the mainland and a peninsula for a good two hundred miles. He certainly had not lied, because after these many hours, the ship had yet to reach its destination.

She stepped to the starboard railing to view the coming dawn. A pale pink glow illuminated the treetops along the ragged eastern shoreline. So close she could almost smell the scent of pine. The cool air that brushed past her cheeks felt surprisingly pleasant for the first week of May, reminding her that the ship sailed the same latitudes as southern Spain.

Spying a dot of light onshore, Rose felt her pulse quicken. Not so far away, some woman had likely risen in the quiet hush to begin another day. No doubt she was in the kitchen stirring banked embers at the back of the hearth, bringing the morning's cook fire to life. By tomorrow, Rose might very well be tending just such a hearth, if the captain had spoken truthfully. According to him, colonials always came to the dock whenever his vessel arrived to bid for the bondservants he'd contracted.

"Good morn to ye, Miss Harwood." A lone sailor made his way from the bow. He sidestepped some lashed-down barrels, a jovial grin revealing a gap in his front teeth.

"Good morning, Seaman Polk." Rose quickly tucked her long night braid inside her hood. Remembering her state of undress, she scrunched in her toes in her bed slippers beneath the dark folds of her cloak's hem. He would think her most common indeed, with barely covered feet.

"We should make port in an hour or so." He paused beside her. "Ye might be wantin' to tell the other womenfolk to start gatherin' their belongings together. Soon as the cap'n reports to the harbor master, he'll be wantin' to. . .to see you folks on yer way."

Rose knew the seaman wanted to spare her feelings by avoiding the plain truth: that Captain Durning would soon be auctioning off the lot of them to the highest bidder as if they were nothing but cattle or sheep. She managed a smile. "We packed our things last eve, but I suppose I should awaken them soon. They'll all want to look their best."

The sailor's sunburned face brightened. "That won't be no work a'tall for you and your sisters, Miss Harwood. 'Specially Miss Mariah."

"That's most kind of you to say," Rose assured him, though the words came hard as she turned back to the railing. She had argued bitterly against Mariah and Lily accompanying her to this new land. But indeed, their contention had been as sound as her own when she had bargained away the family assets. Mariah insisted that if she and Lily left with Rose, Charles would be able to move his young family to Harwood House, thereby eliminating the need for Papa's business to support two homes. Contemplating their logical, if somewhat disheartening reasoning, their father finally relented.

Rose smiled to herself as she recalled Lily's personal reason for coming along. The girl could not suffer the thought of her older sister going to the colonies all alone. After all, Rose had mothered her from her earliest memories.

Mariah, on the other hand, had a far more practical purpose. She had heard that the lines between the classes were less distinct in America and more crossable. She felt she might do quite well for herself amongst what was rumored to be a rather *provincial* people. Despite her own impoverished circumstance, she truly believed her beauty and charm alone to be a more than sufficient dowry. She'd spoken of little else from the moment the three had set sail.

No doubt about it, Mariah would have to be closely watched.

"Rose! Mariah!" Lily rushed through the cabin doorway, her cheeks positively glowing. "Captain Durning says it's time for us to go ashore. I daresay, I cannot abide such excitement."

"Nevertheless," Rose said quietly to calm the younger girl, "he advised us to remain here until his business with our cabinmates and the German family from the adjoining quarters has been concluded." She recalled with distaste the conspiratorial wink he had given Mariah as he related his reputation for "saving the best for last." Rose would have much preferred being present during the earlier transactions for some idea of what she and her sisters might expect, but the man had been most insistent.

Now that the moment to disembark had arrived, her insides quivered uncontrollably. Her one slim comfort was the promise she had extracted from Captain Durning to sell the three of them together.

She glanced around the cabin, noticing how much less crowded it appeared once their luggage had been taken ashore. "Search under the cots, Lily. We shouldn't want to leave anything behind."

Mariah, already in the doorway, swung back. "For pity's sake, Rose. Don't be such a mother hen. We've checked the room from floor to ceiling, and as you can see, not a lock of our hair is out of place, nor has a single wrinkle dared crease our skirts." She whirled out into the corridor with Lily chasing after her.

Compelled to make her own final inspection of the cramped quarters, Rose could only agree. Both her sisters were impeccably groomed. Mariah was stunning in her royal blue taffeta, shawled in white lace—a combination which enhanced the deep indigo of her eyes and her shining black hair. Her wide-brimmed bonnet sat at a tilt as blithe as the girl herself. The blue satin ties and white under-frills would help contain her bountiful curls.

Lily's finely woven wool in muted pink accented her more delicate features and light gray eyes. Her hair had yet to darken from flaxen to golden brown as Rose's had by the time she'd reached her fourteenth year. Mayhap Lily's would remain blond, since her eyes were several shades lighter than Rose's blue gray, and her complexion so fair it burned and freckled in the slightest sunshine. The two of them favored the taller, slender Harwood side, unlike Mariah, who had their mother's more rounded figure.

Rose sighed. What would Mother have thought of her daughters' present circumstances? She'd had such high expectations, such fine hopes for all her children. Her last words had concerned them as she'd extracted a vow from Papa to see the girls safely through the pitfalls of this earthly walk, and she expressly urged Rose, as the oldest, to remain faithful to her Christian upbringing as an example to her siblings.

Now such unforeseen changes lay ahead. But no matter what they entailed, Rose intended to keep that solemn pledge. In this she would not fail her mother.

With a last smoothing of her gloved hands over a daygown of nut-brown linen edged with natural lace, she left the safety of the ship's cabin in search of her sisters. Surely they hadn't gotten too far ahead in the few moments' time since they'd dashed off.

Descending the wooden walkway from the ship to the quay, Rose surveyed the sprawling city with amazement. From the accounts she'd read in the English newspapers, she'd expected the ports to be little more than provincial villages. Yet from this high vantage point, she could see rows and rows of substantial buildings stretching inland. On either side of the *Seaford Lady* a veritable forest of masts jutted up from their moorings, while seagulls circled and darted low, their cries piercing the salt-laden air.

The wharf itself teemed with as much activity as any Bristol dock. Such clamor greeted her after so long at sea, and such an array of smells. Loaded wagons rumbled and groaned beneath heavy loads as they rattled across the wooden planks. Horses clomped and whinnied, while their drivers yelled curses and hawkers shouted their wares. Rose had to smile. On a wharf, every day was market day.

Unable to find her sisters in the crowd, she stepped aside for dockworkers busily off-loading the ship, while a customs agent inspected the cargo manifest. Amid all the hustle and bustle, red-coated king's men kept order. This new land was every bit as civilized as her own England, Rose concluded. She relaxed and took a deep breath, catching her favorite smell, a whiff of the hundreds of hard rolls being baked to supply the outgoing ships.

Rose's gaze lighted on a cluster of men dressed in the attire of tradesmen and merchants. In the center stood Captain Durning and her sisters. She hardly recognized the man, decked out in his best powdered wig, ruffles, and feathered, three-cornered hat. Obviously he wanted to impress the more simply dressed gathering. How sad that his ill-fitting coat puckered between its brass buttons, spoiling the image. With curt motions, he beckoned Rose to join them.

Hesitant to leave the safety of the ship, she waited for the captain's more insistent gestures. When she could delay no longer, she moved toward him. . .toward a very uncertain future. Her pulse quickened upon reaching the landing. *Have faith. The Lord is looking after us.* Papa always said that—even when the opposite seemed true. Squaring her shoulders, she made her way through the gathering to join her sisters.

Captain Durning leaned close, looking none too happy with her. "Tardiness is not a virtue," he rasped into her ear. He pursed his thick lips and stepped onto a platform made of sturdy boards placed on nail kegs. Head and shoulders above the crowd, he scanned his customers as his loud voice rang out. "Gentlemen! As I promised, I have saved the choicest for last. These three young lasses have been schooled in all the social graces, as well as the art of fine cooking. They can also read and do sums. Any one of 'em would make an ideal lady's companion or children's governess."

"Put up the one in blue," a portly man hollered. He wore no frock coat, merely an unadorned vest over his blouse as if he'd just come from a trades shop. "I'll bid on her."

"I'll expect a starting bid of no less than twenty-five pounds for this one." The captain reached down to help Mariah onto the stage.

Rose's gasp went unheard beneath the audience's appreciative comments as they ogled Mariah, who stood up there for all to see. The miser had begrudged Papa the mere six pounds he'd shelled out for Mariah. For Lily he'd refused to go higher than five—scarcely more than a half a pound a year. Out of that stingy sum, their good father had sacrificed two pounds to each of his daughters in the event some calamity should befall them. And this vile man intended to profit a despicable fourfold!

A sudden realization penetrated Rose's consciousness. The captain was offering Mariah separately. This was not to be borne! He'd promised all of them *and Papa* that he'd keep them together. "Captain Durning!" She raised her voice above the confusion. "You agreed to sell us as a family."

Ignoring her protests, he went on with the proceedings. "What do I hear for a first bid?"

"I'll give ye twenty pounds," the portly fellow said. "Not a pence more."

"Twenty-one," another yelled.

"Twenty-two," shouted yet another.

Rose shot a look at Mariah. The girl's eyes fairly danced, and a half smile graced her lips. For some unfathomable reason she actually seemed to be *enjoying* her moment onstage. All the more incentive for Rose to take further action. She stepped directly in front of the captain and raised her voice. "*Mister Durning!* I shall be forced to call the authorities if you do not honor the agreement you made with our father."

The man's florid complexion darkened. His eyes narrowed menacingly as he leaned toward her and thrust a clenched fist beneath her nose. "We have no written contract, wench. I'll thank ye to keep yer mouth shut."

Rose felt Lily edge closer, and the girl's small hands clutched Rose's arm. She could not let the child or her other sister down. Her own hands curled into fists. "And I'll thank you to honor your word as a gentleman, sir."

His mouth twisted into a smirk, and he jutted out his fleshy neck. "What we have, shrew, is yer name on a legal document that says I have the right to sell the three of ye to whomever I please. And if ye don't keep quiet, I'll have ye locked in the hold of me ship until I've completed the rest of me business."

"Not before I summon the port authorities." Rose whirled around. The blackguard would see she was no ignorant street urchin.

"Good sirs," the captain cried, "lay hold of this baggage and hold her whilst I fetch my men."

No sooner had the request been voiced than two men clamped hands on to her, pinning her in place.

She tried to wrench free, but to no avail. Far worse, the ruffians seemed to enjoy their task most thoroughly. "Don't fret, Cap'n," one of the audacious pair called brightly. "We'll see the lass stays put."

"And I'll see you and your manhandling cohorts brought up before the magistrate," Rose countered with equal force. She then felt a tugging on her ruffled half sleeve.

"Please, Rose," Lily urged. "Don't say anything more. They'll take you away."

Rose's heart went out to her baby sister. Only the men restraining her prevented her from pulling the girl into her arms. Looking beyond Lily to Mariah, she saw that her other sister's attention was occupied elsewhere. Up on the platform, Mariah's bold stare was fixed on a young, raven-haired gentleman on the outskirts of the crowd. He sat astride a long-legged bay.

Wearing naught but a loose shirt and tight breeches tucked into tall boots, the smoothly tanned man was as handsome as Mariah was beautiful. And he beheld her with the same blatant interest.

Flirting! Rose acknowledged. *The pair of them! How disgraceful!*

The young man did not take his eyes off Mariah. "I'll bid thirty pounds on the beauty in the blue frock."

The gathering grew quiet. The gentleman had bid quite a tidy sum for a mere four years of household servitude. . .if that was all he thought he was purchasing.

"Thirty-one," came from another quarter.

Grinning lazily, the horseman hooked his leg over his saddle's pommel, as if prepared to stay for the duration. "Forty."

At the enormous bid, murmurings of amazement spread through the crowd. Then expectant silence. All eyes turned toward the challenger—another young jack-a-dandy. At his shrug of defeat, attention shifted to the man who'd opened the bidding.

He rubbed a hand over his paunch and looked from Mariah to the young mounted gentleman. His expression soured and his bushy brows formed a V over his slitted eyes. He did not take kindly to losing.

Observing his stubborn glare, Rose suspected him to be the sort who would be an abuser of servants. She held her breath and sent a fleeting prayer heavenward that the older man would concede.

Abruptly, he grunted and stomped off, shoving past anyone in his path.

"Sold!" The captain's triumphant shout grated on Rose's frayed nerves. He sounded more than pleased with himself and his good fortune. "To the gentleman on the fine stallion."

The man laughed and spurred his mount forward. Edging the animal alongside the makeshift platform, he scooped up a very willing Mariah, whose arms were already outstretched and waiting.

Rose fumed. *The hussy.* Furious, she broke free from her captors' grasps and lunged toward her sister, grabbing a handful of Mariah's stiff taffeta skirt. "Come down from there this instant."

"Miss Harwood has a point. Set the lass down."

The captain's words surprised Rose. Renewed hope flowed through her.

"Ye'll not be taking her anywhere until there's hard cash in me hand and ye put yer signature on the indenturement." He slid a satisfied glance to Rose. "Everything proper and legal."

Rose could not abide such a display of impudence. He should be thrashed. She jerked once more on her sister's blue taffeta.

Mariah gifted the handsome rider with an apologetic smile then complied by allowing him to lower her to the ground, which he did much too slowly.

So appalled she could not speak, Rose tugged Mariah to a spot between her and Lily. But before she could deliver a scathing reprimand, the captain seized Lily beneath the arms and deposited her on the platform.

"There ye go, child," he said sternly.

Rose's heart jolted as her sister's eyes grew round with fright and her face lost all color. Hiking her skirts, Rose stepped a foot onto the stage. "Mr. Durning. Lily and I *must* be sold together. She's far too young to go forth alone. I beg you to reconsider."

Durning booted her foot off the platform. "Stay put and hold yer tongue, or I swear I'll clap ye in chains and sell ye in another port a few days' sail from here."

Rose ignored the vehemence in that statement and met his glare. She would not be intimidated by this blighter of honest dealings.

Gradually his expression eased, and he glanced away. "If someone wants the both of ye, he'll not be prevented from bidding on *yerself* next. In the meantime, I advise ye to mind yer manners." He placed an arm around Lily and ushered her a few steps farther away.

Shy, timid Lily pleaded silently with Rose, her soft silvery eyes clouded with fear.

Rose had to clamp her hands over her mouth to keep from crying out. This was all wrong. So wrong. The villainous captain had lied to her, to Papa. To all of them.

Durning again raised his voice to the gathering growing steadily in the midmorning sun. "This young lass is also of the merchant class. She's had the finest education a maiden of her advantages could receive. She can read and write and has been taught all the latest stitchery designs. She's a good-natured girl and quick to learn."

Unable to bear so many eyes upon her, Lily slid behind the captain.

He dragged her forward again, this time holding her in place with a firm grip. "She may look a bit frail, I'll avow," he went on, "but I assure ye she didn't suffer a day of illness on the long voyage here. She's—"

"The little thing don't look like she'd stand up to much hard work," someone behind Rose challenged. "But I'll give ten pounds for her—if her teeth are sound."

Durning took hold of Lily's chin. "Open your mouth, girl. Let's have a look."

"How dare you!" Utterly insulted by the blackguard's thoughtless ill treatment of her poor sister and humiliated for her as well, Rose hoisted herself onto the stage, only to be immediately plucked off by the same ruffians who had restrained her moments before. She had no choice but to stand by as the younger girl closed her lashes over tears. Helplessly she watched them roll down her sister's pale cheeks. Her own followed suit.

Durning made a show of peering into Lily's mouth then smiled with benign assurance. "As perfect as the queen's own pearls, I must say."

"Ten pounds, one shilling."

The firm but gentle voice came from quite near Rose. Swiping the moisture from her eyes, she noted that this man did not wear the tailored clothing of a city businessman. Wearing plain-spun and simply made attire, he was rather tall and lean, with a build similar to that of their father. He had a kind face.

"Ten and two shillings," came from the vile man who'd wanted to see Lily's teeth.

Frowning, the man beside Rose reached into his pocket and pulled out a fistful of funds. He opened his hand, displaying a heavily calloused palm filled with paper and coin, which she counted silently along with him. Ten and six. He stepped forward. "Ten pounds, three shillings."

His competitor spoke again. "Eleven pounds. That's my final offer."

The gentle-voiced man's shoulders sagged. He glanced at Rose, his disappointment unmistakable. "I was hoping I could get a nice young girl like her for my Susan. She's been poorly for quite a spell now." He turned to leave.

The mere thought of the teeth-inspecting reprobate taking Lily away, having her at his mercy, was more than Rose could accept. She reached out and caught the kind-faced man's sleeve. "Bid more. Please."

He smiled sadly down at her. "I would if I could, miss. Alas, I cannot."

Before he finished speaking, Rose had one of her two precious pounds out of her small purse. She pressed it into his hands. "Please."

Moments later, to her everlasting gratification, she heard the captain award dear Lily to the gentle-faced man. She breathed a quick prayer of thanks. Her baby sister had been properly placed in a good home.

"Hie thyself up here, wench." Captain Durning's voice lacked even a smidgen of gentleness.

Consumed by concern for Lily, Rose had forgotten her own turn would come. She refused to budge.

The two ruffians hooted with laughter and hoisted her onto the platform.

She swung around to give them a piece of her mind but met only more guffaws and clapping from the onlookers. She'd become a spectacle. The morning's entertainment. How she wished she had contracted with a different ship's captain, but it was far too late for remorse. She clamped her jaws together and faced the lying, cheating peddler of flesh who had betrayed her trust.

As the laughter faded, Durning's singsong rang out across the crowd. "Now if ye want a full day's labor for yer money, this *spinster* here is the one ye're lookin' for. The female's five and twenty. In her prime. She's run an entire household since she was thirteen. Raised her four sisters and brothers, and ye've all seen how at least two of those lasses turned out." He cocked an eyebrow for emphasis.

Rose was sorely tempted to announce that she would give no buyer more than eleven pounds' worth of labor during the next four years—the six that Captain Durning paid her and five for the expense of her passage. She loathed the thought of that cur profiting any more than he already had. But no doubt the captain would lock her in the hold and carry out his threat. Should he cart her off to a different port, there'd be no way of keeping track of Mariah and Lily. How could she endure that? They needed her. Especially Mariah, whether or not the flirt would agree.

With her mind in such turmoil, it took a moment for Rose to become aware that every man within twenty yards was staring at her. Scores of eyes raked her from head to toe and back again. The prospective buyers nodded and chatted amongst themselves. A few pointed as they discussed her attributes.

These strangers in this strange land. . .appraising her worth.

Rose had never felt so exposed in her life. Or so helpless.

Chapter 3

"The wench's sisters may have virtues enough," a bystander hollered. "But this one's got the tongue of a fishwife!"

Laughter again erupted from the men gawking at Rose. They'd become a merry crowd, and at her expense. She struggled to retain what little dignity remained to her. If honoring a promise to one's parent and protecting one's family was termed being a "fishwife," so be it. She searched around for the two girls.

Lily stood near her new master, gazing up at Rose with heartfelt sympathy.

Mariah, however, seemed not in the least offended by the derisive levity aimed at her older sister. Her smile was as broad as anyone else's as she and her fancy gentleman-owner stood beside his elegant horse.

Once the revelry died down, the captain continued his spiel. "Ye've merely seen the woman act the way of any mother hen worth its feathers. She's tryin' to keep her little chicks tucked beneath her wings. Of the three of 'em, I'd say she's by far the most experienced worker." He paused. "Now, who'll give me a startin' bid?"

A newcomer attired in a gold-trimmed burgundy frock coat shouldered between two other prospective customers standing just below Rose. "I need to look over them hands of hers."

Rose was tempted to refuse, considering his request was only a little less degrading than being asked to display her teeth. Yet from the man's dress and expression, he appeared quite successful and even earnest, especially compared to the more seedy types who made up much of the gathering. She held out her trembling palms as he and several onlookers crowded closer to examine them.

"Look pretty soft to me," one commented.

"Aye," someone else agreed. "All three of them sisters are wearin' right fine frocks. Mayhap the lasses are more used to givin' orders than takin' 'em."

The captain let out a huff of disgust. "'Tis true, the Harwoods come from excellent stock on t'other side of the water. To see any of 'em put to work as mere scrubwomen would be a pure waste. This one in particular is accomplished in preparin' tasty foods. She can put every spice ever brought to the British Isles to proper use."

Rose found the captain's praise of her talents a bit excessive; nevertheless, she appreciated his generous words on her behalf. Cooking indeed had been the one household duty she truly enjoyed and had never relinquished to a servant.

A shout came from the left. "Fifteen pounds. A good English cook beats any of those Frenchies hired by folks over on the Potomac. Can't abide their runny sauces."

"Sixteen," another called out.

"Seventeen."

"Eighteen."

"Nineteen."

Bids came in such swift succession Rose could no longer ascertain the individuals speaking. Glancing at the captain, she realized the insufferable toad was actually deriving a perverse sort of pleasure from her distress. She clamped her teeth together, determined to bear the shameful outrage with fortitude.

A wagon rolled to a stop at the edge of the crowd, and the driver, an older man with a scraggly, graying beard rose to his feet. The ill-fitting clothes on his short and squat figure looked rumpled and soiled beneath the droopy-brimmed hat he wore. His high-pitched voice rang out above the din. "Did I hear tell the lass is a good cook?"

"Aye." Captain Durning nodded.

"I'll gi' ye fifty pounds fer her."

"Sold!" The captain allowed no time for reconsideration on the part of his customer.

Rose looked at Durning, who grinned like a pirate with a newly captured treasure on this most profitable of days. When he snagged her hand and dropped down to the splintery wharf, she lost her will to resist. Meekly she followed as he pulled her toward the wagon driver ambling his way through the crowd.

Close up, the squat newcomer looked even more shabby and unkempt. His ruffled shirt bore a profusion of smudges and food stains, and he reeked of sweat and other indefinable odors. Rose could not venture a guess as to when he'd last seen a bath, if ever. The mangy, untidy ne'er-do-well was to be her owner? How would she suffer such a fate? Her throat clenched as dismay crushed her soul.

Oblivious to the obnoxious smells resonating from the wagoneer, Captain Durning grasped the man's grubby hand and pumped it with fervor. "Come with me. I've a quill and ink on yon barrelhead. Once ye settle up, I'll give ye her papers to sign." He checked around and gestured to his other two successful buyers. "Ye men that bid on the other lasses come along, too."

Still held in Durning's strong grip, Rose woodenly followed the group now making their way to the barrels lining the customhouse.

Lily rushed over and hissed into her ear, "What are we to do, Rose? You cannot go with that foul man. He's—he's *horrid*."

Mariah whispered in her other ear, "We must not allow that disgusting creature to take you off to heaven knows where. I shall have Colin speak to the captain on your behalf."

"Colin, is it?" Rose swung toward her sister. "And I suppose *Colin* is already addressing you by your given name as well?" She could only wonder what philandering purpose the man had in mind when he'd purchased Mariah.

The other girl's lips drooped into a pout. "Upon my word, Rose. This is not the time for such trivial nonsense." In a rustle of taffeta, she whirled away to join the stylish gentleman and his bay stallion.

Rose traipsed after her. She would have a word with this *Colin* while the opportunity presented itself. Catching up with her sibling, she hooked an arm about Mariah's shoulders and stared up at the interloper. "Sir, before you sign my sister's papers, I'll thank you to relate exactly what duties will be expected of her in your employ."

Not at all intimidated by her question, the bounder smiled. "To be quite truthful, Miss Harwood, I have no duties in mind for her whatsoever. But I assure you, my mother shall be most pleased at my finding someone of your sister's refined qualities to be her companion."

His reply stunned Rose. "You. . .you bought her for your mother?"

"Why, yes. Of course. Surely you didn't think me the sort to have something else in mind for the lass." His forehead creased in amusement.

Surely she had, and in fact, still did. "Then I'm sure you will not mind pledging to see my dear, virtuous sister placed into your mother's watch-care before the sun sets this day. And you'll see to her religious instruction as well?"

"Rose!" Twin spots of color sprung forth on Mariah's indignant face, but her new master placed a staying hand on her arm and met Rose's gaze in all candor. "You have my most solemn word, miss."

"I thank you, sir. I shall rest easier knowing she is with trustworthy folk." From the pocket of her skirt she withdrew a shard of lead and a scrap of paper. "Might I ask where to post my sisterly correspondence? I should hate to lose touch with one of the only two relatives I possess on this continent."

He gave a polite nod. "To Barclay's Bay Plantation at Alexandria. On the Virginia side of the Potomac."

"Virginia? But isn't that another colony? How far away is your plantation?"

"Rest easy, miss. 'Tis within a day's ride."

"A day's ride?"

Mariah eased out of Rose's grasp and turned to Mr. Barclay. "Pray sir, forgive me, but I'm afraid my sister and I have a matter of much deeper concern. We must not let that swarthy old man take her. Would you please speak to the captain? Implore him to withdraw these proceedings?"

He grimaced slightly. "My dear Mariah, the man bid fifty pounds."

"Yes, I'm quite aware of that." She employed her most persuasive smile. "But if you would just try."

Colin Barclay shook his head with sad finality. "I regret to say all closing bids are final. I do find it rather astounding that one so unkempt should have that amount of ready cash. One can only wonder how he came by such funds."

Her last flicker of hope gone, Rose assured herself that her new owner could be set to rights easily enough with a bit of soap and some hot water. Very hot water and lots of it. But Mariah? She sighed and prayed fervently that Mistress Barclay would be a most conscientious guardian to her new charge.

Impulsive, flighty Mariah, an entire day's ride away.

And what about Lily? To what distance might she be taken? *Not so far, dear Lord. Please, not so far.*

Leaving Mariah and Mr. Barclay, Rose approached the farmer who waited in line for his turn with Captain Durning. "Sir, I trust you live nearby?"

"The name's John Waldon, miss. And may I express again my sincerest appreciation for your assistance." He cast a worried glance toward the uncouth fellow leaning over Rose's papers. "'Tis my deepest regret I was unable to return the favor. I've just come from building our new house up in Pennsylvania's Wyoming Valley. Within the week we'll be departing Baltimore."

"Wyoming Valley? Pennsylvania?" Rose's chest began to tighten beneath the heaviness pressing on her spirit. She had read of vast tracts of land existing in the Americas, but she'd been told most people lived along the seaboard. "Pray, good sir, how far from here is that? I'm afraid I'm not familiar with these colonies and how they relate to each other. I must know where my sister will be living."

The sadness she'd seen earlier when he'd mentioned his ill wife deepened. "Several days upriver, miss." He took her hand. "I wish it were closer. But I vow to you, your sister will be kindly treated in my household, and you may consider yourself most welcome to come visit us whenever your master can spare you."

The invitation was hardly comforting. Why had she ever agreed to allow the girls to accompany her to the colonies? Instead of beginning a new life together, the three of them were being scattered like chaff on the far winds. This was such a crucial time in their young lives, yet there'd be no seeing to her dear sisters' spiritual instruction if they did not dwell in close proximity to herself. Mariah, in all likelihood, could easily go astray.

Why has this horrid fate befallen us, dear Lord?

"Rose Harwood." The captain held out a plumed quill to her. "Step forward and put your name under Mr. Eustice Smith's."

⁓

The longest week of Rose's life dragged slowly by on the swift, dark currents of the Potomac River. A vast array of birds, many of which Rose had never seen before, soared and swirled overhead in the bluest of skies. Others flitted among the topmost branches of the trees lining the wide banks, their cheery twitterings barely penetrating her gloomy thoughts. Why were those insignificant creatures free of earth's constraints, while she was being carried farther into the unknown?

On either side of her, virgin forest tangled with such density she could scarcely peer more than a few feet into its growth. Strangely, as she rested atop several meal sacks in the confines of a cumbersome keelboat Mr. Smith had hired, the foliage—like great green walls, high and impenetrable—seemed almost protective, except when the feral screech of some unseen, unknown animal carried to her ears. Then the hairs on her arms stood on end.

Nevertheless, Rose resolved to remain as calm as the duck she spied floating in the shallows with a brood trailing placidly behind. Rose's composure was one of the few things she still clung to as the rough-hewn boat distanced her from everyone dear to her.

She and Mr. Eustice Smith were not entirely alone. The man had hired another riverboat like the one she was on, each being poled upriver by a crew of five—two on each side manning the poles and one at the rudder. Purposely tuning out the annoying din of unseen peepers and tree toads whose endless chorus filled the air, Rose disregarded the good-natured chatter exchanged by the men. She preferred the solitude of her thoughts, however depressing and hopeless they might be.

After the party had taken leave of Baltimore, she had felt safe enough as they passed the array of towns and settlements speckling the region. In between, there'd been vast plantations of tobacco fields. Great manor houses overlooked the river, attesting to the prosperity of the region. She couldn't help but wonder if Mariah would be dwelling somewhere among them.

Traffic at first seemed brisk on the busy waterway. But all too soon the river left the flatlands and began cutting through hill country. This morning she'd seen only one other string of rivercraft. The passing flatboats heading downstream were piled high with what she learned were beaver pelts. Such carnage, she mused, took place in those dark, distant woods—and all for making fashionable men's hats.

A thunderous boom roared across the water. Rose sprang to her feet and searched in all directions as the sound echoed back and forth between the ridges framing the narrow valley.

"Nothin' to fret about, missy." A shabby boatman walking his jammed pole to the rear of the boat nodded toward the noise and spit a brown streak of tobacco juice in that direction. "'Tweren't nothin' but a big ol' tree sayin' its last good-bye."

Rose sat down again, settling her charcoal gray skirt over her ankles. "I thank you for putting my mind at ease."

Her thanks sparked a grin from the rawboned man, his body straining as he maintained pressure on the pole. "Didn't want ye thinkin' a pack o' wild Injuns was swoopin' down on us."

"Indians! I thought the Indians sold all their land on this side of your mountains and moved out to the west."

"Aye," he grunted with a glance back at her. "They did. Fer the most part."

Rose chose not to linger on his last words or question him further, no matter how strong her curiosity. Being a lone woman among so many men, it seemed prudent to refrain from engaging them in conversation, even on the most basic of topics. From their uncommon interest in her every move, a person would think her as fascinating as Mariah.

With her sister once again on her mind, Rose had to admit it now seemed almost laughable how worried she had been that her siblings would be taken away from Baltimore. The irony that she was the one going who-knew-where was not lost on her. And after more than a week traversing this river, Rose had pressing questions for Mr. Smith— questions he seemed adept at sidestepping.

All she had learned from the evasive man was that he purchased her for the sole purpose of relieving his wife of mealtime chores—and that not out of kindness for his missus, but because he deplored the woman's cooking. He'd been extremely closemouthed as to the actual location of their home. She'd gleaned little more from him than the knowledge that the supplies stacked high for transport were to replenish his store. The vague address she'd been able to provide her sisters at their tearful parting was to write her in care of the Virginia and Ohio Company office in Alexandria. . .yet was not Alexandria one of the towns they'd left behind?

As the party traveled northward, Rose could only wonder if she was anywhere near where Lily would be living. But rather than poling into the settlement, the men veered onto the river's southern fork. There'd been no sign of civilization along the banks since. With every endless mile, Rose was being carried deeper into the wilderness.

And nothing could be done about that for four interminable years.

Seized by a sense of desperation, she searched ahead along both banks. If only Mr. Smith's store would soon come into sight, she might be positioned within a day of her baby sister—indeed even less if heading downstream in one of those narrow native boats the men called canoes. They seemed to glide by faster than a man could run.

It was high time she received a straight answer from the storekeeper. Rose hoisted herself off the sacks and, careful not to trip over her bothersome skirts, gingerly navigated toward the front of the keelboat, where the man sat. He could be found easily enough at any time of the day or night merely by following her nose, she conceded wryly. Surely when he reached their destination his wife would make certain he had a good soak in a bathtub. Rose yearned for that luxury herself. . .along with the safety of female company.

Her owner slouched on a crate, his hands clasped between his knees. With his floppy hat shading most of his face, he seemed to be searching ahead with intense interest.

She stopped and placed her feet apart to balance herself on the moving craft. "Mr. Smith, I should like a word with you, if I might."

He looked up and blinked. "Oh, good. Yer here." His high, thin voice rose in stark contrast to his coarse features. "We'll be dockin' 'round the next bend. It'll be the end of our ride on this here river, and I'll expect ya to haul off all that truck ya insisted on cartin' along with ya. I'll not be payin' the men extra fer that."

She bristled. "I've done so at every portage, sir, have I not?"

He grunted like a mean-tempered pig. For a man who had paid such a goodly sum for her person, he seemed unaccountably stingy in the matter of her belongings—one trunk and two valises, leaving her to lug and drag them along herself whenever necessary. But they were all she had left in this world, and she was not about to leave a single piece behind.

Suddenly the import of his last words struck her. "You say we're about to dock? Oh, splendid! Splendid!" Turning away, she could not suppress a huge grin, and she did not care if the other men misread it. They had arrived at last—mayhap she would be within a few days' journey of where at least one of her dear sisters would be located.

Even as Rose cautiously made her way to where her large black chest sat with the valises strapped on top, a horseshoe curve came into view. She could see a wide sandy strand stretching across its inward side, and fingering out from that, a sturdy deck. Two overturned canoes rested in the sand, a pleasing sight.

As the craft moved closer, Rose noticed that inland of the short pier lay a clearing dotted with log buildings, corrals, pens, and fenced pastures housing a number of horses and other animals. The tiny settlement appeared similar to the last place they'd stopped to unload and portage around a small waterfall, but here the current ran smoothly as far as the eye could see.

Beyond the clearing, an endless stand of thick forest closed off further view of the region. Could this isolated outpost be the location of Mr. Smith's store?

On land, an individual charged out on the dock, waving and yelling words that became somewhat jumbled as they echoed off the layered rock walls on the other side of the river.

The men pushing the poles hollered back, "Halloo the landing!" Laughing, they walked their poles toward the rear.

Rose saw people streaming out of the closest cabin and running to the dock. They wore dreary, coarse-spun shirts, and their sagging knee-high breeches met none-too-clean stockings.

With one exception. Tall, stalwart, and ruggedly built, a fine figure of a man strode forth. Appearing quite prosperous in a white ruffled shirt and brocade vest, which he wore with indifferent grace, he had a midnight blue frock coat draped over one arm.

Rose's spirits lifted. Perhaps there was a village of substance nearby after all. She glanced down at her simple linsey-woolsey spotted with pine pitch. She'd worn it for the past week to prevent spoiling any of her better gowns. Even the shawl collar she'd placed atop her bodice was her oldest. But perhaps the straw bonnet with its wide black ties was none the worse for wear and would add a bit of style. She sincerely hoped to make a good impression on Mr. Smith's good wife.

Nearing the dock, one of the crewmen tossed a rope to a waiting fellow who quickly looped it around a thick post and drew the craft alongside. The lumbering conveyance thudded against the pilings and shuddered heavily before another worker caught and fastened a second rope, snugging the rear of the vessel. The other keelboat was tied in similar fashion.

Mr. Smith and the crew hopped ashore and exchanged boisterous greetings with those on the landing.

To Rose's dismay, she saw a brown jug making swift rounds. She could only pray it contained cider. But spirited contents or no, the matter was out of her hands. With the men no longer underfoot, she took advantage of the moment and grabbed the handle of her trunk, dragging it toward the side.

Before she'd gotten halfway there, she felt the boat dip as someone came aboard. She looked up at the man attired in finer clothing who strode steadily toward her in his neat buckle shoes.

"If you please, miss." He kept his voice pleasingly low in timbre as he removed his three-cornered hat and placed it on a crate. "Let me be of assistance." A broad smile revealed straight, healthy teeth, and dark, softly curled hair framed sincere hazel eyes. A jovial crinkling of his brow further disarmed her. Rose found something quite stirring about his appearance. Even though his long face was far too rugged for genteel handsomeness, its hollows and angles had a compelling quality one could not easily dismiss. There was no way to guess his age. Not with skin bronzed by constant exposure to wind and weather. But despite his elegant attire, he carried a sense of recklessness about him, of adventure. And for some reason, the warm friendliness in his eyes made her sense instinctively that she could trust him.

She felt fleeting regret for having lacked foresight enough to begin the day in a more presentable fashion. For the first time since selling herself into bondage, she truly felt the part of the dowdy servant. She managed only a weak smile as the man continued to hold her in his gaze.

The breeze caught a tendril of her hair and whipped it across her cheek. With him staring so intently, should she brush the strand free of her lashes or pretend it didn't exist? Unaccountably light-headed under his scrutiny, she felt her heart quicken beneath her laced bodice.

He bent down and caught hold of the trunk handle with hands as hard and brown as those of any riverman she'd yet encountered. He seemed to Rose a man of substance, yet one unafraid of honest labor, and his assistance was more than appreciated. She preceded him off the boat.

With solid ground beneath her feet at last, Rose assessed the settlement more closely, noting the weathered but sturdy cabins speckled here and there within the wide clearing. Large corrals teemed with horses, while additional pens housed several cows. A few rumpled men and a ruddier individual who she assumed could easily pass for an Indian lurked about, watching the keelboats being unloaded. Aware of the more-than-interested attention her arrival caused the residents, she ignored their grins and suggestive stares and hiked her chin.

"You sir!" Mr. Smith hollered. "Stop!" Despite the straggly beard shrouding most of his face, the trader's displeasure was unmistakable, even from a distance.

Her chivalrous helper glanced over his shoulder. "You yammerin' at me, Eustice, you ol' river rat?" A lazy sort of American accent softened his rumbly voice.

Mr. Smith cocked his head, squinting in the glare of the sunshine. Then he let out a hoot. "Nate Kinyon? That you?"

"Aye. Headin' down to Conococheague to see if Ma's still holdin' up. It's been nigh two years or so since I was back that way."

"Well, you look purty enough t' be a reg'lar party cake."

Mr. Kinyon turned a shade redder above the ruffles at his throat, and a corner of his mouth quirked as he eyed the storekeeper. But he made no response. He hoisted the hefty trunk and the two valises onto his shoulder as if they weighed next to nothing and strode toward the front of the boat.

Trader Smith jabbed a stubby finger at him. "That's jes' what I meant. I want the girl to haul that truck off on her own."

Rose blanched as the onlookers ceased talking among themselves and centered their attention on her, each curious ear perked.

Either her rescuer didn't notice or he didn't care. Without hesitation he leaped onto the dock with her belongings.

Rose shriveled inwardly in discreet silence, knowing—hating—the next words sure to come out of Eustice Smith's mouth.

Her unaware hero, heavily muscled shoulders straining the brocade fabric of his vest, marched right up to the storekeeper and dropped the burden mere inches from his feet. "And why shouldn't I help the lass?"

Rose's throat began to close.

"'Cause she's a stiff-necked female, that's why. Needs to be taught a thing or two."

Knowing Mr. Smith wouldn't leave the matter half told, Rose wished she could crawl inside her trunk and close the lid. In truth, there was no shame in insisting on what few rights she had, or even in being a bondservant. The difficulty lay in making herself believe that.

One of the raftsmen butted in. "She belongs to Smith, Nate. He bought the woman to cook fer him."

Mr. Kinyon's square jaw went slack, and he looked from the storekeeper to her.

Rose detected a subtle change in the way he now viewed her, and she abhorred it. But what could she say? Every word was true. She'd been purchased like any other sack of goods off the ship.

The man's brows knitted over a sharp gaze that seemed to pierce right through her. Then he leveled a glare at Mr. Smith. "He's jestin', right?"

The storekeeper took a small step back. For the first time since she laid eyes on the little man, he seemed unsure of himself. Then he stiffened. "Paid good money for her, Nate. Hard cash. The contract says I'm to provide her with food, shelter, an' two sets of clothes a year. And at the end of her four years, she gits sent on her merry way with a month's supplies an' four pounds sterling. The papers didn't mention nothin' about where that food and shelter was to be provided."

What did he mean, where? Rose trembled as a chill ran down her spine. Something was very wrong. She somehow found her voice. "Where exactly are you taking me, Mr. Smith?"

"Nowhere, that's where." Towering head and shoulders above Mr. Smith, Nate Kinyon widened his stance and challenged her sulky owner with a withering glower. "You ain't takin' this pretty little lass no three hundred miles into Indian country. An' that's that."

Chapter 4

Rose's blood turned cold. *Indian country!* Her lips fell open, and her arms dropped like rocks to her sides. Her gaze darted from Trader Smith to Nate Kinyon and back again. "Surely you're not considering taking me off to where wild Indians live. I cannot— You cannot—"

Smith's slitted eyes hardened. "I can an' I will. An' you can an' you will. You have no say in the matter, seein' as how yer bought an' paid for." He turned to Nate. "My stomach's gone right sour on me lately. I'm in sore need of some good English puddin's an' such to sweeten it up. You can understand that. Hear tell she's a real good cook."

Astonishment clouded Mr. Kinyon's expression, and his jaw went slack. "You mean to say you're draggin' this gentle lass all the way out to that tradin' post of yours just so she can make you up some puddin'? That's plumb crazy, Eustice. Plumb crazy."

"It ain't neither." He bristled, a sneer twisting his grizzled face. "You must not a'heard, but me and my partner, we ain't been hittin' it off these days like we used to. So Branson's fixin' to set up his own post down on the Little Kanawha."

Nate frowned and tucked his chin in disbelief. "How can he do that? I happen to know the fur company requires two men to be posted at each store. Besides, what's that got to do with puddin'?"

The trader sniffed in disdain, as if Nate possessed the thickest skull since the dawn of time. "He's the only one what could make it right—when we was able to get ahold of some milk. But I seen to that." He gestured toward the penned cows.

Nate glanced in the direction indicated. "I did hear you was takin' them beasts overmountain with you. Ought'a be a challenge, I'd say." He smirked.

Her irritation mounting as she stood by listening to the bizarre turn of the conversation, Rose planted her fists on her hips. "Pudding! Cows! I cannot believe any of this. It's simply not to be endured."

"Quiet, woman!" The trader returned his attention to Kinyon. "Me an' Branson figgered we wouldn't say nothin' to the comp'ny. More profit for us both that way. 'Sides, I got my wife's brothers to help me keep an eye on the place."

Kinyon kneaded his chin. "Looks like you two have things all worked out between you, then." He shook his head, appearing to mull something over in his mind. "Well, think on this. What say I get you a couple puddin' recipes an' trade 'em an' whatever you paid for the woman—plus a little profit, a'course—an' that'll make us all happy. How much *did* you lay out for her, anyway?"

For one brief moment, Rose felt a ray of hope that this trustworthy-looking man wanted to save her from her fate. Then she realized she was merely being bartered for again. Hopelessly outmatched, she gave a huff and turned in proud defiance to stride away.

Smith grabbed her arm, halting her midstep, and glared at Nate. "Even if the gal was for sale at any price—and she ain't—when did you ever have fifty pounds jinglin' in that pouch of yourn, I'd like ta know?"

"Fifty pounds?" Kinyon hiked his brows. "You paid fifty pounds for her?" He eyed Rose up and down with an intensity that made her cringe.

Humiliated beyond belief, Rose knew she must look a fright, having worn the same clothes for days. Even her once-fashionable hat was droopy, and when had she last run a brush through her tangled hair? She lowered her gaze to her hands, noticing that Smith's grubby fingers still gripped her arm. She felt as if she was in the middle of a nightmare—only this bad dream was all too real and had barely begun. Hearing the jingling of some coins, she raised her lashes, not entirely ready to relinquish all hope.

Nate Kinyon emptied his leather pouch into his open palm, fingering through the contents as he mentally tallied the sum. "I can give you eleven pounds, two shillings, sixteen Spanish dollars, and four bits on account. How's that? I'll have the rest next spring after trappin' season." He stole a quick glance at Rose then looked at the trader. "I'm good for it. You know I am."

Smith gave a dubious half smirk, a sly spark in his beady eyes. "I'm sure ya are. Only those promises won't do my innards one lick'a good." He shifted his stance and glanced around the settlement. "So where's that huntin' partner of yourn? Thought you two was joined at the hip."

He shrugged. "Black Horse Bob ain't comin' out with me. Right now he's over playin' cards with some of your boys. Said he'd wait there till I get back."

Nodding, Smith cocked his head. "You two'd have more spendin' money if you'd stop throwin' it away at cards. Never did put much stock in gamblin' meself."

A sheepish hue tinged the tips of Kinyon's ears as he looked at Rose. He straightened to his full height. "Spent most of my purse on these city duds I'm sportin'. Didn't want Ma to think I'd gone all woodsy."

Surmising that someone with the name "Black Horse Bob" must have a long, horsey-looking face, Rose peered over the tall man's shoulder and up the bank toward the buildings, trying to spot someone of that description. A jolt of alarm whipped through her when she saw as many Indians as white men milling about now—heathens who, she'd heard, scalped people, skinned them, and ate their hearts. A nervous chill went through her.

Oddly enough, no one else seemed uneasy. She drew a measure of comfort from that. Perhaps the things she'd heard back in England were just talk. After all, Mr. Smith wouldn't be so interested in acquiring a "puddin' maker" if living in Indian country was so very dangerous. His own wife was there, wasn't she? Nevertheless, Rose couldn't help recalling Mr. Kinyon's words: *"You ain't takin' this pretty little lass no three hundred miles into Indian country."*

Indian country. Three hundred miles from civilization.

More than three hundred miles from her sisters.

Lily. Mariah. Stark despair crept into Rose's heart.

Bringing the discussion to a timely end, Trader Smith pivoted on his heel and started up the sloped bank from the river as the boatmen traipsed back and forth, toting cargo off the vessels and piling it in stacks. He raised his voice to a yell. "One of ya go fer the horses I bartered for. We still got half a day's light left, an' we need all of it."

Horses! As if she hadn't endured sufficient indignities already, the sickening dread that now she'd be expected to continue this journey on horseback sank into Rose's heart with a thud. She'd never been on a horse in her life—not even Timmy's pony, Corky. She didn't have the slightest notion how to climb in skirts and petticoats way up onto some hairy, smelly beast and perch there for some interminable length of time, much less control the animal and make it go in the right direction.

"Hey! Bondwoman!" Smith's nasally voice cut into her musings. "Git yerself an' that truck of yourn up here. Time's a'wastin'."

Swallowing her angst, Rose felt an empathetic hand come to rest on her shoulder.

"Don't worry about your things. I'll fetch 'em for you." Nate Kinyon turned then swung back around. "Did Eustice speak true? Did he actually pay fifty pounds for you?" A skeptical dip of his straight brows indicated disbelief.

"Aye. He did indeed, sir."

Kinyon pursed his lips in thought. "For that skinflint to lay out that kind of money for a cook, that stomach of his must be worse off than he says. Not that a good cook wouldn't be worth a hefty price, mind you, if a fellow has it to pay." He glanced up the hill at the trader occupied with stacks of unloaded cargo. "Still, he just shoulda hired a man, is all." He reached down for her belongings and hefted them onto his shoulder.

Not bothering to agree with sentiments that matched her own, Rose had little choice but to follow after her rescuer. Creepy chills made the hairs on the backs of her arms prickle when they passed close by sullen-looking Indians who made no effort to disguise their meaningful ogling as they followed her with their eyes. She could only imagine what the guttural sounds passing between them were saying about her. She straightened her spine and clung to whatever composure still remained as they reached one of the packhorses.

Nate cut her a sidelong glance and set her luggage on the ground. "Don't fret yourself about the Indians, miss. Smith forked over quite a purse for you. He's not about to let no one give you trouble. Soon's I get back from my family's homestead, I'll come out an' check on you myself. Who knows? I might be able to talk some sense into him by then."

Rose didn't know how to respond. This strange land, these strange people with their unknown language, and the fearsome possibilities lying ahead filled her with trepidation. Everything was happening so fast. Nothing was under her control. She was completely at the mercy of Eustice Smith. Nevertheless, she raised her lashes and met Kinyon's kind gaze. "I do thank you for your concern, Mr. Kinyon. 'Tis most appreciated, I assure you."

A gentle smile tweaked the corners of his mouth. "An' I thank you for bein' such a pleasurable sight for these poor, deprived eyes. We don't get to see many womenfolk out here in these parts."

Nor had she. Her sisters were the last women she'd spoken to since the three of them had stepped onto colony soil, adding even more to her loneliness. "No doubt you'll see many more pleasing sights as you travel back into civilization. I shall pray for your safety, as I allow you'll pray for mine."

He opened his mouth as if to reply then rubbed his jaw. "Hmm. Well.

Sure thing, lass. Oh, by the by, what might I call you, if you don't mind my askin'?"

"Miss Harwood. Rose Harwood. And if perchance you should happen to pass through the Wyoming Valley settlements, where my sister Lily has been bonded to a family by the name of Waldon—or travel by Alexandria, where my other sister Mariah is to live on the Barclay Plantation—please be kind enough to inform them you've seen me and that I am. . .safe." *So far, at least,* her mind added as a leering Indian moved noiselessly past her.

Mr. Kinyon tilted his head. "I hadn't planned on goin' downstream as far as Alexandria, but if it'd help you rest easier, I'll make every effort to do so. As for the other lass, I fear goin' off in that direction ain't in my plans right now."

Shoulders sagging in disappointment, Rose knew she'd asked too much of the man, however kind he might seem to be. "That valley. . .'tis farther upstream, then?"

"Well, miss, it's upstream, that's the truth of it, but we're not talkin' this stream. She'll be near the Susquehanna River, likely somewheres around the Wilkes-Barre settlement."

The news quenched Rose's spirits. "Where is that river? I believe Mr. Waldon spoke of it being near Baltimore."

"If I had my map on me, I could show you that the mouth of the Susquehanna is a mite north of Baltimore, an' the Potomac dumps into the bay a few miles south of the city. From its headwaters up in New York, the Susquehannah flows right through Pennsylvania an' on into Maryland. What we're standin' in is Virginia territory."

"Oh my." It was too much to take in, and her mind whirled with the realization of the immeasurable distance that likely would stretch between her and the other girls. Her throat closed up with disappointment, and tears sprang to her eyes, trembling upon the tips of her lashes. She could hardly speak. "The last thing I told our papa before we sailed for these colonies was that I wouldn't let them out of my sight." She cast a despondent glance in the direction of the river that had already carried her far, far from Mariah and Lily. "I promised. Made a solemn pledge that I'd remain strong in my faith and look after them. Somehow I must keep my word."

Kinyon raised a calloused hand and squeezed her shoulder. "Are you sayin' you only just got here from across the water? I vow you're a long way from home, Miss Harwood. But I hope you'll take comfort from knowin' you'll never be outta my thoughts."

Just then Eustice Smith's boots clomped toward them over the uneven ground. "Thought you was on your way downstream, Nate. Ain't that what ya said?"

Aware that Mr. Kinyon's gaze remained on her damp eyes, Rose lowered hers.

"Aye, that I am. That I am." He let go of her shoulder and closed his fingers around one of her hands, and she felt a strange combination of strength and gentleness as he lifted her hand to his lips. "Till we meet again, pretty lass." A last long look and he took his leave.

Rose could not bear to watch him go.

Plunked unceremoniously by her owner atop a mammoth beast with a tangled mane of hair, Rose had no idea how she was supposed to steer it. Fortunately the animal seemed to know what was expected, as it followed Mr. Smith's horse behind the settlement and into a forest of thick trees sporting every shade of green imaginable. Only the palest semblance of sunlight, obscured and fragmented by the canopy of leafy branches overhead, lit the trail. . .a trail so primitive it was hardly more than a deer path.

Rose stole a last backward glance toward the river, where the solicitous Mr. Kinyon had paddled away in one of those swift canoes less than an hour ago. Even though she'd barely met the man, she realized he was the first person who had befriended her in these colonies, and now he, too, was gone—just like Mariah and Lily. Here she was: a lone woman perched on a smelly creature with her smelly master and six equally smelly Indians—*Indians!*—traveling a brush-lined trail leading into the vast, deeply shadowed wilderness to some unknown destination. Would she ever feel truly safe again? As the party plodded along in silence, she resigned herself to her disheartening fate, praying for the grace to endure whatever lay ahead.

Her thoughts reverted back to her arrival at the tiny river settlement a scant two hours ago, to meeting Nate Kinyon. From the first moment he stepped into her life, he'd shown nothing but kindness. . .the only modicum of human decency she'd encountered since disembarking the ocean vessel. She'd felt instinctively that he had a trustworthiness about him, that he was a man of his word. He'd said he'd come to Mr. Smith's store and try again to rescue her. The promise in his voice, in his eyes lingered in her heart after he walked away.

Even now she replayed the scene in her mind, allowing it to fill her with hope. Was it possible that the Lord sent him for the very purpose of reuniting her with Mariah and Lily? Or had he merely acted the part of a gentleman to go along with his fine clothes? Perhaps this whole predicament was the Almighty's punishment for rashly having taken control of her family's situation without so much as a prayer for wisdom and guidance, and now God was leaving her to stew in this mess she'd brought on herself and her sisters. The possibility was too horrid to dwell on, and her heart ached with the pain of loss.

Not liking the direction her thoughts were taking, Rose turned around and met the face of the feathered savage directly behind her. Clad in buckskin trousers similar to Mr. Smith's, he wore no shirt but had a decorative thing made of colored beads around his neck. His hair, parted in the middle, had been plaited and tied with leather strips.

In the shadowed foliage, the mounted Indian appeared darker than ever as a sly, unpleasant smirk brought a sinister glint to his coal-black eyes.

Rose pretended not to notice and gazed beyond him to the rest of the pack train traversing along a path so narrow it could accommodate only a single horse at a time. Each of the five Indian riders trailed a string of four loaded animals behind them. Taking up the rear, another whip-wielding Indian, this one in buckskin trousers and an open buckskin vest, drove a bull, two cows, and a calf. Feathers adorned his braided hair, also. For such a ragtag, motley party of travelers, they made quite an impressive assemblage, Rose decided. Perhaps Mr. Smith's establishment was not nearly so primitive as he and his native helpers appeared.

The Indian at the rear gave a smart crack of his whip, and Rose jumped at the unexpected sound. The rider behind her chuckled under his breath, adding to her already strained nerves. She sat up straighter, determined not to appear like some weak, simpering female as they forged ever deeper into woods so thick with growth hardly a breath of wind stirred through the treetops.

A spot on one of her thinly pantalooned legs began to chafe. Not wanting to draw undue attention, she casually tucked a bit of petticoat between the hard leather saddle and her knee. Traveling at this slow pace had enabled her to adjust quickly enough to riding horseback, but she feared the animal's swaying and bumping would inevitably take its own toll.

Suddenly from off to the side, wild snapping and cracking echoed through the dense brush. Rose's heart pounded, and she tightened her grip on the saddle's pommel. A doe plunged out of the growth in a blur of brown, missing her by mere inches as it leaped across the trail and clattered into the undergrowth on the other side.

Some other wild creature must be chasing after it! Rose held her breath, waiting, listening, but when she heard nothing but the blowing and *clop-clop* of the horses, the straining of leather, and an occasional birdcall or tree toad, her panic eased. Ahead of her, Mr. Smith continued on as though nothing out of the ordinary had occurred, while she still trembled from head to foot—and this journey into the notorious unknown had only just begun.

A familiar phrase popped into her mind. *"Yea, though I walk through the valley of the shadow of death. . ."*

That's where I'm going, dear Lord. As she felt herself losing the last shred of control, she recalled the rest of the verse: *"I will fear no evil: for thou art with me."*

Are You with me, Father? Will You come with me into this dark, mysterious land? Please don't forsake me, Lord. I'm so alone.

Chapter 5

The woodland trail made a gradual ascent to higher ground as the afternoon slipped away. Now and then an occasional break in the dense forest growth provided Rose with a brief glimpse of a nearby stream paralleling the trail. Occasionally she heard disturbing and unfamiliar wild cries emanating from deep in the forest on either side. Determined not to let them affect her, she governed her emotions and watched Mr. Smith for his reaction. Nothing seemed to disturb him.

His horse whinnied then, as did the others. The trader reined his animal to a stop and pulled a pistol out of his belt.

Rose's horse came automatically to a stop behind Mr. Smith's, its ears perked and flicking from side to side. Rose tensed, wishing she had a firearm of her own for protection. She detected the sound of hooves coming toward them from the opposite direction and turned to glance at the Indian in back of her.

He, too, had drawn a weapon. A big, long musket.

From around a curve rode two bearded, scraggly, lean men attired in the fringed garb Rose had become used to seeing since her arrival in the backcountry. They also held weapons at the ready.

"That you, Smith?" the lead rider hollered. "Thought fer sure the buzzards had picked them bones o' yers clean by now."

"It's me, all right. An' still in the flesh, to boot." He tucked away his pistol. "You boys headed in to spend yer money?"

The man in front grinned, drawing up alongside Mr. Smith. "That's the plan. Gonna have me a high ol' time with—" Catching sight of Rose, his mouth gaped open. "Horsefeathers, Eustice. You got yerself a young white woman there!"

He straightened in the saddle and lifted his bearded chin. "No. What I got me is a cook there. An' don't none of you yahoos forget it."

Dragging his eyes off Rose, the man swung around to the rider in back of him. "You see that? Smith's got hisself a—a cook!" Turning again to the trader, his mouth went into a slack grin. "If'n you say so."

"I do." His tone took on a defensive edge, and no smile softened his demeanor. "The gal's me bondservant, bought an' paid for with hard cash."

"Well, I'll be dogged." The newcomer's eyes raked over Rose in a slow survey. "Where 'bouts could a body find a cook like that, I'd like ta know."

"On the docks in Baltimore. That's where." The trader nudged his mount into motion and maneuvered it around the first rider. "Don't have no time to chew the fat with you boys. We're losin' daylight. See y'all later."

Rose's horse started dutifully behind him. As she passed the riders, she was extremely conscious of the way they filled their eyes with her as if they hadn't seen a female in years. But then, all she'd seen for the past several days was men. The sight of another woman would be just as welcome to her. She'd be glad to reach Mr. Smith's store and meet his wife. She was in dire need of feminine companionship herself at this point.

⌐⟋

In the waning daylight, Mr. Smith guided his mount off the path and into a small, level clearing, where he came to a stop. He swung down and approached Rose. "We'll make camp here fer the night. My stomach's not farin' so good. I'll have the boys get a fire started fer ya an' fetch the fixin's fer some mush whilst you go milk the fresh cow."

Still perched on her horse, Rose swept a glance around. "I'm sorry. I don't see a place to cook in."

With an incredulous grimace that scrunched up one side of his scruffy face, he shrugged. "Place! There ain't no place. Just pick a spot." He shook his head in disgust.

She stared dumbly down at the man. "Surely you're not saying we'll be staying here! On the ground!"

"That's right, missy. Right here on the ground. Now get yerself down. I'm hungry." He started to walk away.

"Wait!" Rose tried to come up with some graceful way of getting off her mount while renewed panic filled her. "I'm not sure I know what mush is, and I've never milked a cow before in my life."

Smith stopped in his tracks and turned to gawk at her then narrowed his eyes. "Ya said ya was a cook. Were ya gullin' me?"

"No, sir. Not at all."

"Then it's best ya get busy, ain't it?" He reached up without so much as a by-your-leave and hauled her right off the horse.

It was most fortunate that he kept hold of her momentarily, because her legs felt really strange after riding on a saddle all afternoon. It was all she could do not to sink to the ground in a graceless heap. Doing what she could to gather herself together, she gave him her most forthright look. "I daresay I'm considered quite a fine cook. . .in an actual kitchen. . .with milk already waiting in a pail. And what, might I ask, is mush?" She waved aside a pesky fly.

The trader rolled his eyes and muttered something unintelligible under his breath as he wagged his head in scorn—actions he repeated numerous times over the course of the next quarter hour while he demonstrated how to dispense milk from a cow's udder.

Rose found the squeeze-and-pull chore a touch more difficult than it looked—especially with so many muscles in her lower regions aching while she stooped. And the fact that her Indian audience grinned and snickered at her clumsy efforts didn't make it any easier. Apparently they considered her as inept as Mr. Smith did—these Indians who were supposed to be so dangerous. Though she still felt a bit ill at ease in their presence, they had yet to do anything threatening other than leer in her direction from time to time. Again she concluded that their exploits must have been exaggerated back in England. She purposely disregarded them and continued doing her best while they unloaded several items from the packhorses. She was glad to have a bit of space between her and them. Whenever they were near, she detected a stench she couldn't identify.

After she'd managed to acquire a reasonable amount of milk from the soft-eyed cow, Mr. Smith directed Rose to a blazing campfire, where a tripod fashioned from sturdy sticks held a blackened pot suspended above the heat.

"Watch." If he'd said that once during the last half hour, he'd said it a dozen times. He poured water from his flask into the kettle then opened a gunnysack slumped nearby along with several others. More than a little exasperated, he rammed his filthy hand into the bag and pulled out a fistful of gritty yellow powder. "Cornmeal." Eyeing her pointedly, he tossed the grain into the pot then added a second handful.

It took all of Rose's fortitude to restrain herself from giving the man a piece of her mind, but knowing it would be wiser to hold her tongue, she clamped her lips together. After all, she needed no reminder that she was in the middle of nowhere—a lone female with seven men—a precarious situation if ever there was one.

The trader grabbed a stick from a pile of kindling off to the side and rubbed it across his grubby pants as if that would do more to clean it than recent rains could have done, then used it to stir the contents of the pot. After that, she surmised, he no doubt expected her to eat the nasty mess.

"See?" Straightening from the fire, he turned to her with a smug grimace. "Nothin' to it. Course it'll need a pinch o' salt, an' I'm partial to some sweetenin'. After the water boils down some, pour in some o' that rich milk. That's all there is to it. Mush." He handed Rose the stir stick. "Just don't let it get lumpy."

Determined to remain in the man's good graces, Rose spoke in a casual tone. "I'll do my best. But where might I find the salt and sugar?"

He squinted as if his patience had reached the painful limit and stepped directly in front of her, his foul breath almost smothering her. She held her ground despite the inclination to step back from the stench. "Don't try playin' dumb with me so's I'll send ya back, gal. It ain't gonna happen." He kicked at another large sack. "Salt." And the one next to it. "Sugar." With a "humph" of disgust, he stomped away to where the Indians were rigging tarps between trees.

Despite her intentions not to upset the trader any more than necessary, Rose gulped in dismay. Surely those flimsy bits of cloth would not constitute their only shelter for the night! The very thought made her ill. Mosquitoes had voracious appetites after dark, and already she had more bites than she could count. Each evening during the trip upriver, the trader had managed to secure food and lodging for the party at various villages along the way, so they'd been protected from insects. Tonight would be different.

How many more nights in the open lay ahead? Small wonder that when she questioned him about their destination he'd been so vague. The man was scarcely more than a sneaky weasel. But then she was probably every bit as stupid as he thought she was. Hadn't she gotten herself in this untenable predicament in the first place? Even convicts balked at being sent to America as indentured servants to pay their sentences. She should have thought of that before undertaking such a rash course of action. Had she saved her father from prison only to condemn herself to an even worse fate?

As another mosquito sang in her ear, she swatted it away.

Observing her action, the trader chuckled. "If ya ask one o' them Injuns fer some o' that bear grease they smear on their bodies, ya won't have none o' them bugs botherin' ya."

Bear grease. So that accounted for the stench around them. Rose didn't respond.

~~~

Assorted night sounds magnified in the fading twilight around the camp, adding to Rose's heightened anxiety as she tried to dislodge a piece of dried meat from between her teeth with her tongue. Losing a battle with persistent mosquitoes that seemed drawn to the light, she appreciated the swift bats cavorting overhead, making a meal of the loathsome insects. Across the fire from her, Mr. Smith sipped from a tin mug of steaming tea, straight from a beat-up old pot, leaves and all. She ignored his steady perusal of her, unable to envision what tasteless gruel he expected her to concoct next.

He pointed with a grubby finger toward one of the stained tarps now stretched out about three feet above the rocky, leaf-strewn ground. The poorest excuse for a red blanket she had ever seen had been tossed beneath, apparently for her use. "Over there's where you'll bed down fer the night."

Rose slid a troubled glance from the makeshift bed to the Indians crouched around another campfire a scarce stone's throw away.

Smith gave a snort. "Don't bother frettin', little missy. Them redskins know yer my property, an' they'll think twice b'fore triflin' with anything what b'longs to me."

Thus far the trader had shown no inclinations of a trifling nature either, but Rose dreaded having to attempt sleeping on hard ground that in all likelihood would be damp and lumpy with rocks. Far worse, that disgusting blanket quite possibly housed lice, bedbugs—or some other night-crawling vermin known only to the colonies. A shiver coursed through her at the unwelcome possibility.

Thankful she'd had foresight enough to pack some necessities for the journey from England, Rose got up from the chest she'd used for a seat and dragged it over to the tarp. She'd use the scant bedding she'd brought with her, along with her cloak, to ward off the night chill. Her shawl would do for a pillow, and the trunk itself would provide whatever privacy she could hope for in such a situation. As to whether she'd get a wink of sleep in the company of so many strange men was yet to be determined—especially with unseen forest creatures prowling about. After heading for a nearby bush to answer nature's call, she returned to her designated sleeping spot, swallowing her fear as the mournful howl of wolves filtered through the trees.

Surely Mr. Smith and the others would keep their weapons at the ready, she assured herself as she tried to ignore the incessant chirping of crickets. The men seemed to be used to making their way through the wilderness. Down on her knees while she created her own small haven in the dark, Rose heard the hobbled horses in the meadow whinny as they'd done that afternoon, when they'd signaled the approach of riders. She paused in her work and peered over her trunk.

Mr. Smith snatched up his musket and stepped out of the glow of the campfire, and the Indians melted silently into the shadows.

Rose's pulse throbbed in her throat. She'd heard tales of land pirates— and of savage Indians who tortured and murdered unsuspecting folks. Now she could only wait to see what sort of fate awaited this camp in the wilds. The temperature had dipped lower once the sun was no longer dominating the daytime hours, and a cool, pine-scented breeze wafted through the clearing, adding to her shivers.

"Halloo the camp!" came a shout from the direction of approaching horse hooves. "It's us. Nate Kinyon and Black Horse Bob."

Releasing a slow breath, Rose eased up in her hiding place behind the trunk as Mr. Smith and the Indians moved back into the firelight, their weapons now lowered. The silhouettes of two riders on horseback, followed by a couple of packhorses, met her eyes. And foolish though she knew it was, Rose had never been so glad to see anyone in her life.

Mr. Smith, however, appeared none too pleased to have visitors. His expression in the erratic firelight resembled a scowl as the two riders in fringed buckskin dismounted. Rose couldn't discern the newcomers' features in the dark, but she recognized the taller of the pair as Mr. Kinyon. She focused on his familiar form, still appealing and muscular in the brushed leather clothing as he towered over her owner.

"Thought you was headed downriver," the trader said, his tone somewhat accusing.

Kinyon shrugged, moving closer into the fire glow. "Been gone from home so long I figgered Ma wouldn't recognize me anyway."

Rose noticed that the other frontiersman wore dark braids and had a lithe build similar to those of the Indians at the other fire. He gave a hearty whack to Kinyon's back. "'Specially in them fancy duds. Ol' Nate looked like one of them parrots I once saw down in York Town. All bright colored and struttin' up an' down on some ol' sea captain's shoulder like he was the king of the realm."

Apparently still put off by their unexpected arrival, Mr. Smith gave a grudging grunt at the man's levity.

Mr. Kinyon swept a glance around in the darkness, taking measure of the camp. "Where's our Miss Harwood, Eustice?"

"She ain't *your* anything," the trader rasped. "Don't be gettin' any notions about her in yer head. But seein' as how you two are here, yer welcome to stay. The more weapons the better."

Listening to the exchange, Rose felt silly crouched down in the shadowed confines of the tarp, but she wasn't certain it would be prudent to stand and present herself.

Mr. Smith made the decision for her. "As fer my cook, my property, she's already abed." He didn't bother to gesture in her direction.

The braided fellow tilted his dark head. "Now that's a real shame. I was lookin' forward to seein' this *property* of yours. Reckon it can wait'll mornin'. Think I'll mosey over and see what our Shawnee brothers think of the new gal. That might be pretty interestin'." He flashed an amused grin.

Rose watched from her haven as the man left his friend and joined the Indians sitting cross-legged around the other campfire. From what she could tell in the limited light, he appeared to have a darker complexion than either Smith or Kinyon. Possibly he was an Indian himself, though the easy way he had of speaking like a white man surprised her. She returned her attention to the trader and their other visitor.

"I drunk up most of the tea, but I believe there's some dregs left in the pot," Smith said. "There's cups in that sack by yer foot."

Deciding his tone had taken on a smidgen of friendliness, Rose eased down on her makeshift bed and laid her head on her wadded-up shawl. An owl hooted from not far away, and as she leaned out from the tarp toward the sound, her breath caught at the beauty of the night sky. Millions of stars twinkled like diamonds against the cobalt blue, reminding her of the awesome power of God and His tender care for His creation. She hoped He hadn't forgotten her and her plight. Deep in thought, she breathed in the night air bearing traces of woodsmoke, damp earth, and the ever-present pine.

The firelight reflecting on the tarp was blocked momentarily then reappeared as Mr. Kinyon moved between her sleeping spot and the fire to settle down with her owner. "Don't s'pose you heard anything new from up New York way while you was down in Baltimore."

"Like what?"

"I don't know. I'm just wonderin', since the French sent that large force down from Fort Frontenac on the Ontario. Hear tell they're plannin' to build forts down as far as the Ohio. The Federation's gettin' real nervous."

"You talkin' the Iroquois Federation? What difference would it make to them, I'd like ta know. If anybody should start worryin', it should be us English traders."

"The Mohawks especially are concerned about the Senecas. Pretty much all the Seneca villages have pulled up stakes an' are now hangin' out at the French posts. Lots of gifts an' promises have been made to 'em. The other tribes are afraid the French'll woo 'em into attackin' the English tradin' posts along the rivers."

Listening to the news, Rose edged forward a bit and tugged her cloak more closely around herself. She'd hoped the conflict between the Indian tribes and the settlers had eased long ago as the colonies became more populated.

Kinyon continued in his even tone. "Since the Federation chiefs signed agreements to support the English, you'd better believe they ain't happy. If there's trouble, they say they won't attack their Seneca brothers. They figure that'd destroy their own treaties."

The trader snorted. "Aw, just more of the same ol' gossip. Most of the Iroquois tribes are partial to our trade goods. They'll stick with us.

'Sides, it don't have nothin' to do with me. My store's in a Shawnee town. Way south of all that squabblin' betwixt the governor of New York an' the Frenchies."

Shawnee town? Weren't the Shawnee a tribe of Indians? Why, that awful man was carting her off to the wilds to live in an Indian town! Rose's spirits sank to a new low. Each piece of information she'd heard this day was worse than the one before. She settled into her uncomfortable, lumpy bed, her thoughts awhirl in her head. This whole thing had to be a really bad dream. Soon she'd wake up to find all would be well.

Lord God in heaven, please make this circumstance merely a horrible nightmare. Ever since Mother passed away, I've been faithful to do my duty. I took care of my family just as I was supposed to. I ran a fine household. I lived the life You ordained. But now. . .I feel as if I've been thrown out to be devoured by wolves.

Hot tears trailed down her cheeks, and Rose curled into a ball, pulling her cloak over her head. It was bad enough having had to dispose of treasured family possessions and be forced to leave her beloved homeland to endure endless days of seasickness and weeks on a ship tossed about on angry waves. Then to be humiliated before leering strangers on an auction block and parted from her sisters for an interminable time. But now this! This was far worse. Here she was in the midst of some frightful, unknown wilderness with an uncouth man dragging her off to a village of heathens who spoke a tongue she did not understand—and who might invariably decide to murder her in the end. What had she done to deserve such a horrid fate?

Chapter 6

A cacophony of birdsong drew Rose out of deep slumber. Surmising she must have left the window open, she snuggled deeper into her warm haven for a few more moments of sleep before rising to prepare breakfast for her family.

The raucous *rat-a-tat-tat* of a woodpecker brought her fully awake, to the realization that there was no window, there was no family. She was in the middle of nowhere, a lone woman in a camp full of men, most of whom were heathen Indians.

As she rolled over to take a look beyond her trunk, every bone in her body ached, and muscles she'd been completely oblivious to all of her life protested. The mere thought of having to get on that blasted mangy horse again made her want to groan aloud. Nevertheless, she managed a painful roll onto her side and raised her head enough to peek out at the camp.

The faint blush of dawn was just beginning to make an appearance through a break in the trees. Rose barely made out two men slumbering beneath furry hides near the dead campfire, likely Mr. Kinyon and his friend. Off to one side of them, loud snoring interspersed with the occasional snort drifted from beneath a strung tarp. She smirked.

Mr. Smith, of course.

A number of yards away, the Indians occupying the other camp also lay sleeping. At least it would allow her time to go down to the creek and make herself more presentable. Perhaps more than presentable. She needed to look as good as humanly possible so Mr. Kinyon would feel compelled to do all in his power to redeem her from Mr. Smith and reunite her with her sisters.

She eased gingerly to her knees and crawled out from under her tarp then forced herself to stand, biting her lip at the aches and pains the slightest movement caused. Cautiously picking up her valise so as not to disturb the others, she tiptoed on stiff legs out of the camp toward the sound of the rushing creek.

But. . .fifty pounds. That was a fortune indeed, an insurmountable amount of money for someone to acquire. *Father, it cannot be Your will that I be taken into a land of wild savages. The Bible says that nothing is too hard for You. Surely You can get me back to civilization.*

Detecting movement back at the camp, Rose looked over her shoulder and saw one of the Indians beginning to stir. Once again she was reminded of her precarious situation. She hoped the God who made the heavens truly knew about her. And truly cared.

Nate shifted position on his sleeping mat to alleviate the annoyance of the sharp pebble poking into his hip. The rock wasn't the only thing irritating him. He should be halfway to his mother's by now, sleeping in a soft, warm bed and waking to the smell of bacon and biscuits at some friendly inn. But no. One brief encounter with a single female—an Englishwoman, at that—and here he was, sleeping out in the open on the rocky ground. He stifled a disgusted groan at his insanity.

Lifting his head slightly, he surveyed the camp and surrounding pasture in the faint daylight. Cows! Smith was bringing along cows to go with his new cook! There seemed no end to the man's foolhardiness. At the other camp, he saw one of the trader's hired Shawnee braves at work coaxing a new fire to life. Rumbling snores emitting from a nearby tarp announced Eustice Smith's sleeping presence.

He could not see around Miss Harwood's trunk at the other strung tarp. But maybe if he got up and gathered sticks for a fire he might "accidentally" catch a peek at the lady. He kicked aside his buffalo robe and rose with a stretch onto his moccasined feet. Then, realizing the possibility she might see him at the same time, he smoothed his rumpled buckskins and untied the thong holding his hair at the back of his neck. Using his fingers, he tamed the unruly mess as best he could and retied the leather strip around his queue again. After all, the fact that most women seemed to consider him handsome was not lost on him. No sense spoiling the image. He felt a smug grin tug at his lips.

As he began gathering wood from deadfall at the edge of the camp, he caught a flash of motion coming from the trees. He thought in reflex of his musket's location then realized it was merely the woman returning from the direction of the mountain stream. The same dress she'd worn before still clung enticingly to her young, womanly curves, and he noticed that the brown shade was as soft as that of a fawn and matched her coiled hair. Her complexion, still pink from the cold water, made her gray-blue eyes appear large and luminous. He remembered then why he'd come back.

She walked—or limped, to be more precise—out of the forest and came to an abrupt stop when she saw him. Realizing he'd been gawking unabashedly, he stepped forward. "Excuse me, miss. I musta forgot my manners. I'll get you a cook fire goin' before I go wash up."

"Thank you, Mr. Kinyon. That's very kind of you," she said softly. She turned and dropped her valise on the trunk.

Reveling in the sound of that lovely, refined voice of hers, Nate caught himself staring at her trim figure again. Any man worth his salt would be most fortunate to bask in her attributes. Not that he was of a mind to forfeit his adventurous life just to settle down, but he could understand why others might be so inclined. Giving himself a mental shake, he turned his attention to gathering enough kindling to start a fire.

Moments later, kneeling down to feed dry grass to some banked embers while he coaxed a spark to flame, he sensed rather than heard her light step behind him. He turned on his heel.

She gazed down at him. "No doubt you'll think this sounds silly, but I've not the slightest idea what sort of meal is required of me or what is to be done."

"Meal, miss? When we're on the trail we usually just finish off the game we shot an' roasted the night before. I notice you got a pot of somethin' sittin' on that firestone. What's in there?"

She grimaced. "Some sort of a cornmeal mixture he called 'mush.' Disgusting concoction, I thought."

Nate had to smile. He opened his mouth to reply, but movement on the far side of the campfire interrupted him.

Where he lay on a sleeping mat, Bob propped himself up on an elbow with a lazy grin and peered up at Miss Harwood. "Now I see what the big hurry was all about."

Ignoring the barb he knew was directed at him, Nate gave his full attention to nursing the tiny flame again.

Miss Harwood moved to his side. "How do you do," she whispered to the half-breed Indian. She put a finger to her lips then pointed to the tarp where Mr. Smith still sawed wood. "I don't believe we've been properly introduced. I'm Rose Harwood."

He sprang to his feet, an eager gleam in his dark eyes. "That's a real purty name," he said in a much quieter tone. "From now on, ever' time I see a rose, it'll put me in mind of you." Taking a step closer, he bowed at the waist. "My name is Robert Bloom Jr., Miss Harwood. But if you prefer, my ma's people call me Boy on a Black Horse."

Tucking his chin at his partner's overt display of interest, Nate let out a small huff. "An' the rest of us call him Horse Bob or just Bob most of the time." Glancing up at her, he remembered to smile.

She returned his smile then switched her attention to his partner. "I believe I shall call you Mr. Bloom. If you don't mind, of course."

"No, miss. I'd be pleased. It's got a real respectful ring to it, don't it?"

The guy was taking a real shine to the Englishwoman, Nate realized. Gritting his teeth, he tossed a few sticks on the growing fire then stood to his feet. "I'll take the teakettle down to the stream an' fill it whilst Bob an' me wash up." He nailed his partner with a glare.

Watching after the pair as they took their leave, Rose felt renewed hope blossoming in her chest. Perhaps she could glean some much-desired information from those two frontiersmen if she invited them to breakfast. She sensed that even the dusky-skinned man seemed intent on making a good impression on her. He might be another ally in her effort to return to civilization. With that thought in mind, she stirred some extra cornmeal and water into the pot. With any luck, there'd be sufficient milk left from last eve, and a touch of extra sugar should make it better than yesterday's.

She worked quietly, hoping Mr. Smith would sleep longer. At the other camp, however, she noticed that more of the Indians were up and about. She wished they'd stop ogling her. . .but comforted herself with the assurance that they simply weren't used to seeing many fair-skinned women.

Rose added more wood to the fire and positioned the pot of mush over the flames. As she stirred the mixture, she saw that her hands were now soiled with soot and dirt. Not only that, but a loose wisp of hair was flying about on the breeze. Noticing the two tall, leather-clad men striding out of the trees toward her, she wiped her hands on the smudged apron she'd worn last eve then tucked the strand of hair back into proper order. She focused on Mr. Kinyon, hoping her assessment did not appear anything beyond casual interest. To her own amazement, she decided buckskin suited the man far more than did proper English garb. In that comfortable clothing he appeared infinitely more capable of keeping her safe.

As the two passed her trunk, they each grabbed an end and brought it over near the fire. "For milady to sit on," Kinyon announced quietly. He placed the teakettle among some outer embers.

From his quiet tone, Rose concluded she wasn't the only one who wanted to delay the trader's awakening. "Thank you again. The mush will be ready in a few minutes. I'd be most pleased if you both would join us for breakfast this morn."

Mr. Bloom smiled, the whiteness of his teeth brilliant against his dark skin and much tidier braids. "We were hopin' you'd give us an invite."

"Then do have a seat, gentlemen." Rose felt a rush of heat in her cheeks at the awareness that there were no chairs to be had.

The men didn't seem to notice. They dropped down onto the ground and crossed their legs, while she perched on her trunk. "I have a question to ask of you. . .if you wouldn't mind answering."

"Anything," they answered in unison, then swapped peculiar looks.

Rose did her best to squelch a smile. "Mr. Kinyon, I couldn't help overhearing you speaking to Mr. Smith last eve. About the French and a tribe of Indians, I mean, attacking English trading posts. I—"

Kinyon raised a hand, stilling her. "You needn't be worryin' about that sort'a thing. Where you're goin' is way to the south of the area we were discussin'—unless I figger out a way to talk ol' Eustice into sendin' you back out with me first."

"That's just it, don't you see?" She inclined her head. "I've asked the man at least a dozen times where it is he's taking me. But he has yet to answer me."

"No wonder." Mr. Bloom chuckled.

Glaring at his partner, Mr. Kinyon picked up a small stick and smoothed out the dirt before him. He drew a large square then pointed the stick at the center. "Think of that space as bigger'n your whole England. To the west are these mountains we're crossin'." He sketched a rough map in the dirt. "At the north end are some huge inland seas of freshwater that are as far west as the Mississippi River an' run into each other until they empty into the St. Lawrence River that dumps into the Atlantic. Along them lakes an' both rivers is where the Frenchies have forts an' fur tradin' posts."

"I've read about the Mississippi. Doesn't it flow all the way down to New Orleans, the port on the southern coast?"

"Right." He pointed to the far bottom corner of his dirt map. "An' the French have decided they want everything in the center area that New York an' Virginia have claimed. Them Frenchies are a greedy bunch, so they brought in some soldiers an' established a store. . .about here." He indicated a spot not far below the most eastern lake.

"And just where is Mr. Smith's trading post located?"

He pointed farther south with the tip of the stick. "I'd put it here. On the Muskingum River just before it pours into the Ohio."

"Well, that doesn't look so very far to me," Rose said, trying to sound hopeful despite the niggle of dread spreading through her.

"It might not *look* far on a map," Mr. Bloom cut in. "But what with all the rivers an' creeks we'll be crossin' to get there, it'll take four, maybe five weeks through some not-so-friendly Indian country. 'Specially with the horses an' all Smith's trade goods."

"Not so friendly?" Purposely overlooking the proposition of spending four or five interminable weeks on the trail, Rose mouthed her main concern.

Mr. Kinyon quickly stepped in. "Bob means not so friendly to the French, lass. The English have made treaties with most of the tribes where Smith's store is located. An' the tribes want English goods as much as the English want the furs the Indians provide."

Only slightly comforted by his elaboration, Rose had to be sure. "So then everything is fine at Mr. Smith's trading post, just as if he were in a foreign country like Spain or Portugal." It was more question than statement.

Kinyon cocked his head back and forth. "More or—"

Following his gaze, Rose saw that the trader had risen.

Smith peered at the two men then at her. "I see ya got breakfast goin'. Good. We'll be hittin' the trail soon as we've et." He strode toward the Indian camp. "You boys start loadin' the horses."

"Reckon we better get to ours, too." Kinyon stood to his feet. "No sense keepin' Eustice waitin.'"

As far as Rose was concerned, the later they broke camp and left, the better, because nothing Mr. Kinyon or Mr. Bloom had said made her feel any more at ease about what lay in her future. She'd overheard the frontiersman tell the trader last eve that several hundred French soldiers were heading south. . .and they had Indian allies aiding them in their intentions.

Chapter 7

Rummaging through the sacks by the campfire, Rose unearthed enough spoons, wooden bowls, and cups for herself and the three men to use for breakfast. Now she had to figure out where to set things. What she would give for a proper table covered with pristine linen and lovely china, a real home. She'd taken such niceties for granted back in England, where she had no difficulty acting the hostess and serving guests. But out here in the woods, nearby logs and stones would have to suffice.

The ever-present awareness that the men in both camps observed her slightest movement both perplexed her and filled her with a strange sense of worth. Back home in Bath, most locals had considered her only goldsmith Henry Harwood's spinster daughter. Those who knew how she'd taken her mother's place and cared for her family members looked on her with pity that she'd never experience the benefits bestowed by matrimony.

Lifting the kettle away from the fire to pour in tea leaves for steeping, Rose glanced up to see how far along the men were with tying the bundles onto the packhorses. Obviously this was the accepted mode of transporting goods in the colonies, as normal and common as the freight wagons that rumbled along the cobblestone streets of Bath to deliver wares to the city's wealthy inhabitants.

One particular detail set the Indians apart from the English, however, and that was the variety of ways they dressed their straight black hair. Two of the braves wore braids. Another had his head shaved except for a short, narrow strip running from front to back, and a fourth let his hair flow loose, except for a small braid on each side. The one herding cows had the front portion pulled up in a topknot that exploded with feathers. But all of them used beads and feathers in assorted ways to decorate their hair.

And one of them leveled a bold stare right at her.

Diverting her gaze, Rose walked purposefully over to her bedding, gathered it up, and carried it to her trunk. Except for Mr. Smith's disgusting blanket, she folded each item and packed it away so her things would be ready to be picked up when the men carted off the foodstuff. Thank goodness the trader hadn't required her to load her chest onto a horse. It was one thing to drag her property along on the ground, as she'd done when they'd traveled by flatboat, but quite another to have to lift the heavy belongings over her head.

After she finished packing the chest, she locked it and laid the folded tarp and red blanket on top. Another glance toward the men revealed Mr. Kinyon, Mr. Bloom, and Mr. Smith heading toward her. She reached up and gave a quick pat to her hair to make certain no stray wisps had worked loose before pouring the tea.

"Everything's ready," she said on their arrival. She fixed a cup of half tea, half milk and handed it to the odorous trader.

Slightly out of breath, as if he'd just completed backbreaking labor, he dropped down on a log, eyes closed, and took a sip of the hot brew.

Rose flicked a glance at the other two men. "Would you care for milk in yours as well?"

"No, it's fine like this." Mr. Bloom reached out a hand for his.

Mr. Kinyon nodded as he accepted the one offered to him. "Same here. We don't wanna be no bother."

"An' I'll be holdin' ya to that," the trader announced in his weary

SALLY LAITY AND DIANNA CRAWFORD

tone. He opened his narrow eyes enough to glare at them.

Rose leaned over the pot and scooped a portion of mush into a wooden bowl, adding some crushed sugar, milk, and a spoon. She handed it to her owner. "'Tis such a lovely morn." She dished out a second bowl. "The sun has come up, the birds are singing, and the hand of Almighty God kept us safe through the long night. I do believe we would be remiss if we forgot to ask Him to bless our food and today's journey."

The three swapped dubious looks. Mr. Smith put down his spoon.

Rose handed Mr. Kinyon the next bowl, oddly aware that he didn't meet her gaze this time. He just stood there, cup in one hand, bowl in the other. As she scooped out Mr. Bloom's portion, an awkward sort of silence permeated the air. Nevertheless, Rose was not about to retract her request. If her lot was to accompany these men into the wilderness, she was determined to take the Lord along with her.

Finally the trader cleared his throat. "I b'lieve Nate here's the one who usually gives the blessing, don't you, boy?" He winked at Mr. Bloom.

Mr. Kinyon's eyes flared wide. He glanced from Mr. Smith to his partner, who was losing his battle against a grin. Adjusting his stance, the frontiersman inhaled a sharp breath and turned to Rose. "Once you're settled, I'd be glad to do the prayin'."

Though he'd given in to the woman to be polite, Nate felt as if he'd just been cornered by a pack of ravenous wolves. Nobody had asked him to say grace over food in—in—how many years? Not as far back as he could recall. And both those jokesters knew it.

Miss Harwood remained calm, as if she'd just asked the most natural thing in the world, then she sprang to her feet. "Oh! I've forgotten to bring out the dried meat." She set down her bowl and hurried to retrieve some from one of the sacks.

Given a moment's blessed reprieve, Nate racked his brain for the words his father always said before meals. *Father in heaven. . .Father in heaven. . .bless the food. . . .* What else?

All too soon the woman was back, passing strips of jerky to each of them.

His partner and that snake-in-the-grass Smith still sported mocking grins.

Miss Harwood retook her seat on the trunk and looked expectantly up at him with those luminous blue eyes, eyes filled with so much hope they stole his breath.

Nate shot a quick glance to see if the Shawnee were watching, but they were occupied with their own meal and not paying them any mind. Relieved, he filled his lungs and let out all the breath at once. All right. He could do this. How hard could it be?

Three heads bowed. Waiting.

Nate removed his broad-brimmed hat and cleared his throat. He swallowed. "Father in heaven, bless this food, an'. . .an' thank You for . . .for a cloudless day an'. . .a pretty woman to look at." *Couldn't hurt to be charming.* "Oh, an' amen." Then, realizing he was the only one still standing, he slapped his hat back on, plopped onto his buffalo robe, and balanced his mush along with the cup of tea, glad the ordeal was over.

A snicker issued from the log as Mr. Smith hiked his shaggy brows. "Didn't know ya had it in ya."

Nate branded him with a glower. "There's a lot about me folks don't know, Eustice."

The trader gave a grudging nod. "A lotta truth in that. You long hunters spend most of yer time braggin' and lyin' about how you can shoot out the eye of a squirrel at a hundred yards, or how you outwrestled some she-bear. We never hear the real stuff."

A span of uncomfortable silence magnified the sounds of forest creatures coming to life. Already the tree toads' chorus drowned out the trill of the birds cavorting from branch to branch in the nearby thicket. Overhead a hawk circled against the blue sky, on the hunt for a warm, tasty morsel to carry off in its talons and devour.

Miss Harwood's gentle voice broke into the quiet. "Mr. Kinyon, I believe you spoke of going to visit your mother yesterday. Pray, where does she live?"

Glad for the change of subject, Nate felt his tension ease. "A couple days downriver from where you docked, miss. My older brother took over my pa's place after he passed on. Ma stayed there with him an' his young'uns."

"Then I'm sure she's well cared for." She took a spoon of mush and swallowed it. "It must give you great comfort to know your mother's in good hands when you're deep in the wilderness."

He spoke in all candor. "Never gave it much thought, to tell you the truth. With the farm goin' to the oldest son, I figger the duty of lookin' after Ma fell to him, too. Besides, she's real partial to his offspring. Young Nathan, the one they named after his handsome, adventurous uncle, he's a real corker." Feeling the tips of his ears heat up at the outrageous boast, Nate gave her a lopsided grin. "An' I myself was named after someone in the Bible, Miss Harwood. Ma was pretty fond of a couple of the prophets an' liked to read their writin's over an' over."

At this, Bob set his empty bowl aside and chimed in. "Far as names go, I got Nate's beat by a mile. I was named after Scotland's greatest king, Robert the Bruce."

She smiled. "How splendid. That man was a great leader, freeing the Scots from an oppressive English king." She looked back at Nate. "And Nathan in the Old Testament was a brave prophet indeed to stand up to King David and cause him to face the dreadful sin he'd committed by taking another man's wife. I should like you gentlemen to know I think it's marvelous that you both honor your heritage. . .as I do mine."

Smith snorted under his breath, but Nate ignored him. "From your manner an' speech, Miss Harwood, I can tell you came from a fine family. Whereabouts is it, exactly, that you hail from?"

"Why, thank you, Mr. Kinyon. I do indeed come from fine, God-fearing folk. And had it not been for the untimely death of a young lord who owed my father a great deal of money, I allow I'd still be living in the bosom of my family in Bath, England. But alas, many sacrifices had to be made to spare our family from total ruin."

The trader guffawed with such relish, mush spewed out of his mouth. He wiped his chin on his sleeve. "Woman, I'd say any family what has to sell off its daughters is already in ruination."

She hiked her chin and arched her brows higher, answering him with a tinge of vexation in her voice. "I should have you know, Mr. Smith, that my sisters and I gladly took it upon ourselves to sell our services for a mere four years to save our family's home and livelihood. I've not the slightest doubt that our father will have saved enough funds to send for us by the time we have completed our terms, if not before."

Intrigued by her story despite the limited details she'd provided, Nate wanted her to be sure he was on her side. "Know that I'm at your service, lass, for as long as you need me."

She returned an appreciative gaze to him and opened her lips to speak but was interrupted.

"Me, too," Bob injected. Nate glared at his irritating partner for butting in.

The trader shook his head in disgust and got up from the log, not bothering to dust off his backside. "Just remember, both of ya, she's at *my* service and *in* my service. . .which reminds me. Get done eatin', woman, and git this mess cleaned up. Day's a'wastin.'" Swinging around, he stalked off toward the heavily laden packhorses.

Fifty pounds. Glaring after him, Nate bit his tongue at the man's churlish treatment of such a refined young woman. Somehow, some way, he had to get his hands on fifty pounds. And a profit.

Chapter 8

Settled again on the horse she'd ridden the day before, Rose did her best to ignore her aching thighs—which doubtless would feel added torture by day's end. Ahead of her, Mr. Smith's mount lumbered along, the muscles of its rump twitching, its straggly tail swishing away blackflies. The steady plodding of the horses' hooves, along with their blowing and nickering, made time pass slowly. From time to time a break in the forest canopy overhead allowed a view of fluffy clouds floating across the expanse of blue. Colorful birds flew among the branches, and the occasional squirrel scampered up a nearby tree trunk. In other circumstances, this could be a pleasant day's diversion from one's daily life. Alas, these circumstances were far from that.

Rose reflected back on the panic she'd experienced at the start of the journey. No amount of praying had calmed her fears about accompanying a strange man and five Indians into deep, dark wilds filled with unidentifiable sounds. This morn, however, she had two knights in shining armor—well, not so shiny, attired in buckskin instead of hammered mail—but still, they were in attendance and hopefully would protect her from harm. She smiled thinly, feeling a bit safer.

The ache in her heart, though, she could not dismiss. How were her sisters faring? Had Mariah settled into her life at the Barclay Plantation? Did she get along with Colin Barclay's mother? And was she remembering to act ladylike and not be a flirt?

And what of dear, sweet Lily? Had she reached her new home? Mr. Kinyon said she'd be located quite a distance from Baltimore. Was she safe now and providing the needed care for her new owner's sickly wife? *Please take care of both my sisters, Father. . .and please hasten the day when we'll be together again.*

The trail broadened, and Robert *the Bruce* Bloom moved alongside Rose on his sleek black horse. Strange, he appeared every inch as much the savage as Smith's Indians, yet he seemed as endearing to her as her youngest brother, Tommy. With skin several shades deeper than a white man's, his features were pleasant, his form tall, lean, and honed. Since he and Mr. Kinyon had joined the party, one or the other would ride next to her whenever space allowed, each regaling her with exploits that outshone his partner's.

As Mr. Bloom approached, Rose planned to take charge of the conversation. His civilized ways fascinated her, and she wanted to learn more about his unusual past.

"Miss Harwood." He greeted her with a broad grin.

She started right in. "Mr. Bloom. I'd like to ask you something, if I may."

"What is that?" Concern furrowed his dusky brow, making his dark brown eyes appear almost black.

To put him at ease, she offered him a small smile. "I'm curious regarding your parents. Having just arrived from across the water, I've never had occasion to meet someone with your background."

His smile fell flat. "You mean about me bein' a half-breed?"

"Not at all. That term hardly describes your heritage. You've actually had the advantage of having parents from two different continents. . . a man of two worlds."

His jovial grin reappeared, and he sat straighter in the saddle. "That does have a more pleasurable ring to it." He paused then continued. "My ma was captured and sold as a slave when she was young, and my pa took it on hisself to marry up with her an' take her to live on his farm. So you're right about the two worlds. Trouble is I never feel like both my feet are welcome in either one, an' no matter where I go, seems part of me's left on the outside."

Rose gave a light laugh. "I know exactly what you mean. From the moment I stepped foot on this continent I've felt as if neither of my feet is touching solid ground. In my wildest girlhood dreams, I never expected to be here in the colonies, let alone find myself traversing a wilderness trail to an unknown destination."

"You came as a surprise to us, too." He chuckled along with her. "It's different with me an' Nate, though. His pa's place bordered ours, so him an' me grew up together as boys, playin' together, fishin' together, best friends. I even had me some schoolin' along with him. When we go out on our own, explorin' some new piece of country, my feet's jest where they wanna be. A'course, there was a spell when the two of us was separated for some years, when Ma run off with me back to her own people."

"Mercy. I'm sure going to a whole new world must have been difficult for a young lad."

He shrugged a shoulder. "Not too bad. They was more willin' to accept my English blood than the white man was my Indian side. I got used to bein' looked down on or just plain ignored by folks. But I had some catchin' up to do with Ma's people, learnin' to hunt with a bow an' such. A lot of their ways seemed strange. Pa's Presbyterian teachin's pulled one way and theirs the other."

"I can understand that." But she wanted to know more, so she plunged on. "How were you able to reconcile the two different teachings?"

He laughed. "If you'd a'knowed my pa, you wouldn't ask that. When I was near sixteen, I came back out to see how him an' Nate was doin', an' Pa wouldn't let up on me till he set me straight. He took down his big ol' Bible ever' night an' read it out loud at the supper table after we finished eatin'. An' once when that preacher Reverend Whitefield come through our town, Pa drug me to the meetin' place to hear him. That Reverend

Whitefield was one powerful preacher, a true man of God, an' like they say, I 'saw the light.' I like to think of myself as one of them New Lights. Nate doesn't b'lieve like me yet, though. I'm still workin' on him."

Rose wondered what Nate's beliefs were. He'd prayed that rather odd prayer at breakfast this morn, but it seemed to come from his heart. She barely restrained herself from turning around to look at him. Instead, she moistened her lips and inhaled deeply. "George Whitefield has also preached to great crowds in my country. I never sat under his teaching myself, however. My family's in good standing with the Church of England. And from what I understand," she added with diplomacy, "the Reverend Whitefield's beliefs differ somewhat from our own."

"That makes you an Anglican, don't it?"

"Yes. In my deepest heart."

He nodded his dark head, gazing off into the distance before turning to her once again. "I always wondered about the difference between you Anglicans an' us Presbyterians but never knowed anybody I could ask about things. Would ya be of a mind to talk to me about it some evenin'?"

Rose couldn't believe her good fortune! A true Christian believer traveling with her! *"Oh, ye of little faith. . ."* God had not deserted her after all. "'Twould be my pleasure, Mr. Bloom."

⸺

"Hold up!"

Almost lulled into semiconsciousness by the gentle rocking of her horse, Rose jerked fully awake when Mr. Kinyon yelled from behind. She swung in her saddle to see the men of the party bringing their animals to a halt.

"Why are we stopping?" Barely twenty minutes had elapsed since the group had stopped to rest the horses.

"Riders comin' after us." He pulled his long-barreled musket from its scabbard and checked its load, as did the others.

Rose scanned the forest trail they'd been steadily climbing. Despite its rustic beauty, she couldn't forget the possibility of real danger lurking along the route. If shooting started, should she race ahead? Hop down and take cover behind a tree? Or. . .

When she saw Mr. Smith dismount at the front of the train, she swung a leg over the saddle.

"Stay put," Mr. Kinyon ordered, passing by with his rifle in hand. "Prob'ly nothin' to worry about."

Probably. She turned on her mount to watch then realized she was the only one still on horseback—a perfect target. Not an ideal situation.

Two white men and a pair of brown-skinned Indians rode up to the end of the column and reined in their horses. Without having drawn weapons, the riders remained on their mounts as they conversed with the travelers in her party, all of whom had congregated at the rear.

One of the newcomers flicked several glances in her direction, making Rose uneasy. Had they come because of her? Had Mr. Smith broken some law by forcing her to accompany him into Indian territory? A tiny ray of hope lessened her fear.

The group talked for several minutes, leaving her to sit and wonder about the proceedings. Finally, the members of her party headed back to their horses, and the strangers slowly worked their way past them on the narrow trail. She didn't know what to think and drew a nervous breath.

Nate Kinyon and Mr. Bloom reached her first. The latter nodded a greeting. "Sorry to tell ya this, but I gotta leave. I'll catch up with ya at Smith's tradin' post soon as I can."

"You're leaving?" Distraught, she cut a glance to his partner. "And you. Are you leaving as well?"

He shook his head and flashed an easy smile. "No, miss. Don't worry yourself none. I ain't goin' nowhere. Bob has to go with these fellows down to a Catawba village. Seems a white boy was brought there to be ransomed back to his folks, an' they need my pal to translate for 'em. The two braves they sent out to make a deal don't talk English so good."

A touch more at ease since Mr. Kinyon wasn't going to desert her, Rose checked back toward the approaching white men.

Their demeanors remained serious, even determined. "Hurry up and say your good-byes," one said to Bloom as they came alongside. "Who knows what them savages already done to Billy—and what all they want from us to get him back."

Rose could easily understand their angst, but she couldn't help remembering that Robert Bloom was the only person with whom she'd been traveling who professed to be a Christian—and now he was leaving her behind to go to the aid of a boy some savages had taken captive. But she couldn't help but identify with the lad—who was probably scared to death being held prisoner by wild Indians—and she empathized with the strangers. "I shall pray for you and the boy, that he'll be safe and unharmed, and that your journey homeward will be without peril."

One of the men took off his hat and bowed his head to her. "Thank you for that." He swept a glance around at her motley group then extended his hand, giving hers a warm squeeze. "We'll be prayin' for you, too, miss. May the good Lord keep you safe in His hand as that devil Smith carts you off into that hellish heathen land of his." He flicked a disgusted glance to her owner, who at that moment was lumbering up the trail from the rear.

Rose felt renewed trepidation as the stranger wagged his head and led his party and Robert Bloom away.

Chapter 9

Determined not to cry as the newcomers and Robert Bloom took their leave, Rose watched after them until they reached the top of the ridge and vanished from sight. How frail was hope, she mused, when it could vanish so quickly. She'd grown accustomed to having Bloom around, had counted on his presence, and his unexpected departure filled her with emptiness.

In front of her, Mr. Smith turned in his saddle, a smug smirk twisting one corner of his mouth. "Now I'll only have one o' them moonstruck jaspers to keep an eye on, Miss Harwood." With a glance encompassing Nate and the others, he raised an arm high, heeling his horse into motion. "Forward, ho."

The flame of embarrassment burned Rose's face. Mr. Kinyon had to have heard the trader's comment. What must he think? Without checking behind to gauge his reaction, she nudged her mount to a walk. But the creaks and plods coming from the caravan as it started up did not muffle the low chuckle that rumbled from the frontiersman's chest. Why, the man actually found the crude remark humorous! She pursed her lips and straightened her shoulders.

As they gained the top of the rise and started down a steep incline, it dawned on Rose that Smith—uncouth and tactless though he may be—may have bought her to be a cook, but had assumed the responsibility of being her chaperone. The smelly trader possessed at least a spark of human decency. At this, Rose nearly laughed herself. Who could have imagined that after the monotonous, predictable life she'd endured in her motherland, her world was destined to be turned upside down?

It would be awhile before Nate would be able to erase the memory of the desolation he'd detected on Miss Harwood's face when Bob rode off to help fetch the kidnapped boy. And the leader of the group's parting remark about praying for her safety had only made things worse. Despite her brave front, the woman had fears enough regarding her uncertain future without some stranger adding to her misery. But leave it to Smith to lighten the mood. He chuckled again.

The trader's attempt at levity sure caught the little gal off her guard, though. Her spine went as straight as a ridgepole, and her neck turned beet red. Nate would look for an opportunity to talk to her, ease her mind a bit. She'd fare well enough if she were prepared for what might lie ahead. They'd come to the Cheat River soon, where they'd raft across the water a few at a time. There might be a chance then to allay some of her misgivings.

The sound of rushing water made it to Rose's ears before the river came into view. It grew gradually louder as they ambled steadily downward, drowning out the usual forest sounds. It must be a river of some size, like the Ohio. That name had been bandied about during the trek, and it was reported to be quite large. The group had been traveling for days already. Perhaps the men hadn't exaggerated about the journey requiring weeks. Mr. Kinyon himself had said they'd be venturing three hundred miles into the wilderness. Had even twenty of those miles been covered yet? It felt like a hundred to her backside.

Soon they came to a break in the forest growth, providing Rose her first glimpse of a wide, swift-flowing river. A number of tall trees had been cut down and used to construct a crude wooden dock jutting out over the water's edge. Two layers of rope stretched from the dock across to the other side, where they wound around a pulley, and a raft made of logs attached at both ends to the lower rope bobbed on the current.

"Blast!" Mr. Smith whacked his hat against his thigh, dislodging a puff of trail dust. "We gotta haul the fool thing over to us."

Rose startled. *The man must be mad if he thinks that pitiful-looking bit of wood can bear the weight of horses and goods—and us!* She observed the rapid swells coursing past the dock. Hearing a horse moving up alongside hers, she slanted a nervous glance at Nate Kinyon.

His expression remained even. "We'll be waterin' the stock before we cross. I'll take your mount down to the river whilst you stretch your legs a bit."

"Surely you don't mean we're expected to cross that wild torrent on that useless conveyance!" She pointed toward the raft, hoping her voice didn't sound as frightened as she felt. When she looked back at Nate, he was actually grinning. She let out a silent huff of displeasure. Did he find everything humorous, for pity's sake?

His countenance never did turn serious. "I reckon the ferry does look a mite puny, but don't be frettin' your pretty self. It's sturdier than you think. Besides, I'll be right there with you to see you don't lose your footin.'"

Rose drew little comfort from his words or his smile. Anyone with sense could see that such an ill-crafted thing could very well be the end of them all. Should she find herself in the churning water, her limited ability to swim would be no match for the river's power, especially if she had to contend with cumbersome skirts and petticoats.

When they reached the dock, the frontiersman reined in and dismounted. He caught up the traces and strode to the front of Rose's horse. "Time to get down, miss. I'll be waterin' the animals now."

Gracefully as possible, Rose acquiesced, counting it a blessing that she didn't collapse at his feet. At least the practice of getting on and off the beast over the past few days had been of some benefit, though her legs still retained an awkward, wooden feel and ached after riding for hours. As the shuffle and clomp of the rest of the caravan surrounded her, she dodged her way to the edge of the river and gazed across to the other side. The men and horseflesh surged down to the water for a drink, and the thirsty cows mooed as they lumbered past in a cloud of dust. No one else appeared concerned about the crossing, so Rose tamped down her own foreboding. She vowed she'd give no further hint of her disquiet but couldn't help gauging the swiftness of the current all the same. *Be with us, Father. See us safely to the other side. . .somehow.*

Mr. Kinyon returned moments later with the horses. He handed Rose a leather flask. "You must be thirsty. Have some cool mountain water whilst we wait for the men to haul the ferry across."

"Thank you." Taking the container, she lifted it to her lips and let the refreshing liquid cool her tongue. How she longed for a much-needed bath after the dusty ride. She lowered the flask and watched the raft moving slowly through the current as a couple of the Indians hauled on the lower ferry rope.

The frontiersman cleared his throat. "There's somethin' you need to know."

What else? she wanted to scream. But considering the new vow she'd made not to reveal her emotions, she took a breath for patience and turned to him. "What is it, Mr. Kinyon?"

He grimaced, crimping up one side of his face. "It's all the *mister* an' *miss* business. Don't you think it's time we get past that nonsense? Could you see fit to call me just Nate, or even Kinyon? An' I'd be purely pleased to call you Rose. If you wouldn't mind."

She gazed beyond him to where the rumpled Mr. Smith was checking the straps and tie-downs on a packhorse. Raising her eyes to meet those of the frontiersman, she was lost in the sincerity she saw in the hazel depths, and her insides went still. "I suppose, under the circumstances, it might not be improper for us to address one another by our given names.

'Tis not as if we are among the gentry out here."

That infectious grin she'd grown accustomed to seeing popped into place again. "No, miss, we surely ain't. Now that we got that outta the way, *Rose*, there's another matter I'd like to set your mind to rest about."

Certain it could only be the "moonstruck jaspers" remark Mr. Smith had made earlier, she steeled her expression and waited for him to elaborate.

"About them Indians kidnappin' that boy. You don't need to worry about that none. Long as you don't go wanderin' off by yourself out here, nothin' like that'll happen to you."

A small shiver went through Rose. "Surely you're not telling me that boy took a walk by himself and got captured by sheer chance!"

"No, not a'tall. His pa said the boy an' his brother an' another lad was out coon huntin' with their dogs after dark. Chasin' after the hounds, they prob'ly got themselves too deep in the woods, and considerin' all the racket dogs make, it would'a been easy for some Cherokee huntin' party to hear 'em." He shrugged a shoulder. "Likely the Indians figgered the boys was trespassin' on their huntin' grounds, so they went after 'em. I expect they must'a killed the two older boys who might'a given 'em trouble an' took the young one to their village. Prob'ly figgered he was young enough to retrain, make him part of their tribe, if his kin didn't offer enough of a price to get him back."

Rose's brows arched in shock. "You're saying that Indians do not consider murder or kidnapping an evil act, then?"

"Not like we do." Nate shifted his stance. "They got different ideas on what's right an' what's wrong. Sometimes they capture a person to replace one of their own who might'a been killed by a white man."

That sort of logic didn't sit well with Rose. She glanced toward the dock at the Indians chatting back and forth between themselves as they worked. She then looked again at Nate. "Indeed, they truly are as savage as I've been told, even if 'tis not apparent at first glance."

He tilted his head and studied her. "No more savage than what's been goin' on in Europe for a thousand years, kingdom against kingdom. The word *Indian* is the one Columbus tagged 'em with when he thought he'd discovered the route to India. These people have their own nations an' clans just like in Europe. Actions that might be considered evil in their own towns an' villages are quite acceptable against other tribes. That includes killin' an' takin' hostages. Indians have their own territories an' languages an' rules of conduct just like in Europe an' the rest of the *civilized* world." He stopped talking abruptly and flashed a sheepish grin. "Sorry. Reckon I was speechifyin' a touch."

Rose smiled. "'Tis quite all right. I suppose the more I'm able to understand regarding this foreign land I'm in, the less apprehensive I'll be. So I gather I'll be going to a town where the neighbors are friendly and business is conducted similar to the way it is in the shops at home in Bath. Is that right?"

"Not exactly." His grin broadened, and he rested an elbow on his horse's saddle. "More like the bargainin' that goes on in the weekly markets or down on the docks in Baltimore, I'd say."

Baltimore. Thinking back on her experience there, Rose recalled seeing a ship of African slaves in chains being off-loaded as she was leaving the wharf. The phrase *savage Indian* lost some of its sting. Their actions couldn't hold a candle to the cruelty of the English slavers who captured and sold other humans into a lifetime of bondage just to line their own pockets with gold. "I do thank you for your frankness, Mr.— Nate. I shall look forward to more of your *speechifyin'*. As I gather more information about the daily lives of the natives here, I'm less befuddled about what I might face when we reach our destination." She paused. "Pray, what is the name of the town I'm going to?"

Nate rubbed his chin. "Don't know as it has a proper name. Some Shawnees an' Delawares started raisin' their wigwams an' longhouses in the area when the fur company contracted for Smith an' his partner to set up their store there. Us longhunters call it Muskingum-at-the-Ohio. . . or just plain Muskingum."

"Muskingum. What an odd name. Whatever does it mean?"

"I ain't rightly sure. I think the word comes from the Erie tribe, or mebbe the Senecas. You see, along the Ohio's been mostly free huntin' and trappin'. No tribe in particular claims that territory. Leastways, not yet."

"Hmm. How odd. In England—as well as all of Europe, I believe— every foot of land in existence is claimed by some individual or some government."

Nate chuckled. "Us humans tend to be a greedy bunch, don't we?"

A laugh bubbled up out of Rose before she could catch herself.

The frontiersman tipped his head, studying her, then stepped closer. "You know, that's the first time I heard you laugh. Don't mind sayin' I like the sound of it."

Rose felt unwelcome heat climb her neck and warm her cheeks as she stared back at him. For a moment all thought fled except how very much she admired his stalwart presence, his face, his smile. . . .

"Yo! Kinyon!" Mr. Smith's bellow from the riverbank halted her midthought. "Stop your moonin' an' git down here. We need to git these skittish horses aboard."

Mooning! The trader had no end of ways to humiliate her. Rose felt her face grow even warmer, especially when Nate's grin widened from ear to ear. Then, recalling the rest of her owner's words, she turned toward the dock and watched the men struggling to coax a loaded horse onto the wobbly raft. Ears back, the brown gelding's eyes walled to the side, and the terrified animal went stiff legged. It would not budge. *I know exactly how you feel, poor thing.*

Reaching the others, Nate whipped off his linen hunting shirt and tossed it over the packhorse's eyes. Almost immediately, the animal began to relax. Rose watched the frontiersman lean close to its ear and speak a few words then lead it slowly from the dock onto the gently rocking ferry, where two other horses had already boarded. Once the gate bars dropped into place, Nate and two of the Shawnee braves tugged on the rope that would take the Indians and the first three horses to the other side of the river.

She knew it was less than ladylike to stare at the man's broad back, but Rose could not deny Nate Kinyon made a rather dashing figure without his shirt. Finely honed muscles stood out with his movements, and the June sunshine lent a glow to his bronzed skin. He truly was quite capable when he put his mind to it. Recalling his promise—or almost promise—to take her back to her sisters, she had no doubt he was a man who'd move heaven and earth to stand by his word.

Watching the raft make its slow passage, a mental image made Rose smile. If she balked about setting foot onto that pathetic, rickety raft, would Nate throw his shirt over her eyes and lead her onto it?

No indeed. A gallant champion like Nate Kinyon would scoop her up into those strong arms of his and carry her aboard bodily.

Chapter 10

Nate focused his attention on loading the raft time and again, then watching it cart animals and various members of the party across the river. But he also observed Rose Harwood from the corner of his eye. Each successful crossing seemed to alleviate her fears a little more, and as old Eagle Eye Smith finally left for the other side, Nate knew her trip would be more enjoyable without the man's presence. Now only one cow and a calf remained to be ferried across, along with Rose, himself, and the last Shawnee, who would help pull them to the other bank.

When the wooden raft returned to their side, Nate turned to Rose. "I believe it's our turn."

"So 'twould appear."

He held out a hand, and she placed her fingers in it.

"Thank you." She managed an uncertain smile.

Though bravely spoken, a slight tremor in her hand belied her spunk. It felt small engulfed in his, small and silky as a flower, and he realized how fitting the name Rose was for her.

He also realized with no small shock that he was becoming completely besotted with the woman! A woman who'd likely cost him at least fifty pounds—and possibly considerably more—if he ever succeeded in convincing Eustice Smith to release her. The trader hadn't hesitated to part with that hefty sum to buy her, and all he'd wanted was a cook. Nate had known Rose but a few short days, and for some illogical reason, she occupied most of his waking hours. He'd lived a footloose life for years, picking up and moving on whenever the notion struck, always anxious to see what lay beyond the next mountain, around the next bend in the trail. Why did this pert little female kindle within him thoughts of home and hearth? He needed to thwart those inklings right now!

But as he led her to the railing near where he'd assist the Indian in working the rope, he found it hard to release that delicate hand enclosed in his.

A glance past her shoulder revealed a knowing smirk on the brave's sun-browned face. Nate offered him a weak grimace and reached for the rope, nodding for the two of them to pull in unison.

Rose stood wide eyed, watching the current with a modicum of acceptance, if not enjoyment. And Nate enjoyed watching her.

In midstream, she turned to him. "Cheat River. Are you acquainted with how it came to have such a curious name?"

"Aye." He huffed with effort as he yanked on the rope. "But first, I'd like to hear how you got your name. It suits you fine."

"My name?" She focused her gaze off into the distance, a tiny smile on her lips. "Actually, while my mother was awaiting my birth, she came across a term in her Bible: 'Rose of Sharon.' She thought it was the loveliest name ever, so that's what she and my father decided to call me."

"Rose of Sharon—"

"Kinyon!"

At the Indian's sharp tone, Nate realized he'd stopped pulling. He immediately got back to work, but not before catching the grin Rose tried to contain as she turned her attention to the water. It didn't bother him in the least. She needed to know he was truly interested. "Your parents must care a great deal for you an' miss you sorely."

She gave a sad shake of the head, the brim of her bonnet dipping on the breeze. "I'm afraid Mum went to be with the Lord when my youngest brother came into the world. I've no doubt that Papa misses my sisters and me a great deal, however. We were quite close."

"I'm sure he does." Nate gave the hemp two sharp yanks. "Especially you."

"And my cooking. Let's not forget about that." The teasing lilt of her voice faded along with her smile, and she turned serious. "Ironic, is it not? 'Tis that very skill that has thrust me upon this tiresome journey." She filled her lungs and let the air out in a slow breath. "Speaking of journeys, this small part of it has almost come to an end. So do tell me from whence this river got its name."

"Oh, that." Nate checked ahead to the dock as the small conveyance neared the wooden structure then gave a hearty pull on the rope. "Hear tell this particular river got its name when some hunters left their gear along the bank while they were off yonder dressin' out a buck. They weren't gone too long. But when they came back, that cheatin' river had made off with all their truck. Swept it away while they weren't lookin.'"

"You can't be serious." Rose slanted him a look of disbelief.

"Sure as I'm standin' here. This river's known to be real tricky. It can wash right up onto its banks and steal a pretty little thing like you away before you know it. And that surely would be a cheat if ever there was one."

Rose closed her eyes and shook her head. "Nate Kinyon. As they say in Ireland, I do believe you've kissed the Blarney Stone."

He chuckled. "Mebbe a time or two." And gazing at those tempting lips on his Rose of Sharon, he knew something else he'd like to kiss.

꧁꧂

After making the successful river crossing, the party lined up again to travel onward, and Rose found herself in the middle of the pack train. She found the change unsettling, as the Indians' relaxed behavior took on an ominous change. No longer did they chat back and forth in the low tones of their strange tongue. Instead they became silent and watchful, constantly looking about. Often their hands would come to rest on a rifle or sheathed knife—particularly when a birdcall or the screech of some wild animal echoed through the forest growth.

Added to that, Nate Kinyon, whom she looked upon as her protector, no longer rode directly behind her. He'd taken the lead position, ahead of Mr. Smith. At times he rode even farther beyond, out of sight, sometimes for half an hour or more.

Rose couldn't help remembering the frontiersman's explanation regarding the territory they were entering. No tribe had laid claim to it, he'd said. The land lacked a governing force of any sort, and here young boys could be captured and killed or carted off by roaming Indians and ransomed without fear of reprisal. She could tell from the tension in the backs of the men in the party that unspoken dangers of other kinds could be lying in wait anywhere, anytime in this vast, untamed place.

No one had to remind her that the pack train was a prime target. She was riding in the midst of twenty heavily laden horses weighted down with goods and treasures every Indian coveted—or Mr. Smith wouldn't be hauling them these many, many miles. Remembering how readily he had plunked down fifty pounds for her alone, she surmised his store must be a profitable enterprise. She sent yet another silent prayer for safety aloft.

Late afternoon sunlight through the treetops speckled the rustic deer trail as the party lumbered on, single file. Humidity magnified the woodland scents as they passed rocky outcroppings covered with moss, and as always, Rose's nostrils detected the smell of the horses as they plodded onward. Her thoughts drifted back in time to her English home, where she'd have had a perfumed handkerchief tucked in her sleeve for use at a moment's notice to disguise unpleasant odors. How sweet was the scent of the summer roses that climbed the garden trellis in back of their home, the inviting aroma of fresh-baked bread and raisin scones that filled the house. And the lovely tea Lily would brew. What she'd give for a soothing cup right now on this seemingly endless day!

At the sound of approaching hoofbeats, Rose tensed, gradually relaxing as she spotted Nate returning.

Passing the front of the group, he came to join her, a weary smile intensifying tired lines around his eyes. "We'll be stoppin' for the night soon, but not lightin' any fires, sorry to say." His quiet tones set her on alert again. "We'll just eat up some of those hard buns an' jerked meat we brought with us. Mebbe some of that fresh cow's milk would taste mighty good. Oh, an' I happened across a few berries awhile back, so I picked some."

"No fire, you say?" Wishing he'd elaborate further, Rose decided she'd really rather not know what put him on guard. She'd have to trust God to look after this vulnerable, mismatched group forging ever deeper into the unknown.

Nate untied a juice-stained sack from a saddle ring and handed it to her. "If it's any comfort, you'll be takin' it kind of easy for a spell. There'll be no cookin' tonight or any other night for a couple days." He tipped his head in Mr. Smith's direction and chuckled.

Rose laughed with him. "Quite right. I fear poor Mr. Smith and his tender stomach are hardly getting his money's worth out of me."

A frown crinkled the frontiersman's forehead, and he kneaded his chin. "That purely puzzles me. Ol' Eustice has always been a shrewd dealer. I wonder if a sour stomach is his whole reason for wantin' you so bad."

With a glance at the trader, Rose shivered as a chill shot through her.

Nate's broad hand covered hers on the pommel. "Like I told you before, I'm here, and I ain't goin' nowhere."

Gritting her teeth against the pain caused by riding hours on horseback, Rose hobbled back toward the camp, carrying milk from the cow that now grazed placidly on meadow grass. The hem of her fawn skirt swished with her movements, and she gazed down in despair at how dusty and dismal the daygown now looked after having been worn day after day. It had snagged countless times on protruding brambles. Inhaling the delicate scent of wildflowers dancing in the meadow, Rose wished she looked as fresh and smelled so sweet. She recalled with chagrin her uncivil thoughts regarding the odorous Mr. Smith and realized she could be close to such rankness herself now. But she would not sacrifice another daygown. How long had it been since she had sunk into a tub billowing steam and soaked until the water grew tepid? Or climbed between crisp bed linens of pristine white that still carried the fragrance of the summer wind? Would she know such luxuries again?

Reaching the clearing, where food sacks sat propped against a fallen log, she set down the bowl of milk and retrieved the items for the evening's spartan meal. Not far away, the members of the party worked in harmony while she removed wooden trenchers and cups for her threesome. The men had to be as travel weary as she, yet no one complained as they freed horses of their burdens and hobbled them.

One of the Indians paused in his work and eyed the sky with concern. Rose glanced up and sighed at the sight of clouds rolling in. She'd already had to forfeit the promise of stimulating conversation regarding faith with 'New Light' Robert Bloom and would not be allowed the simple comfort of herbal tea this night. Now a storm loomed. The injustice of it all stung her. But rather than allow herself to sink into the mire of self-pity, she refused to give in to tears that would make her appear weak in the presence of all these men. Lifting her chin with renewed purpose, she resumed her chore, setting out the trenchers and cups and gathering the needed food items Nate had mentioned.

The sounds of repeated thwacking and chopping made her glance toward the thicket, where Indians were cutting branches from fir trees and tossing them into piles. There was to be no fire this eve. What purpose lay behind such a waste of energy? Other men were busy removing tarps from the packs and stringing them between trees. This time the worn canvases were more in number and strung at a slant, likely to provide runoff from the imminent rain. But what would keep water from blowing in from the sides?

The unusual pile of fir branches continued to grow. Then the men gathered them and spread them out, layering some beneath the tarps and leaning some upright against the sides, layer after layer. Primitive shelters took form before Rose's eyes. The fir branches that seemed to have no purpose would surely keep their bedding off the damp ground, as well as keep out blowing rain.

When Nate Kinyon placed her trunk and valises inside one of the crude huts, Rose appreciated his constant concern for her personal welfare—despite her fear that she no longer smelled as sweet as her namesake flower.

From out of nowhere the story of the Nativity drifted into her mind, reminding her of the way the Lord had looked after Mary and her baby when a situation seemed impossible. God provided the unwed peasant girl a confidante in her relative Elizabeth, and a husband who, instead of giving her a certificate of divorce, married her and then lovingly cared for her and her unborn child. When King Herod sought to destroy her baby, the Lord compelled Joseph to take his family and flee to Egypt. Always there were angels to guide and protect them. God truly did care for His own.

Hearing footsteps, Rose glanced up to see Nate walking toward her with that endearing grin that warmed her heart. Was he her own personal angel sent by God when she needed help the most? *Don't be such a goose!* Even after all these days, the man turned red as ever when he offered the prayer at breakfast.

But still, it was an interesting thought. She returned his smile.

Chapter 11

Grateful for the chance to sit down at day's end, Nate sank onto a fallen log at the campsite and stretched out his legs.

Across from him Rose lowered herself with her usual grace onto a slumped flour sack and drew her ivory shawl about her shoulders. She always dispensed with her bonnet when preparing a meal, and wisps of honey-gold hair—though somewhat tangled from travel—formed little curls around her face, giving her an enchanting innocent charm as she looked up at him and Eustice. "Would either of you care for the honor of blessing our food—such as it is—this eve?"

"Sure thing," Nate blurted without thought. He'd been stewing all afternoon about Smith and his covert plans for Rose, and neither a humbling request for prayer from her nor a taunt from the trader would deter him from the questions he intended to level on the man once they were out of Rose's earshot. Alone on his horse earlier, he'd searched his mind for snatches of blessings from his childhood that his deceased father had offered at mealtimes. Drawing on those memories, he spoke with fortitude that had been sorely lacking in his earlier efforts. "Heavenly Father, we thank You for this quiet day an' for the meal we're about to partake. We also ask You to be with Bob on his errand of mercy for the unfortunate lad an' work out the details so things can be put right. . . ."

Wondering if any of the Indians over in their circle might have understood enough English to know he performed a religious rite, he sneaked a peek in their direction while Rose and Eustice had their heads bowed. The redskins were a superstitious lot, and who knew what they might think? But seeing they were involved in their own concerns, he relaxed and concluded the prayer. "In Jesus' name, Amen."

He sniffed in confidence for having discharged the duty adequately and raised his head. Rose still hadn't looked up but wore a sweet smile as she took a sip of milk. He'd gained a little ground with her, sure enough, and the thought pleasured him. But Smith was another matter entirely. The surly man sat rigid as a totem pole on a rock nearby. Nate snatched one of the hard buns off the trencher Rose had set out and tore off a chunk with his teeth. The sooner they all chewed down this tough-as-a-boot excuse for a meal, the sooner she'd be able to leave for her shelter and find the rest she sorely deserved. Then he would see about getting some straight answers from that old geezer.

"Woman," Smith said, "fetch me a bowl. I need to sop my bread in some o' that milk ya' got us."

"Of course." Swallowing down a bite of her own bun, she turned to Nate. "Would you care for some milk as well?"

He shook his head. "Naw. My teeth could use the workout." Glaring at the trader, Nate's ire for him grew as he watched the submissive young woman waiting on a wretch not fit to wipe her shoes.

Holding her wrap closed with one hand, she served Smith the requested bowl of milk and retook her seat, settling her skirts about her. "Mr. Smith? I should like to inform my sisters of my whereabouts. How many days do you assume it will take us to reach your store?"

He shot a wary glance up at the sky. "Depends on the rain. If a lot of it gets dumped on us and the rivers start swellin' we'll have to give 'em time to smooth out b'fore we can cross 'em."

"Rivers? There are more of them ahead?" Her face paled noticeably.

"Yep."

"How many are there?"

Nate snickered. "Go on, Smith. Tell the lady how many rivers, cricks, an' streams we still have to cross." A bit shocked by the animosity he could hear in his own voice, Nate determined to rein it in.

The trader cut him a sullen look. "However many it takes us to get there. That's how many." He went on dunking his bun.

Intense silence settled over the campsite, leaving only night sounds and the murmured conversation of the Shawnee at the other circle to go with the sounds of chewing dried meat and the crunching of hard bread. The wind was picking up, stirring through the treetops as churning clouds darkened the sky and the low rumble of distant thunder echoed. A mosquito whined near Nate's ear, and he brushed the pest aside.

Finally Rose broke the stillness, her voice still amazingly patient. "Mr. Kinyon. I've heard that the colonies abound with opportunities for farming and the trades. Why would an obviously capable man such as yourself choose to leave those things behind to hunt for wild game in the wilderness? Every farm we passed along the Potomac had an abundance of farm animals."

Nate prickled. So that was her intent? To get him to forsake his wanderlust and agree to hitch himself up to some old plow on some old ramshackle farm for the rest of his life? Off to the side he heard Smith cackle around a mouthful that puffed out his bearded cheek, and it galled Nate no end. "What me an' Bob do is more important than huntin'. We hunt so we can fill our stomachs or trade with the tribes for other food an' furs. Furs is as good as cash money anywhere in the nations."

"I see." But the way her slender brows dipped toward each other indicated she was no less puzzled.

Nate explained further. "Me an' Bob, we're explorers, like Columbus. The colonies are sittin' on the edge of a vast continent, an' we chart the rivers an' lakes an' such for folks that'll come after us. There's great tracts of open land that scarcely a man, white or red, has ever set foot on. Folks need to know what's out there, so they can find places to settle an' make lives for themselves."

Her features calmed. "Oh. I see. You're providing a service of true import, then. . .at the sacrifice of comforts offered by home and hearth."

How did she manage to get back to him farming? Nate rolled his eyes. This was not going well. But she had to realize that he would never be tied down. Not to her, not to anybody. Not now, not ever. "I do my best to get home to see Ma a couple times a year. More, if I have good reason." That said, he added his most charming smile.

Rose lowered her lashes without responding.

Good. She was starting to take to the notion. Nate slid a glance at Eustice Smith, eyeing him from unkempt head to scuffed toe. A serious talk with that man was overdue. Long overdue.

⁓

In the fading light of day, Nate watched Rose clear away the meal trappings. He couldn't help but admire her for not voicing a single complaint about the many discomforts she'd suffered during the long journey. Anybody with eyes in his head could tell she was worn out by each day's end. After hours on horseback, she hobbled about on stiff legs to see to her own needs and theirs as well.

The dress he'd thought so comely at the start of the trip was wrinkled from top to bottom, bore a liberal amount of stains and trail dust, and showed numerous snags from bramblebushes she'd scraped past. And her skin, though she managed a quick wash at the creek now and again, looked smudged. He'd wager the gal had never been so rumpled or dirty in her life. She had real spunk. Spunk and grit. He watched her limp to her shelter, where she stretched a kink out of her back before crawling inside.

A light mist was just beginning, and from the look of the dark clouds shrouding the sky, it was a mere portent of the impending storm that would make a royal mess of things. Thunder and lightning would make the horses skittish also, so the Indians would need to stay close to them through the storm and keep them from bolting. Switching his attention to Smith, who sat on a boulder nursing a cup of milk, Nate noted that the man was looking particularly slovenly. But the trader did little but sit around in his trading post between infrequent trips out to civilization. A trivial detail like his appearance wasn't high on his list of concerns.

Lumbering to his feet, Smith rubbed his belly.

Nate cleared his throat. "I'd like a private minute with you, Eustice."

He grimaced, easing back down. "Don't tell me you're fixin' to shove off, too."

"I'm not sure. You still set on draggin' that poor gentlewoman off to that godforsaken Shawnee settlement of yours?"

Smith narrowed his beady eyes. "Look here, Kinyon. I didn't buy that gal just so's I'd have a skirt around to gawk at. Like I tol' ya, I'm in dire need. Her comin' with me's a matter of life and death. Mine."

"Aha. Just like I figgered."

"What're ya talkin' about?"

Nate shook his head in disdain. "Some chief's got it in for you, an' you bought her for him as a way of atonement. Well, I'm here to tell you, that ain't gonna happen." He snatched his hunting knife from the scabbard hooked to his belt and raised it to make his point. "I'll do you in myself first."

The man's eyes flared, and he jerked to his feet, spilling his cup to the ground. "Wait just a minute!" He stretched out a hand to ward Nate off. "Ya got it all wrong. I bought her papers so's she could cook fer me, an' that's the plain truth. My stomach's been ailin' me sore most all the time, and sometimes"—he peered around and lowered his voice— "I even pass some blood now an' again. If I don't get me some soothin' food soon, I could up an' die."

Nate sat back and eyed him closely in the growing darkness. Though grime and the man's frizzled beard hid most of his face, Smith did look a mite poorly, and his eyes had a yellowish tinge.

The trader continued. "I got me some chickens off a passin' raidin' party awhile back, an' now with the cows I'm bringin' home, there'll be milk an' eggs a'plenty. Enough to see me through till my stomach gets put to rights. I even bought some good English spices and healin' herbs the gal knows how to use. So as you can see, no price in this world's gonna buy her off me till I'm in fine fettle again."

Serious raindrops began spattering them as they stared each other down. Nate grimaced and dried his knife on his pant leg then shoved it back inside its sheath. He'd just have to wait Smith out, one way or the other. "Well then, Eustice, I reckon my answer to that question of yours is I'll be ridin' with you the rest of the way." He got up and strode to his own shelter.

Rain, rain, rain. Slogging along the muddy trail, Rose looked woefully up at the gloomy sky and shook her head. At least the thunder and lightning had ceased sometime during the wee hours. From the time she'd left the leaky shelter of the crude hut where she'd slept last night, they'd all sloshed through mud or been splattered by it as the caravan trudged up one ridge and down the other side. Then it was start up yet another mucky ridge and face the inevitable swollen stream they needed to cross at the bottom. All the while, water poured from the sky as if angels were emptying barrels of it at a time.

Whenever Mr. Smith gave the order to rest the horses, Rose hopped down into ankle-deep mud, which saw to the swift ruination of her soft leather shoes. The soles barely allowed her to keep her footing, especially on any sort of grade. Going downhill was hard even on the animals, who also struggled to keep their footing beneath their heavy loads.

Gritting her teeth as the rain continued to pummel her, Rose clutched her soggy cloak closer. Soaked through, its hue was more violet than burgundy. She turned her head slightly to peer around, and the limp brim of her bonnet drooped like a funnel, pouring a stream of cold water down her nose and hands. She winced. If there was anything that smelled worse than a wet horse, it was her smelling like a wet horse!

She knew the rest of the party looked as bedraggled and smelled as odorous as she did. The decorative feathers the Shawnee braves sported in their braids and on their clothes now drooped as sadly as everyone's expressions. Thank heaven it was June and only mildly cool, or they'd all be shivering and covered with gooseflesh.

Up ahead, she saw Nate on his horse, coming back from scouting after nearly an hour. She wondered if anyone—Indian or bandit—possessed gumption enough to lie in wait to ambush a caravan in such abysmal weather. After he stopped to converse with Mr. Smith, he headed down the line to her.

"You look like a drowned chicken." A sympathetic smile curved one side of his lips.

She snickered. "I beg to differ. The Indians with all their soggy feathers look like drowned chickens. I, on the other hand, look and smell rather like a drowned skunk." The sad truth of her words made her grimace.

A teasing spark lit his eyes as he leaned closer, the brim of his hat spilling rainwater onto the ground. "I'd say in that wet wool, you smell more like a dead sheep." He reached around and untied his bedroll, shaking out the fur blanket he slept in. He handed it to her. "Shed that wet cloak of yours and wrap this around you instead. The rain won't get through it."

Rose was touched by his kind offer. "Are you sure you don't need it?" A dollop of water dropped on her hand from overhead branches.

He smiled as she glared up at the tree. "Actually, I'm used to weather like this. Been traipsin' around out in nature nigh onto ten years now. Like it says in Ma's Bible, 'This, too, shall pass,' and all that."

Rose only hoped it would. As gracefully as possible, she shed her sodden cloak and accepted his covering. It was heavier than she'd expected—far heavier than her wet cloak. She took measure of the thick fur, which held little resemblance to the coveted wraps and muffs displayed in the elegant shop windows at Bath. "What type of fur is this?"

He shrugged. "Buffalo. Keeps a body dry when it needs to."

"Dry? Is there such a thing?" Laughing, she pulled it around her soaked clothes.

Nate reached over to help her. The weight of the wrap was no match for his strength, and he hefted it as if it weighed no more than a feather.

But what surprised Rose even more was his gentleness. Suddenly she was acutely aware of how very close he was. She could feel the warmth of his breath feathering her cheek, and it sent a tingly sort of pleasure through her being, the likes of which she'd never felt before. But then, he was the sort of man the likes of which she'd never encountered before. Nate Kinyon was like a protecting angel. Her own protecting angel.

He fiddled with the fur wrap until he had it snugly about her shoulders. His hazel eyes, very near, met hers and lingered there for a breathless moment. Finally he centered himself again on his saddle and gathered his reins. Cocking his head to one side, he flashed a grin. "Keep it warm for me till I get back."

Without further word, he spurred his horse on.

Now, whatever did he mean by that? Uncertain whether or not she liked that particular smile, she couldn't help staring after him. Then she straightened her spine. *The man was such a flirt.*

Chapter 12

The rain gradually slowed and came to an end. Rose swept a thankful gaze up at the sky as late-afternoon sunshine broke through the clouds, slanting shafts of light into the forest. Familiar with Britain's wet climate, she was intimately acquainted with rain, but except for the drenching suffered on her homeward trek from Bristol during a downpour, she'd never felt like a drowned rat until now. And at least the road in England had been cobbled, not a slippery quagmire. Moisture still dripped from the trees onto the soggy trail, making travel precarious, but she knew several hours of strong sunshine would set things to right. As the pack train continued a descent that began half an hour ago, the pathway began to level out, making the journey a bit easier. Perhaps they were coming to the river Mr. Smith had mentioned last eve. She certainly hoped so. They were supposed to stop and make camp there.

The buffalo robe Nate Kinyon had loaned her had protected her from getting any wetter, but she longed to get out of her still-damp clothes and into something dry. How ironic that after fearing for her sisters and being concerned about their welfare, she was the one traveling into the unknown. The girls were undoubtedly warm and dry in substantial homes with tight roofs over their heads, while she herself could easily catch lung fever and slowly waste away.

Shrugging off the temptation to feel sorry for herself, Rose directed her thoughts across the ocean to her father and brothers. She hoped her and her sisters' sacrifices had indeed saved the rest of the family from ruin. But how marvelous it would be to go home again, be snuggled and toasty warm in her own feather bed with a blazing fire in the hearth, the wonderful smell of rich stew from supper permeating the dwelling. She should never have taken such blessings for granted. She breathed a prayer for her sorely missed loved ones, trusting them in God's hands, and vowed that if ever she found herself living a life of ease again, she would express her utmost thankfulness daily.

A sudden gust of wind chilled by the storm swirled around her, and Rose tugged the fur tighter about her. At least she still had that one small comfort, even if it was only a loan from Nate.

Where was Nate? Turning in her saddle, she searched past two of the Shawnee and their strings of horses and discovered him and Mr. Smith conversing as they rode side by side. The frontiersman must have ridden in while she allowed herself that brief moment of self-pity. She didn't dare dwell for long on how truly miserable she felt, lest she fall apart, and when the reality of her situation occasionally did intrude, she strove to quash it as quickly as possible. She had to remain strong—or at least appear to.

Now that the storm had passed and the last of the heavy clouds scudded from view, the bright sunlight cheered her up. But her optimism quickly faded as she detected the ominous roar of a river ahead growing louder by the moment. Rain had probably swollen the volume of water, as Mr. Smith had predicted. Remembering the last crossing, which had been tentative enough to give any brave soul pause for thought, she hoped they wouldn't attempt to cross an even mightier river this eve.

The party emerged into an open meadow, and Rose feasted her eyes on the variegated greens sprinkled liberally with summer wildflowers. Everything looked fresh and clean, and leftover raindrops sparkled like diamonds amid the tall weeds. Even the cool breeze smelled sweet. Then she saw more red men.

A cluster of nearly naked Indians with shaved heads stared at them from the riverbank. They looked nothing like the Shawnee she'd grown used to seeing. Attired only in loincloths and bedecked with feathers, they sported piercings and strange-looking tattoos on various parts of their bodies. They smiled and waved, however, so Rose hoped Providence would find them friendly after all. Still, she couldn't shake off her anxiety.

The man ahead of her appeared at ease after spotting the braves, but Rose saw that his hand now rested on the butt of his musket.

Three long canoes lay upturned on the bank near a ferry raft similar to the one used at the last river crossing. The sight of crude shelters like the caravan had used last evening indicated the Indians must have camped there during the storm. Now they had a campfire to warm their chilled bones and some delicious-smelling meat roasting over the blaze. Rose breathed in the enticing aroma.

Reaching the unfamiliar group, the pack train came to a halt. Nate, Mr. Smith, and the first of the Shawnee riders dismounted and joined the strangers. Rose was not near enough to make out voices or words, but she noticed that as the men talked, they used their hands more than their mouths, communicating with grunts and broad gestures that looked somewhat comical.

Her first impulse was to get off her horse, but since the other Shawnee in the party had remained mounted while they watched the exchange, she resisted any thought of sliding down. Even though she sensed no hint of danger, she assured herself that the Indians at the camp didn't mean any harm.

After a few tense moments, Mr. Smith broke away from the group and headed toward Rose. He stopped at her side and spoke under his breath. "I want ya to stay put till we build ya a shelter. Then ya need to get in it and stay there. We'll bring over some food when it's done."

The thought of actual food, fresh and hot and tasty, sounded inviting, yet a sense of unease slithered through Rose. She glanced beyond the trader to Nate, who continued gesturing and nodding with the strange

Indians. "Surely you don't mean we must stay the night here. . .with these. . .other strange Indians."

"Aye. That's just what I'm sayin'. They come downriver with a mind to do a bit o' tradin'. An' as you'll learn soon enough, redskins don't get in no big rush about it. We might be up half the night dickerin' and parlayin' over what's tossed on the blanket. . .an' I don't want you throwed into the mix. Is that clear?"

Thrown into the mix! What did that mean? Rose wanted more of an explanation and opened her mouth to protest the whole affair but bit back her words. She'd already been auctioned off once, only to be dragged out to this uncharted expanse of emptiness, and she couldn't begin to imagine what horrors might await her were she to be purchased by one of those vicious-looking tattooed Indians. "Rest assured, Mr. Smith, I shall be only too happy to leave you gentlemen to your business."

"*Gentlemen*, eh?" The trader gave a wry chuckle. Then he winced and rubbed back and forth across his protruding belly. "Sure will be glad to get back to my place. This trip's takin' the starch clean outta me." The short, paunchy man took a step away then turned back. "Remember what I said. Stay outta sight."

~~

Stay out of sight! As if Rose needed her owner to tell her that more than once. Despite the day's mild temperature, she huddled within the confines of Nate Kinyon's fur blanket and sat still as a post until the other horses in the pack train had been unloaded. With even her nose buried inside the hairy cover, she'd scarcely even peeked out of it, avoiding all eye contact with the peculiar Indians.

The sound of approaching footsteps made her pulse quicken, until she recognized them as Nate's.

"You can get down now, little missy. And don't worry none about stayin' safe. We'll all of us be keepin' watch."

Somewhat encouraged, Rose opened the fur wrap, but felt somehow as exposed as a flag on a pole. Missing its privacy, she shivered.

Nate reached up to her, and she gratefully accepted his help. Again she was impressed at the way gentleness tempered his strength, and part of her wished she could remain within the safe circle of those strong arms. A man of his ilk would make any woman feel secure and protected. But each nerve in her body sensed that everyone was watching. Her skin crawled as she felt dark, hooded eyes observing her every step on the way to her private shelter.

The low jabbering started up again. Already Rose regretted having parted with Nate's fur robe. She still felt vulnerable and exposed even inside the crude hut with the added protection of her belongings surrounding her. Any thought of shedding her damp clothing and changing into a dry outfit fled her mind. Instead she peered out the entrance toward the fire, watching the goings-on at the gathering.

The men from the pack train clustered around the Indians' campfire, drying out, with the exception of Nate, who occupied himself with the unsaddling of her horse. For ten minutes or more Rose kept an eye on the group. Finally she exhaled a bated breath as she saw them all settle down onto blankets around the fire. One of the Indians turned a spit, which held what appeared to be a wild turkey and perhaps a goose. The aroma of those roasting birds was almost more than her hungry stomach could endure.

She continued to observe the men for several more minutes to be sure no one was leaving the others. Then she hurriedly flung open her trunk and plucked out some bedding and some dry clothes, intending to be changed and have her bed made before anyone started moving about again.

—

Without Bob around, Nate was glad a Cherokee by the name of Two Crows spoke passable English. Nate fared well enough using sign language but preferred being able to talk in plain words whenever possible. The Indian had recognized Nate's name and even asked about Black Horse Bob.

But once they'd waded through all the polite questions regarding mutual acquaintances, the expression on Two Crows's face changed from friendly smiles to stony reserve.

Nate tensed. *Why the sudden change?*

"What you hear about Mohawk Chief Tiyanoga and English governor Clinton at Albany?" The Indian's black eyes narrowed as he studied Nate.

Nate and Eustice Smith swapped a glance and shrugged.

"We ain't heard nothin'," Smith replied evenly. "I been down in Baltimore. There was talk about some French soldiers an' a black robe movin' aways south of Lake Erie to build a fort. Nobody's happy about it. That's the last I heard." He sniffed.

The Indian hiked his chin. "Chief Tiyanoga say they build forts from big lake to Ohio River. He say to Clinton, 'We make treaty with you. Why you no go stop the French?' Then Tiyanoga say, 'Mohawk support English allies, but English allies no support Mohawk.' He say the Dutch buy small piece of land from Mohawk, but say piece is bigger." Two Crows spread his arms wide. "Tiyanoga say no more. He say he send wampum belt to the Six Nations, say chain is broken with the English."

Neither Nate nor Smith moved, but their eyes met and held for a brief second.

The trader shook his head offhandedly. "That bunch up in New York is always gettin' things wrong with the Nations. But them Indians up there got William Johnson to speak for 'em. He's a fair man. He'll sort things out sure 'nuff."

"Aye, that he will." Nate gave an emphatic nod. But inside, he knew that if Governor Clinton did nothing and allowed the French to gain control of the Ohio, Smith's trading post and every other English enterprise this side of the Alleghenies would be at risk.

Inhaling a troubled breath, he glanced around the circle of Indians, wondering if even the Shawnee and the Cherokee farther to the south would turn on them. If so, what would become of Rose. . .his Rose of Sharon?

Chapter 13

A canopy of stars twinkled in the blue velvet sky, while around the camp and off in the distance, fireflies flickered like so many more miniature stars. An occasional bat darted among the leafy treetops, and the hobbled horses stirred at the plaintive howl of a wolf. Used to nature's sounds, Nate chewed a bite of turkey and relaxed, enjoying the rush of the dark water not far away.

In the group ringing the campfire while they ate the roasted meat, Nate had the distinct impression the Cherokee seemed more inclined to be friendly toward the Shawnee braves than the Shawnee were toward the Cherokee. While the Cherokee talked with the help of hand signs, the Shawnee kept their replies short and blunt. Nate figured the Shawnee didn't want their red brothers to the south to think they could blithely intercept the pack train and get first pick of all the best trade goods. No doubt the Shawnee were already coveting a few particular items among the lot.

Switching his attention to Two Crows, Nate sensed the Indian's interest lay elsewhere—in the direction of Rose's haven—and the knowledge set him on edge. Nate had taken her a turkey drumstick moments earlier, and since then the interpreter seemed more occupied by the possibilities of what might be inside her small shelter than in the goods from the sacks and crates awaiting the group's inspection. He took another bite of the roasted turkey that had been flavored with some of Eustice Smith's seasonings, watching as the dark hooded gaze of Two Crows drifted often to Rose's hut.

The Indian wiped the back of his hand across his greasy mouth, puffing out his chest as he sat up straighter and turned to Nate, a frown rippling his tattooed forehead. "Why you serve woman? Why she no serve you, the man, like good squaw?"

Nate opened his mouth to reply, but Smith's voice cut him off. The trader leaned forward and cocked his grizzled head to one side. "The gal don't b'long to Kinyon. I bought her. She's my property, jest like ever'thing else on this here pack train." Having made the announcement, he sat back with a satisfied "harrumph."

Perhaps it was the man's stern tone of voice that caused the other Indians around the fire to cease talking and turn their attention to him, but Nate was quite sure they understood little, if anything, of what the trader had just said.

Not to be dissuaded from his question, Two Crows eyed Smith steadily. "If woman belong to you, why she not serve you?" His sullen eyes narrowed in confusion.

The trader raised his chin and stared hard at the Indian for several seconds before replying. "She's up there b'cause that's where I told her to stay, that's why. She don't need to be out here prancin' around fer you youngbloods to be gawkin' at. As it is, I'm already havin' to put up with more prancin' an' preenin' than a body should have to." He shot a surly glance at Nate as if challenging him to deny the accusation.

The interpreter still appeared perplexed, but he didn't comment further. His party had come many miles downriver with a load of furs to trade, and Nate was certain that, despite his curiosity about the ways of a white man, Two Crows knew better than to anger the trader who possessed the goods they hoped to barter for.

The other Cherokee began to stir restlessly—not a good sign. Then one of them said something in their language to Two Crows, who responded with a few words that seemed to mollify the Indian somewhat. He and his companions settled down again on their blankets and helped themselves to more meat from the roasted birds.

Nate decided it was time for a change of subject. "How is it that you braves knew we'd be comin' through here today? I find that mighty curious."

Two Crows let out a small huff. "Hunting party see when Smith go east. He take many horses loaded with furs for trade. We bring many prime furs in canoes. Wait at river crossing. Three suns." He held up a trio of greasy fingers. Then his gaze wandered again to Rose's hut with a knowing grin. "Smith's number-two wife, she make happy man under blanket."

Nate was sorely tempted to wipe that leer off the Indian's mouth but knew the prudent thing would be to refrain. They were crossing lawless Indian lands, and only an idiot would want to deliberately invite trouble.

Keeping the peace seemed the least of Eustice Smith's concerns, however. He leaned toward Two Crows with a meaningful glare and shook a turkey wing in the red man's face. "You'd best forget about the woman, or I won't so much as let ya get a sniff of what's in them packs of ourn." He gestured with a thumb toward the goods waiting to be displayed.

Two Crows's eyes widened for a second. He then composed his features into the more normal unreadable demeanor most Indians adopted and settled back on his blanket, eating as if nothing whatever had transpired.

Stifling a grin, Nate took another big bite himself. Up until now, he'd always assumed Eustice Smith would trade away his own mother if the price was right. But apparently that was not so when it concerned his stomach. Even more surprising, the man wasn't about to brook any vulgar insinuations about his lovely new cook. Would wonders never cease!

Then a more unwelcome realization dawned. Getting Rose out of

Smith's clutches was going to take a lot more effort than he'd figured on.

A lot more.

Having devoured the delicious turkey leg Nate had been kind enough to bring to her the previous evening, Rose still basked in the memory of the savory meat the next morning, wondering when she'd last enjoyed such a treat. Even without the roasted potatoes and fresh bread that would have accompanied it back home, it had been a most welcome change from the tiresome mush and cold jerked meat that made up most meals on the trail. Now what she would give for a spot of tea to warm her insides. But knowing there was little chance of that luxury, she disregarded the activity from the camp and concentrated on the lovely songs of the birds cavorting among the trees nearby. Already the tree toads were in fine harmony, and the steady drone of cicadas promised a hot day ahead. Meanwhile the ever-present river continued to surge and gush past the camp, though the volume had lessened somewhat from the previous day.

Rose's thoughts turned heavenward. *Dear Lord, how I thank You that Mr. Smith rode up to the auction when he did and not a moment sooner. I could not begin to imagine my sweet Lily being in my position here, not with her youth, her innocence. . . .*

On the heels of that notion, the mental picture of Mariah came to mind, and Rose felt a droll smile tug at her lips. Even a man as obstinate and stubborn as Mr. Smith would have sent someone as spirited as Mariah packing once she started whining and complaining at the sight of the first smudge on one of her gowns. And the dire comment she'd have made about his smell! La, either the man would have traded her off at first opportunity, or he'd have resorted to gagging her. Even then, however, the girl's nose would have curled in utter disdain at the odor whenever he passed by.

On the other hand, he might have traded Mariah off to those Indians he'd bargained with half the night. That realization sent a chill through Rose. And what if their dear father ever found out about such an unforeseen turn of events! How such disastrous news would break his heart. The poor beleaguered man had suffered trials enough, with the betrayal that left him in financial ruin. Surely the Lord would reward him in full measure for his patience and unfailing faith throughout the whole sorry affair.

She wondered if her family in England gave much thought to their loved ones who'd sailed across the wide ocean to the colonies. . .or for that matter, if Mariah even once wondered about her sisters' well-being. Perhaps she was consumed mostly with thoughts of herself and her own surroundings. Rose knew that Lily, having been so attached to both her sisters, undoubtedly kept her and Mariah in constant prayer. Rose suppressed a pang of longing for the dear girl. *Please keep her in Your tender watch-care, Father. I miss her so.*

As she sat in her shelter, observing the movements outside, Rose sighed. The early morning sun glistened off the river, casting golden outlines around the first members of the caravan making the crossing. Fortunately, the queer-looking Indians were hastening the trip by loaning their canoes to transport the goods, while the horses were hauled across the rapid water on another pitiful raft.

And here she still sat, relegated to stay out of sight as she had the night before.

Far from being the dull, overlooked spinster she'd been back home in England, it seemed the tattooed Indians considered her a lady of mystery. Now and again they'd pause in their work and glance toward her shelter, which grated on her nerves. How drastically her life had changed in such a short amount of time. Nibbling the inside corner of her lip, she wondered if it might have been wiser to display herself out in the open last eve in all her rained-on, rumpled glory. But when still another pair of beady black eyes flicked her way, she knew she had to trust that Mr. Smith and Nate knew best. After all, they'd had previous dealings with these natives of the land and knew some of the intricacies of their nature.

At last the goods and animals completed the tedious journey across the river. When the Cherokee began their slow paddle upstream with their load of pots, knives, bolts of cloth—and muskets—Nate came ambling up the bank toward Rose's hut. He waved, his friendly grin a most pleasing sight, as he called out to her, "Time to go, pretty lady."

His presence on the trip made it seem less of a trial and more like an adventure to Rose, especially since she knew he was making the journey for one reason only. For her. Smiling, she stood from her pallet and folded the blankets. Then after placing them and her other belongings inside her trunk again, she clicked it shut.

Time to go. . .into her still unknown future.

Chapter 14

O n her very first seemingly endless day of travel, Rose had decided it was pointless to try to memorize passing landmarks in hopes of making her way back to Baltimore some future day on her own. Now that a fortnight had passed, she relinquished even the hope of escaping by her own efforts. As the caravan plodded up one mountain and down again, crossed another stream or creek or river like the one they'd forded a day or two or three ago, she concentrated on the beauty of God's untouched wilderness.

Her eyes beheld huge moss-covered boulders and majestic, sheer cliffs jutting out of the mountainside along the route. Strange new animals peeked from behind trees and shrubs and massive ferns, and bright red birds reminded her of Mariah dressed in all her finery. Just then a pair of orange-bellied birds resembling the orioles in England flitted among the trees, adding splashes of vivid color among the many blends of green.

Bluebirds with prominent crests and black, white, and red woodpeckers were also quite colorful, she admitted, but they had the annoying habit of breaking the blissful silence by making cacophonous calls and rapping on trees.

Inhaling the fresh scent of pine and the fragrance of the meadow flowers and tall grasses growing beside gurgling brooks, Rose couldn't help comparing the alluring perfumes of nature to the rank, odorous sewers of Bath, the acrid smell of smoke and falling ash from a thousand British chimneys. During the long voyage across the Atlantic, she had not experienced anything akin to the wonders of this new land, America. It was so filled with life, she felt exhilarated.

"Caught you smiling again." Nate surprised Rose as he guided his mount alongside hers.

"I'm afraid you did. I just saw a greedy little squirrel with the fluffiest tail ever trying to stuff one more acorn into his cheek. . .and all the while he's squealing at another squirrel in the next tree. See him?" She pointed up to a branch not far away.

He nodded, and that easy grin of his stretched across his face. "Thought you'd want to know we'll be reachin' the river in a couple of minutes."

"Another river?" She rolled her eyes. "And which one will that be, not that it makes the slightest bit of difference."

"Which one?" His straight brows sprang high on his forehead as he stared at her. "The Ohio. It's the one all the others we crossed drain into."

"Oh. Well, now that you mention it, I believe I can almost hear the roar. Did you not say the Ohio's near the river where Mr. Smith has his store?"

"Aye." His grin widened. "Where the Muskingum forks in. It's a mile or so downriver from here."

Rose felt her pulse quicken with excitement. . .and fear. "As I recall, you said a Shawnee and Delaware Indian village has formed near his enterprise."

"Right. But don't fret. Those Indians never gave him a lick of trouble, so they shouldn't bother you none. Like I said, they value the trader and the goods he supplies too much to give him reason to up an' leave here with all his merchandise."

After all this time, we shall finally reach our destination, then. Splendid! Still feeling some trepidation at the thought of being presented to the trader's wife, Rose schooled her features and did her best to dredge up a smile. Surely Mrs. Smith, another white woman, would be glad to have some female company around.

Rose cast a despairing look down at her hopelessly faded and worn brown dress, which she'd sacrificed rather than spoiling any of the few other daygowns she'd brought with her. All the natural lace that had adorned it at the start of the trip had frayed and worn away, and with all the snags and tears and stains the pitiful garment now bore, its best fate lay in the burn barrel. While the men were occupied with constructing the rafts the party would need, there had to be time to spruce up before meeting the trader's wife. Rose decided to don the indigo blue gown she'd worn briefly while her rain-saturated clothes dried. She'd prevail upon Nate to get her trunk down from the packhorse.

How odd, though, that Mr. Smith had not volunteered a single piece of information about his wife during this journey—except that he didn't like her cooking. Whenever Rose attempted to bring up the subject, mentioning that the woman must be very lonely with him gone for such a long time, he'd merely shrugged and said that her brothers were there to keep her company. *More men.* Rose supposed she'd be cooking for them, too.

Within moments, the midnight blue of an immense river came into view, certainly much larger than any of the others they'd crossed along the way. Dark and deep, it moved so massively that scarcely a ripple disturbed its surface.

"I've never seen such a wide, powerful river," Rose murmured.

Nate emitted a chuckle from deep inside. "I canoed down it once as far as the Mississippi, an' as big as you think the Ohio is, the Mississippi's a good four or five times bigger."

Rose gasped. "Mercy me. This surely is a wondrous new land." She turned to him.

As he gazed at her, Nate's eyes took on a warmth she'd never before glimpsed in them. Then he looked off into the distance. "That it is, Rose. That it is."

Could she possibly have been the cause for such a tender gaze, or was it merely evidence of how much he loved his frontier life? She reined in the romantic fancy lest he read something in her own expression. "I do hope Mr. Smith's store is on this side of the river. I can't imagine a rope long enough to ferry us to the other shore."

He threw back his head and laughed. "Now that would be a powerfully long chunk of hemp, wouldn't it? Unfortunately, his store does happen to be on the other side, so we'll have to build us some rafts for crossin'. By the time we rudder our way across, we'll probably have floated down to just about where the Muskingum town is. I'd say we should have enough trees downed an' cleaned an' the rafts put together before the day's out."

Looking about as men began chopping down trees, Rose knew this would be far from just one more crossing for them—it would be crossing the hard way. With Britain being tamed and settled from shore to shore, bridges, walls, buildings, tradesmen, and exotic trade goods were all a matter of course. Though her life had been quite busy there, compared to the American frontier it had been quite easy. Food was as near as the local marketplace, clothing as close as the nearest seamstress. And Papa's livelihood hadn't involved providing a necessity like food or shelter or clothing. He made adornments for the frivolous rich folk to wear about as they attended socials and parties.

Yes, life had been much easier in Britain, more tranquil, and shamefully taken for granted by everyone. Rose breathed in her surroundings. Perhaps circumstances had been more comfortable there, but in some strange way, she'd never felt so alive as she did now.

She looked up at Nate. "While you men are building the rafts, is there something I might do to help? I cannot sit about doing nothing."

He gave a decisive nod. "Food. Lots of food. I know the Shawnees'd appreciate whatever you fix, same as the rest of us. Choppin' down trees for rafts is real hunger-makin' work."

"As you wish. I shall make the lot of you a royal feast. . .even if it is jerked meat and mush and beans. And could you possibly get me my trunk when you have a moment?"

Raft construction took longer than expected, and rather than attempt a
night crossing, Nate was glad when Smith decided they'd make camp one
last time. Some of the men had gone hunting and returned with a pair of
fat geese, which Rose immediately prepared and roasted for supper. They
were quickly devoured, fresh game always being appreciated much more
than dried jerky. Nate admired the outdoor cooking skill his very refined
Rose had acquired along the journey. She'd come a long way from having
to depend on a proper hearth.

The following morning, the log rafts were loaded and launched one
by one. Eustice Smith oversaw the loading of the first two, figuring that
by taking one in the middle of the line, he'd be able to keep an eye on all
his goods and be onshore when they were unloaded. Now on the third
one with Rose and the trader, Nate watched Rose observing the lead raft
as it slowly made its way across and downstream, aided by the river.

"We'll reach the village just before the Muskingum merges," he told
her, "an' be at the tradin' post soon enough." Keeping a steady hold on
the rudder, he studied the slender English beauty perched on her trunk
as she looked ahead, her expression heart-wrenchingly expectant. The
dark indigo of the new gown she'd put on added depth to the blue-gray
of her eyes. Even her hair had been washed and brushed and lay in
shiny, silky amber waves he wished she hadn't tied back with a ribbon.
She looked so feminine and delicate, yet he'd witnessed her strength of
character and determination dozens of times. If only she knew what lay
ahead. . .

Nate swallowed a huge chunk of guilt. He should have prepared
her for her first visit to a Shawnee village instead of allowing her to
believe Smith's store sat in the middle of a civilized town. But she had
so many fears to work through already, he didn't have the heart to cause
her more worry. Things were sure to come as a shock to her. He eyed the
trader slouched on a flour sack with his grubby hands dangling between

his knobby knees. Just what would the old geezer take to let her go back where she belonged?

Catching the eye of the Indian riding with them, Nate motioned for him to take over. The brave obliged and handed Nate his pole then took control of the rudder stick while Nate made his way gingerly across the logs to Smith. He cleared his throat.

The man peered up at him and grunted.

Speaking in tones Rose would not overhear, he met the trader's narrowed eyes. "Look, Eustice. You know an' I know that Indian village is no place for a proper lady like Rose Harwood. Tell me what I can give you to let her go back to her kind. Do the decent thing for once in your life."

The man fingered his beard as if considering the matter and let out a deep huff. His bony shoulders rose with a shrug, then he looked up at Nate in all seriousness. "The truth of it is, if I had me enough furs or cash money ta quit sellin' stuff to folks an' go off where I'd be able ta live in comfort the rest o' my life, I'd take it. This trip's prit'near been the end o' me, Kinyon. It's all I can do to put one foot in front o' the other. I'm too old to be gallivantin' back east for goods ta sell then hike over mountain trails an' sleep on the hard ground in all kinds o' weather. Thing is, right now I need that gal to cook me some good food till I'm able ta consider packin' up an' leavin'. That's all I can tell ya."

A tide of discouragement swept over Nate. *Enough furs or cash money to live on for the rest of his life! How could a body come up with that?* Awhile back, he remembered hearing rumors about silver, about some Shawnee chief downriver toward the Mississippi having a secret silver mine. Could it be true? Well even if it was, rumor had it that some Frenchies had set up a trading post of their own down there, and they sure wouldn't want any competition. Still. . .one never knew. He turned to admire Rose again. Somebody had to do something, and there was nobody to do anything but him. He'd just have to find a way, that's all there was to it.

Chapter 15

Rose didn't know what she expected to see when she arrived at the settlement where Mr. Smith's trading post was located, but it wasn't anything remotely compared to what she found. Before her lay fenced, cultivated fields that flanked a goodly number of dome-shaped and cone-shaped dwellings covered with bark and animal hides, and even some long, low lodges. When the raft passed some of the conelike structures near the riverbank, bronze-skinned men, women, and naked children had charged out of them, whooping and yelling as they ran alongside, keeping pace with the raft. Others, many attired in pale deerskin, streamed from other huts to join them. Her anticipation mounted with the excitement of the gathering throng.

Scanning the enthusiastic revelers, Rose searched for Mrs. Smith among the mass, but to no avail. Obviously the woman was shy or perhaps used to such displays and reluctant to be jostled by such an eager crowd. She grabbed hold of the railing as the raft floated next to one of the others and dug into the moist riverbank. Nate's strong arm saved her from pitching forward as it lurched to a stop.

Mr. Smith hollered some harsh orders in the Indian language, and the crowd backed away, though they continued to chatter in their guttural way and laugh among themselves, pointing at the newcomers. Most of their attention centered on Rose.

Uncomfortable with their unbridled ogling, Rose gasped as Nate scooped her up into his arms and jumped ashore. Amid the ear-splitting racket going on all around them, she could barely make out his explanation about not wanting to ruin her shoes as he set her on dry ground and returned to the raft.

Left on her own, she found herself instantly surrounded as a mob of Indians of all ages closed in around her, babbling in their foreign tongue. The stench of bear grease on their shiny bodies filled her nostrils. Eager voices of men, women, and children drowned out every other sound as frantic hands shot forth from all directions to touch her, grabbing at her clothing, her skin, and her hair. The stylish bonnet was torn away, and her hair tumbled from the pins she'd so carefully placed in order to look nice for Mrs. Smith. As locks of it were yanked one way and then another, some fell before her eyes, nearly blocking her vision. Overcome by mounting panic, she couldn't even speak. She wanted them all to stop touching her and step away. *Dear Lord, help me. Protect me. I do not know what to do.*

From behind, someone suddenly whisked her up, and her heart nearly exploded from fright. Recognizing Nate, she regained her senses, and her heightened breathing slowed to normal. He'd come back, saved her again, and bullied his way through the crowd. To Rose's utmost relief, the Indians did not follow after them as he carried her away from the melee.

This was not the welcome she'd expected. Wanting no more than to relax into the comfort of his embrace, Rose knew it was not proper to do so. Instead she assessed more of the settlement, amazed at its size and the extensive array of crops. But as Nate strode away from the cluster of dwellings and headed toward the outskirts, she looked ahead and saw they were coming to a building completely different from the rest. Made of logs piled one on top of the other on three sides, the open front had only a canvas covering, which had been pulled to the side. Rose blew a wisp of hair out of her disbelieving eyes and her heart stopped. *This—this decrepit hut—was the profitable enterprise the trader owned?* She didn't know whether to laugh hysterically or burst into tears. Shocked beyond words, she could only gape at the wretched structure, where a pair of unfamiliar braves who looked younger than she by a few years sat on the ground, cross-legged, leaning back against posts flanking either side of the entrance, their black eyes glittering. Peering as hard as she could within the shaded confines of the store, she could not make out Mrs. Smith anywhere.

"Sorry I left you alone like that, Rose," Nate said as he set her down. "I should've figgered they'd be meddlesome, seein' somebody so pretty as you outta the blue. Anyway, looks like Eustice can get along fine without my help." He motioned with his head toward the crowd, where the trader was directing the unloading of his merchandise. Following Nate's gaze, she saw horses and cows being led ashore, goods hauled off, and workers being greeted and hugged by loved ones. The accumulating piles of supplies drew considerable attention as curious inhabitants of the village craned their necks to peer inside the crates, while Mr. Smith continued to yell at them in their language. Obviously he didn't want anyone making off with any of his precious cargo.

Considering everything she'd endured since her arrival in this land, Rose wondered why any of these circumstances surprised her. It was actually a fitting ending for an incredibly unbelievable journey. After all, the trader had sloughed off every question she'd asked regarding his store.

Even Nate, *her protector*, had given only the barest hint of a response when she inquired about specific details, she reminded herself. But having known him long enough to appreciate his stalwart character, she gave him the benefit of the doubt, surmising that he'd only been trying to be merciful. She moistened her lips and took a deep breath, doing her best to smooth her hair into some semblance of order with her fingers as she looked up at him. "I had no idea that they were like this. I'd heard so many stories about the noble savage, I thought they'd all be. . .proud.

Self-controlled. Instead, they bring to mind the poor street urchins in the slums of London. Wild, smelly, and loud."

Nate's hazel eyes radiated gentleness, and a sheepish half smile played across his mouth. "I'm truly sorry for bein' so remiss. I shoulda warned you not to dress so fancy-like. Most of 'em have never seen such fine women's clothes. Thing is, I was so caught up feastin' my eyes on how pretty you look, I just plumb forgot. I hope you'll forgive me."

At Nate and Rose's approach, the unsmiling Indians at the store's entrance unfurled their legs and sprang to their feet, catching up muskets as their ferret eyes squinted with suspicion. Both men had tattooed arms and wore their hair loose with cloth bands tied above their brows, and they were attired differently from the braves Rose had ridden with for the past weeks. Instead of wearing long buckskin trousers, they had on only breechcloths and beaded moccasins, leaving their legs bare. Each wore an intricate breastplate of beads over their hairless chests. Trying not to gape, she nodded a polite greeting then started into the trading post to see if she might have missed Mrs. Smith behind a stack of kegs or barrels. Moving past the braves, she felt their intent gaze following her.

A touch roomier than it appeared at first glance, the trading post had several kegs and barrels occupying its corners. She noted some cooking pots and kettles hanging on hooks, along with wooden bowls of different sizes. Crates of tomahawks and hunting knives sat on the dirt floor beside half-a-dozen muskets. A rustic shelf fastened to one of the log walls held yard goods, folded blankets, and an open box containing an array of mismatched buttons. Brass looking glasses nearby reflected light from the entrance onto a variety of colored beads, and the odor of cured animal hides stacked almost waist high permeated the structure.

She heard Nate greet the pair from the open doorway where he stood. "Running Wolf, Spotted Elk. How're things goin' for you boys?"

"No trouble," one muttered, his tone more cool than friendly.

Rose stopped to glance over her shoulder. None of the Indians she'd traveled with had spoken a word of English in her presence, though they seemed to understand whatever Mr. Smith said to them.

"We let no one in," the young brave continued. "Trade only on blanket out here. No one steal from Fawn Woman when Smith not here."

Nate nodded. "That should please Eustice. I'm sure he'll reward you and Fawn Woman with somethin' real good for bein' so diligent. By the way, Miss Harwood here would like to meet Eustice's wife. Where might she be?"

The brave pointed toward the crowd surrounding the rafts being unloaded. "She waits to see what gifts husband bring."

Hearing that information, Rose turned and came forward to look toward the crowd. So Mrs. Smith had been there all the while. Strange that she couldn't be seen amid the onlookers pressed shoulder to shoulder at the river. And where were the woman's brothers? Becoming aware that neither stone-faced brave had smiled as yet but stood erect, eyeing her, Rose thought they reminded her of the Royal Palace Guard at London's Windsor Castle. Ignoring their leering stares, she searched the milling throng chattering near the trade goods, but she still could not spot the trader's wife among them. Obviously the woman must be quite comfortable around the Indians, or she wouldn't mingle so closely with them. No doubt after living among these people she'd become rather fluent in their language the way her husband had. As yet unable to make out even the simplest of words, Rose marveled. Would she ever be able to converse with them herself?

As Rose wandered again among the goods in the store waiting for the trader and his wife, Nate moved closer to the guards. "Do you boys know if any of the Miamis or Illinois from downriver have come up this way with metal bracelets to trade?"

The pair exchanged wordless glances; then one of them shook his head. "Metal bracelets come from over great sea, not from setting sun. English make good bracelets." He rubbed his tanned fingers over the wide brass circlet clasped around his upper arm. "French bracelets no good."

"Aye. The English ones are best." Gratified that no one here had become aware of the silver discovery farther west, Nate glanced toward the river where supplies from the rafts were being carried to the store. He leaned inside the entrance. "They're bringin' stuff up from the river now, Rose. Come outside an' have a seat. I'd like a word with you."

"Of course. I shouldn't want to be in the way while the goods are being stored." She followed him to a log in front of a dead campfire and sank down onto it.

He propped a foot alongside her, and they watched the parade of crates and sacks being transported into the trading post. "In a few days I'll be headin' out," he said at last.

"I beg your pardon?" A flicker of fear sparked in her eyes as she met his gaze.

He gave a nod. "I spoke to Eustice, an' I believe I can get him the price he wants to sell you to me."

Her fear evaporated. Anger took its place. Her mouth dropped open in a look of shock, and her face grew white.

Her reaction floored him. Hadn't it been clear all along that he'd come on this journey with the intent of getting her free of Eustice Smith? He reared back with a frown. "What's the problem? I thought that's what you wanted."

Chapter 16

Rose's fists closed around handfuls of her skirt, and she clenched her teeth together so hard they hurt. This man—this *rescuer* she had counted on all this time—wanted to *buy* her, not free her. She did want to be out of here, but not as merely another man's property. Surely the bounder did not expect to purchase her from Mr. Smith so he could drag her off somewhere for his own amusement!

She fought for words to express her fury so Nate Kinyon would have no doubt as to how despicable a cur she thought him to be. But before she could verbalize her opinion of him and that plan of his, Mr. Smith emerged from the group of Indian workers toting cargo to the trading post and strode over to her. He gestured with his thumb toward the rear of the store.

"Back there, woman, there's a pen o' chickens. An' off to the right o' that you'll find my wife's garden. Make me up a pot o' rich chicken soup with plenty o' cooked-down vegetables. My sleepin' quarters are in that wigwam left o' here. There's a dutch oven inside ya can use. Oh, an' milk the cow first off. I need some milk to soothe my innards right quick."

Rose stared at him, completely dumbfounded. She was quite capable of plucking chicken feathers, but he expected her to go and kill the poor bird herself? The swine! Already in high dudgeon over Nate Kinyon's announcement moments ago, she felt her stomach tighten further. This was all too much.

"Well, get to it, gal." His scowl darkened. "Now."

"But—I've yet to meet your wife. I'd hoped—"

He rolled his squinty eyes and shook his head. "Ain't no use. You'll get no help from her."

"Please."

His bony shoulders sagged. "Oh, all right." He swung on his heel and turned to Running Wolf or Spotted Elk—Rose didn't know which was which—who stood speaking to a squaw. "Fawn Woman! Get over here."

In total disbelief, Rose felt the single wish that had sustained her throughout the endless journey crumble to ashes as a slender Indian woman grimaced to the young brave and approached on silent feet. Near Rose's own age, the dusky-skinned woman with a beaded leather headband above long, shiny braids and a beaded dress of soft doeskin would have been considered quite a beauty, were it not for the obstinate expression of sheer disgust that hardened her features. She cut a wordless glance to Mr. Smith, then to Rose.

Her husband tilted his head toward Rose. "This here's Rose Harwood. I brung her to cook fer me. Miss Harwood, this is my wife, Fawn Woman Smith."

Too devastated to utter a response, Rose merely stared as the woman raked her head to toe with her deep brown gaze and grunted. She reached out and felt Rose's gown. "Want gown." She pouted at her husband.

That Indian woman wants my clothes! Not only is she not English, she wants my clothes! Rose all but choked.

Mr. Smith steered his wife away. "Ya don't need that rag o' hers, Fawn. I brung you a gown of yer own. Better an' much grander than hers. You'll see."

"Hmph." Only slightly mollified, the squaw crossed her arms in defiance. "She cook for you. I no eat pale-woman food. Woman no sleep in my wigwam."

"She won't have to," the trader agreed, "soon as ya build her one next to ours."

"Me?" The squaw raised her chin and sneered.

"Aye, woman. You."

She huffed and pursed her lips. "Want gown. Give now."

Smith appeared noticeably weary of the situation, but his determined stance showed he wasn't about to give in to his wife or any other female. "First ya build the wigwam. Then ya get the gown. That's final." Shaking his grizzled head, he turned to Rose and lifted a hand palm up in question. "What're you still standin' there fer? Git a move on. I need that soup quick. I got a powerful ache in my belly."

Rose fully understood. Her own stomach wasn't feeling so wonderful at the moment, imagining the chicken she'd have to butcher with her own hands.

Having witnessed the conversation, Nate cleared his throat and stepped up beside Rose. "Think I'll give the little lady a hand, if it's all the same to you, Eustice."

The trader shrugged and stomped away, while his wife cast a scathing glare over her shoulder at both of them and went to see to her task.

Rose gave the frontiersman a wavering smile. He'd come to her aid again. How could she stay mad at him? Once again God had shown His faithful presence, His mercy. As Papa always said, *"God is a sure help in time of need."* She sent a thankful prayer aloft and followed Nate behind the trading post to the chicken pen, her feet dragging the entire way.

The village lay quiet. Night sounds from the surrounding forest drifted across the area as the moon shed its light on the sleepy settlement. Lounging on his sleeping pallet with a cup of tea at the campfire in front of Rose's thrown-together wigwam, Nate shook his head, wondering when a gust of wind would blow the pitiful thing clear out over the next ridge. Fawn Woman had put the least effort possible into its construction, her disdain for Eustice's new cook almost tangible.

He redirected his thoughts to Rose, already asleep inside the structure's barely adequate shelter. This day had been a hard one for her, likely the first of many. He'd make her hovel more secure in the morning. Sure had been a sight to behold, though, her chasing after that poor squawking chicken earlier. A smile twitched his lips. How could she be that old without ever having killed a chicken before? Must be because city folk had butchers and bakers at their beck and call. Proper little Rose Harwood was out of her depth, but she did have pluck. She stuck to something till she saw it through.

Hearing footsteps coming out of the woods, he glanced up to see Eustice Smith returning from answering nature's call. Nate sprang to his feet and went to intercept the man before he entered his wigwam. "I'd like a private word with you."

"What? Now?" Smith let out a weary breath.

"It'll only take a minute." He handed him his leftover tea. "Let's sit over on your log."

Lumbering beside Nate till they reached the fallen wood, Smith sank onto it. "Make it quick. I'm bushed."

Uncertain about how to start, Nate decided to go for broke and blurt out the words plain and simple. "Far as I know, Bob still has most of his money from the furs we traded, an' I'll be gettin' some mighty fine pelts myself for that fancy suit I bought before the trip. If you'll take all of that, plus whatever money I still have on me in trade goods, me an' Bob'll go downstream and do some sharp tradin' in some of the tributaries that don't have no store. Mebbe get enough in those untried areas so you could retire to that life of ease you was talkin' about."

The old man chuckled. "Ya really do want that little gal I bought, don't ya'?"

Not relishing being made sport of, Nate felt his hackles go up. "That's why I'm here."

"That's French territory you'll be headin' into, ya know." Smith took a sip of the tepid tea.

Nate shrugged. He'd discerned a hint of interest in the trader's voice, a good sign. "All the better. Think on it, Eustice. You got finer quality cloth an' weapons than those Frenchies do. Besides, me an' Bob can take care of ourselves."

Rubbing his shaggy beard in thought, Smith grunted. "Do what you want. I don't see as how I can lose. I wasn't much cottonin' to ya hangin' around here, distractin' my cook, anyway."

"Distractin'? That what you call help? You should be thankin' me, man. If it wasn't for me showin' her the how-to, Rose'd still be out back tryin' to catch that chicken you had for supper, an' you know it."

Smith sputtered into a laugh then clutched his belly with a wince and glanced over at Rose's deplorable wigwam. "That ol' bird gave her a run fer her money, eh?" He handed the empty cup back to Nate. "Well, there's no denyin' the gal cooked me up a fine meal. These innards o' mine don't feel near as bad as before. I knowed she'd do me some good." He nodded in thought and got up.

Nate watched the man amble away to his wigwam, holding his midsection.

On his way back to his sleeping pallet, he looked across the moonlit Indian village. It had swelled in size since he'd come through last spring. There had to be thirty-five or forty wigwams now, and at least three longhouses. He could see light streaming from one of those gathering places. Some tribe members must be inside tossing bone dice. Indian men weren't so different from most footloose men he came across in his travels. They all liked to gamble.

For a few seconds, he toyed with the idea of joining them. He'd probably get a lot more for his fancy clothes with several men vying for each piece. But then he glanced over at Rose's shelter and knew she wouldn't like him gambling. Shaking off the unwonted conviction, he recalled his promise to sleep near her entrance tonight. She'd been pretty jumpy, this being her first night in such a foreign environment. Besides, he really didn't want to chance losing the few pounds he possessed, not when he needed so much more than that to fulfill his plan.

He wondered how much money Bob had on him. That partner of

his was such a miser, he habitually sent most of his money to his father's sister for safekeeping. Nate glanced toward the river. Bob should have beaten the caravan and been here long before the party arrived. What was taking him so long? The sooner the two of them went looking for that silver he'd heard about, the sooner they'd get back. . .and the sooner he'd get his Rose, his Rose of Sharon.

A small shaft of light fell across Rose's eyes, awakening her. Blinking against the brightness, she peered up to see sunshine streaming through one of several holes in the cone-shaped wigwam Fawn Woman had slapped together. Rose grimaced, thankful it hadn't been rain that disturbed her sleep. When she found some free time, she'd patch those spots. Sitting up on the sleeping pallet of furs, she vowed to save up chicken feathers until she had enough to make a softer bed. She took a leisurely stretch as she took stock of the cramped living quarters, half of which was cluttered with sacks and kegs and small chests containing Mr. Smith's personal foods. There had to be a way to stack them neatly so she'd have more room.

Sounds from outside drifted to her ears as the village residents began to stir. Rose bolted up from her pallet and opened her trunk, snatching from the contents the now-stained brown gown and its equally spotty apron. No one could possibly envy those. She dressed quickly and ran a brush through her hair before tying it back with a ribbon. Then she opened the flap of her wigwam.

As he'd promised, Nate slept nearby. His thoughtfulness touched her, and she tiptoed quietly past him to take care of her morning needs at the bubbling creek she'd discovered yesterday in a shallow gully behind the crude chicken coop and pen.

While at the brook, Rose wondered what day of the week had just dawned and calculated it must be Wednesday. She must not lose track again. Scanning the area around her, she found a sharp rock and used it to scratch a line into a nearby tree. She'd make one mark for each day so she'd always know when the Sabbath came.

In the morning's quiet freshness, she sat with her back against the beech tree and bowed her head. *Dear Father in heaven, thank You that my long journey has finally ended. I don't understand the reason You brought me here, but I ask for strength and patience as I fulfill my contract. Please help me to be an example of Your love to the Smiths and to remain faithful to my faith, as I promised Mum. And as always, I commit my loved ones into Your loving care.*

On her way back, Rose spied Mrs. Smith emerging from the much larger rounded wigwam in a gaudy red gown more suited for a theater performer than a respectable lady. Her husband's taste in women's fashions left much to be desired. Rose kept her features composed as she nodded a greeting to her owner's wife.

The Indian woman deliberately averted her face, ignoring her.

Rose tucked her chin. *Surely Fawn Woman Smith doesn't imagine I'm out to steal her husband. As if I'd be tempted by that filthy old goat!* With a shake of her head, she hoped that once the squaw realized there was no possibility of that particular danger, she might become friendlier. After all, they'd be living in close proximity to one another, with wigwams and campfires separated by no more than fifteen feet. With the wigwam belonging to the store's two guards on the other side of the store, the arrangement was actually quite cozy. A touch too cozy.

Not wanting to disturb the men, Rose nursed a fire from some banked coals then poured water into the kettle suspended above, all the while adding up how much time being a cook in this primitive setting was going to take. There were chickens to feed, a cow in the makeshift stable to milk, the growing calf and other cattle to drive out to graze in the large pen. Then, of course, there was the garden. That responsibility would probably fall to her as well. Yesterday Nate had mentioned gathering berries and nuts when they were in season. But she'd draw the line at chewing leather to soften it for clothing, as she'd seen an old woman doing in front of a village wigwam. That couldn't possibly be a cook's job.

Once she'd fed the chickens and gathered the eggs, she noticed that

Mrs. Smith had started her own fire and stood chatting with another squaw, no doubt showing off that silly red gown.

"Mornin', pretty lady," Nate called with a grin as he came out of the woods.

She smiled back. "Good morning to you. I'll have the tea steeping in no time." She started toward her wigwam for the supplies, intending to ply the frontiersman with a hundred questions. She'd done the same thing yesterday and hoped he wouldn't lose patience.

"I'm glad to help," he said, following after her.

He always seemed eager to assist her, and she wondered idly if he'd be so accommodating if they were married and he was sure of her. Her cousin back in England complained constantly about being taken for granted. Of course, actually marrying Nate was the furthest thing from Rose's mind. She got out the ingredients for biscuits and began mixing them. Besides, he seemed more interested in buying her.

"I'll see to the milkin'," Nate remarked. "You're busy."

"That would be wonderful." *And I know you're hoping to be invited to breakfast.* Rose smiled to herself. Mr. Smith wasn't the only man who appreciated good cooking.

Moments later, the salt pork sizzled in the pan, and Rose knew its aroma was a magnet, drawing Nate back with milk in a very short span of time.

"Cows are out grazin'." He gave a nod, looking rather pleased with himself as he handed her the milk pail, only a quarter full. "That's all that glutton of a calf left me."

"Thank you. It's plenty." Rose moistened her lips. "When winter comes, will I be expected to cook outside in the rain and snow?"

He shook his head. "Folks cook inside then. There's a flap up top of your wigwam you can open to let out the smoke. Works pretty good. 'Cept—"

She paused in her work and met his gaze.

"Well, you don't have to worry none about that. I'll see you're outta here before then."

Rose didn't want to think about how he planned to accomplish that little detail, and there wasn't time to dwell on it anyway. She caught a flash of red out of the corner of her eye. An unsmiling Mrs. Smith sauntered up to them, her dark eyes glinting with anger. She stepped right in front of Rose and grabbed her hand, drawing her along with her toward the store, where one of the guards sat slumped over, fast asleep. Fawn Woman gave him a swift kick with her moccasin, and he jerked awake as she tugged Rose past him into the store.

The woman stopped before bolts of material in a variety of colors and patterns. "You." She pointed to Rose then took hold of her skirt and shook it. "Me."

Confused, Rose frowned. "Yes, we both are wearing daygowns."

The squaw shook her head and pouted. She placed a hand on some shiny yellow satin.

"I believe she wants you to make her a new gown," Nate supplied, having come into the store without Rose noticing.

Mrs. Smith grabbed the bolt and thrust it at Rose. "Gown. Make."

Rose gave her a pleasant smile. "Of course. I shall make you a gown right after we've eaten breakfast."

She gave a decisive nod. "After eat." She whirled around, her red skirt flaring into the surrounding goods, then walked away, her nose in the air.

Nate chuckled.

"What's so funny?" Rose asked, fighting irritation.

"Your 'mistress' is makin' sure she ain't losin' her exalted position as the storekeeper's only real wife. She wants everyone to know you're not just Eustice's slave, but hers, too."

Rose sniffed in scorn. "I cannot imagine anyone would want to be that man's wife."

"Now, see? That's where you have it wrong." Nate put a hand on Rose's shoulder and steered her out of the store, back to the cook fire. "Fawn Woman doesn't want to be Smith's wife. Fact is, he bought her some time back. But the title does hold importance in this village, plus she has the protection of her two brothers Smith hired to come along when he brought Fawn Woman out here. The three are Susquehannock."

"Those two guards outside are her brothers?" Rose rolled her eyes. "Oh mercy. Classes exist even here in the wilderness, and she's an outsider who wants to be part of the aristocracy."

He nodded. "Somethin' like that. Just do like she says an' always stay close to Smith an' the Susquehannocks. No matter how Fawn Woman postures, none of 'em will let any harm come to the 'cook' while I'm gone."

"Gone?" He'd told her before that he was going to leave, and it remained in the back of her mind, but Rose had dismissed that fact.

"Any day now." Reaching the fire, Nate bent to turn the side pork with a long fork but avoided meeting her eyes. "Soon as Bob gets here." Straightening up again, he stared out over the wide river, his straight brows dipping together in a worried frown. "Funny, I was sure he'd beat us here."

Rose glanced from him to the village of people milling about now, all of them speaking words she would never understand. . .and Nate was going to leave her. How would she manage without him?

Chapter 17

Rose struggled to keep the slippery yellow material from snagging on the rough crate top she was using as a worktable to cut out Mrs. Smith's gown. No matter what ill opinion Fawn Woman held of her, Rose determined to do her finest work on the garment. There had to be a way to encourage friendship with the squaw, since they'd be living near each other for the next four years.

From several yards away, children's laughter drifted like music to her ear. Looking toward the youngsters at play, she spied three little Indian girls kneeling in the shade of an oak tree, putting together a miniature wigwam for dolls. Several naked boys with small bows and arrows shot at a thick tree trunk nearby. Rose smiled at the way girls always played house and boys always tried to outdo each other. They weren't so very different from white children.

Suddenly one of the boys dropped his bow and pointed toward the river. He bolted for the bank, and the others scampered after him.

Rose turned to see what had drawn his attention and spotted a lone Indian in a canoe paddling toward shore. Laying aside the scissors, she stood for a better look. "Robert Bloom!" Relieved that Nate's partner remained alive and well, she felt a twinge of sadness as well, since his coming would precipitate his and Nate's departure. But at least it was comforting to know Robert was a practicing Christian, unlike his pal. The short, perfunctory prayers Nate offered at mealtimes did please her, but she sensed that pleasing her was his motivation. She would have preferred seeing evidence of some real faith.

Perhaps the frontiersmen would remain at the village for a while. Rose dreaded being left here with Mr. Smith as the only other white person in residence. She remembered Robert's desire to have spirited conversations with her about the teachings of George Whitefield and other new Christian thinkers coming into prominence, like John and Charles Wesley. She hoped there'd be time for some good talks.

A deep sigh came from inside. If nothing else, Robert would have information about the lad taken hostage and how the Lord had answered their prayers. This eve she would make a delicious meal for the men. Out in the wilds they had to exist on whatever fish or game they found along the way—or worse, eat only cold jerky for days on end as the caravan had often been forced to do. Perhaps after some good English cooking, they wouldn't be so eager to head for parts unknown.

~~~

Finishing up his improvements on Rose's wigwam, Nate heard the commotion at the riverside and saw Bob paddling ashore. He dropped his tools and went to meet him. Half the village already swarmed the water's edge, and the Shawnee braves he and Bob had traveled with threaded their way to the front of the crowd as Nate waded into the water to pull in the canoe. "Glad to see you still have your scalp, buddy. But what'd you do? Swap your horse for this thing?"

Bob grinned. "No, I came across it hidden in some reeds." He hopped out and helped shove the bark-covered canoe onto the beach. "Knowin' how you love raft buildin', I thought mebbe you'd like to go back over with me to build one for my horse."

Chuckling, they strode together up the shallow rise. They scarcely gained the top before Indians and hired braves from the village crowded around them and started jabbering to Bob in their language. Words flew back and forth so quickly Nate could only pick up one or two but suspected they were discussing the hostage situation. Bob wore a satisfied expression as he answered questions, but oddly, the Indians seemed far more pleased than he was. A couple of them snickered and swapped knowing glances.

Nate elbowed his pal in the ribs. "I take it you were able to rescue the lad in question."

"Aye. But the Indians are happy about what all the Cherokees got in the trade."

"Good trade." One of the hired braves smirked.

Nate's brow furrowed. "What'd those men have to give up to get the boy back, anyway?"

"All their trade goods an' every cent they had with them, plus all the cash money I had on me."

"All of it?" Nate saw his personal plans for Bob's money evaporate like dew in the sunshine. "But you're talkin' only what was left after the funds you sent home for safekeepin', right?"

He nodded. "Aye. But the kid was lookin' real beat up. I had to help him. You'd've done the same."

"You're right." Nate felt the chink in his plan grow wider, but nothing could be done about that. "Well, let's get a couple of volunteers an' retrieve your horse before some wildcat gets wind of him."

"Good thinkin'." Bob cleared his throat. "How's Rose, by the way?"

Irritated by his partner's interest in her, Nate gave a curt response. "She's here an' she's fine. I'll tell you all about her on our way across the river. Think I've come up with a plan to get her away from Smith." *One that'll take a mite of adjusting, in the light of things.*

Bob laughed. "You haven't settled on killin' the man, I hope."

"Actually, the thought did cross my mind." Nate flashed a sheepish grin. "But the way these Shawnees love that store of his, I figured they'd scalp me for sure." *On the other hand, Smith might not go for the new plan. . . .*

From her position near the store, Rose watched in disappointment as Nate and Robert shoved the canoe back into the water then hopped into it. Two Indians joined them, and the four men began paddling back across the river. Nate said he and his partner would leave as soon as Robert returned, but how could they go so suddenly without so much as a brief farewell? Her throat closed up, and her chest began to ache as hot tears stung her eyes. She blinked them back, determined not to cry. She needed to stay strong before these village people.

Mr. Smith came up behind her. "Those two're prob'ly goin' over to fetch Bob's horse. The river's too deep fer it to swim across. They'll have to build a raft to get the mare to this side."

A wave of relief swept over Rose, but she was still confused. "Why did they not take one that's already beached here?"

He looked at her as if she were daft. "'Cause o' the swift current. They'd have a time of it tryin' to paddle one o' them lumberin' things upstream. It's too deep fer polin.'"

Rose tamped down her embarrassment. She should have known that, remembering how swiftly the raft moved yesterday when she arrived. At least she had hope that the men would soon return.

"Another lazy hunter to feed." The trader grimaced and started away then turned back. "Don't be killin' another chicken. I'll get ya some venison to cook fer 'em. I'll eat whatever's left o' last night's chicken stew. But make plenty o' puddin.'"

An hour later, Rose added a pinch more seasoning to the venison stewing in the kettle, hoping to make it smell and taste more like meat she preferred. To her nostrils it smelled worse than the bear grease the Indians lathered on themselves to fend off mosquitoes. She gazed out across the river yet another time, wondering how much longer it would be until the men returned. How she wished she could see past the bend

ROSE'S PLEDGE

where they'd paddled out of sight. Mr. Smith had never actually lied to her, but it would be nice to have proof he'd been right about their constructing a raft.

As if her thought had conjured the man up, the trader again strode up to her without her noticing, quiet as an Indian in the moccasins he now wore. "Don't be wastin' all my good flour on them upstarts. Make 'em some corn bread instead."

"As you wish." She slid a weary glance after him as he sauntered back to the store. Would he be that stingy with his food once the men had gone? *Gone.* Even the word was depressing. How she would miss the two once they left. She'd be entirely friendless then and would have God alone to turn to.

Chapter 18

After hours of felling trees and constructing a raft for his partner's horse, Nate wanted nothing more than to bed down for the night. But the enticing aroma wafting his way from Rose's kettle revived him as he and Bob climbed the rise to Smith's trading post. Not far from the store, Rose bent over the fire, stirring the suspended pot, and his gaze drank in the picture of grace and femininity she made with her honey-colored hair streaming over her slender shoulder.

Before they reached her, Running Wolf and Spotted Elk left their posts and came to greet Bob, eager to hear the details of his exploits.

Nate gave them a polite nod and looked again in Rose's direction. She'd seen him, too, and the surprise on her face warmed his insides. . . until her gaze shifted to his partner and really lit up.

"You're looking rather well," she told Bob when the four of them arrived. "Were you able to rescue that boy?"

He grinned from ear to ear. "Aye. He should be back in the arms of his ma by now. It'll prob'ly be a long time before he strays far from home again."

"Praise the Lord."

"Amen to that." He laughed and moved closer to her.

Rose continued to regard only him. "We must give a sincere thank-you to the Almighty when we bless the food this eve. 'Tis just about ready."

"And it smells mighty good." Nate managed to wedge into the conversation.

His partner glanced across the distance between Rose's cook fire and Fawn Woman Smith's, where the squaw tended her own pot. "Does she eat separate?"

Nate answered for Rose. "Her an' her brothers. That's how she wants it."

"Hmm." Leaving Nate and Rose, Bob walked over to her.

She looked up at him with a pleasant expression. Smiling warmly, she spoke to him in her language, gesturing toward her own cooked meal.

He gave a nod but responded in a voice too low to be heard at a distance.

The woman's smile flattened momentarily, but as Bob kept talking, her glum demeanor brightened, and she turned with a stiff smile toward Nate and Rose.

Grinning with satisfaction, Bob rejoined Rose and the men. "Mrs. Smith's invitin' us to join her. Help me tote this good-smellin' food over to her fire, boys."

Noticing how eagerly the braves grabbed up trenchers and cups, Nate suspected they'd been yearning to try some of Rose's good cooking.

As Bob snatched the board holding the corn bread and the pail of milk, Nate released a long, slow breath. He much preferred it when there'd been just Smith and him and Rose.

Or better yet, just him and Rose. But that was not to be. Yet.

Reluctantly, he plucked a rag to protect his hands from the hot kettle handle and unhooked the pot from the tripod then reached to pick up a smaller pot at the edge of the coals.

Rose looked up. "Oh, that one's not to be shared. 'Tis for Mr. Smith and his poor digestion."

"Don't forget to bring some fur robes to sit on," Bob called over his shoulder.

Rose had yet to move. Nate could tell she was no more thrilled about the unexpected arrangement than Mrs. Smith was. "It'll be all right," he assured her. "Bob always wants folks to get along, whether they want to or not. It's his way."

"Well, I'm afraid *she* has the opposite desire," Rose said wryly.

"Mebbe. But try to make the best of it. While we're gone, it'd be better to have her for a friend than an enemy." He tried to cheer her with a grin.

Rose looked all the more troubled and quickly turned away. "I'd best go tell Mr. Smith dinner's ready."

Watching after her, Nate could tell from the sad droop of her shoulders that she didn't want him and Bob to leave her. But he also knew that the sooner they left, the sooner he'd be able to come back for her and take her with them.

Rose found her owner trading with an Indian who'd come from downstream earlier that day. She waited for him to finish his business dealings before announcing supper, hoping his presence at the meal would lend the support she needed to face his unpleasant wife.

A touch of the day's heat still lingered in the early evening, and when Rose and the trader joined the group, everyone had gathered in a circle away from the cook fire. They'd piled food on their trenchers but had yet to begin eating. By the eagerness in their expressions as she and Mr. Smith approached, she assumed Robert had mentioned that most white people began their meal with a blessing, a custom not followed by Indians.

The brothers' nostrils flared as they inhaled the aroma of the food before them, and Rose hoped their eager display would not anger their sister. Fortunately all the men had been wise enough to take portions from both women's cooking pots.

Robert nodded to Nate. "If it's all the same to you, I'll do the prayin' this time."

"Sure, go ahead." Unsmiling, Nate gave a nod.

Rose saw a muscle work in his jaw. He seemed disappointed. Perplexed, she bowed her head along with the others as Robert began speaking.

"Thank You, heavenly Father, for Fawn Woman's kindness in askin' us to share some o' her fine cookin'. We ask You to bless it as we eat. Thank You, too, for allowin' Billy Wexler to be restored to his family. Now please protect me an' Nate as we leave tomorrow to visit new tribes. Make 'em curious to know about You. In Jesus' name, amen."

"Amen," Rose whispered. She needed a chance to collect herself after hearing of his and Nate's departure on the very morrow, so she took her time filling her trencher over both pots. When she turned back to take a seat on one of the pallets, all the men were eating with great gusto—especially Fawn Woman's brothers. Even more amazing, the woman herself took a gingerly sniff of Rose's stew, which encouraged Rose. She scanned the group. "Did you know that Rome was once saved from savage hordes from the north with pepper?"

Robert hiked his brows. "You don't say."

"'Tis true. The Romans bought them off with all the pepper they had in the city. It seems everyone enjoys a variety of spices." Mrs. Smith had yet to sample any of the meat from Rose's kettle, so Rose decided to plunge in and taste the squaw's stew to show her appreciation. She deftly avoided the fatty meat and tried the woman's greasy mixture of corn, beans, and summer squash. A grisly chunk of fat hid beneath the vegetables, but she managed to keep from gagging as she forced it down whole with a smile and a nod.

Alas, Fawn Woman wasn't even looking her way.

"Muskrat." Nate grinned. "Tasty, eh?"

The squaw gave a smug nod while Rose struggled to keep the food down. "Rat?" Her gaze darted across the fire, where Robert and Mr. Smith both sat chuckling.

Robert reached over and gave Rose's arm an empathetic pat. "It's not really a rat. More like a beaver. That robe you're sittin' on is made from muskrat pelts."

Her hand automatically went down to touch the brown fur and found it thick and soft to the touch. It was rather sweet of him to comfort her. How she wished she was attracted to the dedicated Christian instead of to Nate.

While the men took their time eating the meal, Rose and Fawn Woman picked at theirs. Rose noticed that her hostess continued to ignore her presence.

Nate broke the silence. He turned to the trader. "Eustice, when that boy got ransomed, his pa an' his companion didn't have enough goods or cash on 'em, so Bob had to use all his own money to help out. That got me to thinkin'. You front us a canoe loaded with trade goods, an' I'm sure we'll get a lot more prime pelts for the truck out where there ain't a tradin' post for a hundred miles."

The trader lazed back a moment, pondering the matter, then sported a sly smile. "If I git my cost back off the top, then I'm willin' to be generous. I'll split the profit with ya, since you boys'll be riskin' yer necks—or should I say scalps."

That last statement struck Rose hard. The caravan hadn't had any real trouble on the way here—but there'd been seven well-armed men in the party.

Nate looked from Robert to Mr. Smith. "We'll give you all the furs. All I want is Rose."

This time she really had to fight not to retch. How mortifying to have a man bartering over her—and in front of Mr. Smith's already haughty wife! A gleam in those sullen eyes proved the squaw understood quite a bit more English than she spoke.

The trader toyed with his beard. "It'll take more'n one measly little tradin' trip to set me up fer life, ya know. I 'spect you boys'll be paddlin' down there a whole lot more times than ya bargained fer."

Nate narrowed his eyes and studied the man. "Exactly how much do you figger you're gonna need to set yourself up, anyway?"

Rose wanted desperately to put a stop to this outrageous conversation, but the thought of bringing notice to herself at such a humiliating moment seemed even worse.

Mr. Smith rested an elbow on one knee and leaned his bearded chin on his fist, appearing to give the matter serious thought. "I'd say about five hundred pounds."

Nate set down his trencher. "Three's more like it."

"Not hardly. But I mebbe could squeeze by on, say, four hundred."

To Rose's astonishment, she saw the frontiersman reach over to the trader with his hand outstretched. "Deal. An' I'd like that in writin'."

Four hundred pounds! He'd never be able to earn such a fortune in ten years, much less one summer. Even two or three. "I must see to cleaning the kettle," she mumbled. She needed to leave before she broke down in front of them all. Rising, she snatched the pot from where it sat near the fire, not caring that the handle was still hot, and hurried away. For all Nate Kinyon's big talk, they both knew she'd be here for the full four years of her indenturement.

—

Tears blurred Rose's vision as Nate and Robert Bloom took their leave. To help with the unfamiliar dialect needed in the Wabash area, they hired a Miami lad who'd been stolen as a youth, and the three of them paddled downriver in a long canoe piled high with bundles of trade goods. *Please watch over them, Father. Keep them safe.*

When the boat vanished from sight around the river's bend, she inhaled a wavering breath and trudged slowly back to her wigwam. The fact that the return of the young brave would guarantee Nate and Bob a hearty welcome eased her mind a bit, but she couldn't help wondering if her two frontiersmen would come back alive. Mr. Smith's caustic remark about their scalps still rang in her mind.

From the corner of her eye, she spotted Fawn Woman coming her way.

The squaw didn't bother with any sort of greeting. "You. Go. Me gown."

Rose sighed and went to fetch her sewing, which had been interrupted by the men's departure. Nate had divulged a second reason

SALLY LAITY AND DIANNA CRAWFORD

why the Indian woman was so adamant about a new gown. Shawnee women didn't have the fine thread or needles Rose possessed. Instead, they used leather thongs and reed strands, along with what looked like hair or whiskers from animals. The clothing they made appeared sturdy, but they were also coarse. Mrs. Smith would be quite the envy of the others in the village, having not one, but two cloth gowns.

Rose briefly considered selling two of her own better gowns out of the mere four she had brought from England. If what Mr. Smith predicted turned out to be true and Nate came up short of pelts even after several trips, the money her gowns might bring in could help out. Once the other squaws caught sight of Fawn Woman's gown, they'd probably be willing to pay for one of their own.

Sinking down onto a log, Rose opened her sewing basket. Her thread supply was shrinking fast. She wished she'd had the foresight to bring much more along. Picking up the partially sewn gown, she set to work.

Her thoughts drifted to the possibility of leaving Mr. Smith's protection and riding off with Nate Kinyon. Could that actually happen? And if so, would it be a wise choice? What exactly were Nate's plans for her? Did he truly intend merely to return her to her sisters after everything he'd have to do to earn four hundred pounds? That was hard to believe. And he'd never even hinted at marriage. *Dear Lord, this is such a dilemma. I need Your wisdom to show me what to do.*

Just then a shadow moved across her basket, and Rose looked up.

Her heart froze.

Chapter 19

Rose's mouth dropped open in shock. A pitiful-looking white woman stood before her in a filthy, ragged daygown. Her puffy blue eyes were rimmed with red, her skin sallow and blotchy, and hair that once might have been the soft gold of a wheat field hung in matted strings. But far worse, cuts and bruises covered her face and all exposed skin. A whimpering infant was slung behind her slumped back.

Setting her work aside, Rose placed her sewing basket on the ground and stood, trying to compose herself. "What can I do for you?"

"Milk." The word came out in a croak. "For my baby. I dried up." With effort she drew a ragged breath. "I'm. . .dyin.'"

"That cannot be." Rose glanced out across the village, but no one was paying them any mind, as if a woman so obviously suffering didn't merit the slightest consideration. Swallowing her abhorrence, Rose motioned toward the sitting log. "Please, sit down. I'll get milk for both of you."

Trembling, the woman dropped down with a gasp.

Her heart crimping, Rose moistened her lips. "I'll take the baby for you." She lifted the infant out of the ragged sling, noticing that though the baby was thin and dirty, it seemed unhurt. She estimated its age to be four or five months at most. The little one gazed up with wide blue eyes, hungry eyes that made her wonder when it had last eaten.

Leaving the child's mother, Rose hurried down to the brook, where she kept a pail of milk cool in the water's flow, and fetched it back. She shifted the baby to one hip then plucked a couple of dipping gourds from her wigwam, along with one of the few small metal spoons Mr. Smith possessed and returned to the slumped woman. Setting down the pail, she quickly dipped some milk for her. "Here. This may make you feel a bit better."

She raised a discolored arm and pushed the gourd away. Her hand burned with fever. "Jenny needs it more."

Rose shook her head and thrust the milk back to her. "I've plenty for your baby girl. This is for you. Please drink it." Satisfied when the woman acquiesced and raised it shakily to her lips, Rose dipped the second gourd into the pail and took a seat on a nearby fur blanket within eyesight of the baby's mother. She began spoon-feeding the infant. The poor little thing slurped at it so greedily, Rose's eyes swam. She could hardly get it to her fast enough.

The mother looked longingly at the baby devouring the milk, and she tried to smile. "My name. . .is Hannah Wright." The strangled whisper seemed to sap much of her strength, but she took a sharp breath and went on. "I come from a homestead up near. . .the west fork of the Susquehanna." A pause. "My husband's name was Adam."

As Hannah Wright drew another breath, Rose felt a sudden ache in her throat. *Past tense. He must be dead.* The baby squawked and kicked its tiny feet, and Rose resumed feeding it.

"Adam's folks live east of there. . .near the main branch. Names are Edith and Chadwick Wright. Take Jenny Ann to them. Please." She coughed. "You. . .only hope."

"But you're a hostage, are you not? Will the Indians allow me to take the baby?"

The still half-full gourd slipped from the feverish hand, and Hannah moaned, rocking back and forth as if consumed by pain.

Seeing the poor woman's struggle to speak further, Rose propped the fur securely around the baby and stood to her feet. "We can talk later. First we need to take care of you. My name is Rose."

Hannah held up a hand and wagged her head. "It's. . .too late." Moving aside her ragged skirt, she exposed a swollen leg that looked as if it had been hacked at with a tomahawk. Discolored and covered with dried blood and oozing pus, it smelled like rotting fish.

The hideous sight almost caused Rose's stomach to heave. Unable to fathom such vile cruelty, she quickly inhaled to keep from fainting.

Mr. Smith ambled up to them. He stared at the woman but did not appear surprised or appalled upon seeing her. "Who's this?"

His indifference angered Rose. "We must get this poor woman out of this place."

"Too late," Hannah whispered again. She tried to raise a hand but barely succeeded. It fell back onto her lap. "Take my Jenny."

Furious now, Rose swept Hannah's skirt aside, displaying the putrid injury the unfortunate young woman had suffered. "Look at this, Mr. Smith. Have you medicine at the store that might help her?"

He took one look then shrugged and shook his shaggy head. Bending over, he gave the woman's shoulder a sympathetic pat. "Sorry as I can be, missy. It's past any helpin' at this point. Should'a been tended days ago."

Her reddened eyes filled with tears.

Rose stared at him in dismay. "But we *must* do something."

"Fawn Woman!" Smith hollered, straightening up.

The squaw looked over at him with a sour face as she sat stringing some shiny beads near their wigwam. She grudgingly got to her feet and came to join him.

He glared at her. "When was this gal brought here? Why weren't her wounds tended to?"

The baby began to fuss, so Rose stooped down and fed her a little more milk while Fawn Woman rattled off an explanation in her language. Then, as if Hannah didn't exist, she turned around and sauntered off to her beads again, obviously devoid of interest in the matter.

Such heartlessness and savage inhumanity revolted Rose. So the stories she'd heard about the hellish treatment whites received from Indians were true, after all. Hannah Wright was proof. The possibility that such vicious cruelty could one day be inflicted upon *her*, but for the trader's presence, made Rose's blood turn cold.

Mr. Smith turned to her. "This is how it is. The woman an' babe were brought here as slaves by the son-in-law of an old woman. He was replacin' his wife an' son, who both died during the birthin'. The brave's not real fond of his wife's mother, an' he decided to rid himself of havin' to care fer the ol' gal. Problem is, the girl was hurt pretty bad when she ran the gauntlet. Worse, the baby's not a boy, so the mother-in-law says she's been cheated. She threw this one an' her babe out an' is refusin' to claim them. Nobody else wants a dyin' woman, an' nobody wants the babe, either, 'cause there's already a lot more women than men in the village, what with all the warrin' betwixt the tribes. She's been draggin' herself around fer days, fightin' the dogs fer scraps to eat."

It was hard for Rose to get words past the clog in her throat. Tears coursed down her cheeks as she went to Hannah and wrapped her arms around the poor woman.

Hannah made an effort to stand, finally managing with Rose's help. She gasped for breath. "Now *I* understand."

Rose struggled to support the weakened girl's nearly dead weight. "Mr. Smith, help me to get her to my bed. I'll do what I can."

She began to cry. "Thank you, Rose," she whispered between gulps. "God bless you."

Giving little thought to her clean bedding, Rose and Mr. Smith lay Hannah gently down onto her pallet. Filth could be washed away. Help could not wait. Rose touched the burning brow. "I'll get some cool water and a washing cloth. We'll have you clean and comfortable soon."

"My baby."

"Don't you worry about Jenny. We shall tend her as well." She slanted a pointed look at Mr. Smith and arched a brow. "Will we not?"

"Aye." He grimaced. "Fawn Woman'll see to her right away."

Moments later, Rose brought some washrags and a bucket of water into the wigwam. Hannah appeared to be fast asleep but startled when Rose ran a cool cloth gently over one of her arms. She closed her bruised fingers around Rose's hand. "My name is Hannah Wright. My. . .husband's folks are near—"

"Shh," Rose crooned. "I remember. The Susquehanna. Rest now. You and your baby are safe here." But a new worry assailed Rose. Wasn't the Susquehanna the river up which Lily had been taken? Was any white person truly safe in this wild land? She breathed another swift prayer for God to watch over her little sister.

"Jesus promised. . .to send someone," Hannah whispered. "And He sent you." She closed her eyes, and the slightest smile played over her cracked lips.

The sentiment stunned Rose. *Me, sent by God?* Had God planned months ago, before she'd ever left England and sailed to America, that she would be here at this very place to help Hannah Wright? Freshening the rag in the cool water again, she felt renewed hope spring to life in her heart. God truly did have a purpose for bringing her here.

Hannah mumbled something unintelligible just then.

"What did you say, dear?"

Her eyes still closed, she drew a labored breath. "I don't mind dyin'. I'm goin' to my Adam. He's. . .waitin' for me." She smiled again, a real smile this time.

Blinded by her own tears now, Rose continued to wash the precious woman. She needed to be beautiful for her husband.

Chapter 20

Rose felt the little warm baby stir beside her as it breathed in soft content. Having gotten only snatches of sleep, she opened her eyes to the pitch-dark night and listened once again for Hannah's raspy breathing.

Ominous silence filled the air.

Pulling back the light cover over her and Jenny, Rose crawled across to where the child's mother lay. Her heartbeat throbbed in her ears as she reached out and found Hannah's face. Where there had been a raging fever, the skin was cool to the touch, and no breath issued from Hannah's lungs. Already on her knees, Rose sank the rest of the way down onto her folded legs with the realization that Jenny's mother had died. She'd put up a valiant struggle to stay alive until she knew her little one was safe, and once she had that assurance, she'd let herself go.

Tears Rose had banked earlier that day broke through her resolve and streamed down her cheeks. Hannah was the second young mother whose untimely death she had witnessed. Rose's own mother had been only a few years older than Rose was now and had been in the process of giving birth to a new babe when the angel of death had paid a visit. It seemed so senseless at the time—just as Hannah's dying seemed senseless now. And it, too, had left Rose in mourning and burdened with the responsibility of a baby.

She crept back to the slumbering little one and snuggled close to her softness, breathing in her little clean smell and seeking comfort for herself and for the tiny orphan.

Then terrible doubt surfaced. *Father God, the Bible says our times are in Your hand, but I cannot understand how You could allow such a tragic thing to happen to someone so undeserving of this horrid fate as Hannah Wright. She was Your child. Surely she must have cried out to You to save her. But You did not. Are You really there? Do You really care?*

A wracking sob swelled within her breast, and Rose sat up to stifle the sound before she disturbed Jenny. She clamped her hand tightly over her mouth as her cheeks and hand were washed with her tears.

Completely unexpected, a soothing sense of peace spread through her, and she recalled plainly the words of comfort her father had given her when her beloved mother breathed her last. *"The Bible tells us that our days are numbered by the Lord before we are born, Rosie-mine. It says there's a time to be born and a time to die. He alone knows when those times come to us. Even though there will always be suffering in this life, He knows all those who love and trust Him. He never leaves us or forsakes us. He stays by our side through all the hard times. And He will always see us safely through to the other side. God is waiting to welcome us home."*

The gnawing ache inside her lessened as her sorrow eased with hope. Hannah Wright's last words played across her memory. She was looking forward to being reunited with her Adam. . .and the two were probably even now embracing in the presence of the Lord, happier than they had ever been. Despite the evil torture the poor woman had endured, her ultimate victory was her everlasting joy in a place where sorrow and pain and death would never again intrude.

The baby made a sighing sound.

Rose lay back down and drew little Jenny close. The tiny girl was her sole responsibility now. God had put the precious child into her care. From this moment on, she must remember that her coming here— despite the hardships and fears she'd endured along the way—was no accident. The Lord had placed her here in His time and for His purpose. Whatever she had to face, she would be strong in her faith, just as she had promised her mother so long ago. Strong for God and strong for Jenny.

⟜

Rose chose a small knoll just out of sight of the Shawnee village where she felt Hannah would finally rest in peace. Mr. Smith had Running Wolf and Spotted Elk dig the grave in a spot shaded by a towering maple tree, and the two lowered her body, wrapped in a clean blanket, into the ground. Rose held Jenny close as she and the trader watched the braves fill in the gaping hole. Then Rose placed the few late wildflowers she'd found nearby atop the mound of fresh earth.

After the two Indians walked away, Mr. Smith pulled a thin book from inside his belted shirt and exhaled as he opened the worn volume. His high-pitched voice broke the silence as he began reading. " 'Jesus said unto her, I am the resurrection, and the life: he that believeth in me, though he were dead, yet shall he live: and whosoever liveth and believeth in me shall never die.' " Rose recognized the familiar passage from the apostle John's writings and looked up at the trader while he finished. "Ashes to ashes, dust to dust."

Astonished that the man actually had a New Testament in his possession and made sure Jenny's mother had a Christian burial, Rose tried not to let her surprise show.

Mr. Smith reached out with his gnarled hand and ruffled Jenny's silky hair. "We should bow fer a word o' prayer." He cleared his throat. "Almighty God, Ya know what took place here that put this young gal in an early grave. Ya say in Yer Word that vengeance is Yourn, an' I guess we have to leave it at that. I know Yer lookin' after her, an' we'll do our best to look after the little one she left behind. Amen."

Touched by the heartfelt prayer, Rose raised her head. . .only to be assaulted by laughter a short distance away. This unfortunate white woman died because no Indian deigned to tend her wounds, and these people found humor in something so despicable?

She swung toward the noise and saw three native girls about the same ages as her sisters playing some sort of game. Each had a short-handled paddle of sorts and repeatedly hit into the air what looked like a small ball with a tail of feathers.

Rose wiped perspiration from her brow and relaxed. At least the girls hadn't been laughing at the death of Hannah Wright. Nevertheless, it irked her that life in the village went on as usual. As she and Mr. Smith returned to the trading post, she could see older women seated in front of their wigwams weaving reeds into baskets or stitching leather. Another kneaded a lump of clay. A few collected vegetables in their gardens, while some of the men stood in the river casting nets for fish. Not far from them, youngsters splashed about in the shallows near the bank. No one cared a whit about the fact they'd caused mortal injury to an unprotected woman—an innocent baby's mother—and then allowed her to die an unspeakable death.

Still, Mr. Smith had cared. For all his gruff talk, the man truly cared. Rose's respect for him went up a notch.

From the corner of her eye, she caught him rubbing his stomach as he so often did of late. As she turned to him, he stretched out his arms. "Let me have that sweet little gal fer a spell. I had me four sons b'fore my Ellie passed on. Never did have us no little gal."

Rose smiled and handed the baby to him. "I didn't know that. Where are they now?"

He tossed his head as if it was of no import, but Rose didn't miss the spark of pride in his eyes. "Scattered about back in Virginny with fam'lies o' their own now. I seen to it they was all set up in a prosperous trade. Good boys, one an' all."

Listening to him imparting personal information, Rose realized she wasn't the only melancholy one today. Hannah's funeral must have brought back memories of the first Mrs. Smith's death. "Have you and your present wife been blessed with any children?"

He snorted. "No. An' we ain't likely to, neither." His jaw tightened.

Rose had more questions, but from the derision in his voice, she thought it best to drop the matter. "If you'd be kind enough to entertain little Jenny for a while, I'll go cook you both a nice rice pudding with raisins and cinnamon. How's that?"

He laughed and lightly tweaked Jenny's button nose, making the little one catch a breath and giggle. "We'd like that right 'nough, wouldn't we, sweet thing?"

Watching the two of them, Rose knew she had certainly misjudged Mr. Smith. He wasn't nearly the heartless man he'd led her to believe. It was all a big act.

During the long weeks that followed, Rose kept a number of pressing questions to herself. Days were growing noticeably shorter. Many of the village crops had been harvested and dried or stored for the coming winter. As the weather began to cool, the leaves started turning the magnificent colors of autumn. Yet Nate and Robert Bloom had still not returned.

Mrs. Smith now paraded before the other squaws in another daygown Rose had made her, a blue checked one. But the trader's wife couldn't hold a candle to her two brothers, who strutted around in matching green-and-yellow-striped shirts Rose had sewn for them.

Now besides caring for the baby and doing the cooking, Rose was learning the fur business—which animal furs were the most valuable and the subtle differences within a species that determined the quality of each pelt. Mr. Smith was her teacher, and he also had her bargaining with the Indians whenever they came to the trading post with canoes loaded down with bundles of furs. She still hadn't mastered any of the Shawnee language, much less the dialects of any of the other tribes, but she'd picked up on a primitive sort of sign language that was used in trade and got by fairly well with it.

Rose had never questioned the man regarding his reasons for these new duties, but she knew instinctively why he'd been so intent on having her learn his trade. He did not trust Fawn Woman, and no matter how mild and smooth the food was that Rose made for him, it was obvious he continued to suffer pain in his stomach. His straggly beard no longer hid the sunken cheeks bearing witness to a noticeable loss of weight. She suspected he was much worse off than he let on.

One day after an Indian who bore multiple scars and disfigurements left the trading post and headed back upstream with his goods, Rose could not contain her curiosity. She straightened some of the pelts the red man had left in trade and approached her owner as he jiggled the now healthy Jenny Ann on his knees. "Mr. Smith, how could one man be covered with so many scars, like that Indian was, unless—" She paused for breath. "When Jenny's mother was dying, you said she'd had to run a. . .a. . ."

"Gauntlet," he supplied. "An' yes, that brave might'a had to run it, too. Likely he was stole from his people by some other tribe. An' ya might say, runnin' the gauntlet is like bein' initiated. If ya make it through, yer good 'nough to be adopted into the tribe."

"What is a *gauntlet*, exactly? I've often heard that word." She noticed the baby's eyelids were growing heavy, and the trader did as well. He laid her gently down onto a plush pallet of furs they'd put between some crates and smiled as she put her thumb into her rosebud mouth and nodded off. Then he looked up at Rose.

He let out a slow breath. "It's like this. The whole tribe lines up in two rows facin' each other, an' they all got sticks. The captive has to run betwixt 'em whilst they're swingin' the sticks at 'em. They get a real kick outta tryin' to trip a poor fella up, 'cause then he has to start over again. Afterward, though, if he was brave 'nough to make it the whole way, they take him in and patch him up, an' he's part o' the tribe. Might be he's still a slave, though."

"But they didn't help Hannah Wright, even though Spotted Elk told me she actually did make it through."

He nodded. "I heard that, too. 'Fraid that little gal was unlucky enough to get herself caught in the middle of a family squabble."

Rose mulled over his response. "Well, if Nate or Robert was set upon by some other tribe, would they have to run the gauntlet?"

He rubbed his bearded chin. "That there's a different case. Them boys is down tradin' in country them Frenchies is tryin' to claim as their own. Those two would prob'ly get treated a mite rougher than Miz Wright."

Sobered by that statement, Rose felt the blood drain from her face. "Surely you don't mean. . . ."

He didn't answer right away. Then he shrugged a shoulder. "If them Frenchies get wind of 'em, those two could be in fer some real trouble. But don't start worryin' overmuch. Them boys is real good at takin' care o' themselves. They don't take no foolish chances, neither." He grimaced and pressed a hand atop that spot on his belly that seemed to give him the most trouble. "Reckon them eggs I had this mornin' didn't set so well. Think I'll go lay down fer a spell." He glanced lovingly down at Jenny Ann, sleeping sweetly on her soft pallet, then met Rose's gaze. "Keep an eye out fer customers."

"I will." Still awed by the tenderness he displayed around the baby, Rose sensed he was as attached to the child as she herself was. As she watched him head for his wigwam, she wished she'd managed to squeeze in a few more questions. Nate and Robert had been gone weeks now, much too long for them to dispose of one measly canoe load of goods— and they'd taken on that dangerous mission just for her.

To keep her mind off the plaguing thought, she began lining up knives and hatchets neatly on a crate top. Those items were some of their best sellers, and the stock was dwindling.

A voice from outside interrupted her chore. "Harwood."

Rose pivoted and glanced out the store's wide opening. Running Wolf, in his green-and-yellow shirt, pointed down toward the riverbank.

She followed the gesture with her gaze and saw two men beaching a canoe.

White men! Nate? Robert?

But as they looked up toward the store, her joy plummeted to her toes. Strangers. Merely strangers.

Chapter 21

Muskets in hand, the newcomers broke away from the curious villagers and started up the rise to the trading post. Rose saw their jaws go slack when they caught sight of her and knew they must be wondering how a white woman happened to be standing at the store entrance. No doubt they'd be full of questions. Well, she had questions of her own for them.

Both men were attired in the typical buckskin garb worn by hunters and frontiersmen alike, and both sported beards. The taller of the pair had a droopy mustache which moved when he spoke. "You sure don't look like most hostages I've seen."

Ignoring their lack of a polite greeting, Rose tilted her head slightly. "Welcome to our store. Miss Harwood at your service." She fingered the edge of the long apron she wore over her cobalt daygown.

Both quickly swiped their fur hats off their heads. "Beg your pardon, miss," the shorter, stocky man said. "I'm Mr. Gilbert. My partner's Mr. Townes." He blinked his hooded eyes as he and the other man stared unabashedly. "Where'd you come from?"

"As to your kind remark," she said in a businesslike tone, "I'm not a hostage. I'm Mr. Smith's servant."

"Servant! Are you saying Eustice Smith brought you, a woman, out to this wild place—and you agreed to come?" Hiking his brows, he eyed her up and down.

Rose regretted having to explain. She'd never get used to the sting of her lowly position. "I should have said I'm his bondservant. I had no choice but to come."

Their expressions hardened, and Mr. Townes spoke. "Where is the trader? We need to talk to him." They started to move past her.

Rose put up a staying hand. "Please. I'm afraid Mr. Smith isn't feeling well just now. He's abed, taking a nap."

"That's not our concern, miss. We have important business to discuss."

"Gentlemen, please. I shall go and wake him if I must, but first, I've a few questions to ask, if you'd be so kind as to indulge me."

Both men relaxed, and Mr. Gilbert even managed an obliging smile. "Of course, Miss. . .Harwood, was it? What do you need to know?"

Rose noticed by his manner of speech that he seemed more educated than many of the other white people she'd encountered in her travels into the wilderness, and she found it quite refreshing. She smiled, alight with hope. "I was wondering if you happened to come across Nate Kinyon and Robert Bloom on your way here. I believe you came upriver, did you not?"

He gave a negative shake of his head. "Sorry, miss, but no. We came downriver from up on the Allegheny."

Profound disappointment flowed through her.

"We've been checking on the infringement of the French up north," Mr. Townes added, "by order of Governor Dinwiddie. We just stopped by for fresh mounts so we could report back to him. We hoped Smith could provide us with a couple of good horses."

Rose focused on that disturbing information. "The French are to the north and east of us?"

Townes stepped forward and took her hand, a calming look in his eyes. "Don't you worry your pretty head. No officer, even a Frenchman, would allow harm to come to a lady like yourself. You can be sure of that."

Rose sensed the statement held little truth, if any, but remained silent.

"Now, if you don't mind," he went on, "we'd really appreciate a word with Trader Smith."

"Of course." She paused then searched their faces. "But might I ask a favor of both of you?"

"Anything, miss. What is it?"

"I'd appreciate it if you'd carry some missives with you when you go. I'd like my family to know I'm well. They've had no word from me for some time, and 'twould set their minds at ease."

Mr. Gilbert nodded. "I've pretty decent penmanship. Would you like me to write the words for you?"

Rose nearly smiled. They probably hadn't come across many bondservants who could write. "That won't be necessary. I have my own writing implements. I'll go and wake Mr. Smith, and while you conduct your business, I'll write my letters."

—✒—

Putting quill to paper, Rose was careful not to cause her sisters needless worry. She did want them to know Mr. Smith had turned out to be a kind employer and that she was faring well in a village to the west. They didn't need to know it was a Shawnee village or that it was hundreds of miles to the west. She encouraged Mariah to remember to give priority to her spiritual well-being while she honored her commitment to her employer on the plantation. To Lily she mentioned that the Lord had placed a darling baby girl into her safekeeping, and she asked her to let the baby's relatives know that though the child's mother had passed away, the little one was fine and—

For a split second, Rose considered sending the baby back with the men but quickly discarded the notion. Even if they happened to be adept at caring for a baby, they'd be hard pressed to provide suitable food for her. Besides, Rose had already grown attached to Jenny Ann and wasn't ready to give her up just yet.

"Is that within Your will, Father?" Realizing she'd spoken aloud, she shot a cursory glance around to see if the braves at the entrance had noticed her talking to the air.

She needn't have worried. They sat with Mr. Smith and the others at his fire while Fawn Woman served them food and drink. Amazingly, the squaw hadn't demanded Rose come to help. A closer look indicated she was paying close attention to the conversation. Her posture suggested she was every bit as interested in the news the men brought as Rose had been.

Within the hour, the men selected two mounts. While the supplies they'd purchased were being loaded, Mr. Smith continued conversing with Mr. Gilbert.

Rose picked up her wax-sealed letters and a few coins and walked out of the store to Mr. Townes as the man stuffed the last of his purchases into a sack. "I do appreciate your taking my correspondence with you, sir. I don't know what the post might cost once you reach a town, but this should suffice." She handed him the money and the letters.

He looked down at them, then at Mr. Smith, who was speaking with his friend. Toying with his mustache, he met her gaze. "Miss Harwood," he said under his breath, "I don't know what Trader Smith has told you. But no court in the colonies would hold you to your indenturement bond if you'd leave this place with us right now. Just walk down to that raft with me and get on. I'll shoot the blighter if he tries to stop you."

Rose's heart took flight. Leave? This minute? Return to civilization and her sisters?

For a few seconds she entertained the thought. Then her gaze slid to Mr. Smith, who was wasting away by the day before her eyes. She could not desert him in his time of need. And Jenny Ann. . . The baby had been sleeping since the men arrived. In all likelihood the trader hadn't bothered to mention anything about her presence, or the visitors would have gone inside to see Jenny for themselves. If they took her with them, it would be weeks before the milk she was thriving on would be available again—and besides, Mr. Smith was so attached to her.

And Nate. She couldn't possibly leave before he returned. . .*if* he returned.

Rose exhaled a wistful breath and looked up at the man, wearing the most sincere expression she could muster. "'Tis a kind and generous offer. I thank you from the bottom of my heart. But I know for a certainty that the Lord placed me here, and I cannot and will not shirk my duties— no matter how tempting your offer may be."

He opened his mouth to object.

"Truly, kind sir." She placed a silencing hand on his arm. "My place is here. At least for now."

He stared hard at her then eased his stance. "As you wish, miss. I respect your decision, even if I don't agree with it. I'll not forget you in my prayers."

"That is all one can ask." Glad to learn he was a man who sought God, she tipped her head toward her employer. "And please add Mr. Smith's condition to your prayers. He's been poorly for some time. Pray that his recovery will be swift and complete."

Even as she spoke the words, Rose feared her request held little hope. She'd been trying to ignore the trader's rapidly failing health for days, telling herself it was her imagination, that he'd perk up soon. She was plying him faithfully with soups and broths and puddings, but they seemed to have lost their effect. Now she had to wonder what would become of her if Nate didn't come back and Mr. Smith were to die. Fawn Woman had never befriended her, and who knew how the Shawnee in the village would look upon her once Mr. Smith was no longer around to protect her.

Her troubled gaze followed the travelers as they walked their newly purchased mounts down to the raft, and a sudden panic gripped her in its icy fingers. What *would* become of her? It took every ounce of willpower she possessed to stay where she was and not run down to them and plead that they take her and Jenny with them.

As a last resort, she turned her face up to the cloudy sky. *Have I made the right decision, Father? Do You truly want the baby and me to stay here. . .or did You send those men to deliver us from this place? Please, I need to know Your will before it's too late.*

*

Jenny's airy giggles blended with Mr. Smith's nasally laughter, drawing Rose away from her sewing. She gazed over at the pair and watched Jenny Ann crawling all over the trader. Smiling at the enchanting sight, she tucked her cloak more securely around her legs against the cool draft finding its way past the store's partially covered opening.

Jenny Ann had begun to crawl and pull herself up to whatever happened to be within her reach. To Rose, she seemed to be early in her accomplishments—at least earlier than her brother Tommy had been at that age. To corral the active little one, Mr. Smith fashioned a little walled area from crates and grain sacks, and on this clear, crisp day the two of them sat inside it on a fur robe, his back propped against one of the crates.

A fire in the small fireplace nearby kept the back of the store fairly warm, and the trader sat near its heat most of the time now. Rose tried not to think about how much weaker he seemed with each day. . .yet he never tired of sweet Jenny. He called her his little bundle of blessing, his joy. It seemed the baby ate more solid food than he did, since he subsisted on nothing but milk and pudding now.

Rose had spent most of the morning sewing. To rest her strained eyes, she blinked and peered out of the store's opening toward the village. Since the episode with Hannah Wright, she still harbored the opinion that the Shawnee were savages, but she couldn't deny that their daily life proved to be pleasant. In some instances they seemed kinder than some English people she'd known. Rose rarely heard an angry shout from the village inhabitants and had never witnessed a hand being raised against a child, yet the children hardly ever misbehaved. The younger ones were quite happy as they mimicked their parents in their games, while the older ones seemed eager to learn needed skills from the grown-ups.

From out on the water, Rose heard echoing shouts and checked to discover the source. There she saw two village canoes bearing several enthusiastic young lads racing each other across the river, even on this chilly day.

She thought back on the surprise she'd felt upon learning that Indians bathed in the river quite regularly. And now that mosquitoes no longer presented a problem, the people ceased to wear that odorous bear grease.

How unfortunate that Mr. Smith had never taken up the habit of cleanliness. Rose wondered how Fawn Woman slept in the same wigwam with him. But then, perhaps that was one reason the squaw was unpleasant much of the time.

Aside from Mrs. Smith, most of the villagers seemed content. But despite their congeniality, Rose knew they could turn vicious and violent in an instant, becoming heartless and uncaring about any unfortunate soul they deemed their enemy.

She cut a glance at the trader's wife. Sitting at her own fire and adorning her yellow dress with an assortment of colored beads, the woman still treated Rose with loathing and spoke only when there was an order she wished to give.

Attired in doeskin leggings and shirts these cool days, Running Wolf and Spotted Elk sat with their sister, their moccasined feet stretched out toward the fire. They'd completed their chores with the stock and had milked the cow for Mr. Smith, so they were enjoying a few moments' relaxation.

It was hard to believe how gruff the trader had been when she first joined him, how angry he'd been to learn she'd never milked a cow or killed a chicken. He'd mellowed so much, especially since Jenny Ann had come along. Now he relegated only the care of the store and the baby to Rose and assigned the outside chores to the brothers. The two hadn't balked when ordered to take over those responsibilities, but Rose had noticed that the three siblings spent much of their time in covert conversation of late. As they happened to be doing now.

One of the braves saw her peering out at them and made a comment, and the talking stopped.

Rose wondered if Mr. Smith had been cognizant of their secrecy, or had he been so caught up with little Jenny and his bad digestion that the Indians' conduct didn't seem of import? Perhaps they'd always been that way. But how she wished she understood their language.

She looked over at the trader as he kissed Jenny's short, blond curls. "Mr. Smith?"

"What's up?"

"Nothing. I'm just curious. 'Tis one of my worst faults, I know."

He smirked. "So what bee do ya have in yer bonnet this time?"

"Actually, 'tis you and Fawn Woman. You don't seem to show much affection for each other. How is it that you married her? If you don't mind my asking."

He tossed his head and patted the baby's diapered bottom. "Ya might say it was mutual attraction."

Rose frowned in confusion, and he chuckled.

"I thought she was purty to look at, an' her pa was real partial to a new musket with fancy scrollwork I'd just brought into the store."

"Surely you don't mean you traded a musket for a wife!" The concept disgusted Rose. A woman was of far more value than that.

Adept at reading her expressions by now, Mr. Smith rolled his eyes. "That ain't no different from them English aristocrats an' all that business of swappin' lands and dowries an' such, is it?"

She mulled over his remark in her mind. "No, I suppose not. I just never thought of it that way."

"Besides," he went on, "Fawn Woman wasn't no innocent victim. She made her own requests. She went through my store pointin' to all manner of useless truck she just had to have." Jenny tugged at a handful of his beard, and he chuckled and pried her little fingers away. "All them beads an' shiny baubles she wanted is long since lost or traded off by now." His grin widened. "But she's still got this fine ol' man o' hers."

His words rekindled thoughts of Mariah and her desire for the better things. Rose hoped and prayed her sister would not turn out to be as foolish as Mrs. Smith. She picked up her sewing and resumed working on another warm dress she'd started for Jenny out of a bit of woven fabric.

The trader continued his tale, his voice thoughtful. "When I seen how unhappy Fawn was, 'specially since she never birthed a young'un, I was fixin' to divorce her. But then me an' my partner was ordered to leave her village an' head overmountain to set up a store out here on the Ohio. We figgered if we took her along, those two brothers o' hers could be persuaded to come along, too—fer a price, a'course. She's still ever' bit as greedy as she always was, an' them boys did love the new rifles we give 'em."

Pausing in her work, Rose slid a glance their way. The two were never without their muskets—or the knives and hatchets tucked in their waistbands. They looked formidable enough and seemed proud of being the store's guards. No doubt it gave them a sense of power. Rose was just glad they were there to protect this little encampment and not to attack it.

Nevertheless, something about their taciturn conversations and occasional sly looks made Rose feel apprehensive. . .particularly with Mr. Smith in his weakened condition.

Just how much did Fawn Woman hate Rose. . .and her own husband?

Chapter 22

"Harwood! Up!"

Someone was shaking her shoulder. Rose struggled to open her eyes. It was still dark. Still cold.

"Up."

Recognizing Fawn Woman's voice, Rose felt for the baby sleeping beside her then sat up. Something was amiss. "What is it?"

"Husband. Come." The squaw's shadowy figure hurried to the flap and pulled it back. "Come. Now."

Shoving her feet into her shoes, Rose collected her cloak off her trunk and threw it about herself as she followed after the woman. Since no unusual sounds or activity drifted from the village, Rose's worst fears filled her with dread. Only one thing would cause the trader's wife to summon her in the dark of night. Mr. Smith must have taken a turn for the worse. . .or—

She couldn't finish the thought.

Inside the larger wigwam, the fire pit blazed, providing welcome warmth that surrounded Rose. Fawn Woman stopped near the fire and stoked it with a stick.

"Rose?" Mr. Smith's faint croak came from the far end of the dwelling.

The quaver in his voice made her heart lurch. She went immediately to where he lay among some furs and sank down to her knees beside his pallet. In the glow from the flames, she could see his face had lost all color. His eyes appeared sunken, and his breath came out in jerky rasps. Deep trepidation settled its weight on her heart.

"Rose?" he said again, even more weakly.

She leaned close. "I'm here. What can I do for you?"

"I need. . .my tin box. Get it."

She glanced around. "Tin box?" It seemed every available spot around the wigwam was stacked high with goods of all kinds. Nothing resembled a tin box.

Fawn Woman, now sitting opposite the fire, pointed with her stick. "There."

Rose crossed to it and picked it up then returned to him. Kneeling, she held it out to him.

He gave a slight shake of his head. "Open it."

She did as bidden and found it was filled with legal documents and writing paper, a couple of plumed quills, and a considerable number of coins in various denominations. In the corner was a bottle of ink.

"Take out. . .your indenture papers," came his halting whisper. "Dip a quill." He paused and took a breath. "I need to sign 'em off."

He was releasing her? As she followed his instructions, the trader struggled to roll onto his side and raise his head. With a shaky hand, he used his dwindling reserve of strength to scratch his signature. His head fell back to his pillow.

Overwhelmed at her owner's kind act, Rose tucked the papers inside an inner pocket of her cloak. Then, after returning the box to its proper place, she sank down at his side again. "Please, Mr. Smith, I want to help you. There must be something I can do."

"Nothin', child." She detected sadness, finality in his voice. "My innards must'a. . .popped a hole." Another pause. "I'm bleedin' out."

Rose's heart plummeted to her toes. She shot a frantic look at his wife. As though detached from the situation, the squaw sat staring at the fire, idly toying at it with the stick she held. A wicked twitch of her lips looked a whole lot like a sickening smile.

The trader's bony hand wrapped weakly around Rose's, drawing her attention away from the insensitive woman. "Give her brothers. . .another musket each. . .so they'll stay till. . .Nate comes to git ya outta here." The pressure of his hand waned. "Take any money I have. . .to get started on."

No. No. Rose's throat thickened with anguish. Panic raised gooseflesh on her arms. "Please don't die. Don't leave me." She barely choked out the words.

"Can't help it." He drew another laboring breath. "Should'a had them governor's men. . .take you an' the babe with 'em." Nodding sadly, he gave a wry grimace. "Didn't think I was this bad."

She cupped his icy hand in both of hers and held it to the warmth of her cheek. "I wanted to stay. I did. You needed me here. I wouldn't have left you."

The trader attempted a smile. "Yer my brave gal." With a groan, he blanched even whiter and let out a shuddering breath. "My boy Charlie. . .has a cooperage in Fredericksburg." Another pause. "Git word to him. He'll tell my other boys." He gave her hand a slight squeeze with his colder, weaker one. "Yer the daughter I never had." He peered up at her with a slight nod. "Good an' kind, ya are. . . . Knowed it when I first seen ya. . . . May the good Lord bless an' keep ya."

"But—Mr. Smith—"

"Git little Jenny fer me. . . . I need one more look at my joy."

———

When Rose brought the half-asleep little one to see Mr. Smith, she found with dismay that he'd stopped breathing. His passing left her completely bereft. That he had not lived long enough to set his eyes upon his sweet angel added sorrow beyond words. After Rose took the sleepy child back to their wigwam and settled her once again on her fur pallet, an emptiness beyond anything she'd yet experienced gnawed at her heart. She and Jenny were now the only white people left at the trading post on the edge of the Shawnee village and without the protection of Mr. Smith—a reality that brought deep unrest. But at least no one was around at the moment to see her cry. Rose no longer fought against the tears she'd been holding back. Sobbing quietly, she let them run unheeded down onto her pillow until she had no more left inside.

In the morning, the Susquehannock brothers took care of the burial. Speaking around the tightness in her chest, Rose read some scripture verses and said a prayer over the trader's grave. It took all the strength she possessed to maintain her composure in the braves' presence, when what she wanted more than anything was to give in to her grief and wail for all the world to hear, the way she'd heard an Indian woman grieve the loss of a family member last month. Heart aching, she placed a small bunch of lacy ferns atop the lonely mound near Hannah Wright's resting place.

After she and the brothers returned to the store, she offered Running Wolf and Spotted Elk the new muskets Mr. Smith wanted them to have so they'd stay and continue guarding the place. Nodding and smiling, they took them with obvious gratitude. They had always been friendly to her, especially after she made them the matching shirts.

But their sister was another matter entirely. Rose had no idea what Fawn Woman was thinking.

When Rose had asked for Mr. Smith's frayed New Testament to read at his grave, the woman had handed it over. . .but did not deign to come and see her husband's body laid to rest. With a very determined look on her face, the young woman took all of the trader's clothing and bedding and set them afire then swept out the wigwam with a vengeance. From a deerskin pouch she wore around her neck, she sprinkled some kind of powder across the floor.

For all that frenzy of work, Fawn Woman never demanded help from Rose, which made her even more leery. The squaw had always derived perverse satisfaction from ordering her around. She wondered if the woman was actually mourning her dead husband in her own way but knew that would be one huge stretch of the imagination. Fawn Woman had made no secret of the contempt she harbored for the trader. Or for Rose and Jenny.

Far more disturbing, all trading at the store ceased upon Mr. Smith's death. Groups of Indians would talk among themselves and stare now and then toward the trading post, but not one ventured forth to trade or do business. The few canoes that did arrive from up or down the river were intercepted and the goods or furs were taken to one of the longhouses instead.

Nightfall arrived all too soon, closing in on Rose with its strange sounds and black coldness. She feared having to cross the short distance from the trading post to her wigwam, but the canvas covering the storefront did little to keep out the cold after sundown. It was too chilly for Jenny. There was no other choice. She'd already started a fire in her wigwam, so carrying the baby with her, Rose banked the hot coals in the hearth. Then after collecting a musket and the fixings, plus a hatchet and a sharp hunting knife, she went at last to her meager dwelling and prepared for bed.

Lying on her sleeping pallet, she couldn't decide whether it was the occasional night sounds that kept her on edge. . .or the ominous silence. After lying awake for hours, she slept only fitfully, dozing then jerking awake at the slightest noise, real or imagined. She was now completely alone in this vast wilderness, and the stark realization made her shiver in the fearsome chill of night.

She had no one to turn to now.

No one but God.

Dear Heavenly Father, You promised never to leave me or forsake me. Please take away this fear I have inside. Help me to be brave. Please, give me rest. And please, please, bring back Nate.

Something pulled Rose's hair. She opened her eyes to see a smiling Jenny Ann with her tiny hand entwined in Rose's night braid.

Remembering the uncertainty of the night before, Rose felt for the loaded musket lying on the dirt floor beside her pallet, where she'd tucked it beneath the edge of her top blanket for protection. She'd caught only short snatches of sleep, and from the brightness of the light seeping past the flapped opening, she must have overslept.

She got up quickly, noticing she still wore her clothes from the previous day. She'd been too nervous to change into her nightshift, but here she was, just as safe as before Mr. Smith passed away. The Susquehannock brothers proved to be honorable men.

Once she got the banked embers going to warm the wigwam, she changed the baby's diaper layered with its crushed moss for a dry one while Jenny giggled and played with the braid dangling over Rose's shoulder. Then she bundled the little one up and walked out with her into the cold morning.

Rose had hoped to find someone else up and about to take the baby while she took care of her own morning needs. But no one else was around. She gave a small grimace. It seemed once the trader was no longer present, his widow and her brothers didn't see a necessity to rise early.

Rose sat Jenny in the little pen the child and Mr. Smith had played and napped in together the day before yesterday. In her mind, she could still hear the two of them laughing. The reminder of her and Jenny's loss assaulted her with sorrow as she headed for the woods.

On her way back, Rose heard the chickens squawking to be let out of their coop. She looked past their crude hut to the corralled stock. Unless it was her imagination, there didn't seem to be as many horses as there should be. She took a quick count. Sixteen—out of twenty-two! Six were missing—including a gelding Nate had left there for safekeeping.

She rushed to the brothers' wigwam. "Running Wolf! Spotted Elk! Come out! We've been robbed!"

There was no response.

Rose grasped the flap and tore it aside. The wigwam was empty!

She then dashed to Fawn Woman's wigwam and pushed that flap aside. The squaw—and most of her belongings—were gone. And Mr. Smith's metal box lay open, emptied of his money.

The scuffling sounds that had disturbed her restless sleep last night hadn't been forest animals scurrying about, after all. A quick check of the store revealed a number of items missing, the worst of which was the bundle of the best furs.

Rose stood seething for several moments. But gradually it dawned on her that Mr. Smith's widow was probably due an inheritance. After all, she had stayed with the man for six years. Whatever money he'd saved was rightfully hers. Rose could do nothing about the rest.

Knowing it was now her responsibility to look after the animals, she put Jenny into the baby sling the trader had fixed for her and slipped it on. Grabbing the sack of feed, she headed for the chicken pen.

Walking outside, she noticed a group of Indians standing at the entrance of one of the longhouses a short distance away. All were staring at her. The dire reminder came again that she was here in this Shawnee village alone, with no protector, and nothing between her and them but a single-shot musket.

Chapter 23

Afraid to let Jenny Ann out of her reach, Rose spent the morning with the child slung on her back while she took care of the chores. The entire time she worked, she kept one eye on the Shawnee in the village, aware of their furtive glances in her direction. What were they thinking, planning?

She alternated between praying for God's protection and debating whether or not to take Jenny and some supplies and ride away. But she'd need help to cross the river. . .and the Shawnee hadn't even tended Hannah Wright's wounds. What were the chances they'd be willing to aid her and Hannah's daughter?

Of course, there were plenty of goods available to pay for assistance, which might help. On the other hand, what would prevent the Indians from coming to the trading post at will and helping themselves to whatever they wanted?

Father, what should I do? Give me courage. . . . Please, God, please bring Nate back.

But no answer was emblazoned across the sky, and no assurance of what action she should take brought peace to her heart.

As Rose cooked oats with dried fruit for her and Jenny's noon meal, she spotted two Shawnee approaching. They carried no weapons, but considering she was a mere woman, would they even feel they needed them? Her pulse throbbed in her throat.

She glanced down at Jenny nearby, who was crawling after a bean-filled rattle Mr. Smith had made from a gourd. Then she checked to make sure her musket was still propped against the sitting log.

The two had warm fur robes wrapped around them against the cold. As they approached, Rose noted that along with the usual buckskin breeches most villagers wore, the round-faced older of the two sported an elaborate feather headdress adorned with an abundance of decorative beading. A necklace of bear claws peeked from an opening in the robe. She recognized him as one of the chiefs of the village. He raised a brown hand in greeting.

The action didn't seem hostile, but still. . . Forcing herself to relax, she returned his greeting.

"Harwood woman," the younger brave said.

She nodded, grateful that one of them spoke English. "Good afternoon." She checked to see Jenny was still nearby then motioned to the sitting log not far from the fire, where the warmth from the flames along with the sunshine would keep them comfortable. "Please, sit down." She'd learned early on that visitors were always invited to sit and always offered food or drink.

The two lowered themselves to the log, an indication they'd come to talk.

"Would you care for some tea?" She gestured toward the pot where she'd been brewing some for herself.

The young man spoke to the elder, then they both nodded.

Good. Rose managed a smile and rummaged through a sack for a pair of extra cups. There was no point in complicating things by asking if they wanted sugar or cream. She felt their eyes following her every movement as she removed the pan of cornmeal mush from the coals. She hoped the cooked mixture wouldn't get too lumpy before they took their leave—assuming they left peaceably.

After pouring tea into the three cups, she handed each Indian one then took hers and sat across the fire from them, waiting for them to say something.

They didn't. Not right away. They sat on the log, presumably enjoying their drink while steadily observing her.

Rose breathed a prayer for protection yet again while she took a sip and tried to appear calm. This time, however, she added a request for wisdom to her growing list of desperate needs.

At last the chief set his cup down and said something to the interpreter.

The younger man, elaborately tattooed, with earrings made from animal teeth dangling from his lobes, smiled. "Red Hawk say Susquehannocks no good. Steal horses. Run away. Shawnee no steal."

The chief spoke to him again and he continued. "Smith know he die. Smith make you good trader. Red Hawk say stay. Is good store. Red Hawk give guards. Keep store safe." He pointed to himself. "Cornstalk. Cornstalk stay. Fast Walker come, stay." He nodded, his straight brows raised in question. "Good?"

Rose couldn't believe what she was hearing. Not only were they not planning to harm her; they were going to protect her and the store. Astounded at God's mercy, her heart all but burst from thankfulness as she nodded and smiled at both of them. At least she'd learned one word to say in trading, so she used it now. "Oui-saw." Good. She hoped she pronounced it half as well as Cornstalk spoke English. Their languages were so different.

Jenny started fussing just then, and Rose immediately picked her up. She didn't want the child to cry, since Shawnee considered that to be rude behavior. From what Mr. Smith had told her, if a Shawnee baby persisted in crying, it would be strapped in its cradleboard, taken into the woods, and left alone to hang in a tree until it learned crying would not get it any attention.

The Indians raised their cups and drained them then stood to their feet and raised a hand in farewell.

The tattooed one gave a nod. "Cornstalk get Fast Walker. Come here."

Rose smiled with an answering nod. "Thank you."

As they walked away, relief surged through her. Moments ago she'd felt abandoned by everyone she knew. Now her circumstances had taken the opposite turn, and she'd be under the protection of the Shawnee. Better still, if she stayed and traded with the Indians until all the supplies were gone, she might possibly be able to save up enough money to buy back her sisters—perhaps even secure passage for the three of them back home to England.

But before she could revel in that unexpected prospect, unbidden thoughts of Nate Kinyon crowded in. . .of his hearty laugh, his teasing smile, his concern for her. Was returning to England and life as a spinster what she truly wanted? "Nate, where are you?"

Rose drew her cloak around herself and Jenny on the log as she gazed across the wide river. All afternoon, distant banging sounds had carried from the other side. Someone across the way must be building a raft. She didn't know whether to be glad or concerned. The only time a raft was used was to transport livestock, and Mr. Smith had mentioned that officials from the fur company sent men out every couple of years to check on the trading posts. Had the time come for that?

Jenny squealed and grabbed at Rose's arm.

"Forgive me, sweetheart. Mama stopped feeding you, didn't she?" With a shake of her head at her carelessness, Rose spooned some smashed beans and squash into Jenny's mouth and gazed lovingly at the child. How like a rosebud were the tiny lips that could smile so sweetly. No one could deny she was growing cuter by the day. And the little one's nearly white-blond hair now curled about her ears. Whenever Indian squaws happened into the store, they could not resist fondling Jenny's silky ringlets. All their babies had straight black hair.

Reaching for another spoonful of food, Rose realized she'd called herself "Mama" to the baby. She'd become far too attached to Jenny, which was not prudent since the day would soon come to hand her over to her grandparents. Rose tilted her head with a sigh and grinned at the infant. "But you're mine for now." She blew at one of those flaxen curls as she scooped in another bite.

A village dog began to bark. Then others joined in, and they loped down toward the water. Rose glanced across the river, where two men and four horses were making the crossing.

Mr. Smith's employers, perhaps? Surely they'd insist upon her leaving. No way on earth would they allow a lone female to run one of their stores. But would they at least give her recompense for the profitable trading she'd conducted during the weeks since Mr. Smith had passed away? They probably wouldn't be pleased by the small number of fur bundles that remained on hand or the amount of missing trade goods. Nate and Robert Bloom had taken a fully loaded canoe with them when they left, and the Susquehannocks had helped themselves to both goods and furs when they stole away in the dead of night. Fortunately she'd saved the remainder, pitiful lot though it was.

Rose glanced at the two Shawnee braves who had provided protection since the Susquehannocks deserted her. How she wished the men coming were Nate and Robert. As hard as it was to accept, she was beginning to believe they were never coming back.

Jenny cooed and smiled one of her sweet baby smiles, and Rose's heart crimped as she picked up the child and hugged her close. She'd never be able to erase from her mind the terrible condition Hannah Wright had been in before she died. . .nor could she dwell on similar thoughts of what might have happened to Nate and Robert. She sloughed off the morbid turn her mind had taken and caught Jenny's little fist with a playful shake. "We should find out who the visitors are, should we not?" Standing up with Jenny in her arms, she started down the slope.

Already the enthusiastic villagers were assembling on the riverbank, awaiting the newcomers' arrival. With the baby propped on one hip, Rose waited behind the noisy crowd, awed by the change in her perception of the Indians. At home in England, she'd believed them to be nothing but half-naked savages bent on butchering anyone who ventured into the frontier. Now, she kept a slight distance between them and herself merely because she didn't want to get jostled in their excitement.

After beaching their raft, two bearded men dressed in the rough attire of frontiersmen came toward her through the crowd, trailing their horses after them. Both halted at the sight of her then continued their approach. "Rose Harwood?" one asked, the eyes beneath his bushy brows squinting as if unable to believe what he saw. He nudged frameless spectacles higher on his hooked nose.

"Yes, I'm Miss Harwood." Her heart plummeted. They knew her name. Surely they had to be the fur-company men. But they looked scruffier than the last men who'd come through the village.

"I knowed I had letters to deliver to a Rose Harwood," the man with glasses went on. "But I never expected no white woman."

"Aye," his partner agreed, daylight glancing off a scar that ran down one cheek. "We thought it was an Indian wife or a half-breed. But you don't look like no half-breed I ever seen. An' with a towhead baby yet!"

The word *letters* dawned on Rose. "You have letters for me?" She stepped forward, holding out her free hand.

"Yes, ma'am, in one of our bags," the first said. "For you an' Trader Smith. When we stopped by the Ohio an' Virginia Fur Company they asked us to drop 'em by on our way in."

"Then you're not in the employ of the fur company."

"No, ma'am. We're trappers. Goin' downriver for winter beaver."

She breathed a sigh of relief. This meant she had more time to trade with the Indians for furs. More time to make money. "Please," she invited, "do come up to my fire. I've got chicken stew in the pot."

"Chicken! That does sound temptin'." Tugging on his horse's reins, the man started up the hill, past her and the baby. "Ho! Smith! Where you hidin' out, you ol' skinflint?"

Before Rose could say anything, the scarred man paused beside her. "One more thing."

"Yes?"

"Jest so's ya know, some men from the fur company are on their way. They was startin' out a couple'a days behind us."

Her chest tightened with dread.

He cracked a gap-toothed grin. "But don't ya go feedin' them no chicken. 'Possum's good enough for them greedy misers."

A few days after the trappers left, Rose heaved a sigh as she gazed down at Mariah's letter again. Would the girl never change?

Salutations, Rose, the missive began.

Salutations! How pretentious! One would think Mariah was composing business correspondence. But at least she'd taken the time to put plume to paper and had given her older sister some thought. She read further:

I was quite surprised to hear from you. I had been rather concerned about your welfare at first, considering the appearance and ghastly odor of your employer. But Colin assured me that any man who could hand over the sum of fifty pounds for you without batting an eye was surely a man of far greater prospects than he appeared. Since receiving your letter, I see Colin was correct.

Although you must be living in quite remote circumstances without shops or other niceties, I assure you I am not much better off. I have been relegated to the lowly position of tutor to Colin's three sisters and secretary to Mr. and Mrs. Barclay. For as wealthy as these colonials are, the females especially lack most severely in penmanship.

The girls tag behind me wherever I step, and Mistress Barclay is forever finding something for me to do, so I have precious little time to myself. Would you believe that the woman actually had me serve food at their annual summer gathering? I was sorely mortified!

To make matters even worse, I am allowed only one day to myself a week, and Mrs. Barclay refuses to let Colin escort me anywhere. I have been to the shops only once since my arrival here, and that was as a companion to the old biddy and two of her spoiled daughters. I need not tell you how little money I have to spend. Fortunately, Colin slipped me a few coins. He really is a dear, as generous as he is handsome.

Alas, the mistress is calling me. I shall try to write more in a few days.

I remain your obedient sister,
Mariah

Rose laughed at the absurd ending. *Obedient? Rarely! Willful? Often! And quite often concerned only about herself.* But the girl did have her moments of generosity, and Rose knew she genuinely cared for her family.

Laying the letter aside, she picked up the one from Lily and pressed it to her heart. Sweet Lily. She unfolded the thick missive which she'd read so often she'd nearly committed it to memory. The words penned in her younger sister's fine hand were so like her, Rose could imagine Lily speaking them in her airy voice:

My beloved sister Rose,

I cannot express in words how unbearably deeply I miss you. I wish so very much that I could have gone with you that day we were all auctioned off. I was so distraught about your welfare I grieved for you daily, until I received your precious letter. But know that every night the Waldons and I pray for your safety and your happiness in your strange and scary circumstance.

When I read how you came to possess the baby of that unfortunate woman, it brought me to tears. Soon after we arrived here, we heard that a band of savages had swooped into the Wrights' farm, intent upon burning and destroying, as they are prone to do. It was no surprise to hear they took Mistress Wright

*and her baby hostage. How terribly sad that the poor woman died.
However, Mr. Waldon assures his wife and me that we are in no
danger. The Wrights lived at the very edge of the frontier on land
sold to Mr. Wright by one tribe of Indians, while a different tribe
also laid claim to that very land. Mr. Waldon is certain his deed for
the property we dwell on is in no way questionable. Still, whenever
I venture outside, I always check the woods. I am sure I shall grow
more comfortable with my surroundings as time goes by.*

*I could not be happier here. Mr. Waldon is a kind and gentle
husband, father, and employer. Mistress Waldon somewhat
reminds me of you. She treats me like a younger sister, though
she is not nearly as energetic as you, dear Rose. Some days she
can scarcely walk, for the pain in her joints is severe. Other days
she seems much improved. Before all our meals, we pray for her
healing.*

Smiling, Rose laid down the letter. She'd been right about giving Mr.
Waldon the extra money he'd needed to purchase Lily's papers.

Or had she? It sounded like Lily lived far too close to where Indians
had conducted a murderous raid. Rose flicked a glance to the store's
front, where her guards relaxed just outside near their fire, their muskets and hatchets lying nearby to ensure her safety. . .these 'peaceful'
people who decorated their dwellings with bloodied scalps and other
severed body parts. She shuddered.

An icy breeze tugged at the lowered canvas at the front of the store,
loosening the ties, and an edge began to flap. Rose left the limited warmth
of the crude fireplace and checked on Jenny. All but swallowed by furs as
she napped, the child had one tiny hand peeking out. Rose reached down
and tucked it beneath the warm covering then went outside to retie the
loose thong holding the canvas in place.

No one had come up the river to trade for several days, and even
the Shawnee were staying inside their warm wigwams. Rose knew if she
didn't have Jenny Ann to keep her company she'd be unbearably lonely.

The weather had turned much colder. Except for the evergreens, all trees and shrubs were devoid of their brilliant fall colors. Their bare forms looked forlorn, like so many skeletal fingers poking up at the sky. After tightening the flap's ties, Rose gazed toward the river. Crackly ice fringed the dark water, and overhead, a dull, gray cloud bank threatened snowfall.

Whatever had possessed her to remain here through the harsh winter with a little baby? Perhaps the men from the fur company would arrive soon and give her orders to leave. . .and hopefully escort her back to civilization.

Spying a canoe coming into view around the bend, Rose grimaced. Likely it was just some Indians willing to brave the cold to come and trade.

Cornstalk and Fast Walker straightened, alert at their posts. Rose felt at ease knowing the two had promised to keep her safe.

Stepping back inside the dimly lit store, she began straightening things, making certain the goods were displayed to their best advantage. She hoped Jenny, in her little warm cocoon, wouldn't be too fussy when awakened by the arrival of customers. From the shouting and hullabaloo of barking dogs that had already begun, the visitors would be surrounded by welcoming villagers any minute.

It would take time for the furs to be unloaded. Rose added water to the kettle over the fire and stirred the coals. The travelers would probably be chilled to the bone and would appreciate some hot India tea, always a treat from the usual bitter herb teas almost everyone here served. And a few leftover biscuits remained from noon. She'd get those out as well. Not quite an English high tea, but thought of serving afternoon tea as if she were at home in Bath brought a bubble of laughter. Rose clamped a hand over her mouth so she wouldn't disturb Jenny.

Sudden light flooded in from the front of the structure, and she swung toward it.

"Rose? You in here? It's me, Nate. I'm back."

Chapter 24

Out of breath after racing up the bank from the river, Nate searched frantically in the dim light of the log-built trading post. Then in a blur, Rose flew to him and threw her arms about his neck.

"You're alive! You're actually alive! Thank God!"

Wrapping his arms around her soft form, he hugged her tight. "So are you. When we got word that Eustice had died, I was so worried, I—"

An ear-piercing wail came from farther back in the store.

Going rigid, Nate pushed Rose to one side and went for his hunting knife.

The wail turned into sobs. He moved toward what sounded very much like a very unhappy little one. He couldn't believe his eyes. There, walled in by a few crates and sacks, sat a baby. A blond, blue-eyed, squalling baby.

He felt the blood drain from his face as he wheeled back to Rose. "You—you never told me you were with child."

"Me?" Rose's expression was one of shock. Then she burst into laughter. "I'm not her mother," she sputtered between giggles. "But she is mine to care for until I'm able to deliver her to her grandparents." She reached down and picked up the towhead, who stopped crying almost immediately. "Nate Kinyon, I'd like to introduce Jenny Ann Wright. Her mother, unfortunately, died after suffering grievous wounds while running the gauntlet. She asked me to look after her little one."

His brow furrowed. "That's really regrettable. . .but not unheard of."

Clinging to Rose, the child peered at him from rounded blue eyes as if taking his measure, then reached out a tentative little hand, still moist from her mouth.

Nate took hold of the slimy fingers, and the little curly-top gifted him with a darling, two-tooth grin. The little one was every bit as irresistible as the woman holding her.

"Robert Bloom is with you, is he not?" Rose searched his face.

"Aye. He's seeing that everything's unloaded. He's brought back quite the surprise. Wait'll you see." Nate chuckled then sobered. "It's true, then? Smith's dead? You were left here by yourself?" Concerned over her sad situation, he drew her and the baby close to him, burying his face in Rose's hair, breathing in her unique scent. She felt so good in his arms. He made a solemn vow not to let her out of his sight before he had her safely away from here.

After a long-spun moment, she leaned her head back and gazed up into his eyes with such warmth he thought he'd melt. "I feared you were dead. Whatever took you so long?"

The store's flap flung wide again, and Robert Bloom strode in, all smiles, with his arm around a slip of an Indian lass. A thick hat of rabbit fur hid most of her raven hair but not the perfect oval of her olive face with its huge, dark-chocolate eyes. Wrapped in a soft fur robe, she looked small and shy beside Robert's lean form as she lowered her lashes with a faint smile.

Robert drew the girl along as he came forward and took Rose's hand. "Rose, I'm so glad you're alive an' well. If you hadn't been, I reckon I would'a had to shoot Nate for leavin' you here in the first place."

Pleased they'd both finally returned, yet still surprised, Rose glanced from the Indian girl to Nate, who offered a sheepish shrug.

"And this must be the baby Red Hawk was telling me about down at the river." Robert reached over and ruffled Jenny's hair with his free hand. "Cute little thing." His gaze met Rose's again. "Praise the good Lord you were here for that little gal."

Rose nodded. "I feel the same way. I've no doubt Jenny Ann is the reason God allowed me to be brought here. He knew she'd be in dire need of someone to care for her."

"Aye. He does work in mysterious ways. Speakin' of that, look what the Lord gave me." He gazed lovingly down at the girl at his side. "This here is Swims with Otters, but I can't help myself. . . . I call her Shining Star 'cause I can't seem to take my eyes off her."

Smiling at his words, Rose lifted the willowy girl's hand, drawing her liquid brown eyes up to her. "I'm very pleased to meet you, Shining Star." She motioned toward the back of the store. "Would you like to take a seat by the fire? I've water heating for tea." She smiled at the men, including them in the invitation.

Robert quickly translated what Rose had said, and they all moved to the warmth of the back of the store, removing their outer clothing along the way. Without her hat, Swims with Otters's glossy braids, entwined with thin strips of leather, hung to the middle of her back. She brushed a few stray strands from her eyes.

Rose noticed the girl also wore an intricately beaded headband, which complemented her beaded doeskin Indian dress and calf-high deerskin moccasins. "While I prepare the tea," Rose said, "you men will have to tell me why you were gone so long. And Robert, how you happened to bring along this lovely girl."

꧁꧂

"It's a pretty sad story," Bob said, taking a sip of steaming tea as the four settled on grain sacks they'd pulled close to the fire.

Nate peered over the top of his cup and cut his friend a pointed look, a warning not to let the reason for their delayed return slip out. No sense frightening Rose any more than necessary.

Bob reached beside himself and squeezed the Indian maiden's hand. "You see, Rose, Shining Star's part of the Miami nation. She lived in a village not far from Mascouten territory, an' them two tribes've been feudin' back an' forth for some time. I reckon it got pretty bad, 'cause the Miami women outnumber the men a good four or five to one these days."

"Mercy." Rose hugged Jenny close. "How dreadful, all those widows and orphans." She gazed down at her own little orphan.

Nate chimed in, hoping to ease her mind. "The men take on more wives. That helps some."

Rose tucked her chin and arched her brows. "Surely you don't mean plural marriage. That's a rather pathetic solution to such a problem."

"Anyway," Bob said, "Shining Star's pa was killed in a raid last spring. Then when her brother never came back from huntin'. . ." He shrugged a shoulder. "What men are left already have more wives an' daughters than they can hunt for an' feed. So her mother came to me."

Looking from him to the Indian lass and back, Rose met Bob's gaze. "To ask you to marry her daughter."

He slid an uncertain glance to Nate before responding. "More like she wanted to sell Star to me." At Rose's gasp, he rushed on. "You see, if the widow had trade goods, she could bargain with the village hunters for meat now an' again. . .to see her an' her other little ones through the hard winter."

"So you bought her? You actually bought her?" Rose rolled her eyes and grimaced.

Nate could see this was not going well for his partner. Not well at all.

Bob offered a weak smile. "No, not at first. But her ma kept comin' back to me with her, pleadin'. An' I felt so sorry for my shy little girl, I gave in." He lifted his chin a notch. "But rest assured, Miss Rose, I won't be beddin' or weddin' her till she comes to know the Lord as her Savior."

Rose arched her brows. "Don't you mean, *if?*" she challenged.

Watching her reaction, Nate shifted uncomfortably on his seat. Rose Harwood was one stiff-necked woman, especially when it came to religion. A body would think she was one of them Puritans.

But Bob didn't seem the least put off by her remarks. "I already thought about that. A lot. I figger if she don't become a believer, then I'll look for a suitable husband for her among the other tribes."

Nate was pretty sure he discerned a hint of triumph in the smile that played across Rose's lips. "In that case, I shall make room for the girl in the wigwam with Jenny and me."

Looking from her to Bob, Nate released a tired breath. He couldn't believe he'd just risked life and limb for such a hardheaded woman. But he had to admit he was as besotted as Bob. No doubt about it.

Chapter 25

As they all continued sipping their tea, Rose rocked back and forth slightly with Jenny Ann asleep in her arms. She studied Swims with Otters, or Shining Star—whatever Robert wanted to call her—then glanced at Robert, seated beside the lass. "I must say your young lady scarcely appears older than my youngest sister."

He tipped his head. "She was born durin' the time of fallin' leaves, fifteen years ago. I know she's a little thing, but she's full growed."

"Fifteen." Rose shook her head. Papa wouldn't have considered an offer for any of his daughters until they were at least seventeen years of age. Thoughts of Mariah came to mind. The girl had been too picky for her own good. . .and then it was too late. And here sat a shy girl who reminded Rose so much of young Lily, already given to a man—*sold* was closer to the truth. The very concept was appalling.

Remembering the leftover biscuits, she used her free arm to reach behind herself for the covered plate then removed the cloth and offered one to Nate and then the girl.

The lass glanced from the plate to Rose, then to Robert, with questions in her dark eyes. He smiled and nodded, and she took one but held on to it and stared, as if she didn't know what it was.

Robert also took one, bit into it, and said something to her.

Finally the girl took a small nibble. After a few seconds she took another bite.

"Oui-saw?" Rose asked, using her one and only word of Shawnee.

The bashful smile appeared, and the lass nodded.

"So," Nate cut in, taking a second biscuit, "seems you been pickin' up a bit'a Shawnee."

Rose chuckled. "I'm afraid that's the extent of it. Mr. Smith taught me the word when he was training me in the business of trading."

Grinning, Robert gave a nod "That's what Red Hawk told us. About you in here dickerin' just like you knowed what you was doin'."

"I actually do know what I'm doing." She flashed a wry smile. "Most of the time."

"Red Hawk said that when the Susquehannocks left, they run off with several horses an' a bunch of your best furs," Robert said.

She nodded. "Along with all the cash money, I'm sad to say."

"Well, no need to fret," Nate assured her. "Bob an' me did real good, all considered. An' with Smith gone, you ain't bound to him anymore."

Remembering the trader's final act of kindness, Rose smiled. "Quite right. In fact, before he died, he signed off on my papers to make everything legal. So I'm hoping to earn enough from the furs and trade goods still left in the trading post to buy my sisters' papers and free them, as well." Having divulged that information in a rush, she waited for their reaction.

Nate turned and surveyed the goods stacked against the side wall. "Don't look like that'll be a problem. We'll buy back your sisters, take that baby back to wherever she belongs, an' still have plenty leftover to have ourselves one fine time in Baltimore. Or mebbe you'd rather go to Philadelphia. Hear tell they got a lot more shops an' taverns an' playhouses an' anything else we fancy."

A fine time? That was his proposal? To offer her what some bigwig would offer a loose woman? Crushed and not wanting him to see the disappointment on her face, she stood with the sleeping baby and went to stoke the fire.

All those long days and weeks she'd spent longing for Nate Kinyon to return—wasted. So was her deepest hope—that he'd taken steps to strengthen his faith, since he knew how much it meant to her—so that when he asked her to marry him, she could say yes. But the horrid truth was her chances of wedding Nate were no better than Robert Bloom's were of marrying Star. Probably worse. Shining Star had yet to hear enough about the Lord to accept or reject Him. But Nate. . .

A plan formed in Rose's mind, and she swiveled on her heel, hardening herself as she looked at Nate. "I'm sorry, but your plans won't do. I'm not footloose as you are. I have serious responsibilities. Not only do my sisters need to be bought out of bondage, I need enough money to purchase their passage back to England, where they can be properly looked after by our father."

Nate reared back. "I thought the whole point in comin' to America was because your father couldn't look after you girls."

She gave a small shrug. "I'm sure he and my brother have managed to take care of the problem that beset our family by now. In any event, I plan to make money enough for each of my sisters to have a sizable dowry so they'll be able to make a good match." She knew she was probably overreaching, but she was too hurt to care.

Standing to his feet, Nate towered over her. "An' how do you propose to do that? If you don't mind me askin'."

Rose wished he weren't so much taller than she, but she did her best to straighten to her full height as she looked up at those steely hazel eyes of his. She mustered as much force in her voice as possible so he'd hear her determination. "By continuing to run this trading post as I've been doing since Mr. Smith passed on. The villagers want me to stay. The store is good business for them as well as for me, with people constantly coming and going. There's no reason for me not to go on looking after things until I've earned sufficient funds. I could not earn a fraction of what I'll make here anywhere else."

Still seated with his Indian maiden, Robert gave a light laugh. "Looks like she's been doin' fine so far. Course, on the other hand, there's the problem of restockin' an' such. Plus I don't see them boys out at the Virginia an' Ohio lettin' a woman run the place, when it comes right down to it."

"Well. . ." That was so true. How would she? An idea slowly surfaced. Rose took a deep breath and averted her gaze from him to Nate. "As it happens, a pair of trappers came through a few days before you arrived, and they told me representatives of the company would be here any day to check on things. And I thought. . ." She glanced at Robert. Noticing he was talking quietly to the girl, Rose drew a breath and stepped nearer to Nate so she could speak softly. "I thought if you two would stay on till they leave, you could pretend. . .to be. . .my husband." There. She'd said it.

Nate clamped a hand on her shoulder and pulled her closer, his mouth agape. "Did you say what I thought you said?"

⁓

Rose had no idea how she suffered through Nate's snickering and teasing. The maddening frontiersman was having a lot of fun at her expense. Granted, it took awhile for him to see the logic behind her scheme, but once she explained her reasoning, he was quick to come around—even if he did have a mischievous gleam in his eye. Surely he did not imagine he could attempt anything untoward during their little deception. In any event, she was more than glad to have *her protector* back again. . .along with Robert Bloom, of course.

She got up from her seat on the flour sack. "I'm sure the three of you must be hungry after paddling all day upriver in such cold weather." She moved toward Nate with an impish smile. "Here, let me have *our* baby. You need to bring in your pelts before one of the villagers takes a liking to them."

"You're right about that." With no indication that he'd noticed her suggestive statement, Nate rose to his feet and handed Jenny to her. After shrugging into his warm outer garment, he headed out.

Robert also came to his feet, and so did Shining Star. He turned to the lass and spoke quietly in her language first, repeating the words in English. "Stay here." He gestured toward Rose. "With Miss Rose." Obviously he was attempting to teach her some basic English, which Rose appreciated.

The Indian girl sank back down onto her seat and looked timidly at Rose. "Wi' Mi' Rose." She checked back at him with a tentative smile.

"Oui-saw. Good girl." He cupped her cheek in his palm and smiled into her eyes.

Observing the loving expressions passing between them, Rose felt a twinge of envy and, for a brief moment, felt like crying. But she'd been doing quite enough of that of late, she reminded herself, and sloughed off the emotion.

Robert grinned over at her. "I'm sure Star'd be happy to hold the baby while you tend to things."

"If you're certain. I could put Jenny in her little pen."

He shook his head and spoke a few words to the lass, and she got up. As Star approached Rose with her arms outstretched, he threw on his fur robe and started to leave. But reaching the flap, he stopped and turned. "Rose, what you really need is a cradleboard like Indian mothers use. Babies love 'em 'cause they never have to be left with someone else while their mothers work. I'll see if I can trade some squaw outta one."

"Thank you," she said in her most polite tone. Having given Jenny over to the Indian girl, Rose pondered the concept of cradleboards versus a cloth sling. She'd noticed babies strapped to their mothers' backs and thought the stiff contraptions looked too restrictive. Yet the wee ones all seemed happy, snuggled and warm inside their little cocoons. Perhaps Jenny would feel more secure in one. She glanced at the little one and saw her smiling and toying with one of Shining Star's braids while the lass sang softly in her ear.

Nate came back in on a blast of winter air, his arms straining with the weight of a large bundle. "Where do you want these?"

Rose quickly dragged a couple of crates away from the side wall. "Put them here. 'Twould be best to keep them separate from the others."

Dropping them with a thud, Nate bent over and pulled out what appeared in the dim light to be a beaver pelt. "Feel how thick this is, Rose." He held it out to her.

She smoothed her hand over it. "Oh yes. Very prime. A lovely pelt."

"Aye. We only traded for the best. That wasn't the main reason we went tradin', though. We heard rumors that one of the tribes had a secret silver mine, and we were hopin' to get our hands on some of that silver we heard about. Enough to satisfy even ol' Eustice." Taking the beaver hide, he caressed her cheek with the silky fur. "Almost as soft as your skin."

Gazing up at him, Rose couldn't move. There was such passion in his eyes it made her knees feel weak. She couldn't believe how easily she fell beneath his spell.

Robert strode in just then with his arms filled with furs, and the tension lightened noticeably. Rose moved out of his way. "Put them there with Nate's."

He dropped the load onto the first pile. "Did I hear Nate mention the silver?" He stepped nearer to Rose and grimaced as he pulled up a sleeve, displaying a bracelet. "One of the two we managed to get our hands on."

She gasped. "Then you did find the silver mine."

Both men laughed, and Robert elaborated. "Mighty strange, the way a story gets started an' grows into somethin' a whole lot bigger an' better with the tellin'."

Smiling and frowning with confusion at the same time, Rose was all too aware that Nate had yet to take his eyes off her. She hoped her idea of pretending they were husband and wife before the fur-company officials wasn't giving him any more improper ideas. She found it difficult to focus on his partner's words.

"Turns out," Robert continued, "the bracelets came from Spanish Mexico. Been traded here an' there till they made it up to the Ohio Valley. All that way. Ain't that somethin'?"

"It truly is," she responded. Still feeling Nate's eyes on her, she steeled her emotions and faced him.

A one-sided grin emerged, and he rejoined the conversation. "Aye, and us paddlin' up one stream after another, like we was Ponce de León, searchin' for his fountain of youth."

So that's why they were gone so long. Rose looked from one grinning face to the other then decided to get their minds back on business. "Since Mr. Smith, may God rest his soul, has passed on, 'tis only right you should have all the profits from your venture. I have the bills of lading from the goods he purchased and the record of the items you took with you, so when the furs are taken to the company, it should be quite easy to figure."

"That'll help make up for the trouble we had," Robert muttered.

"What trouble?" Her heart skipped a beat.

"Nothin' to speak of," Nate blurted. He slid a significant glare to his friend.

That really piqued Rose's curiosity.

Nate's expression eased to one more innocuous. "Well, now. That's mighty nice of you, givin' Bob and me the profit. Speakin' of ol' Eustice, did he treat you decent after we left? I told him I'd—well, let's just say I told him to be nice to you."

Another bittersweet memory came to the fore, and Rose smiled. "Thank you. But I must say, once little Jenny Ann came to us, Mr. Smith became a different man. No matter how bad he felt or how his stomach pained him, he loved playing with her. We spent nearly all our time together after she came along—mostly here in the store, with him teaching me the business." Remembering her treasured book, she pulled the slim volume from her apron pocket and held it to her breast. "This New Testament was his. We read from it quite a lot, particularly toward the end."

"Well, I'll be." Nate's smug expression vanished.

Robert, however, looked pleased. "You have a copy of the scriptures!" His gaze veered from her to the Indian lass. "That'll make things easier. I won't have to rely on just the verses I know when I talk to Star about the Lord."

Seeing the delight in the man's demeanor, Rose appreciated the tenderness, the innocence of their new love. She glanced at Nate to gauge his reaction to his friend's comments. But there was no shared joy in his expression. He looked more like a cornered rat.

It was her turn to give him a smug smile.

Chapter 26

Nate and Bob left Shining Star settled in with Rose and the baby in Rose's wigwam and headed for the Shawnee council lodge, as Red Hawk had requested earlier. Nate's insides felt pleasantly sated after enjoying Rose's delicious cooking. It had been ages since he'd downed such tasty eggs and side pork—especially with the added treat of fluffy biscuits slathered with butter. Eustice certainly knew how to pick a cook! He stifled a grin at the ridiculous notion. Cooking was only one of Rose Harwood's many fine attributes.

As he and Bob reached the lodge and entered, most of the talking ceased between the villagers assembled in the immense ninety-by-fifty-foot structure. Always amazed by the size and spaciousness of a longhouse, Nate surveyed the toasty interior with interest. A sturdy framework of thick, upright poles, interlaced with a series of thinner poles, was overlaid with sheets of flattened elm bark. Shafts of waning daylight slanted through a number of smoke holes in the roof and cut through the gloomy, smoky interior, glinting off a grisly collection of scalps displayed on poles like trophies. Nate observed that though many sported black Indian hair, several were blond, red, and assorted shades of brown. Even a couple of gray ones. He caught a troubled breath, inhaling a blend of tobacco, wood, earth, and Indian.

Because of the cold weather, all the fire pits along the length of the lodge were ablaze, and what smoke didn't rise to the smoke holes above mingled with that coming from several long, decorative pipes making the rounds.

It appeared every man in the village had come to the gathering, along with several women who sat on pallets behind the circle of men. Obviously everyone wanted to hear the latest news.

Red Hawk motioned for Nate and Bob to be seated between him and another chief named Barking Dog.

While lowering themselves down onto the packed earth floor, Nate tried not to show his amusement over the second chief's name. He wondered if, as a boy, the chief had gone around barking like a dog, or had he merely teased the mangy camp dogs into incessant yapping? Judging from the rapid rate at which the man spoke, Nate guessed the first assumption was correct.

A pipe came his way, and Nate took it and drew a few puffs then passed it on and settled into a comfortable position. He knew from experience he and his partner would be here for quite some time, with Bob doing all their talking.

As always, conversation began with the polite blather regarding health, how the hunting and fishing had gone this fall, and the usual inane pleasantries. Then Bob's expression turned serious, and he leaned forward. Nate knew the important subjects had finally come up.

In seconds the men sitting around the circle began muttering in low tones to one another, their expressions sober, often bordering on sullen.

Nate decided it was high time he started learning enough Shawnee to make out the gist of what the Indians were discussing. He elbowed Bob. "What'd you say to them?"

He angled his head Nate's way. "I told 'em about the scores of canoes we saw beached where the Scioto River merges with the Ohio. An' that when we sneaked up on the camp, we saw almost as many French soldiers there as Indians."

Red Hawk frowned and said something to Bob.

Nate managed to catch the word *Miami*.

His pal gave a negative shake of his dark head and made a correction. "Mostly Seneca."

The others present relaxed visibly. Nate surmised it was because several of those gathered around the fire happened to be Miami braves.

An interminable hour or so dragged by before Bob finally stopped conversing with the leaders and turned to Nate. "We can go now."

Nate resisted the urge to rub his numb backside as he stood with his friend to shake hands with the men nearby. Then, smiling and nodding, he and Bob took their leave.

As they left the village and covered the short distance to the trading post, Nate drew in a deep breath of fresh air and let it slowly out. "Prob'ly if I took time to learn some Shawnee, meetin's like that wouldn't drag on so."

Bob laughed. "It would help, no doubt about it."

"Well, tell me. Did the Shawnees give you any idea of how they felt about the French movin' south from Fort Ouiatenon?"

His friend shrugged. "They weren't concerned about it. They said the French tried to go that far down the Scioto a few years back, and the Shawnee chiefs at Sinioto told them politely but firmly that they weren't welcome in the Ohio Valley. They kind of *suggested* they go back to their fort, where they'd be safe. What Red Hawk and the others didn't like was those northern tribes coming south into their huntin' grounds."

Recollecting their own recent experience in that area, Nate was thankful the two of them made it back in one piece. "Personally, what I didn't like was all the time we had to stay hidden once the French found out we were tradin' in those parts. We lost more'n a month before they finally moved on."

"Well," Bob said with a grin, "beats havin' our scalps hangin' on some Seneca's lodge pole, don't it?"

"Aye. That it does. I'm kinda partial to mine after all this time. I just hope them Frenchies keep themselves down that way, seein' as how Rose has her heart set on bein' a storekeeper. With me." He grinned and looked up the hill toward her wigwam silhouetted in the moonlight.

It was going to be a lot of fun getting that little gal off that high horse of hers.

Rose awakened to a mild sunny morning, a rarity for late fall. Feeling gloriously alive, she gave a languorous stretch. Nate and Robert were back! If that weren't bounty enough, she and Jenny now had the company of Shining Star in their wigwam, the baby slept soundly through the night, and by all calculation, today was Sunday!

Thank You, dear Lord, for my many blessings. Please, please don't give up on Nate. With both Robert and me pointing him toward You, he just might find his way.

She raised her head and peered across the cold fire pit to the mound of fur where only the top of the Indian girl's dark head was visible. *And please open Shining Star's heart and mind that she might see Your light. She seems like such a sweet girl. She reminds me so of Lily. And thank You for the safe return of the men. You know I'd all but given up on them.*

Easing slowly out of her bedding so she wouldn't disturb Jenny, Rose used a stick to dig to the bottom of the fire pit. After finding some live coals, she blew on them and added wood shavings until enough of a flame sprouted for her to add some thin sticks.

Movement across the wigwam revealed Shining Star beginning to stir. The girl opened her heavily lashed, doelike eyes. At first sight of Rose they registered panic; then she relaxed and smiled shyly as she started to get up.

Rose gestured for her to lie back down. Then, hugging herself tight, she made shivering motions. "Cold," she whispered.

"Cold," the lass repeated softly. With a soft giggle, she snuggled down once again into her lush coverings.

Rose had to smile. Star truly was a joy, just as Robert had said. Perhaps with her around, Rose wouldn't miss Lily so much. . .or the rest of her family. *God bless Papa, Tommy, Charles and his family. . .and do keep after Mariah, since I am not there to do it.*

━━

What a treat, having an extra pair of hands, Rose mused, as she and the Indian girl walked with the baby to the store. Getting herself and Jenny dressed and bundled for the day had been only half as much work with Shining Star a willing helper.

They found a roaring fire already blazing in the hearth when they entered the trading post. Better yet, the water kettle already hung suspended above the heat. Emotion swelled within Rose at the touching surprises, but she reminded herself they were just small acts of kindness. Yet how she appreciated kind acts now. . .so much more than she had before Nate left with Robert.

She carried Jenny closer to the warmth of the fire, noting that neither of her knights in shining armor was present in the store's shadowy interior.

Shining Star also glanced around, appearing frightened as she caught Rose's hand. "Bob."

Knowing the men were most likely out tending the livestock, she smiled at Star. "Horses." She cupped her hand and put it to her mouth. "Feed horses."

"Horse." The girl nodded and turned toward the entrance.

Rose caught her hand. "Shining Star watch Jenny." She handed the baby to her then pointed to herself. "I cook. Feed bellies." She rubbed her own midsection.

An understanding smile curved Star's lips. She patted her stomach then the baby's. "Feed bellies."

Delighted, Rose laughed. They were going to get along just fine.

At that moment, Nate and a blast of sunshine burst through the opening. He held his hat upside down in his hands. "Mornin', ladies." He flashed that infectious grin of his. "Fed your chickens and collected the eggs." He tilted his hat slightly so Rose could see them nestled within what looked like some wilted weeds. "Loved the eggs so much last night, I sure hope you won't mind cookin' us up another helpin'. I pulled a onion outta the garden, too. Thought we could add some to the eggs."

"You did, did you?" She grinned at his enthusiasm.

"Aye. Them biscuits were mighty good, too. An' I dug up a turnip an' a couple carrots an'—"

Shining Star interrupted with a tug on his sleeve. "Bob."

Nate gave a nod and pointed toward the entrance. "Bob come." He switched his attention back to Rose. "He'll be in soon as he finishes milkin' the cow."

She shook her head in wonder. "The two of you are such a help. With my morning chores done, I can start on the biscuits right away, so we—"

The flap opened again, bringing Robert, along with another momentary shaft of sunshine.

"I'll get those biscuits going," Rose continued. "That way we'll have plenty of time for a nice leisurely church service. 'Tis the Sabbath, you know."

"Church service?" Bob set the milk pail on a crate and walked toward Shining Star. "Now, that's what I like to hear. We'll have some Psalm singin', too." He smiled down at the girl.

"Yes, we'll sing, as well." Rose glanced at Nate.

His grin had flattened, but the second he noticed her looking at him, he propped it up again. "Singin's fine with me. I like singin'." But the dull glint in his eye matched his forced enthusiasm.

Rose quickly pivoted back toward the flour sack. It wouldn't do for him to see her smirk.

~

" 'From all that dwell below the skies,' " Nate sang as he and his friends sat outside, his voice determinedly joyful and robust, " 'let the Creator's praise arise: Alleluia! Alleluia!' " Truth was, he did love to sing, and it wasn't as if he was a heathen. He'd been to Sabbath services every Sunday as a kid. " 'Let the Redeemer's name be sung, through every land, in every tongue. Alleluia! Alleluia! Alleluia! Alleluia!' " Even as he belted out the words, he realized their little group truly had caught the attention of the villagers, since they, too, had come outside to enjoy the warmth of the winter sun.

Nate could feel Rose watching him before they started into the next verse of the hymn, and that was the most fun of all. He knew she had to be flabbergasted that he even knew the song. She'd barely squeaked out her alleluias.

He focused on the next stanza. " 'In every land begin the song, to every land the strains belong. Alleluia! Alleluia! In cheerful sound all voices raise, and fill the world with joyful praise. Alleluia! Alleluia! Alleluia! Alleluia!' "

Rose finally caught the spirit of the hymn and raised her voice. She sang the chorus in a surprisingly beautiful soprano, the perfect blend with his baritone, Nate thought. Fact was, the two of them went well together in a lot of ways. They'd have a great time of it, if only she would quit insisting on being such a Puritan and admit it.

As they started into the next verse, Nate feasted his eyes on her as she sat across from him on a crate with Jenny Ann in her lap, like a beautiful Madonna holding the babe. Then his gaze drifted to Bob's Indian girl. If anyone was uncomfortable in this impromptu church service, it was poor Shining Star. With her dark head lowered, she darted glances around the group then out to the villagers down the slope.

Nate couldn't help feeling sorry for her. He knew her bewilderment must be acute. When she looked at him at the start of the final stanza, he sent her a reassuring smile. Her transition into the white world was going to be hard. Bob's mother had never been accepted by the good people in the area where they lived. *Lord, if Shining Star comes out with us, please make them so-called Christians in our neighborhood treat her with the kindness she deserves.*

Realizing with no little shock that he had actually said a real from-the-heart prayer, it dawned on him that he hadn't joined in at the start of the third verse. So he jumped right in. " 'Alleluia! Thy praise shall sound from shore to shore. . . .' "

As the hymn came to an end, Bob held up Mr. Smith's New Testament and bowed his head. "May our Father God bless the reading of His Word, and may He open the ears of understanding to all who hear, in the name of our Lord and Savior, Jesus the Christ."

He then drew Shining Star down on the sitting log beside him, opened the Bible, and began reading aloud. Nate recognized the first verse of the Gospel of John as one often read in his childhood home. " 'In the beginning was the Word, and the Word was with God, and the Word was God.' " Marking his place with his index finger, Bob closed the Bible and turned to the lass, translating what he'd just read. She frowned in puzzlement and asked several questions.

Nate noticed that Rose wore a soft smile as she watched the exchange between the couple. She didn't appear to harbor even the slightest prejudice against the Indian maiden. She turned that lovely smile on him, and his heart grew suddenly warm. "I can see how confusing that first verse could be."

"Aye." Standing to his feet, he reached over for the fidgeting Jenny Ann. "Even if I knew enough of her language, I sure wouldn't wanna try and translate that to the girl. She wouldn't have no problem with the idea of two gods, but"—raising the baby aloft a bit, he then brought her to his chest and nuzzled her neck till the cutie giggled—"Star's problem'll be with the Father an' the Son bein' just one God with one set of purposes. Wait'll she hears about how we're supposed to love everyone, even our enemies!"

He sat down on the log beside Rose and set Jenny Ann on his foot to give her a horsey ride. The little one laughed even harder. "Star is used to war gods an' Mother Earth an' spirits in lots of different forms, like the raven, for one. It has the spirit of a trickster. An' the spirit of the bear? Now, that's big power. Tobacco smoke, that can be real special. The Indian holy men use it to call in the spirits whenever they feel the need. Come to think of it, they're a very spiritual people—in their own way."

The two of them glanced over at Bob and Star, who were still occupied with their discussion. Rose tweaked Jenny under her chin and gave her a motherly smile then looked up at Nate. "Robert has been praying that the Lord will give her understanding. And I know He will. The choice of whether to believe and, more important, to become a disciple, a follower of the Lord, is hers alone."

Nate knew inside that the *disciple* part was actually directed at him. But he knew something else, as well. If Rose wanted him to be one of those Christians who shunned anyone who came from another country or had darker skin, she was barking up the wrong tree. As far as he was concerned, his God didn't mind folks having a little fun now and then either. He opened his mouth to tell her just that, when two musket shots in rapid succession came from across the river. He sprang to his feet.

Rose stepped beside him. "What is it?"

He shrugged. "Folks wantin' some canoes sent over for 'em, I reckon."

"Most likely them fur company men," Bob added as he joined them. He and Nate peered toward the opposite riverbank, where a party of men stood waving their arms.

"Aye. Looks like." Propping their little fluffy-haired cherub in his one arm, Nate slipped his other one around Rose's waist and drew her close. "Just one happy family, right?" He glanced down at those blue-gray eyes of hers. "Time to start lyin'."

The scared-rabbit look on her face was priceless.

Chapter 27

Rose had been in Nate's arms before, when he'd helped her down from horses or carried her to and from rafts, but this was nothing like those occasions. She knew he was in high humor watching the Shawnee paddle three long canoes across the river to fetch the officials from the fur company. She could see the mischievous gleam in his eyes and sensed his tightly contained mirth just begging for release. She also detected a certain possessive quality about the way he tucked her close. Of course, they were *supposed* to look like a married couple—after all, it was her idea. But why did her silly heart go all fluttery as if it was real? And to think this farce was right after their church service, for pity's sake. He must think her a hypocrite.

She inhaled a shaky breath and eased from his grasp, opting for the coward's way out. "I'll go kill and pluck a couple of young chickens. No doubt those men would appreciate a hearty Sunday dinner."

"I'll kill 'em for you." Nate offered the baby to her, but she quickly stepped back.

"No. Keep Jenny with you. She looks perfectly happy, and I've become quite capable of doing a number of things since you were here last. You and Robert go down and greet our guests. 'Tis only right." She arched her brows and smiled, hoping he'd agree.

He did.

On her way to the chicken pen, however, her conscience wouldn't let her alone. Here she was, a stalwart Christian—so she'd thought—planning to deceive the fur company men. And much worse, enlisting the aid of the very person she was judging for his unchristianlike proposal! She truly was a hypocrite.

A familiar Bible verse floated across her mind. *"Judge not, that ye be not judged."* Rose wished she'd never heard it.

But Lord... She unlatched the gate and stepped into the small penned area. *Surely You can see I'm trying to set to rights the suffering I caused my family last spring when I acted rashly and took matters out of Papa's hands. Had I waited on You, Father, You certainly would have made another way for us. Just as You've made this way for me right now.* She gave a righteous nod. *Absolutely. I am doing the right thing. This small deception is for the greater good.* And it's not as if she and Nate couldn't be married. It was a harmless lie, really.

Having packed that irritating conscience away once again in its tidy little box, Rose started after a young red rooster.

The usual crowd of inquisitive Shawnee lined the bank above the river, awaiting the arrival of the men being paddled across from the other side with piles of goods. Weaving through the bystanders with Bob a mere step behind, Nate realized he hadn't informed his friend of his decision to help Rose out with the scheme she'd proposed. He shifted Jenny to his other arm and stopped, turning to face Bob. "I. . .uh. . .need you to go along with whatever I tell those company men."

He frowned. "What're you talkin' about?"

Hoping to come up with the right words, Nate motioned with his head for Bob to follow as he made his way to the edge of the people and their steady chatter. "It's like she told us. She's determined to stay an' work at the tradin' post till she can save up enough money to send her sisters back to England. She's mighty sure of herself now that she can hear the jingle of some money. A far cry from when she first started out here. But you an' I both know no company officials are gonna let a lone woman run a store, no matter how good she's been doin' it." He put a finger up for Jenny Ann to tug on while he worked up nerve enough to admit his willing duplicity. "So we decided to, well. . .pretend to be husband an' wife."

Bob snorted. "An' that's your way of wormin' your way into her good graces?"

"Nay. I'm tellin' you the whole thing was her idea."

Bob tipped his head in thought. "It don't sound a bit like her."

"I know." Nate grinned. *That's the beauty of it!* "But I have to help her out."

Bob studied him for a moment. "Well, for the time bein' I think I'll let your conscience *and hers* be your judge."

That wasn't exactly what Nate hoped to hear. "Does that mean you won't say nothin'?"

"I won't say nothin'. But don't expect me to be a party to this little plot."

"Whatever you say. Not sayin' nothin's all I ask." Breathing a sigh of relief, he changed the subject and edged closer with Jenny in his arms. "Ever see a cuter little gal?"

The Shawnee paddlers delivered five men in the first ice-crusted canoe— three officials from the fur company, attired like easterners, and two frontier guides. When the craft beached in the icy slush lining the edge of the water, the first newcomer gave dubious consideration to the short span he'd need to leap over to make it to the bank. Then, obviously certain his boots were tall enough to ford the shallows, he hopped out.

The next two, however, didn't fare so well. Nate couldn't squelch a snicker when the pair splashed water halfway up their backsides. They yelped and let out a few choice words as they dashed onto the shore.

Their guides weren't far behind. Instead of climbing up the rise, however, those men waited for the remaining canoes to come in.

The Shawnee didn't appear particularly interested in the white men. They focused on the two other canoes loaded with goods for the store.

Careful to maintain his own footing for the baby's sake, Nate gingerly stepped down the slick grassy bank with Bob to greet the visitors. "Welcome. You must be the fur company men we been expectin'."

The first man peered over his long nose as he brushed slush from the bottom of his trousers. "Hawkes is the name. And who might you be, young man?" A suspicious note rang in his tone, and his expression registered surprise upon catching sight of the white baby.

"Kinyon. Nate Kinyon," he answered quickly. "We been lookin' after the place here since—"

"Where's Eustice Smith?" the official interrupted. "Our business is with him." He repositioned his fur hat atop his salt-and-pepper hair.

His two companions—the much younger one, short and stout, with a pasty complexion; the other tall and thin as a beanpole, with sleeves and trousers barely long enough to cover his limbs—joined him. Neither exuded the slightest hint of pleasantry in his posture or manner, but looked Nate up and down as if taking his measure and finding him in dire want.

Bob edged forward. "Sorry to have to say this, but Trader Smith passed away a few weeks back, may the good Lord rest his soul."

"So me and the missus has been keepin' the place goin' ever since," Nate cut in.

"You and the missus?" A sneer curled the edge of his thin lips as Mr. Hawkes exchanged a skeptical glance with his cohorts.

The little round fellow began to shiver. Remembering the young man's rather wet disembarking, Nate nodded to the threesome. "We got a nice fire goin' in the tradin' post. An' the wife keeps a pot of hot tea brewin'. Come up and dry off by the fire whilst we talk."

Once he and Bob had the damp newcomers wrapped in blankets and fur robes, each holding a steaming cup before the crackling fire, Nate related the story, keeping it simple. "So me and Bob went off to do some tradin' for Mr. Smith. My wife stayed behind to cook for him. Her and our baby, that is."

Rail-thin Mr. Parker tucked his chin. "I cannot believe you'd bring a white woman and an infant out here among these savages."

Nate flashed his most disarming grin. "My Rose, she has a real tender heart. Once she heard tell that Eustice was havin' so much trouble with his innards, she come along to cook him up some soups and puddin's to help him get back on his feet. But nothin' she did made him any better off. Poor ol' feller passed on whilst me an' Bob was downriver tradin'." Nate congratulated himself for not having uttered a single lie in that statement.

Hawkes had yet to crack a smile. "I haven't seen Smith's wife or brothers about. Where are they?"

"Them no-accounts?" Nate scoffed. "They hightailed it outta here. Snuck off in the night with a bunch of the best furs, all Smith's cash money, an' six of the horses—an' one of 'em was mine. Bob an' me brung in a load of real prime pelts from downriver, though. That sort'a makes up for their theivin'. Sort'a."

The explanation still did not satisfy the man. He looked askance at Nate. "What about that wife of yours? Where is she, if I might ask?"

Nate gave a proud smile and puffed out his chest. "Soon as she saw you comin', her and Bob's woman went out back to kill some chickens for dinner. She knowed you was travelin' in this cold weather an' wanted you to have a fine meal." Sneaking a quick look at his friend, Nate noticed Bob still wore a grim expression. No reason to make him suffer through any more of this. He glanced at the visitors. "Did you men leave your pack train across the river unattended?"

As Hawkes deepened his stare, stout young Mr. Jenkins spoke up. "We left three of our men with the horses."

"Well, I'm sure them boys'd feel a whole lot better if we sent over a couple braves to help guard 'em. Bob, why don't you ask Cornstalk an' Fast Walker to paddle over there an' spend the night?" He turned back to

Mr. Hawkes. "You fellas are stayin' the night, ain't you?"

Still steely-eyed, he nodded. "Yes. In fact, we are."

Shortly after Bob took his leave, the frontier guides and several braves arrived with supplies from the canoes.

"Put the goods anyplace in here," Nate said. "We'll sort through 'em later."

"*If* we decide to leave them here," the obstinate one said flatly.

Time for another change of topic, Nate decided. "Like I said, me an' Bob just come back from downriver. Things ain't lookin' good down thataway. A large party of Frenchies—plus some Indians from up north, Senecas maybe—was down on the lower Scioto where it merges with the Ohio. They caught wind of me an' Bob tradin' with the Miamis, an' we had us a bear of a time getting' shuck of 'em. Had to hole up for a couple weeks before they paddled down toward the Mississippi."

This news tidbit piqued interest from all three. "The Scioto, how far down is that?" Mr. Parker asked.

"Depends on which way you're goin'." Nate grinned. "Canoein' downstream, it takes near a week if you stay on the river most of the day. Upstream it takes more'n twice that long."

Stocky Mr. Jenkins wrapped his hands around his cup. "You say they went downstream."

"That's right."

"Yes," Hawkes added, "but you don't know how far downriver they went, do you?"

Nate wagged his head. "No, I sure don't, sir. And I'd appreciate it if you wouldn't be mentionin' it to my Rose. No need for her to be worryin' 'less there's real reason to. Me an' Bob had a palaver with the Shawnee chiefs here, an' none of 'em heard tell of Frenchies snoopin' around these parts."

"Well," he commented, "they're doing more than merely snooping around north of here. They seized Joe Frazier's trading post up on the Allegheny. At a Seneca village, by the by."

"You don't say." Nate straightened his spine at the disturbing news.

The Allegheny River flowed into the Ohio. "What about Frazier? What'd they do to him?"

"He didn't happen to be there at the time, but two of his men were captured."

"Aye," Parker added. "It's in territory claimed by Pennsylvania, but the only governor that seems to understand the seriousness of the situation is Governor Dinwiddie of Virginia. Mr. Hawkes"—he indicated the man with the long nose—"went to see him about it, and the governor immediately sent a letter to King George. Dinwiddie is sure His Majesty will grant him permission to act."

Nate's fingers clenched into fists. "You mean to tell me that governor's just sittin' there twiddlin' his thumbs till the king sends word all the way back across the ocean?"

"My sentiments exactly," Mr. Hawkes said with a negative shake of his bony head.

"When did the letter get sent?"

"In October." Hawkes let out a disgusted breath.

Nate snorted in disbelief. "So the answer's still weeks away. No wonder the French are bein' so bold." Peering out the canvas opening, he spied Rose and Shining Star coming from the direction of the chicken pen. A headless bird dangled from each of Rose's hands. Standing up, he met Mr. Hawkes's gaze. "Like I said, don't say nothin' about this to the womenfolk."

Chapter 28

Surely there'd been time enough for Nate to speak to the company men about her and him staying on as traders, Rose thought on her way back to the store. She put the dead chickens in a tub alongside the structure and hurried to the campfire for a kettle of heating water.

She knew three officials had arrived and were now in the trading post, but now two others, most likely their guides, warmed themselves outside at the fire. She'd forgotten there were more men. "Good day," she said pleasantly.

The pair in typically soiled frontier garb stared openmouthed at her. "Good day to ye," one managed.

"There's tea inside the trading post, if you'd like to have some."

"Nay, miss," one with a frizzy red beard said. "We'd just as soon do our restin' outta the way, if ye know what I mean."

"Aye." His ragamuffin partner chuckled.

"As you wish." She bunched a handful of her apron in one hand and grasped the water kettle suspended over the fire. "We'll be having our Sabbath meal in an hour or so."

"Sabbath meal," one murmured. "Ain't had one o' them in a coon's age."

Starting away with the hot water, Rose turned back with a smile. "Well, I'm pleased to say that today you shall have one."

She returned to the tub, where Shining Star stood staring at the lifeless carcasses. No doubt the Indian girl was curious about the English way of doing things. But Star wasn't the only one engrossed. The men at the fire circle also stared—at Rose. As if she wasn't already nervous enough about the businessmen inside.

She pretended not to notice their ogling as she poured the entire kettle of steaming water over the chickens to loosen the quills. Then she wiped her hands on her stained apron, removed it, and checked her hair. Taking the girl's hand, she headed toward the trading post and entered with Star in tow.

"Good Sabbath, gentlemen." She hoped her smile appeared cheerful.

The fur company officials sprang to their feet, along with Nate, who held Jenny in his arms.

"Good day to you, madam." A man with a long face and a nose to match gave her a slight bow of his head. His gaze made a swift assessment of her appearance but revealed nothing. "I presume you are Mistress Kinyon. Allow me to introduce myself and my companions. I am Mr. Hawkes. To my right is Mr. Jenkins, then Mr. Parker."

Each nodded his head in turn.

She bobbed a curtsy, surprised that Star followed her lead. "I'm pleased to meet all of you. This is Shining Star, our friend Robert Bloom's young charge. I hope you've had some tea. The days have been terribly cold of late."

"Yes," the stocky fellow named Jenkins agreed. "Your husband has already seen to our comfort."

"I was certain he would." Rose gave Nate an adoring glance. "He's always been quite the thoughtful type." She smiled at her frontiersman. "We'll have our Sabbath meal soon."

"Why, I've hardly had a decent meal since we left Virginia," the taller man named Parker mused.

"Nor have I," Mr. Jenkins commented wistfully. "My wife's a wonderful cook."

"Well, today you'll all share our Sabbath meal with us." Travelers—even well-dressed ones—were a sad reminder that men without the comforts of home were quite pitiful creatures. She flicked another glance at Nate, who obviously appreciated her performance. His grin softened his rugged features, adding a spark to his hazel eyes.

Rose returned his grin with flair as she hooked the kettle above the coals again. "Do be seated, gentlemen. And since it will be awhile until our meal is ready, I'm sure my husband will be only too happy to refill your cups, won't you, dear?"

"Of course. Only too happy," he mimicked sweetly.

Ignoring the incorrigible man, Rose could hardly restrain herself from asking the all-important question. Would they accept her as a trader for them or not? Regardless, if Nate had not as yet broached the subject, perhaps the officials would be in a better mood once their stomachs were full. "If you will excuse us, gentlemen, Shining Star and I need to return to our meal preparations. We want this dinner to be especially festive in your honor."

Mr. Hawkes remained standing. "Mistress Kinyon. Am I to assume you are the Miss Harwood for whom I've received letters?"

Rose's pulse throbbed. "Why, yes. Harwood was my maiden name. Have you mail for me? Perhaps a letter from my family in England?" The possibility of hearing from her father made her heart pound.

"No, madam. England, you say. I was quite certain I detected a refined accent in your speech. And you're wed to this. . .woodsman?" He frowned in puzzlement.

How to respond without adding to her guilt. She swallowed the growing lump in her throat. "Cupid's arrow takes the strangest paths, does it not?" Without daring to glance at Nate, she added a little laugh. "If you'll excuse us, we must get to preparing the chickens."

As Nate watched the two women sashay out to the deceased chickens, he had to admit he was quite impressed with his little actress-wife. Rose hadn't spoken a single lying word. Of course, the deception was still there. Smiling, he turned back to the men. "If you're all finished with your drinks, I'll show you the fine pelts we brought in."

Hawkes elevated a haughty brow. "Yes. And the ledger." Without further adieu, he set down his empty cup and stood to his feet. The others got up as well.

Jenny Ann had nodded off, so Nate laid her down in her little pen and covered her. Then he led the three officials to one side of the store, stopping near the pile of prime pelts. "I think you'll like what you see here. Once Eustice caught on to Rose's writin' skill, he had her keep the records."

Hawkes did not reply as his gaze briefly skimmed the bundle. He ran his fingers across Rose's neat display of trenchers filled with different-colored beads. "So where's that ledger?"

Nate plucked the volume off a stack of crates and handed it to the arrogant man. "You'll see everything's in order. After Smith's wife took off, Rose made a full inventory to see what all was missin'—not includin' my horse, that is. A good, sure-footed chestnut gelding. He has two notches in his right ear. If you run across him in your tradin', I'd sure appreciate you buyin' him for me. I'll even give you a profit."

"Yes, yes." The man did not bother to look up from the ledger pages while his cohorts inspected the piles of pelts. After a couple of minutes he raised his head. "Come over here, Jenkins. I say, it's a delight to see everything recorded so neatly and with proper spelling."

Both lackeys hurried to his side and peered over his shoulder at the columns of figures. "Quite right." They nodded in agreement.

"An' if you look around," Nate added, "you'll notice my Rose has a real eye for makin' things look nice. The customers are always sayin' how they like the way she keeps the place. When Eustice died an' them Susquehannocks took off, Chief Red Hawk sent some of his best braves over to protect her an' the store till me an' Bob got back. Everybody here's real pleased with her." He moved a touch closer and lowered his voice. "So we was wonderin' if we could take over for Eustice on a permanent basis. What d'you say?"

Plucking feathers at the tub, Rose craned her ears toward the canvas opening, trying desperately to hear what was transpiring inside the store. She'd sensed from Nate's tight expression that he had yet to speak to suspicious Mr. Hawkes about becoming the new proprietors of the trading post. But alas, the men's conversation was too indistinct for her to make out the words.

Even when Nate's voice ceased and the official began speaking, it was still too quiet to be heard. Waiting, hoping, Rose wished she was inside so she could see their expressions and hear what was being said about her, about the store, about the future.

Abruptly, Nate let out a burst of enthusiasm. "Thank you. You won't be sorry. You'll see." Her heart leaped with joy.

"Now let's have a look at those pelts you've been bragging about," Hawkes said distinctly.

Rose tried to contain the stubborn smile spreading from ear to ear. Leaving Shining Star scraping carrots and squash for the meal, she wiped her hands and approached the entrance, lifted the flap, and stepped inside. "I hope you found everything to be in order, Mr. Hawkes."

He turned to her with his first genuine smile. "Why, yes, Mistress Kinyon. I can certainly see the woman's touch here. It was not what I expected, to be sure. But perhaps I should induce more couples to man our trading posts." He shifted his attention to Nate and gave him a peculiar look.

Wondering if it was a doubtful one after all, Rose let out a breath. "I just came to fetch this kettle." She started toward the hearth. "'Tis delightful having all this company. And with this unexpected gift of a mild, sunny day, 'twould be wonderful to set up a long table outside so we can all share the meal together. Could you fix one up for us, sweetheart?"

Nate glanced around. "I reckon we could make a table out of some crates. Anything for you, honey-pie."

"And a bolt of color covering it would look rather festive, don't you think?"

As the men all came to their feet with ready grins, Rose had a comical thought. If only her ever-so-proper family could see her holding court for an assortment of well-dressed businessmen and their unkempt guides at a splintery crate table! A table covered with—she glanced across the bolts of material—turquoise cotton. Yes. Turquoise to go with today's brilliant sky.

By the time all was ready to serve at the crude dinner table which occupied a spot between the trading post and the outside cook fire, Rose caught a flash of deerskin from the corner of her eye. She saw Shining Star running down the hill to meet Robert Bloom, returning from escorting a pair of braves across the river to help guard the horses of the company men.

Thank You, Father, that he's back in time to join us. Since it was the Sabbath, it would be only proper to ask Bob to give a reading from the Bible. Travelers likely heard the scriptures read about as often as they partook of a proper Sunday dinner.

Stripping off her apron, she went to summon the men to the table. It amazed her to find them still gabbing in the trading post. Wasn't it women who were supposed to be the talkers?

"No," Mr. Hawkes was saying as she walked in. "Venango is—Oh, here comes our lovely hostess." He offered her a polite smile.

Rose couldn't help noticing the sudden halt to their conversation caused by her arrival and smirked. Most likely they'd been swapping naughty stories, as men at the taverns in Bath so often did. Strange, though, she heard none of the usual laughter in this case. "Gentlemen, I've come to announce our Sabbath meal is ready."

As the assembly got up from the sacks and crates on which they'd been sitting, she noticed that all of them had removed their hats and every last one had combed his hair and tied it neatly in a queue. How touching of them to put forth an effort to look presentable.

Outside, Rose hurried to greet Robert, who walked hand in hand with Shining Star, chatting with her.

"I seen that dinner table on my way across the water," he said with a grin. "Couldn't miss the tablecloth. Even the people in the village are gawkin.'"

Rose glanced toward the settlement, noting a number of Indians seated around a fire outside the council house, staring their way. "'Twould seem I've given them something new to talk about, have I not?" Smiling, she turned back to him and Star. "I'd appreciate it very much if you would read a selection of scripture before I ask Nate to give the blessing."

A grin broadened Bob's face. "You're askin' Nate to pray? In front of all them men?"

Rose couldn't stop her own smile from growing. "It seems only proper, since he's the head of the house, so to speak. You sit at one end of the table, and I'll be sure he takes the other."

"What about those company men?"

"Why, Mr. Hawkes will sit at Nate's right hand, of course, and Mr. Parker will sit at your right. They're the two older ones. Mr. Jenkins shouldn't mind."

A laugh rumbled from deep inside Robert, and Star looked up at him with a puzzled expression. Sobering, he spoke a few words to her in her language, and they started walking again. "Everybody's standin' 'round the table, Rose. You'd best get up there to that fancy little tea party of yours."

Chapter 29

B e careful for nothing,' " Bob read, " 'but in every thing by prayer and supplication with thanksgiving let your requests be made known unto God.' "

Seated on a keg at the opposite end of the makeshift table, Nate's mind drifted from the scripture reading and floated to Rose, on his left, while Jenny, dozing on a pallet on the ground beside her, nuzzled with a handmade rag doll. Rose had accomplished so much in two hours. Not only had she put together a fine meal, but she'd found time to don a daygown he'd never seen before. The cornflower-blue material seemed to light up her azure eyes, and the faint scent of rose water she had used on her long, honey-colored hair danced across his nostrils on the light breeze. A few loose silky strands glistened in the firelight, free from the blue ribbon that tied the remainder at the nape of her neck.

The heady aroma of chicken and dumplings overtook her sweet scent and made his mouth water. He couldn't wait to taste them and the beans, carrots, squash, and biscuits lining the table, along with a metal pitcher of fresh milk and a container of butter.

Everything looked appealing on the sea of turquoise fabric, despite the mismatched trenchers, tin plates, and utensils that had been gathered for use. His English Rose had come a long way from the frightened young woman he'd first met. And glancing around the table, he realized his was not the only admiring glance she drew. When the men weren't staring wide eyed at the array of food, they were enthralled with Rose. His *wife*. To make certain everyone understood he had prior claim to the British beauty, he reached over and took one of her hands where it lay on the table.

Her gaze flew to his then quickly calmed. A soft smile lit her eyes, and she lowered her lashes.

Nate leaned close and whispered in her ear, "Everything's nice. Real nice."

Thank you, she mouthed then returned her attention to Bob.

Keeping hold of her hand for good measure, Nate made a real effort to shift his attention to his friend for the remainder of the reading.

" 'Finally, brethren, whatsoever things are true, whatsoever things are honest, whatsoever things are just, whatsoever things are pure, whatsoever things are lovely, whatsoever things are of good report; if there be any virtue, and if there be any praise, think on these things.' "

Nate wondered if Bob had deliberately chosen that scripture to chastise Rose or him. Most likely both. How much longer was the chapter, anyway?

" 'Those things, which ye have both learned, and received, and heard, and seen in me, do: and the God of peace shall be with you.' " Closing the Bible, Bob looked up with a satisfied smile. "May God bless the reading of His Word." His gaze moved to Nate. "And now our host will bless the food."

Caught completely off guard, Nate barely managed to keep his mouth from falling open.

Rose squeezed his hand, and an impish spark in her eyes went right along with her pleased smile.

Well, he played his games and she played hers. He could do this. Drawing a calming breath, he stood and bowed his head. "Our Father, which art in heaven, bless this food an' the lovely hands that prepared it, in Jesus' name, Amen."

A rather contrite "Amen" echoed around the table as he regained his seat and the men reached eagerly for bowls of food. Once everyone had filled their plates and commenced eating, compliments rained on Rose.

"I can't tell you," a guide named Davis gushed for about the dozenth time, "how good these here dumplin's be. I ain't had none like these in two, three years."

A slight pink tinge heightened Rose's coloring as she smiled. "I do thank you. When we've finished, I've a surprise for you all."

All eyes swung to her as the visitors continued to stuff themselves.

"There are trees in this area that bear a lovely red-orange fruit the Shawnees like to cook. Nate told me they're called persimmons. I've added some persimmon, along with nuts and spices, to a pudding I hope you'll find quite tasty."

One of the longhunters slid a sidelong glance toward Nate. "If'n you ever take a notion to get shed o' that useless man o' yourn, I'd be mighty pleased to take you to wife."

"And I'd be mighty pleased to crack that head of yours wide open," Nate grumbled. He started to get up.

Rose caught his arm. "Darling, he's merely jesting."

Uncoiling, Nate sank back onto the keg. He felt a little foolish, but her calling him "darling" did much to ease his ire. Too bad it was all for show.

Mr. Hawkes, on his other side, chuckled. "Being the husband of the only white woman in the whole of the Ohio Valley must be quite a challenge."

Turning to the man, Nate propped up a smile. "You might say that, especially since you brought this wolf pack here with you."

"And especially since you're wed to an exceptionally lovely lady." Hawkes gave Rose a gracious nod.

"Thank you, kind sir." She graced him with a smile then looked down the table toward Bob.

Nate caught her worried glance but breathed with relief when he saw his partner totally absorbed in quiet conversation with Shining Star.

Mr. Hawkes shifted his gaze toward the village. "I've noticed an unusual amount of attention coming from the Indians, as well."

Since most of the villagers were taking advantage of the unseasonably mild temperature, reminiscent of an Indian summer day, a good number of them did happen to be looking toward their festive gathering. "We never took our Sabbath meal at table before. Most of 'em have prob'ly never seen such a sight, us eatin' out here like this."

Rose touched his arm. "Sweetheart, we should invite the chiefs and their families to a Sabbath meal soon."

Hawkes returned his attention to her. "Ah. So your true goal, Mistress Kinyon, is to civilize the savages, then."

She shrugged a shoulder. "The Good Book says we're to love our neighbors, and they are my neighbors."

"We can only hope and pray it will always be that way." The official relaxed on his seat. Nate sensed a covert meaning hidden within those benign-sounding words and wasn't surprised when Hawkes turned to him. "I'm rather surprised that none of those *neighbors* dropped by the trading post as yet to look over the new goods we brought."

Nate cocked his head back and forth. "They'll hightail it up here once you leave."

"Mebbe the redskins don't like the way we smell." The red-bearded longhunter whacked his thigh in mirth then sobered. "Beggin' your pardon, ma'am."

Hawkes cut a glance to his partners then back at Nate. "I'll settle up with you, so we can load up the bundles of furs and be out of here at first light. And if I don't see you then, I want to thank you again for manning the trading post so efficiently since Mr. Smith's untimely death, and for locating so many prime pelts for the company on your trip downstream."

Rose came to her feet, and every man present started scrambling to his. "Please, gentlemen, remain seated. I'm merely going to fetch the spiced persimmon pudding."

"Spiced persimmon pudding," young Mr. Jenkins echoed on a wistful breath. "Sounds like music to my ears."

Kinda like her voice sounds to mine. Nate followed Rose's movements as she walked away. He liked the way she moved. In fact, he liked a whole lot of things about Rose Harwood. She seemed to grow on him more with each passing hour.

If only she'd change her mind about *him.*

⌒

As the sky darkened and bright stars spangled the clear, cool expanse overhead, Rose took the baby inside her wigwam to settle her down for the night. Nate was relieved and gladdened as he sat bundled in a fur robe around the outside fire with the three company men and Bob, and Bob's Indian maiden, of course. She was never far from him. The last of the counting in the trading post was done, of stock coming in and furs going out. And Nate had a cup of hot tea in his hand and plenty of coin jingling in his pouch. Rose would be real pleased.

Music from a reed flute drifted from the Shawnee village, with drums throbbing a beat.

"What does that mean?" Alarm rang in Mr. Parker's voice.

"Just makin' music." Bob's gaze gravitated to Shining Star. "Prob'ly just some young bucks tryin' to impress a shy maiden."

Nate chuckled. "Or they're lettin' us know we're not the only ones who can have a party."

Mr. Jenkins nodded. "They did seem quite interested in our dinner. They must have been curious about what we were all saying."

Leaning forward, Mr. Hawkes's expression looked deadly serious in the firelight. "There's something I forgot to mention earlier. The reason Joe Frazier wasn't at his trading post was because he was out looking for his villagers. They'd all disappeared during the night. They knew the French were coming and didn't want to get caught in the middle. Even though they prefer our goods, they're more than willing to trade with whoever sets up a post, English or French."

"That's good to know." Nate rubbed his chin in thought, wondering if these Shawnee villagers would prove to be as disloyal.

Shining Star seemed to detect the seriousness of the moment. Her slender brows knitted with concern, she quietly spoke to Bob. His answer seemed to satisfy her, and she relaxed against him again.

From the corner of his eye, Nate caught a flash of movement. "Here comes Rose," he said in a low voice, then raised the volume. "Has the Potomac started freezin' yet? The stream behind the corrals was frozen half the mornin' yesterday."

"No, not yet." Mr. Hawkes rose to his feet. "Mistress Kinyon, do join us."

"Why thank you." She came into the light, her heavy woolen cloak snug around her.

Nate flashed her a grin. "I take it you got our little Jenny-girl all settled down for the night, my love."

The smile she offered did look genuine as she plucked a cup off a nearby rock and poured some tea from the kettle. "Hopefully, yes."

Pulling back the robe covering his legs, he patted the spot next to him on the sitting log. "Come sit with me, sweetheart." He sure did like playing the part of her husband. Maybe soon. . .

As Rose complied, Nate draped an arm about her shoulders, surprised when she actually leaned into him—even if it was only ever so slightly.

She took a sip of her tea. "I've a fire going in all the wigwams to warm them up. And I've placed blankets and fur robes in the large one over there." She pointed to the one the Susquehannock brothers had used. "Of course, you may want to add your own bedding. It seems to be turning quite chilly."

"Thank you," Mr. Hawkes said with a polite bow of his head. "You've been a far more gracious hostess than we could ever have imagined."

"Well, I do hope your workmen won't mind staying in the trading post."

"That's better accommodations than they've had on the trail thus far."

Young Mr. Jenkins leaned forward. "Where exactly did you come from in England, Mistress Kinyon? I hope to go to Britain for a visit one day soon."

Rose smiled at him. "Were you to make port at Bristol, you'd not be far from my city, Bath."

"I've heard of that place. Isn't that where all the rich people go on holiday?"

"Why, yes, it is." She settled more comfortably at Nate's side. "They come to soak in the hot mineral springs and to take in the plays and balls, of course. But I prefer to think that more importantly, they come to see and be seen. I'm sure you'd enjoy a visit there most thoroughly."

Watching Mr. Hawkes, Nate perceived the man's suspicious nature coming again to the fore as he stared at Rose as if she were telling lies. He had the greatest urge to blacken that company man's judging eyes.

"And you left all that for *this*?" Hawkes made a wide arc with his arm.

She stiffened a bit. "I'm afraid you misunderstood me, sir. Bath was my home, not a place I visited. My father owns a small shop there."

Jenkins brightened. "Perhaps you could persuade your father to carry some of our furs."

"That sounds quite lovely, but for the shops in Bath they'd need to be fashioned into elegant wraps and other accessories."

Thin Mr. Parker finally entered the conversation. "No wonder Mistress Kinyon is well accomplished in the art of display, being the daughter of a shopkeeper."

Nate felt Rose relax again as a small laugh bubbled out of her. "Actually, I learned far more from visiting other shops, if you must know."

The statement puzzled Nate. He'd never thought of her as a spendthrift.

Jenkins looked from her to Nate and back to her. "From what I've heard, the English have the finest shops in the world, with treasures brought in from all the most exotic places around the globe. Coming to the colonies, and then out here to the wilderness, must have been quite a dramatic change for you."

Still smiling, she tilted her head. "More so for my sister. More often than not, I was accompanying her in her quest for the latest fabrics and trims."

"I see."

Mr. Hawkes frowned. "Your sister came to America with you?"

Even Nate felt Rose's sharp intake of breath, as if their nosy employer was beginning to wear on her the way he was on Nate.

"Quite right. She currently resides with a plantation family adjacent to the Potomac River."

"You don't say." His interest obviously piqued, Hawkes straightened. "Perhaps I know them."

"Are you acquainted with the Barclay family?"

"The Barclays! Of Barclay Enterprises?" He shook his head in disbelief. "Why in the world would a lady like yourself allow Kinyon to drag you this deep into Indian country?"

At this, Nate reached the boiling point. Employer or not, the bounder needed his face smashed in. Pulling his arm from behind Rose, he—

Her elbow jabbed sharply into his rib, effectively stopping him. Then she casually stood to her feet. "I prefer to think of my sojourn here as a wondrous adventure. It's been a rather long day, however, so if I don't see you before you leave in the morning, it's been a true treat having you visit us, even for such a short time."

All the men got up, and Nate put his arm around her again. "Aye. It's been a big day. Good evenin', gents."

Leaving the others behind, Nate escorted Rose to her wigwam. Reaching it, he pulled back the flap for her then entered behind her. He dropped the covering closed with a smile.

She swung to face him, hands on her hips, eyes flashing in the light of the fire. Her harsh whisper broke the silence. "What do you think you're doing?"

"Your *husband* is coming to bed," he countered in a blithe whisper of his own, definitely not wanting to wake Jenny.

She flung a look of panic in the direction of the others then turned back to him, her jaw set.

Just then the flap opened, and Shining Star slipped in.

Ruining the moment.

Nate had forgotten the girl stayed with Rose. Worse yet, Bob had probably sent her running in here. Black Horse Bob, the guardian of everyone's virtue.

His gaze returned to Rose. Her expression of panic was now one of renewed confidence as she tipped her head.

"You're absolutely right. We must not make our employers suspicious, must we?" A smile spread across her face. "You may sleep across the fire on Shining Star's pallet, Nate, and she"—Rose rested a hand on the girl's shoulder—"can sleep over here, with Jenny Ann and me."

Chapter 30

Rose felt something tickling her nose. *Nate?* Her eyes sprang open and met Jenny's sweet smile. Capturing the baby's little fingers, Rose kissed them. Was anyone else awake? She raised her head to peek over Star's sleeping form and saw Nate also asleep on the opposite side of the fire pit. It must be very early, or only a little past dawn on a gray morning. Her eyes roved over the fur-shrouded frontiersman as he lay there, and a smile tugged at her lips. After all his tossing and turning last night, he needed the extra sleep.

Still in her clothes from yesterday, she bundled Jenny, eased up off the sleeping pallet, and slipped outside with her.

Mr. Hawkes and his two companions sat with their backs to her around a roaring fire. They'd truly be off to an early start, Rose mused, heading for the woods.

After seeing to her morning needs, she plucked the covered milk pail from the thin film of ice surrounding it in the stream and started back. Jenny Ann would be patient for only so long.

She could see the workers loading bundles of pelts down at the river as she came up behind her three employers. "Good morning, gentlemen."

The threesome turned to her, all smiles, and spoke as one. "Good morning, Mistress Kinyon."

"I trust you slept well."

Mr. Hawkes nodded. "It was a pleasure not to have to erect tents. The fire kept us quite comfortable."

She smiled and set down the pail. As she reached into a sack and removed a small pan, he got up and came forward. "Let me hold your little one for you. She reminds me of my grandbaby back home."

"Why, thank you." She handed Jenny to him then poured milk into the pan and set it on one of the rocks surrounding the fire pit. "I like to warm her milk on cold mornings." She glanced up at the official. "What's your grandbaby's name, Mr. Hawkes?"

"Arthur. Arthur Hawkes. My daughter-in-law insisted on naming him after me. We call him Arty. He was seven months old when I left on this trip. How old is your little girl?"

"She's—what's the date? I'm afraid I've lost count." Rose felt her cheeks warm.

The man chuckled. "That's easy to do out here, so far away from everything. Today's the third of December." He patted Jenny's back then turned to his companions. "You two go join the others. I need to speak to Mistress Kinyon alone. I'll be along directly."

A niggle of unease made Rose's heart skip a beat. Had he discovered the deception?

His expression gave no indication of censure. After the men had left, he met her gaze. "I must ask you, are you truly here of your own free will, mistress? You may speak frankly to me."

Relieved that he was merely concerned for her welfare, Rose gave a polite nod. "Yes, of course. Point of fact, 'twas entirely my idea. A way for us to earn a goodly amount of money in a relatively short time."

A frown furrowed the man's forehead. "But a decision of that magnitude requires considerably more experience than you possess."

Rose's pulse increased. Surely he was not reneging! Not after all her and Nate's efforts to convince him of their capabilities.

"You came out here with Eustice Smith this summer, did you not?"

She reached down for the pan so he wouldn't see her face. "Yes.

237

'Tis true." Had Mr. Smith informed the fur company about her, his bondservant?

"Then you weren't here during the time of the spring raids, when captives are brought in, were you?"

Remembering Jenny Ann's mother, Rose barely kept herself from shuddering as she poured milk into a tin cup. Amazing how she'd blocked the poor woman's dreadful fate from her mind already.

Hawkes stepped closer. "Torture is the Indians' favorite entertainment. They delight in keeping their victims screaming for days on end before the poor devils finally die. They derive some kind of perverse pleasure in causing people to suffer unspeakable horrors."

Her chest tightening, Rose reached for Jenny and took her from the official. "I'm sure you must be exaggerating. I've heard of the gauntlet captives must run through to be worthy of joining the tribe. 'Tis an initiation, I believe. The lads at university do no less."

Mr. Hawkes wagged his head and scoffed. "Listen to me, you silly woman. That's only for the ones the Indians intend to adopt into the tribe. Captured braves and other unfortunate individuals are another matter entirely. Some of them are taken with the prior intent to *be* tortured for the tribe's amusement."

Stunned, Rose sank down onto the log to feed the baby. What a fool she'd been to excuse so lightly the mind-set of the Indian.

"I can understand your wanting to be here to trade when the trappers bring in the winter furs. Granted. But know this—" He flicked a gaze beyond her.

Giving the baby a sip, Rose looked up to see Robert striding toward them.

Hawkes gave him a courteous nod. "It's just as well you're here to hear this. I'll be sending replacements out here no later than April 1. I will not be party to having Mistress Kinyon and her babe around when the spring raids start. Is that clear?"

Robert glanced at Rose then back at the official. "I wholeheartedly agree. We'll be packed an' ready. Don't much relish bein' here myself then."

Hawkes tipped his hat to Rose. "I shall look forward to seeing you at our headquarters this spring." He pivoted on his heel and started to leave.

"I bid you Godspeed, Mr. Hawkes," she called after him. "We shall pray for your safety."

He stopped and swung back, looking from her to Robert and back again. "You look after yourself, too."

Rose sensed from the queer looks passing between her friend and the official that something serious was being left unsaid. But what?

Allowing grabby little Jenny to hold her own cup, Rose could wait no longer. She looked up at Nate's partner. "Robert, 'tis quite obvious you and Mr. Hawkes went to great lengths to keep something from me. I must know what it is."

From his demeanor, she could tell she had him cornered.

"I'm not— Oh look. Here comes Nate."

Approaching the fire, Nate gave a huge grin, directing his gaze at Rose. "Mornin'." Then he tipped his head in the direction of the riverbank. "I see the men are ready to push off. I'd sure hate to be out on that icy river before the sun has a chance to warm things up." He gave the departing company men a jaunty wave, then grabbing a cup from the sack, he poured himself some tea and came to sit next to Rose and the baby.

She took a slow, calming breath. "It seems Robert and Mr. Hawkes are keeping a secret from me, Nate. One I'm sure you must be privy to." She arched a brow.

He shot his pal a serious glower. "You don't say."

Robert shrugged. "Hawkes says he's sendin' replacements out here by the first of April. Looks like all that fine playactin' of yours didn't make much difference. You're still gonna be tossed out."

"'Twas not like that." Rose let out a huff. "Not like that at all." She took the cup from Jenny and wiped the child's face and neck with her apron. "Mr. Hawkes doesn't want me here in the spring when the Shawnees start bringing in captives."

239

Nate kneaded his chin in thought. "Ah yes, the spring raids. I'd say the decision's for the best. You an' Jenny Ann need to be away from here then. Somewhere safe."

Recalling Hannah Wright and her needless death, Rose couldn't fault any of them for their reasoning. "I suppose you're right." She picked up the baby and kissed her plump cheek. "But I shall hate having to give up Jenny. I'm afraid I've become quite attached to the little angel."

Nate ruffled the towhead's silky curls, making her giggle. "She is a cutie, no doubt about that."

"And then of course," Rose continued, "there are my sisters. I shan't have nearly enough money by April. Nor will I have this sort of opportunity ever again."

"Greedy, greedy." With a teasing smirk, Nate got up.

The accusation irked Rose. She stood to face him straight on. "'Tis not for me, and you very well know it."

"Aye. I know." His expression sobered. "Tell you what. I'm willin' to give you whatever I earn in tradin' between now an' then to help. How's that?"

She opened her mouth to protest, but he turned to his partner. "What say we go take care of the stock while the gals fix breakfast?"

Robert slid a longing look over at Rose's wigwam.

Clapping him on the back, Nate snickered. "Don't worry, pal. Your little darlin'll be up an' about soon enough. I saw her sneakin' peeks at me while I was gettin' up."

He grunted then started after Nate for the animal pens. "Shining Star knows you had no business spendin' the night in there."

Rose couldn't let that pass. "'Twas all my fault," she called after them. They swiveled to face her. "What webs we do weave when we try to deceive. . .or something to that effect." Blushing, she hung her head.

But not before she caught Nate's grin. "No. Exactly like that!" He gave a hoot over his shoulder as he continued toward the stock. "Exactly like that."

A cluster of Shawnee on their way to the trading post passed Nate and Bob as the two of them hiked toward the center of the village. "They're over there, in front of Red Hawk's wigwam." Bob pointed with his decorated Indian pipe.

"Good. Cornstalk's there, too." Nate picked up the pace. "Might as well get this over with."

Obviously having spied them approaching, Red Hawk raised his hand and motioned for Nate and Bob to come join him. "Greetings," he said, the word heavily accented as they reached the campfire. "Sit."

Nate knew that was pretty much the extent of Red Hawk's English, but he appreciated the attempt, since his own knowledge of the Shawnee language was equally lacking. "Greetings." He smiled and nodded at Cornstalk and a couple of older Indians as he took a seat alongside Bob on a coarse buffalo hide.

Bob took a tobacco pouch from his pocket, pouring and tamping a portion into the bowl of his pipe. He plucked a stick from the fire and lit the pipe, drawing a couple of puffs to get it going. He then handed it with both hands to Red Hawk.

As the chief took his time smoking the pipe, Nate sensed the man was particularly enjoying tobacco that had been cured on the plantations back east.

While Red Hawk was occupied, Bob started a conversation in Shawnee with Cornstalk. After the brave's response, he turned to Nate. "He says the music last night was as I figgered. One of the young bucks was tryin' to make time with a maiden by impressin' her with his skill on the flute."

"Oh, the webs their sweet smiles weave for us to get caught in." Nate chuckled, remembering Rose's remark.

Bob laughed also, and Cornstalk interrupted with a question. When Bob translated for him, all the Indians present laughed and nodded at Nate.

Once the pipe had made the rounds and returned to Bob, Nate nudged him. "Mebbe it's a good time to mention that invite to dinner for the chiefs an' their families."

"They're gonna consider it pretty strange, you know."

"Aye." Nate shrugged. "But no more strange than all of us sharin' the same pipe is to me, a white man."

Bob turned his attention to the two chiefs. Nate recognized Rose's name a time or two in the conversation and watched the older men exchange disbelieving glances.

Finally Red Hawk's feathered headdress bobbed as he met Nate's gaze with a nod and laughed.

Bob grinned along with them. "They say they'd be pleased to accept."

"Yeah, but what's so all-fired funny?" Nate frowned, looking around at all the amused expressions.

"I'll explain later. First, I'd better ask if they know anythin' about the attack on the tradin' post at the Seneca village at Venango."

Unable to understand the proceedings, Nate could only watch expressions and draw his own conclusions. The Indians seemed surprised that the French had seized Frazier's trading post, but he couldn't tell if it was an act being put on for his and Bob's benefit.

Nate was pretty sure he knew what Bob was relating, and he watched especially close for the slightest flicker of an eye, any telltale fidgeting. Still, nothing sinister seemed apparent while Cornstalk and Red Hawk both took turns answering. But then, red men were noted for being stoic when they wanted to be.

After a few moments of lighter conversation, Bob hiked his chin at Nate. "I reckon we better get back an' help Rose. There's prob'ly a crowd at the store by now."

Once they'd said their good-byes and were far enough away, Nate turned to his pal. "Well? What'd they say? Are they willin' to stay loyal to us, knowin' the French are both downriver an' upriver from here?"

He shrugged. "They gave me the same ol' speech. Our trade goods are better, an' the Shawnees are stronger an' braver than any Seneca ever thought of bein'. An' Cornstalk said the French bleed just like the Seneca."

"That sounds fine an' good. But did they come right out an' say they'd stay loyal?"

Coming to an abrupt halt, Bob looked him square in the eye. "Come to think of it, they never actually said those words."

Nate gave him a thoughtful nod. "Winter's almost on us. Not even the French should be out makin' trouble this time of year." He paused. "By the way, why were the Indians laughin' at me when you asked the chiefs to dinner?"

"Oh that." A grin crawled across Bob's irksome face. "They said Rose was—what was that word? Oh yeah. She's got you *henpecked* real good."

Nate drilled him with his most menacing glare. "An' who, might I ask, gave 'em that idea?"

Instead of showing the least amount of remorse, Bob threw back his head and howled with laughter. His next words came out in a sputter. "You're even startin' to sound all uppity, just like her."

Chagrined, Nate gave a resigned nod. "You're right, ol' buddy. But if I'm henpecked, you're nothin' but a flop-eared hound, moonin' after your Shining Star. That's some lovesick name you labeled her with, by the way."

Bob gave a helpless, palms-up shrug. "Right. Absolutely right. Looks like both of us have turned into nothin' but a couple of ol' lap dogs. But ain't it fun!"

Chapter 31

What a long, busy day. Though chilly from the store's flap being opened so often, Rose was elated at the number of Shawnee who'd come to check out the trading post's new stock. She waved good-bye to one of the few Shawnee squaws who'd actually made a purchase, as the woman left with yard goods and a pair of scissors. Rose had also sold her a needle and thread from her own sewing basket, knowing that when she returned to civilization in a few months, her sewing supply could be replenished.

She marveled at the bargain she'd made and entered the sale into the ledger. Then, as she folded a muskrat robe, a smile twitched her lips. Not long ago she'd eaten Fawn Woman's muskrat stew and envisioned a wiry-haired, beady-eyed rat was in her mouth. Rose shook her head at the memory. Fortunately she'd never had to eat muskrat stew again.

Laying the robe in the now empty corner where only yesterday huge bundles of furs had been stacked, she heard excited Shawnee voices at the other end of the store. She turned to see an older squaw talking animatedly to a younger Indian mother toting a baby in a cradleboard on her back.

Rose looked at Shining Star, who picked up Jenny Ann, and together they crossed to the chattering pair. Rose smiled as the older one held a pair of eyeglasses up to her face and moved her hand in front of them. "Ah, the eyeglasses." Rose plucked another pair from the basket and unfolded the arms then placed the glasses on her own face to demonstrate their purpose.

The squaw grinned and nodded then took the spectacles in her hand and held them out to Rose.

Rose cupped a number of beads in her palm and showed them to the woman, who laughed with joy and said something to the young mother and Shining Star. Rose wished she'd learned a little of the language so she could share in the woman's discovery.

The squaw turned to Rose again and pointed to a large wooden comb fastened above one of her coiled ebony plaits. A pair of deer were intricately carved across its width. She pointed to the spectacles, indicating her desire to trade the comb for the glasses.

Rose smiled sadly and gave a negative wag of her head.

At that, the older Indian looked herself over then scanned her young companion. Surely she didn't covet the spectacles so much she'd offer to trade the mother for them! But the squaw nudged the mother around and grabbed hold of the cradleboard instead.

Rose's mouth gaped in surprise. No one would offer a baby in trade!

Just then, Nate and Robert entered the store, their faces glowing from the cold. Rose was vastly relieved to have an interpreter. She looked up at Robert. "Is this woman hoping to trade the baby for a pair of eyeglasses?"

Robert spoke to the squaw in her language, and she laughed and shook her head vigorously. Her answer set Robert, Star, and the young mother all snickering.

Chagrined, Rose knew the joke was on her.

Still chuckling, Robert let her in on it. "Bird Woman wants to trade the cradleboard for the eyeglasses."

With a surge of relief, Rose sought Nate's advice. "Do you consider this a good trade, Nate? I'm not accustomed to trading in anything but furs."

He winked at her, a spark of devilment glinting in his eyes. "Honey-pie, a trade's always good if both parties're satisfied. Are you satisfied?"

In no mood for his antics, she ignored his playful tone and stuck to business. "Yes, of course. But we're partners, you and I. What profit would there be for you if I were to accept a cradleboard in trade? The fur company pays only for furs."

He grunted. "I know one thing for sure. My poor arms would profit. I must'a toted Jenny around half the day yesterday. What've you been feedin' her, anyway?"

With a good-natured glare, Rose relented. "Oh, very well." She turned to the squaw with a smile. "Oui-saw."

When the last customers finally left the store, Star took Jenny to the wigwam to change her diaper and lace her into the cradleboard.

Watching after the Indian maiden, Rose caught Robert observing his young charge's departure with longing and gave his arm a pat. "She's such a dear girl and so helpful. I do hope she comes to know the Lord. I'd be very disappointed if we had to leave her here."

He tilted his dark head at Rose, his expression serious. "That's somethin' I pray about all the time. But if I can't marry her myself, I should be checkin' out some of the unmarried Shawnee braves. I wouldn't want her with a man who already has another wife to lord it over her."

Warming himself at the nearby hearth, Nate swung around. "You ain't still thinkin' about leavin' that gal here, are you?"

His friend turned somber eyes on Nate. "I ain't mentioned anything about it to her yet, 'cause I'm afraid she'll pretend to become a Christian just to please me. I want her to become a true believer. It should come from her heart."

"But how could you just hand her over to some brave?" Nate tucked his chin. "You love her. Any fool can see that."

A long braid fell forward as Bob hung his head. "Aye. I love her. But it was wrong to let myself grow so fond of her. The Bible makes it plain that a Christian shouldn't be unequally yoked. I'm thankful I got Rose around here to keep me thinkin' straight." He narrowed his gaze and turned to her. "'Cept you're doin' a better job with me than I done with you over that playactin'."

Humbled by her own guilt, Rose nodded. "I'm so sorry. You're quite right. I now realize things would've turned out the same with those company men had I not resorted to lies. I shall do my best not to weaken again, no matter what." Her gaze gravitated to Nate. *No matter how hard it might be.*

Nate's eyes flashed with anger as he took her by the shoulders. "Are you tellin' me that unless I toe that holier-than-thou line of yours you won't ever marry me?"

Rose yearned to inch back from his accusation, but his strong hands clamped her to the spot. She inhaled a calming breath. Then the full meaning of his words dawned on her. She raised her lashes and peered up into his eyes. "You've never asked me to marry you."

His mouth opened with a confused sputter, and his expression became gentle. "Well, I am now." Releasing her from his grip, he lowered his arms to his sides and gazed into her soul. "Marry me, Rose."

Aching at his vulnerability, Rose moistened her lips and shot a helpless look to Robert but found no help there. She lifted a silent plea to heaven for the right words, words that she had to utter, even though she knew they'd wound Nate deeply. She tried to delay the inevitable. "I had no idea you actually wanted me for a wife."

He rolled his eyes and shook his head. "What do you think we been dancin' around all this time?"

"I was of the opinion you cherished your wanderlust too much to settle down in one place. You told me as much, if you recall."

Averting his gaze for a second, he shrugged. "I know, but I'm sure we could work somethin' out that'd make both of us happy."

"Possibly." Her pulse throbbed in her ears. He wanted to marry her! It was the deepest desire of her heart! Only. . .the time had come to lay out the truth. "But there's still the matter of my obeying the Lord's instructions not to be yoked to someone who hasn't put God first in his life. Expecting that standard from Robert but not myself would be unpardonably hypocritical, would it not? I must be true to my faith."

He took a backward step. . .inches that felt like a mile to Rose as he glowered at her through pained eyes. "You have the nerve to say that to me? After all the lyin' we done yesterday?" He let out an exasperated huff. "I gotta get outta here." Wheeling around, he stormed out of the trading post. The flap closed with a resounding *slap*.

The clog that formed in Rose's throat made it hard to breathe, hard to talk. Her first impulse was to sink to the floor and weep. But gathering all her strength, she turned to Robert. "He's right. I've been such a hypocrite. May God forgive me."

He came closer and wrapped an arm around her, hugging her close. "Ain't none of us gets it right all the time. I'm real glad Jesus died to pay the penalty for our sins, or we'd never get to heaven on our own."

The tears Rose struggled so hard to suppress spilled over her lashes and down her face, and it was all she could do to utter a reply. "But what I did was worse than mere lies. I became a stumbling block to someone who desperately needs the Lord. I made it even harder for Nate to seek after God."

Robert didn't respond for a few seconds. He tipped his head with a soft smile. "Well, missy, I reckon the two of us'll have to pray that the Lord'll keep after both Nate and Star, while we try harder to stay outta God's way. The Bible does say nothin's too hard for God."

~

Waking up *again*, Nate gritted his teeth. It wasn't bad enough lying wide awake on his sleeping pallet for hours, jumping at every night sound, before finally nodding off. Now he was fully conscious again. And it was all that blasted woman's fault. Staring into the pitch darkness, he gave a disgusted huff. Dawn was nowhere near coming.

If it was light out, at least he could get up and go chop wood—or better yet, wring Rose's neck. Anything to work off the rage churning inside him. Funny, he'd actually expected her to loosen up from her judging ways after living out here without all the stuffiness of the rigid do's and don'ts from back east. He snorted in scorn. Sure, he was good enough to come to her rescue and save her skin now and again, but not good enough to be her husband. She was nothin' but a user. A useless, mealymouthed user. That woman could give the worst hypocrite a few lessons.

He smirked. And wasn't she nice as pie at supper, smiling that timid little smile as she served him first, givin' him the biggest chunk of corn bread. Oh yeah, she wouldn't think of marryin' him, but she still wanted to keep him on her leash. She—

A scraping sound interrupted his musings. Scraping and crunching. . .ice crunching from the direction of the river. Like canoes coming ashore!

Lunging to his feet, Nate sprang to the wigwam's opening and peeked out.

The faintest silhouettes of several large canoes were gliding to shore, canoes holding a good twenty men each. Two had already come in, and the disembarked men were sneaking onto the beach.

Why hadn't the village dogs announced the arrival of strangers?

Moving away from the opening, Nate turned around and knelt beside Bob, placing a hand over his partner's mouth. "We're bein' attacked!" he rasped under his breath. "They're comin' ashore now!"

Chapter 32

Bob shot to his feet, fully alert. "Attacked! Who is it? French or Indians?"

"Can't tell."

Both men grabbed their moccasins and fur robes in one hand and their weapons with the other. Crouching low in the darkness, they bolted from their wigwam to the one housing the girls.

"Don't make a sound," Nate cautioned under his breath as he slipped inside.

A step behind him, Bob went immediately to Shining Star's pallet and murmured quiet words to wake her.

Nate knelt by Rose and gently shook her shoulder.

"What?" came her groggy voice.

"Shh. Get up!" he whispered. "Grab your shoes an' cloak. We gotta get out of here. Now." Stuffing his hatchet and knife in his belt, he gingerly lifted the sleeping baby and her coverings.

"But we're not dressed," Rose protested softly.

Nate tried not to lose patience. "Shoes, cloak, an' follow me. Now!"

Peering out the opening while the women grabbed what they could, he saw that the invaders onshore were waiting for the other canoes. He was thankful that the trading post's location, near the edge of the forest a good hundred yards from the beach, gave them the precious time needed to slip into the woods.

There was no moon to give away their presence, but that meant there was no light to guide their way either. Still in his bare feet, Nate handed the baby to Rose and tugged her along by the shoulder. "Keep low," he whispered, leading her behind the wigwam.

Hastening after him, Rose emitted a grunt of pain, and Nate regretted none of them had shoes on as yet. The ground was bitterly cold and damp from recent snow flurries, not the best for undetected flight.

They passed the chicken pen and skirted the corral.

Rose stopped. "Are we not taking horses?" she hissed.

"No. No time. Come on."

"But—we could go faster."

"And noisier. Anyway, they'll serve a better purpose right now."

He nodded to Bob and his friend opened the gate of the corral, shooing the horses out so they'd scatter and cover any trail they left behind. Feeling his way through the snagging brush and trees, Nate wished he had the luxury of a torch to light their way, but that was out of the question until they were sure they weren't being followed.

In back of him a twig snapped. "Try to step softly," he muttered to Rose without bothering to slow down.

From off in the distance they heard triumphant shouts and blood-curdling Indian yips.

Nate raised an arm to stop his small group. "Don't make a sound." As they halted, he craned his ears to the ominous melee echoing from their camp. The glow from several fires began to flicker through the forest growth.

"Our wigwams," Bob muttered. "Just ours, from the look of it. Has to be the French an' some of their Seneca buddies."

"Aye. And wasn't it nice of 'em to send us a beacon to keep us goin' straight," Nate grumbled bitterly.

"Well, let's get our shoes on whilst they're busy an' lace the baby in the cradleboard," Bob suggested.

"You brung the cradleboard?"

"Shining Star thought to grab it. That an' some extra blankets."

"Bless her," Rose said on a breathless whisper. "Someone take Jenny while I put on my shoes. Then Star can strap the carrier onto me."

Nate took the baby and hugged the sweet darling close. "I can't believe how quiet she's bein'."

"She's always been a sound sleeper. But somehow," Rose mused, "I think she knows our lives depend on her silence."

In the gradual lightening of a misty predawn, Rose could see the ground in front of her a bit easier as she followed Nate. And having her stockings and shoes on did much to save her feet from further stubbed toes, scratches, and bruised heels. They'd crossed a couple of streams that were mostly frozen over, but enough water had gotten through the soft leather to keep her feet icy cold. Her toes felt numb and her shoulders ached from the unfamiliar weight of the cradleboard straps, but no one else had voiced a complaint, and she refused to be the first. The Lord and Nate were seeing them to safety. They hadn't detected sounds of anyone following. . .so far.

Fatigue was quickly overtaking her. Rose took a deep breath. How much farther must they go before Nate considered it safe for a few moments' rest?

As if reading her mind, the frontiersman stopped. He turned around and peered over her head at Robert. "There's a good-size stream up ahead. It's mostly frozen, but out in the center the ice looks thin. I'm goin' upstream a little ways. There's bound to be some boulders or a fallen log we can use to get across. Stay with the women. I won't be long."

Watching him go, Rose unhooked the straps from her shoulders and brought the baby around to face her.

Jenny Ann showed all four of her little white teeth in a big smile. Apparently the little imp was enjoying the ride. "Thank You, Lord,"

Rose said in a bright voice to the baby, "for bringing us this cradleboard yesterday." *Yesterday! The Lord provided the item exactly when He knew I'd need it.* The amazing thought awed her.

"Aye," Robert added, "an' thanks for Nate's keen ears last night."

Rose sank down on a decaying log then looked up at Star and patted the spot beside her. As the girl took a seat, Rose turned her gaze toward Robert and saw him retracing their footsteps.

Several feet into the brush, he went still, musket in hand, and swiveled around to check the rear, like the intrepid frontiersmen she'd heard stories about all the way back in England.

"Surely not even Indians could follow our trail in the dark," she ventured. "I could barely see my hand before my face."

"No, they couldn't," he answered over his shoulder. "Not without a torch. The horses probably did much to obliterate our footprints—at least in the beginning. But now that it's gettin' light, they'll pick up our trail soon enough. Then they'll track us. That's why we gotta keep movin.'" He glanced in the direction his partner had taken.

His answer puzzled Rose, and she couldn't keep her emotion from creeping into her voice. "But why would they follow us? They've got the store. Is that not enough?"

He came back to join her and Star. "True, they have the store. But they ain't fixin' on lettin' us go tattle to the English. Leastways not till they finish sewin' up the rest of the Ohio Valley."

Shining Star made a comment to Robert and unhooked a bag from her belt that Rose hadn't noticed before.

Robert strode over to the girl with a smile and lifted her to her feet. He gave her a long hug—the kind Rose wished she'd get from Nate about now. But she knew better than to expect one after the way she'd offended him and the way he'd avoided her all yester's eve.

Releasing Star at last, Bob took the sack and handed it to Rose. "She brought along a bag of cornmeal."

Tears Rose had managed to keep banked throughout the hard night sprang into her eyes, and she gave Shining Star a grateful smile. "Thank

253

you, thank you. Oui-saw." When it came to surviving in the wild, the lass knew ever so much more than she. "We'll be able to feed Jenny a bit of mush, albeit very cold mush."

Leaning the cradleboard against the log, she stood to search around. "What can I use to mix it in?"

"Here." Bob opened the flap of a pack he had strapped across his chest and pulled out a gourd cup.

Deeply appreciative, Rose felt even more inadequate as she took hold of the rustic handle. All of the others had possessed the foresight to bring necessities along, while she'd been so frightened when they'd fled the wigwam, she'd been grateful to discover she'd left her stockings from yesterday stuffed in her shoes.

Nate trotted back downstream along an animal trace shortly after leaving the others. Spotting them up ahead, a rush of relief shot through him to see they were still there and still safe. He slowed to a walk. Unwonted tenderness for Rose crimped his chest as he watched her feeding the baby from a gourd. Drawing closer, he saw mush smeared over half of Jenny's face. Thank goodness someone had thought to bring food for her.

Bob swung from guarding the rear as Nate approached, his expression easing noticeably. "Ain't heard nothin' so far."

All three girls turned their heads toward Nate, and the baby gave him a big smile. Rose and Star sprang to their feet.

"Finish feedin' the little one. I found a crossin' not too far from here." He motioned with his head for Bob to follow him a few feet away from the females, where he spoke in low tones. "How long do you think it'll take them boys to catch up to us?" He eyed the path they'd trodden through the woods. . .more than obvious in the moist ground.

Bob tipped his head. "Three, four hours at most."

"That's what I reckon. When we get up to the log I found, I don't think we'll be able to fool 'em no matter what we do. We can't keep from breakin' up the ice shroudin' it. They'll know we crossed there."

"Then we gotta get these women movin' a whole lot faster." Bob tossed a glance back at them.

"I think our best chance is to make it down to the Ohio as soon as we can."

"Aye. Once we're across, we can do some backtrackin', try to fool 'em then."

"In the meantime, keep on prayin' to that God of yours that we do."

"You, too."

Nate smirked. "I reckon your prayers'll carry a lot more weight than mine."

Bob shrugged. "Do it anyway."

Grunting his doubt, Nate shifted his attention to the women. "Let's go. They're up an' waitin'."

Knowing they had to get to the other side of the stream and down to the river before the trackers made it this far, he set a fast pace up the narrow trace. *If You're listenin', Lord, please let us find a canoe or a raft waitin' on the Ohio when we get there.* Nate knew it wasn't much of a prayer, but he meant every word.

Moments later they came to the pine log he'd found that stretched across the stream. A few thin, broken-off branches stuck up here and there along its length. He leaped off the bank then turned to lift Rose and the baby down to it.

Instead of accepting his assistance, however, she backed up, bumping into Star. She stared at the fallen tree trunk, pointing at the thing in horror. "But—it's covered with ice! Surely you don't expect me to cross on that!"

Rose heard Nate's exasperated huff as he scowled and motioned her forward. His demeanor hardened, and he spoke in a stern but even tone. "We got no choice. 'Sides, it's not as hard as it looks."

She knew he was lying. The likelihood of slipping off the log and crashing through the ice into the dark water beneath sent chills of sheer terror through her. She glanced over her shoulder.

"Go on," Robert urged as Shining Star nudged Rose's shoulder. "We don't have time to waste."

Trembling from head to toe, Rose clenched her teeth and dropped down into Nate's arms.

"I know you got on them slick, leather soles," he said, still holding her. "But I'll be crushin' the ice in front of you. Just hang on to my belt."

She still wasn't convinced. "But—I'm afraid. Not just for me. It's the baby. What if I fall?"

Robert spoke quickly to Star, and the Indian girl immediately unhooked the cradleboard from Rose's back then swung the baby up behind herself with Robert's help.

"Now come on." Nate grabbed Rose's hand and practically dragged her to the log, just past where the roots stuck out. "Stay right there." Leaping onto it with the help of a root, he reached down to her. "Give me your hand, Rose. Now."

Her panic continued to mount. "But. . .I cannot swim."

"You won't have to. You ain't gonna fall. Give me your hand—unless you want me to sling you up over my shoulder an' cart you across that way."

The poor man had come to the limit of his patience. Rose raised her trembling hand. He closed his around it and in one swift haul, had her on top of the log.

One of her feet slipped off the slick tree trunk. She wobbled.

Nate pulled her close. "You can do this."

She looked at him in a silent plea. Beneath her feet, she could tell the log was just as slippery with icy moss as she suspected it would be.

He exhaled a weary breath. "Look, sweetheart, I have my musket right here to help steady me. See?" His gaze softened to one of concern. "I won't fall. All you need to do is hang on real tight an' take one step at a time."

Aware that every moment she held the group up meant their pursuers would get that much closer, Rose swallowed. It had been rather comforting that he'd called her *sweetheart. . . .*

"I'm turning forward now." Nate let go of her hand.

"All right." Quickly she clutched on to the back of his thick leather belt, the knuckles of her cold hand turning white as snow. "I'm ready." *Please help me, Lord. Keep us safe. All of us.*

Nate slowly edged forward. And slippery as the going was, Rose amazed herself by managing to follow him as she carefully placed one foot in front of the other.

Nearing the halfway point, he stopped. "You're gonna have to let go whilst I get around this here branch."

Her heart stopped then pounded double time. Did she have good enough footing?

"Let go, Rose. It'll just take a second, then I'll help you around it."

She knew Robert and trusting little Shining Star watched her from behind, and she felt like such a coward. *Father in Heaven, I need Your help again.* She forced her fingers to uncurl from Nate's belt and stood there, holding her breath.

Using the broken-off branch for support, he stepped around it to the other side then balanced himself with his musket and reached for her.

Rose had to take a step forward on her own, over moss she knew was exceptionally slippery out here over the water. She was already bone tired, and now her whole body started to shake. Her legs felt rubbery.

He met her gaze straight on. "You can do it. Go for the branch. I'm here."

Afraid to take a breath lest she lose her balance, Rose determined to take the terrifying step. Gingerly she put her foot down then shifted her weight, leaving the safety of the previous spot. She reached for the branch. Her foot slipped! She felt herself starting to fall!

"I've got you." Nate caught her arm, pulling her back up. "Grab on to the branch."

Shaking like a leaf in the wind, she grabbed hold with both hands.

His big hand covered hers, and he flashed an encouraging smile. "Soon as we get to the other side, I'm slicin' some grooves in the bottom of them shoes of yours. That should keep 'em from slippin' so much."

He truly did know how difficult it was for her to keep her footing. He did care. The realization warmed her insides.

His voice brought her back to the moment. "Now, hang on to the branch with your left hand, an' I'll pull you around with your right. Don't worry about losin' your footing. I got you."

And Rose knew he did have her. Not just her hand. He had her whole heart. If only. . .

Chapter 33

Nate had to admire Rose. She'd managed to keep up with him for the past half hour as they followed a narrow trace downstream. It did help having Shining Star carrying Jenny Ann on her back. But Rose. His Rose. By the time he'd gotten her across the stream and off the fallen log, she'd been shaking so hard he'd wondered if he should pick her up and carry her. His compassion won out, and he pulled her into his arms, soaking in her nearness, never wanting to let go—until Bob gave him a playful shove.

Her strong religious convictions still taunted Nate, but no matter how desperately he tried to harden his heart toward her, the need in those dusky blue eyes drew him, tore at him. The thought of her being taken captive by the Senecas and made to suffer unspeakable horrors made his knees buckle. And little Jenny Ann. . .

He called himself every fool name he could think of for not insisting on taking the two of them back to civilization the minute he and Bob got back to the trading post. He knew what the French were up to, that they were closing in, and that it was only a matter of time before they had Smith's trading post in their sights.

He became aware of the sound of rushing water. They were coming up on the river at last. Eager to search the bank for a craft of some sort, he turned to his friends. "I'll run ahead an' see if I can find a canoe hidden in the reeds."

"Don't show yourself till you're sure no one's out on the water searchin' the banks," Bob cautioned.

In moments, Nate reached the edge of the trees overlooking the river. A quick visual scan of the area revealed no pursuers, but the river curved about a quarter of a mile downstream. Men could come paddling around that bend at any second.

In his urgency, he slid, more than scrambled, down the steep bank. It wasn't a likely spot for someone to stash a canoe, but he had to look anyway.

His moccasins became waterlogged in the ice-crackled edges as he slashed through reeds and cane in his frantic search for a craft of any kind. But by the time the others called down to him from above, he'd found nothing. Nothing! Not that he'd expected a real answer to that pathetic prayer of his.

They needed to get across the river and onto the trail back to civilization. Time was running out. He called up to Bob, "Send the women down to braid some reed strips into rope. Give Star your knife."

Rose didn't wait to be told twice. She slid down the muddy bank to him.

He pulled his own blade out of its sheath and handed it to her as she gained her feet.

"What are we doing?" She headed for the nearest reeds even as she asked the question.

"Buildin' a raft faster than you'll ever see, that's what."

She tucked her chin but set right to work without further questions.

"Baby's comin' down," Bob said as he lowered Jenny Ann in the cradleboard.

Nate caught hold of the bottom of the carrier and brought it the rest of the way, astonished at how good the tiny girl had been. He'd heard somewhere that babies loved being walked outdoors, and this little gal was sure proof of that. He propped the cradleboard against the bank and started crawling up to the top as Star slid past him.

Bob was already at work with his hatchet, slicing small branches off a fairly straight limb from a downed fir when Nate reached him. A second tree had fallen nearby, shearing branches from smaller trees on its way down. *As if God knew we'd need those limbs.* Nate scratched his head in wonder.

Maybe the Almighty had heard his prayer after all and knew there was no canoe to be found. Maybe that's why He'd allowed the trees to fall where they had. Nate reached for another limb to strip. God truly was with them! It wasn't for his sake, of course, but for Rose's and Bob's. . .and maybe even Shining Star's.

Bob tossed a stripped limb aside and reached for another with barely a pause. "I've been thinkin'. The village dogs weren't barkin' their heads off when those canoes came in. Did you notice that?"

"I did." Working swiftly, Nate stripped his branch and heaved it onto the steadily growing pile. "I'm thinkin' they might'a been muzzled. If you noticed, there was only three spots of light from fires. Our wigwams. Somebody must'a come in and made a deal with Red Hawk beforehand."

Pausing for a second, Bob met his gaze then resumed working. "When we was havin' our friendly little talk with 'em yesterday, do you s'pose they already knew what was comin'?"

"Who can say?" Nate didn't slow down as the unreadable Shawnee expressions came to his mind. "All I know is they didn't come right out an' make us any promises, did they?"

Bob glanced back toward the path they'd traveled. "No, they sure didn't." He sliced his hatchet down another limb. "But I guess we can't blame 'em. Why get kilt over who's gonna run the tradin' post?"

Nate mulled over his friend's words. "Right. But it still galls. Them gals could'a been torched in their sleep. Thank the good Lord we came back when we did."

A grin spread across Bob's face. "Right, Nate. Thank the good Lord."

Rose gawked at the pitiful raft Nate and Robert were pushing across the shelf of ice to the frigid water and vowed not to panic the way she had earlier. The two frontiersmen had gotten them this far. They were all tired and hungry and cold, but they were still alive and relatively safe. She took a closer look at the newly built contraption. Limbs no more than three inches thick were tied together with reeds and leather strips cut from the men's leggings. Still, she had no choice but to trust it would hold together and not sink. Even if the rickety thing did manage to somehow stay atop the water, the fir fronds blanketing the raft weren't enough to keep them all from getting thoroughly soaked—but she refused to think about that.

Nate had been true to his word and ridged the soles of her shoes, so Rose stepped carefully behind the men on the slick ice without slipping. She glanced over at Jenny Ann happily bobbing along in the cradleboard on Shining Star's back. Hopefully the baby, at least, would stay out of the icy flow.

Nate motioned her forward. "Crawl to the front and lie flat."

As she did, Rose tried to convince herself it was a warm summer afternoon, and she was going punting on the Thames for the simple pleasure of it. She struggled to ignore her thrumming heart. Mustering a brave smile as she passed Nate, she followed his instructions, working her way to the front of a space that measured a scant five feet wide and had an uneven aft not more than seven or eight feet long.

Unbidden panic started to rise when Shining Star slid into place belly-down beside her. The cradleboard on the Indian maiden's back resembled an upturned cocoon. Jenny Ann looked over at Rose and grinned, innocently oblivious of the danger facing them all.

This was crazy! Someone needed to get the baby out of here! But just as she reached to snatch up the child, Nate and Robert shoved the makeshift craft out and dove onto it.

It dipped under the water! She gasped as shockingly cold waves rushed across her legs. Then the raft bobbed up again. It was actually floating!

Nate loomed above her. "Scoot to the center. I need room to paddle."

Paddle? The men hadn't even chopped off the ends of the branches for fear the noise would draw their pursuers. Still, she inched toward Star and looked back at Nate.

He dipped a slab of bark into the water and began using it to propel the rude craft.

Rose rolled her eyes. The current was dragging their little raft downstream, toward the trading post they'd just fled, yet they expected to get across this wide expanse before it reached the settlement—with those pieces of bark? They couldn't have covered more than five or six miles during the night before veering toward the river.

Glancing back to Robert, she saw that he'd wedged a slab of wood between two of the central limbs, like a rudder.

Slightly encouraged, she arched her upper half toward the side. Cupping her hand, she reached into the icy current, to help.

"Here." Nate handed her the bark. "Use this."

As she took it and began paddling, he picked up another chunk and paddled with her. On the other side, Robert did the same.

To her surprise, they started to make progress! But would they make it across to the other side before drifting down to the village? The river was so wide. And canoes could slice across to them in no time at all.

Oh man. . .this was a mistake. A big mistake. The farther out on the river the raft got, the more vulnerable they were. The realization sank in Nate's stomach like a boulder. A single canoe coming around the bend carrying armed men was all it would take to do them in.

Still, bad choice or not, they had to keep going. He and Bob could probably outrun persistent trackers, but not with two women and a baby along. *Lord, did I make the right decision? We're sittin' ducks out here.*

He kept a steady eye focused downriver. Ignoring his aching shoulder muscles as he dug his bark shard into the water time and again, he willed the sluggish raft to move faster.

"Let it drift downstream a little," Bob said. "Look. The ice juts farther out over there." He pointed at a spot not far away.

Hallelujah! Nate stopped paddling and let the river take them farther downstream, where a chunk of peninsula with overhanging trees had shaded that frozen stretch from the heat of the sun.

"Only fifty or sixty more feet! Paddle! Paddle!" he urged. They were going to make it!

Once they came to the solid ice, Nate indicated some roots poking up out of the frozen water. "Climb up them roots," he told Rose and Star. "We don't wanna leave no trace of where we came out."

Bob was already at work chopping the raft apart and tossing the remains into the current. Nate yanked out his own knife, and within a minute no evidence of their rude little craft remained. They swapped satisfied grins, and the two of them grabbed their muskets and mounted the roots to join the women.

As Nate climbed up behind his pal, Bob let out a hoarse whisper. "Duck!"

One foot still dangling off the edge, Nate flattened himself to the ground. He lifted his head a fraction and peered around the mound of roots out toward the river.

Out in the middle of the flowing current, a long canoe loaded with a dozen men, half of whom wore French uniforms, sliced silently upstream. One of the Frenchmen had a telescope but at the moment had it pointed at the opposite shore.

Nate slowly pulled his foot up and crawled behind some brush just as the soldier swung the long tube in his direction. Keeping low and peeking through the branches of the shrub, Nate held his breath, watching, watching, as the telescope focused on this shoreline. Had they left any visible sign? Would Jenny pick this moment to cry out?

The canoe sped on with no order to change course. When the soldier switched his attention to the far shore again, Nate hauled in a lungful of air, only now realizing he'd been too tense to breathe.

He scrambled up the rise to where the women lay beneath some low evergreen branches with the baby between them. Rose was kissing Jenny's eyes, one after the other. She'd been keeping the baby entertained and quiet.

Coming to his feet, Nate reached down and tugged Rose gently off the ground. Her hands were so very cold. Cupping them between his own, he rubbed them to generate some warmth and get the circulation going. "We're safe. For a while, anyway. Once we get far enough away from this river, I'll start a fire so we can dry off."

"And warm up," she breathed around chattering teeth as she shivered from head to toe. "That would be heavenly." Her eyes glowed with gratitude.

Nate couldn't stop looking at her. Even all bedraggled, her hair askew, her heavy cloak smelling of wet wool, why did she have to be so alluring? Knowing he had to get her warm, he picked up the cradleboard. "Here, let me help you get Jenny hooked on."

Chapter 34

Nate could hardly believe their good fortune. Surely God had a hand in leading them to the cavelike recess in the hillside. An outcropping of rock sheltered it overhead, and the natural shape of the concavity offered protection on three sides. When they found some dry wood scattered in back of the space, as if Someone knew they'd be coming, he was tempted to believe in miracles. Maybe all those prayers Bob and Rose kept sending up, to say nothing of his own pitiful pleas, really did make a difference.

Removing his partially dry fur robe, he spread it out on the ground for the women to sit on. Their quiet cooperation throughout the ordeal seemed to him another miracle. . .especially since Rose had never been too shy to express her opinion about things.

He and Bob were used to maintaining silence during these past years since they'd been exploring, and they worked together just as quietly now as they knelt down to get a fire going. While Bob struck his knife repeatedly against a piece of flint, Nate nudged fragments of dry moss beneath the flying sparks.

A tiny flame soon burst forth. Nate blew on it gently until it grew enough to add twigs.

Sighs of pleasure erupted from Rose and Shining Star, and he looked up to see admiration in their eyes. At least for the moment, it seemed he and Bob were their heroes.

"We should be safe here for a while," Nate said. "Long enough for our clothes to dry, anyway, an' maybe get something into our stomachs." He knew he shouldn't keep looking at Rose, but she seemed like a magnet to his eyes. He drank in the sight she made, cuddling Jenny Ann within the warmth of her damp cloak. Giving himself a mental shake, he tore his gaze away. "Have any jerky tucked away in that haversack, Bob?"

"Some, I reckon." He broke a twig in half. "I'll check once we get this fire goin' good." He added more sticks to the growing flames.

Nate nodded. "I prob'ly have some in mine, too. We're gonna want somethin' to flavor that cornmeal."

"I wish I'd have had the foresight to bring something as well." Rose's sad comment drew Nate's attention back to her.

He flashed an indulgent smile. "You looked after Jenny an' kept her quiet when it mattered. That was more than enough."

A tender glow of gratitude returned to her blue-gray eyes, and the sight was almost enough to be his undoing.

He shot to his feet. "You can handle this, Bob. I'll go down to the river for some water."

"Be careful, Nate," Rose called after him, her voice soft and low.

He opened his mouth to reply then clamped it shut and turned on his heel. Didn't the woman know that was what he was desperately trying to do?

―⁓―

The overcast sky added dampness to the day, making Rose's search for dry moss difficult, since she'd been instructed to remain within sight of the camp. She moved aside a clump of dead leaves with her foot and found a small strand of green to add to the meager supply she'd already found. A gust of cold wind swirled her cloak open, and she used her free hand to tug it more closely about herself while she continued her search.

Detecting footsteps not far away, she glanced up to see Nate returning to camp, gingerly balancing his gourd cup and a small pan in either hand as he walked. She thought it odd that he'd used such little containers to tote water back to the shelter.

Even as she moved out of sight behind a tree trunk, she knew it was silly to not want him to know she was there.

He joined Robert at the rocky cave and set down both vessels with a faint *clink*. "Can't believe it. How could both of us go off without grabbin' our flasks?"

Smiling to herself, Rose tilted her head enough to peer out at them.

Suddenly Nate straightened with a start and swung around, accidentally bumping the gourd. Water sloshed to the ground.

She ducked behind the tree again.

"Where's Rose?" A distinct note of panic tinged the frontiersman's voice.

Robert snorted. "Calm down. She just went to find moss for the baby."

"Oh." Nate released a lungful of air. "You did caution her not to wander too far, right?"

"I did. Take it easy, pal. She's not gonna take any chances."

"Hmph." He paused. "Guess it's just as well she ain't here right now."

Rose inched forward and saw Robert look up at Nate in question.

"I saw some Senecas across the river runnin' along the bank. They're prob'ly the bunch that followed our trail. They must've found where we built the raft, and now they're searchin' the banks to see where we landed. They know we ain't stupid enough to let ourselves drift very far downstream."

Rose moistened her lips and let out an uneasy breath.

"You're right about that," Robert agreed. "Let's pray they don't find a canoe before gettin' back to the village an' spreadin' the word."

Nate lowered his voice, making his next words barely audible to Rose. "Don't mention nothin' to the women. They're scairt enough as it is."

As we have every right to be. Shrinking out of sight again, Rose thought about Nate, her knight in shining armor, always doing his utmost to protect her, always taking care of her—regardless of anything thoughtless or hurtful she said to him. Why, she'd even refused to marry him, all because she was *too good* for him. What a laugh. Truth was, she didn't deserve him! The very thought of how she'd berated him, how she'd so callously dismissed his proposal, made her loathe herself.

Still, the reasons for her refusal—no matter how tactlessly she might have expressed them—remained valid. She belonged to the Lord, and Nate Kinyon did not. God's instructions must stand. She could not be bound for life to a man who did not seek after the Lord. No matter how her heart ached about it.

God had seen them through thus far. She had to believe He'd continue to do so. *Please, Father, give Nate and Robert wisdom for whatever may lie ahead. Stay with us. Keep us safe.*

The foursome gathered around the tin pan of mush. Holding Jenny in her lap, Rose couldn't help thinking back on the sumptuous Sabbath meal they'd enjoyed a mere two days past. The roasted chicken had been tender and moist, the vegetables cooked to perfection. Yet this simple fare of mush with jerked meat could be no less appreciated. Nate and Robert had carved crude spoons from a couple of broad sticks they'd found, and Rose held hers poised and ready to attack the meal.

"We need to give thanks," Robert said, bowing his head. "Lord God, we thank You for providin' us with this food. I thank You for Shining Star, too, an' ask a special blessin' on her for rememberin' to bring the cornmeal. In Jesus' name, amen."

About to thrust forth her spoon, Rose stopped midmotion as Nate's voice interrupted.

"And one more thing, Lord," he added as she closed her eyes again. "We need to thank You for all You've been doin' to keep us safe." He chuckled. "The fact that You had Rose make me so mad I couldn't sleep was the first of 'em."

She sneaked a peek through her lashes at him, wondering if he was trying to get back at her, but the expression on his rugged face was the most sincere she'd ever glimpsed there.

"An' since then it's been one thing after the other," he went on. "You know better than me all You been doin' to look after us. I wanna thank You for that. Really thank You." Abruptly he raised his voice. "Well, eat up, y'all." He dug his makeshift spoon into the mush.

Still mildly stunned, it took a moment for Rose to remember to join the others scooping food from the communal pan. What was she to think about Nate's prayer? She simply didn't know what to make of it.

"Uhh. Uhh." Jenny reached out a little hand toward the food, returning Rose to the moment. She quickly dipped her spoon and gave the child the first bite then alternated with her, making sure Jenny had no reason to fuss again.

Across the campfire, Shining Star said something to Robert that sounded like a question. He answered, his voice casual as they spoke back and forth throughout the meal.

Rose could think of nothing worthy to say to Nate. Fortunately, he wasn't speaking to her either. Fact was, he seemed to be going out of his way not to look at her, even when he passed her the gourd of water. He kept all his attention on the food before them. So she did as well.

Eventually Robert broke the tense silence. "Shining Star asked me to thank you, Nate, for your prayer." A smile added a spark to his dark eyes. "She says it's a great comfort to know she's with men who seek the favor of our God. An' she believes that He must be very powerful."

Nate tipped his head to the Indian girl. "That was a real nice thing to say."

As Robert translated, Rose sprang to her feet, bringing the baby up with her. Truly overwhelmed with the incredible change in the frontiersman, she didn't want anyone to discover the tears brimming in her eyes. Wiping Jenny's mouth with her already-ruined cloak, she went to the cradleboard to fasten her in. Without chancing a look back at the others, she cleared the clog in her throat. "Time's a'wasting"—words she'd heard Nate say so many times during their journey to Muskingum.

"But you gals' clothes are still damp," Robert protested.

"They'll dry soon enough," Rose assured him airily as she laced the baby in her warm cocoon.

Nate stood up. "She's right. He used his foot to kick dirt over the fire, effectively snuffing it. Then he swung his gaze to Rose and locked with hers for the first time. He grinned. "Time's a'wastin'."

Chapter 35

Rose scarcely noticed the weight of the baby and cradleboard digging into her shoulders. The seriousness of the pursuers chasing after them made even the discomfort of her battered feet of little import as she followed Robert and Shining Star into the woods, skirting leftover patches of dismal snow in their path. Nate had smiled at her. Sensing he was no longer angry, she walked on in silence, basking in the sweet memory of his grin.

No one had to remind her that two skilled frontiersmen like Nate and Robert could easily elude the French and Seneca trackers, were they on their own and had minds to do so. Instead they were willingly risking capture, torture, and even death just to protect their women. *Their women.* Rose didn't dare dwell on the significance of that thought.

She tossed a worried look over her shoulder, hoping to see Nate coming. He'd remained behind to cover any evidence of their presence at the cave. Her last view of him as the party left the campsite revealed him spreading moldy leaves across those they'd disturbed and raking over imprints of their feet with a leafless tree branch. *Watch over him, Father. Surround him with Your angels. . . .*

The image of his priceless smile drifted across her thoughts again. But dear as the sight of it had been to her, Rose hesitated to assign it much significance. He could easily have changed his mind about marriage, considering the heartless fashion in which she'd crushed him by voicing her strong religious convictions. Even now the memory tormented her. But at least he was back to his old teasing self again. . .and how she loved that side of him.

She loved *him*. The prospect of having to give him up in the near future while they went their separate ways was worse than torture. How would she ever find the strength to do it? *Dear Lord, help me to bear in mind that just because Nate turned to You in a time of dire need, it doesn't mean he won't revert to his old ways the minute the danger is past.* Slowing her pace to step over a protruding root in the path, she deliberately steered her mind onto a different course. *And thank You so much that Jenny has been quiet and happy all this time. She truly loves being outdoors and traveling. Were I a Shawnee mother, I'd give her the name Traveling Woman.* With a smile, Rose stepped cautiously through a low, muddy spot.

Somewhere behind her twigs snapped. She and Robert both halted and whirled around. He raised his musket to his shoulder.

Rose caught her breath as the clatter intensified, growing closer. Nate? Was he being chased?

Then, a few yards in back of them, a doe leaped out of the brush, its eyes wild with alarm as it crashed on and vanished into the forest growth, a young fawn clattering after it.

Something had frightened the animals. A shudder went through Rose as she detected the yipping of wolves echoing in the distance.

"Come along," Robert ordered, his voice low and sharp.

Her pulse still throbbing, Rose cast a fearful look around. Then she started up the hill after Robert and Star with a longer stride, dodging snags and whips from brambly bushes she pushed past. *Oh Lord, please don't let Nate get caught. Keep him safe.*

Nate grimaced as he half jogged, half walked, following the broken twigs and footprints the threesome had left in their wake. He'd done his level best to cover their tracks from the river so the Senecas would be unable to detect the point where they'd emerged from the water. Then he buried the campfire and cleared a good fifty-yard radius around the cave, hoping the sharp-eyed trackers would be unable to decipher signs of their resting place. Hopefully they'd be long gone before anyone stumbled upon this fresh trail.

It was taking him longer than expected to catch up to Bob and the others. But that was good. Obviously his friend had set a rapid pace as the party headed for Gist's Trail, a trace that would lead them back toward civilization. Both he and Bob knew they'd have to keep off the actual trail, but by staying within close proximity of it, they'd at least be going in the right direction.

He stopped now and then to cock an ear in the direction of the cave, listening for any signs they were being followed. So far he'd heard nothing unusual. *And don't let there be none, Lord,* he prayed for the dozenth time.

Nate had to concede that prayer was becoming the best weapon he and his friends had in these dire circumstances. He could no longer discount the amazing way they'd managed to elude capture thus far. The gut-wrenching fear that had clutched his insides through the first part of the day had gradually eased, and a sense of peace had taken its place. If it really was God looking after them, Shining Star had been right about the Lord being powerful. And Rose was right that He took care of His people. Surely God's hand had helped them cross that river, and it had to be Him keeping Rose and the others safe now till Nate could catch up to them. That was a mighty comforting thought. And quite humbling.

Continuing to follow the trail for an hour or so, Nate caught the scent of smoke in the air. A terrible sense of foreboding tightened his chest. The others couldn't be more than a mile this side of Gist's Trail. Why in the world would Bob start a fire? He had to know the smell would lead the Indians right to them!

He broke into a run. The blaze needed to be put out before the trackers behind them caught wind of it.

Suddenly someone darted into his path. Nate dove off to the side in reflex.

"Partial to dead ferns, are ya?" Bob asked quietly, a grin broadening his dusky cheeks.

It was quite tempting to illuminate his pal on his partialities, but Nate rolled his eyes instead as he picked himself up and dusted himself off.

Bob held a warning finger up to his lips and motioned for Nate to follow him. Not far away, he parted the low, straddling limbs of a fir. There beneath an evergreen canopy sat Rose and Star, sharing one of the blankets Star had brought, with Jenny Ann between them.

All three girls favored him with smiles, but Rose's was the one that warmed Nate's heart.

He was about to crawl in and join them, when Bob released the branches and motioned for Nate to go with him several feet away from the others. There Bob spoke under his breath. "There's some Senecas up on the trail. They must've figgered we'd head for it. But thank the good Lord they decided to make camp before we accidentally stumbled into their nest."

Nate clamped a hand on his friend's shoulder and gave a squeeze. "Aye. He's been watchin' out for us today. That's for sure."

"I figger we're far enough away from 'em here that even if the baby starts to fussin' they won't hear her."

"How close are we to the trail, anyway?"

Bob gave a casual shrug. "I snuck up a ways. I'd say 'bout half a mile."

As they turned and strode back to the fir tree, Nate checked the sky, gauging the remaining light. The day was almost over. Finally. This had been one of the longest of his life. He stopped near the tree and turned to his friend. "We need to save the cornmeal for Jenny. For now, I reckon we can get by on what cracked corn's in my haversack. Plus I found two small pieces of jerked meat. How much you got?"

"None." Bob winced. "Me an' the gals ate what little cracked corn I had. Baby's been fed, too. Tomorrow mornin' we better snare a critter of some kind."

"Right. Can't afford to make noise shootin' somethin'."

Pulling aside the floppy limb, Bob motioned Nate inside. "I'll take the first watch. You get some rest. The women already piled up a goodly amount of needles for beds."

"Ain't you tired? You been on the trail as long as me."

Bob gave a snort. "I already had plenty of sittin' time, waitin' for you to git your lazy self up here. Go ahead. I'll wake you in an hour or two."

Sleep. The very thought made Nate yawn. He let the branch swing back into place, effectively closing him inside the small haven.

He met Rose's gaze as she patted a welcoming pile of needles. "Here." Her sweet whisper lulled him even further. "Lie down and rest."

She was here. She was safe. He could rest now. He dropped down to the makeshift bedding and closed his eyes, warmed by her presence.

A long, miserable night dragged by. The bitter cold intensified when freezing rain began to fall from the heavens, drenching the branches of the fir tree and dripping relentlessly over the limited shelter. If not for the three shared fur robes, they'd have been soggy messes. In the wee hours the sleet turned to snow, whipped about by a sharp wind. By the time morning dawned, not a hint of a smile graced a face in the bedraggled group. Even Jenny squirmed restlessly in her cradleboard.

"Think I'll make us a fire." Forcing a note of optimism into his voice, Nate scanned the area for something that might burn.

Rose glanced up in alarm. "But—won't that give away our position?"

He shrugged. "Naw. At first light, I hoofed out to the spot where Bob an' me figgered the Senecas made camp, an' it was deserted. We're pretty safe now."

"You mean they returned to Muskingum?" Giving his sodden moccasins a cursory glance, she released a slow breath.

Shaking his head, he took the bundled-up baby from her when Jenny grunted and looked at him with rounded eyes. He nuzzled the little darling. "They left tracks in the snow. Headin' east."

Bob unwrapped a few pieces of dry wood from his haversack and knelt down with his knife and flint to coax a blaze to life. "That's what I expected. They'll prob'ly go up several miles an' wait for us to come to them." His gaze gravitated to Shining Star as she stepped past Rose, tying the end of her ebony braid. He said something to her, and she gave him a shy smile. "I should have a fire goin' in a minute or so," he said to no one in particular.

A concerned frown drew Rose's brows downward. "Are you quite sure a fire won't be dangerous?"

"Trust me," Nate said, drawing her attention to him. "The Senecas had a pretty good-sized one goin' through the night. They'll think any smoke that drifts their way is leftover from theirs."

Her gaze clung to his for a heartbeat before she let it slide to the babe in his arms.

As Rose wrapped her hooded cloak more tightly around her, Nate couldn't help but glimpse the muddied, ruffled edge of her flannel nightdress. Though at times she wrapped in one of the two blankets Star had brought, the nightdress and her damp cloak were all she had to ward off the morning's bitter cold, while the rest of them wore thick fur robes. He had to do something about that.

"Ya know. . .I've been covetin' that cloak of yours," he told her.

That brought her eyes back to his as she looked from him down to her limp wrap. "I can't imagine why." She gave a wry shake of her head.

"Well, think about it." He handed Jenny to Shining Star and tried to sound earnest as he nonchalantly stooped down beside Bob to help with the fire. "This here heavy robe of mine sorta gets in the way times when I need to be movin' real fast. Your cloak I could belt down good an' tight an'—" He watched a slow smile of disbelief add a twinkle in her eye. "What's so all-fired funny?"

She snickered. "The sleeves wouldn't even reach halfway down your arms."

The woman was making it hard for him to maintain a straight face, especially when he pictured himself in it. Without cracking a smile, he gave particular attention to feeding dry needles to Bob's tiny flame. "See? That's what I mean. They'd be outta the way for sure."

"You're right." Bob's lips twitched at the corners as he made an effort to quell his own grin. "Mebbe I'll outbid you for it."

Nate slanted him a meaningful glare. "It was my idea," he blustered to keep from laughing out loud.

"Well," Rose said ever so innocently, "if you're positive you must have it, then I'd welcome the extra warmth of yours."

"It's a deal." Managing to control his features, Nate stood up.

Rising, Rose pushed the burgundy-colored hood from her head. Her hand went to the messy night braid uncoiling down her back. "I really must do something with my hair. Perhaps if we've time before we leave."

"I'd be willin' to help out," Nate blurted. The teasing provided him an excuse to stop trying to hold back his grin.

She arched her brows. "Yes, I'm sure you would." She slipped out of her cloak and held it out to him.

Nate's heart crimped as she shivered before him in nothing but a loosely draped flannel nightdress. Wasting not a second, he whipped off his fur robe and wrapped her in its warm confines.

"This," she sighed, "is so much better." She lingered within his arms for several seconds before easing away.

Nate gulped. The way he felt right now, he doubted he'd need to put on her pitiful wrap for some time to come. He flicked a glance down at Bob.

His partner stared back, all trace of his former humor gone. Bob the chaperone was back.

Nate shifted his gaze away while he shoved his hands through the wide sleeve holes of Rose's cloak then strode off. "I'll go break through that pond ice down yonder and bring us back some water."

Chapter 36

Rose had never been more deeply thankful than she was the moment Nate wrapped her in his warm robe. Chilled to the bone, she'd begun to fear she'd never be able to keep up with the others on one more day's journey in this cold, much less ever reach civilization. But in the heavy fur wrap, she felt herself beginning to thaw. After taking care of her morning needs and getting Jenny tucked inside the cradleboard, she finger-combed her hair as best she could and fashioned it into long braids that would cover her cold ears.

Nate had yet to return with water from the pond they'd passed at the bottom of the last rise. What was causing the delay? She tried not to think the worst but couldn't stop her angst from building.

The marvelous blaze Robert had going dispelled the cold for a radius of several feet, and they all took advantage of the simple, yet vital pleasure. But Rose caught the repeated glances he flicked in the direction his partner had taken. His expression revealed nothing, but Rose sensed his concern over Nate's absence.

He cleared his throat and stood. "Think I'll go see what's keepin' Nate." As he retrieved his musket propped against a nearby tree, Rose noticed with a jolt that Nate's weapon remained there.

She watched Robert start down the hill.

Just then Nate came into view coming up the rise. Rose's knees nearly buckled with relief as he grinned and held up a dead rabbit by its hind legs.

Robert shook his head and joined him.

Meat! Fresh meat! Rose's mouth watered at the concept of actual food—fresh, hot, and glorious.

The frontiersman looked so comical with her too-small cloak belted around his muscular form, his gear dangling against his long legs as the men strode to the fire, but who could think of laughing at someone who'd part with his own garment out of concern for her? After they all ate, she'd insist they swap back. One blanket Star had brought along had been sacrificed as diapers for the baby, but the other, wrapped around the cloak, provided Rose sufficient protection from winter's cold.

Nate handed her the pan of water he'd brought from the pond and held the critter aloft. "This li'l fella took one look at me in this pretty cloak an' was so dumbfounded he stood there, stock still, starin' for all he's worth. I figgered it was only kind to put the poor confused fella outta his misery. One swift throw of my knife did it."

The man was proud of himself. . .but not half as proud as she was of him. He'd brought the food they'd need to make it through the day.

Shining Star, however, was more interested in getting to the necessities than in hearing about the daring deed. Snatching the creature from Nate's grasp and the knife from his sheath, she slapped the rabbit down and began skinning it right there.

Rose squelched her amusement by setting the water near some hot coals. Straightening, she changed the subject. "How long should it take us to get back to the Delaware River?"

The men traded glances before Nate answered. "Considerin' the snowfall an' the fact we won't have a cleared trail to walk on, I'd say two weeks. What's your reckonin', Bob?"

He cocked his head. "That an' mebbe a day or two more. . .unless we can get to usin' the trail fairly soon."

Rose looked from one to the other. "But isn't this the same one we came in on? It took more than a month to get here riding horseback."

"With a loaded-down pack train and cows," Nate added. "We had to load an' unload 'em every day, plus get all that truck across all them rivers. Then we had horses comin' up lame, an'—" He paused and stared at her. "Speakin' of comin' up lame, there's some tricky ground ahead. Lots of ups an' downs. I don't want you women takin' no chances. If you need help, holler."

"I seem to recall doing a bit of hollering while we crossed that slick log yesterday—for all the good it did me." Rose stifled a teasing smile.

"That does bring back a faint memory." Nate flashed a grin but quickly sobered. "I got you across that thing just fine. But up ahead there'll be holes for twistin' your ankle in an'—" He stopped and glanced into the woods.

Rose followed his gaze, wondering what he might have heard.

"Anyway"—his expression exhibited no new concern as he continued—"I'm gonna hunt you gals some walkin' sticks while you cook our breakfast. Me an' Bob'll have you all fixed up."

He turned on his heel and started away but swung back after taking only a few steps. "By the by, Miss Rose. You're lookin' mighty fine in that fur robe. Yessir. Mighty fine." A playful grin lit up his hazel eyes. "I'll make a mountain woman outta you yet."

For three tension-filled days, the men took turns hiking close to the trail, waiting, hoping, praying for the moment the Indian war party would give up searching for them and turn back. The weather remained bitingly cold, but at least there'd been no more snow after the last storm. The ground retained some drifts in spots, but where weak rays of sunshine managed to melt it away, the earth was frozen too hard to be muddy. . .or to leave their footprints. Whenever Rose was not within his sight, Nate had to remind himself continuously that the Lord was looking after them.

From time to time, however, discomfiting memories of periods in the distant past ate at him, times when Christians had been martyred for their beliefs or thrown to lions. He could only trust that his party would not meet such a fate.

As the overcast afternoon began to wane, Nate veered off the eastern trail and headed north in search of Bob and the others. Soon it would be time to make camp for another night—another cold night without a fire. Or maybe just a tiny fire, just big enough to roast the beaver he'd come across earlier that day. He'd heard a loud *snap* near a stream and discovered a beaver caught in the claws of a white man's trap. It seemed the Lord had once again provided supper for them as He'd done for Moses and the Israelites in the wilderness. Nate hefted the critter high to admire his catch, imagining the tasty feast it would make.

Perhaps instead of martyrdom, he should concentrate on manna. But try as he might to recall the Twenty-third Psalm, which he'd memorized as a child, he could only resurrect one phrase: *"though I walk through the valley of the shadow of death."* That part had really caught his imagination.

Bypassing a moldy reed bog, Nate reminisced on his days as a lad, remembering his pa. The big strapping man had set a fine example for his sons. He'd been a faithful, hardworking disciple of God, but that had not kept him from being taken from his family while they still needed him. And little Jenny's folks had both been cruelly torn away from her. So many happenings seemed to lack purpose. Unanswered questions kept challenging Nate's faith, and all the while he was away from Rose and the others, worry was a constant companion.

On his way here, he'd crossed a creek with noticeably thin ice. What if it broke open when Rose tried to cross it? He should be there to see her safely to the other side, not way out here where he couldn't help.

Movement on the edge of his vision interrupted his musings, as a group of people stepped stealthily through a stand of birch trees. They were too close to the trail to be his friends. Lowering the heavy beaver to the ground, Nate slipped behind a thick oak and raised his musket as they came steadily, silently, in his direction.

Had they found the rest of his party and killed or captured them?

Were they now searching for him?

Deftly, he inched forward to peer around the tree.

A huge whoosh of relief left his lungs. Rose. . .Bob. . .and Shining Star, toting the baby on her back! They'd made great time in this section.

Clutching the beaver more securely in his grip, he stepped out from the cover of the tree.

Instantly, Bob's musket swung toward him. Then, emitting a frosty cloud of breath, Bob lowered the weapon and strode to meet him.

Nate's attention went to Rose, who gave him a weary smile.

A hard lump centered inside his chest. If only they could afford to take a day to rest, but that was one luxury they could ill afford. Someday soon he'd make up to her for all she'd endured since arriving in America. . .or die trying. "What are you doing so close to the path?" he asked in the same quiet tone they'd used the past four days.

His partner gave a noncommittal shrug. "Couldn't be helped. The last ridge was too steep that far out an' covered with ice. How close are we to the trail, anyway?"

"'Bout a hundred yards, easy."

Bob's brown-black eyes clouded as he frowned. "Any sign of the trackers?"

"They're still on the move."

"Well, at least we know they're a ways ahead of us."

Nate huffed. "Only if they didn't decide to start backtrackin' today."

Concerned as he surveyed the area, Bob turned to him. "Since we're this close to the trail, let's cross over to the other side. They could easily figure out what we're up to and send some of their men down this side, like I'd do if I was leadin' 'em."

Nate kneaded his chin. "If we do go over to the other side, we could keep on goin' down to where Smith's partner set up his post on the Little Kanawha. Course, for all we know, the French could've sent men there, too. They've been pretty busy."

"Aye." Bob eyed the tired women. "Best we just keep workin' our way out where we know it'll be somewhat safe."

"Well. . ." Nate looked up, judging the remaining daylight. "If we're gonna cross, we better do it now."

"Aye." Bob gestured for Rose and Star to join them. "We're gonna move to the other side of the path."

"Why?" Rose's features scrunched up in puzzlement.

Leave it to her to always have to know the reason for everything. Nate slid an exasperated glance heavenward. "The trackers are less likely to look for us on the south side. That's why."

She nodded in chagrin then followed after Bob and Star, who had already started off. She smiled at Nate and pointed to the dead beaver as she walked past him.

He returned her smile and fell into step behind his Rose of Sharon. Just having her near again calmed him. And even if she did insist on knowing all the answers for everything, he knew her trust in him was growing with each passing day. He wondered if his trust in God would ever be that strong.

Lord, I suppose You know how hard it is for me to trust You when I don't know if Your plan for us is to be saved or martyred. An' You must know I got a powerful hankerin' to spend a whole lot of time lovin' that woman.

Chapter 37

Snow still shrouded the uphill terrain in spots the sickly December sun could not reach. In the week since they'd set out on this arduous journey on foot, Rose knew her legs and ankles had grown much stronger. Even her shoulders had become accustomed to the weight of Jenny's cradleboard when it was her turn to carry the child.

Little Jenny Ann was having the time of her life on her never-ending piggyback ride. She seemed to sense when everyone's mood was light, and then she'd coo and giggle during her waking hours. If the mood was tense, she'd clam up and look from one morose face to the next without making a sound. She seemed especially drawn to Nate and would tangle her fingers in the beard he'd acquired along the way. When he nuzzled her, the wiry hair on his chin made her laugh.

The Lord enabled the men to find meat every day now, and Rose began to look on the trek as an amazing adventure. *How do I thank You, dear Father, for allowing us all to witness Your wondrous workings? I pray that both Nate and Star will come to realize that You do care for Your people and are in control.* She emitted a tremulous sigh. If only she could be sure of Nate. He was becoming dearer to her with each passing day, and she knew her life would be empty if he weren't part of it.

An icy breeze whipped across her face, and she pulled his fur robe tighter around herself. The brawny frontiersman still swapped it for her cloak now and again, though it offered him pitiful protection from the elements. Even the bottoms of his leggings hung in shreds since he'd cut off strips to build the raft. But comical picture or not that he made, she loved her backwoods longhunter with every fiber of her being.

At the front of the group, Robert signaled for her and Shining Star to stop and hide. He raised his musket.

Rose felt only a modicum of concern. The men took this precaution whenever an unexpected sound or sight caught their attention. Detecting the noise herself, she scanned the area for a wild animal.

But it was Nate whose footfalls made the incredible racket as he came sprinting toward them through a stand of dense pines.

Had they been discovered? Her heart pounded hard as she crouched with Star behind a boulder hardly large enough to conceal one of them.

Panting as he caught up, Nate grinned from ear to ear. "The Indians turned back!" He gasped, gulping another breath. "Passed right by me about an hour ago."

Rose slowly stood from her hiding place. "Are you saying. . . ?"

"Aye." He came closer, his eyes sparkling in a way she hadn't seen in weeks. "We can get on the trail now."

Robert wasn't quite ready to relinquish all caution. "You're sure *all* of 'em went by? The whole search party?"

"Ever' last stinkin' one of 'em. I counted all eight Senecas trottin' on by me. An' they looked real eager to get back. I figger they must be as tired of this as we are."

His friend thumped him soundly on the back. "By tomorrow eve we should be able to do some real huntin' then."

"Not only that." Nate laughed as he caught Rose's face in his hands. "We can have us as big a fire as we want."

"Tonight?" she breathed, almost unable to speak for joy.

His smile faded and his shoulders sagged as he released his hold. "I should'a said tomorrow, love. Tomorrow night."

She took a deep breath and tipped her head. "Well, now. That's something for us all to look forward to."

"That it is." He drew her into a hug. "We got a whole lot of things to look forward to now."

He called me his love. Rose could hardly breathe.

"*Looking forward to* is more like what I expect you to keep in mind," Robert reprimanded from behind.

Easing away from her, Nate turned to his friend, who stood with his arm around Shining Star's shoulders. "Don't you think you oughta be takin' some of your own advice, *pal*?"

Rose covered a smile with her hand as Robert glanced from Star to Nate. "It's different with the two of us. We were married by the Miami chieftain."

"Well, you ain't married in the sight of almighty God."

Rose burst out laughing. The danger was surely over now—the men were bandying words back and forth, like old times.

Raising her mud-caked hem to step over a root on the trail as she walked alongside Nate, Rose noticed that the leather uppers of her shoes had become unrecognizable, though they'd somehow held together. The trusty walking stick Nate had fashioned for her did make walking easier.

Not even the cold could put a damper on her mood. A couple of hours from now, the men would build roaring campfires—one for toasting themselves and one for roasting whatever game they'd shoot. Better still, in a few more days they'd walk down to the Delaware River and beyond, to safety. She hoped the river wasn't frozen over. A time of drifting down its current would be a lovely change from walking.

Extending her once-creamy hands out before her, she grimaced at how rough they'd gotten, how browned by the sun. And she didn't have any clothing to wear, having left every last stitch behind in the burned wigwam. If her family could see her now, they'd be appalled.

"I'm glad I didn't write to my sisters and let them know exactly where

I was," she said, doing her best to match Nate's long-legged strides. "By now the colonies must know about the attack on Mr. Frazier's tradin' post. The girls would've been beside themselves with worry."

He looked down at her and took one of her hands in his. "Tell you what. When we deliver the baby to her grandparents in the spring, we'll go visit those sisters of yours an' see how they're farin'."

She felt comforted by his words but could only manage a sad smile. "I had so hoped to be able to buy them out of servitude. If only one of us had thought to bring the money Mr. Hawkes paid us."

Nate chuckled. "We had other pressin' matters at the moment."

"Quite right." She nodded thoughtfully. "But speaking of Jenny Ann, it's going to be terribly hard to give her up. I shall miss her so much."

He gave an empathetic squeeze to her hand. "Me, too. You know, we could write to her kin an' tell 'em how attached we are to her. Mebbe they'd let us keep her."

"What are you saying?" Surely he didn't mean he'd be willing to settle down in one place and help raise her!

Nate came to a halt, stopping her along with him. "I may not be as thick with the Lord as you'd like me to be, Rose, but me and Him's been havin' some real interestin' conversations lately."

Conversations? Was there no reverence? Did Nate assume he could treat almighty God like one of his pals? "Nate—"

He dropped her hand and stepped back, his eyes narrowing. "I can tell by the look on your face. You still don't think I'm good enough for you. Now that you're all free an' clear an' goin' back to civilization, you figger you don't need a rough guy like me no more. Figger you can snag yourself some bloke who's a whole lot more upstandin', more—"

Robert turned back abruptly, almost bumping into them. He glowered and held a finger up to his lips. "I hear horses up ahead. Get off the trail, Rose, till Nate an' me see who it is."

Seeing that Shining Star had already ducked into the woods with the baby, Rose felt her blood turn cold. "More Indians?"

"I doubt it." Nate's words came out on a harsh note as he sprinkled gunpowder into the flashpan of his musket. "Most likely trappers comin' in for winter pelts. Best not to take chances, though. Hurry!" Anger still sparked in his eyes.

Rose grabbed his shoulder. "Not till I tell you your *figuring* is a bunch of nonsense."

"Go!" He replugged his powder horn. "We'll talk later."

Nate and Bob positioned themselves behind trees on either side of the trail, waiting for the source of the creaks and groans of leather and the hoofbeats to crest the hill. Two bearded riders came into sight, each pulling a pack animal.

As they drew nearer, Nate let out an easy breath. "Looks like Reynolds an' Stuart," he called across to Bob. Stepping out onto the trail, he waved his rifle overhead in greeting as a relieved grin spread across his face.

The rawboned men, bundled in heavy fur wraps, gave a jaunty return wave. The first one shook his head. "Well, if it ain't Nate Kinyon an' Black Horse Bob. An' still sportin' their scalps, yet."

Nate grinned back. "Aye. Barely." He turned and hollered into the woods, "You gals can come out. They're friends."

Bob strode forward. "Howdy, boys. Sure is good to see a friendly face."

Rose emerged from the stand of trees, checking her hair and drawing her worn cloak snugly about herself. Nate had to chuckle at the sight. *Women. Always worryin' about their looks.*

"How—" The greeting died in Stuart's mouth as he spotted the women stepping onto the trail. A white woman never ceased to catch everyone by surprise. He and his partner dismounted and walked straight to Rose.

"Ya poor thing." Reynolds's bushy eyebrows dipped into a frown. "Don't ya be frettin' none, yer on yer way home now." He turned to Nate. "What'd you boys have to fork out to ransom the gal back?"

"I wasn't a hostage," Rose said. "I worked for Eustice Smith until he went to be with the Lord."

Reynolds whipped the coonskin cap off his wiry hair. "You was at Smith's tradin' post? Well, I'll be a—" He clamped his mouth shut before uttering something Nate was sure was not fit for feminine ears.

He and his partner crowded close. "Well, I'll be," they said in unison, wagging their shaggy heads.

Not appreciating the way the hunters were surrounding Rose, Nate edged to her side. "We're in a real hurry to get back to the Delaware."

"Aye." Bob nodded. "Some Frenchies an' a big party of Senecas from up north came sneakin' into Muskingum b'fore dawn a week ago. They been chasin' after us. They finally gave up an' turned back the day b'fore yesterday."

"Turned back, did they?" Surprise tinged Stuart's expression. He narrowed his beady eyes.

Nate slipped closer to Rose. "We covered our tracks real good when we left then did our best to stay off the trail, so they were never sure we was comin' this way. They passed us by that first day and kept right on goin'. They must'a waited up ahead, hopin' we'd come to them. When we never did, they gave up and went back. I'm sure they sent out trackers to the north and south, too. Figgered we might'a went thataway."

Reynolds scratched his head. "'Bout how far ahead of us would ya say them Injuns be?"

"Two, mebbe three days," Bob answered as Shining Star moved alongside him. "You should pick up their tracks in a couple'a miles." He helped unhook the cradleboard on Star's back and brought Jenny around to the front.

Both hunters gawked.

"Whose babe is that?"

"Mine." Nate blurted the word without thinking. He didn't like the way the pair kept ogling Rose. He caught Bob's glare and attributed it to the lie, but he still didn't correct the error. He maintained a steady glare.

Reynolds kneaded his scraggly beard and looked from Nate to Rose and back. "I didn't know ya had a young'un."

Stuart picked up on Nate's not-so-subtle warning and changed the subject. "So Smith's tradin' post was taken by the French, too. Make sure ya get word to Governor Dinwiddie. He'll be mighty interested. Last month he talked to the Virginia House of Burgesses about them forts the Frenchies are puttin' up on the south side of Lake Erie. Dinwiddie told the assembly the Crown wants 'em to take some tax money an' raise a militia. Well, the House was already up in arms about some fool taxes the king started slappin' on the colonies. The whole meetin' turned into such a ballyhoo over the new taxes, nothin' was done about raisin' a militia a'tall."

"That's it?" Nate was appalled.

The hunter cocked his head. "Far as the House is concerned. When Dinwiddie found out the Frenchies took Logstown, too, he—"

Bob's mouth gaped in dismay. "They took Venanga an' Logstown? Both?"

"'Fraid so. An now from what you say, they got Smith's."

"Aye." Nate let out a weary breath. "Guess they figgered on gettin' themselves one more before the hard winter sets in. What galls me is there ain't nobody doin' a blasted thing to stop 'em."

"That ain't entirely so." A slow grin widened Stuart's weathered face. "The governor dubbed some young surveyor named Washington a major an' sent him forth."

"Then Dinwiddie did raise a militia despite the House of Burgesses."

"Not exactly." The other hunter swapped grins with his partner. "He sent Washington with a letter, him an' a couple'a longhunters an' a interpreter. Now ain't that just a hoot! 'Monsieur Frenchie, would y'all please leave? We ain't got no militia, but we'd sure appreciate it if ya'd go.'" Both men howled.

Nate failed to see the humor in any of it and noted that Bob didn't either. "Well anyways, you boys know what you're walkin' into."

"That we do." Reynolds sobered. "That's why we're fixin' to turn south when we reach the west fork of the Monongahela. Goin' down Cherokee way. Winter furs won't be as plush, but we'll still have our scalps."

Nate nodded. "That fork was froze over when we crossed it."

"We ain't plannin' to go over it again. Figure we'll stay on this side. We best get a move on, too. Only got a couple more hours before dark."

Even with his dismissal, both hunters turned to Rose, looking much too pleased at the sight of her. They tipped their caps as Nate wrapped a proprietary arm around her.

"Been a real pleasure, ma'am."

Chapter 38

Y ou're back to lyin' again." Robert accused with a scowl.

Hiding her amusement, Rose busied herself with Jenny Ann, handing her a piece of meat to chew on.

Nate snorted in disgust. "Easier than goin' into the whole story, ain't it? Them two blabbermouths don't need to know Rose was a bondwoman."

"Ah. So now you're lyin' to me *and* yourself."

Leveling a glower on his partner, Nate snatched up the cradleboard. "You sure are gettin' fussy in your old age." He helped Rose into the straps. "Come on, let's get goin'. Time's a'wastin.'"

There wasn't much point in trying to start a conversation, considering the mood the two frontiersmen were in. Struggling to keep up with Nate, Rose tossed a backward glance at Star, who appeared to share her opinion as she and Bob lagged behind.

Out in front of everyone, Nate's fast pace only increased as time went by. Rose finally took hold of her shoulder straps to ease the cradleboard's weight and ran to catch up, latching on to his arm. "Are you trying to run off and leave us, or what?"

His mouth in a grim line, he slowed a bit but didn't look down at her as he normally did.

Something was definitely wrong. Recalling that he'd mentioned something about the two of them and the baby being together before the longhunters came along, she moistened her lips. "Nate, what you said before. . . I want you to know you had the wrong idea entirely."

He marched on, still not deigning to look at her, even once.

Rose felt a lump growing in her throat. "I would never use you and then callously cast you aside. I—"

"I know that." His eyes remained on the terrain ahead, but his demeanor eased a fraction. "It's just. . .I been takin' too much for granted. Once we get back, you'll see."

What did that mean? She wished she could look into his eyes, see his heart.

"I'm real rough around the edges, an' you talk an' write all refined-like. I have a hard time just figgerin' out how to spell even easy words."

"That may be true. But you know many other things—important things—that I don't have the slightest idea about."

"Mebbe. But they won't count for much where you come from."

"And my papa's skills wouldn't be worth much in the wilderness, either."

"It don't matter. I just been thinkin' fool thoughts about us. God ain't about to let me have a lady like you. You hear how I talk. I ain't never gonna get it right."

Before she could respond, he stretched out his stride again, leaving her in his wake.

Rose's spirit sank to her toes. Did the man actually think she was that shallow? That judgmental?

No, there was a whole lot more to it than that, and well she knew it. What had the housekeeper often asked Mariah when the girl fancied herself married to some rich Arabian prince? Oh yes. *A fish and a bird might fall in love, but where would they build their nest?*

And where would she and Nate build theirs?

The grueling pace Nate set that afternoon continued throughout the remainder of the day. Thankfully the trail stayed fairly level, with only an occasional iced-over brook to cross. Rose found the walking stick a welcome asset.

Finally they angled off the trail into a dense stand of firs that would provide a good windbreak and some shelter for the night.

Rose hoped Nate would be in a better frame of mind when he turned to speak to her. Alas, he didn't even make eye contact.

"I heard a gobbler back yonder. Tell Bob I'm goin' huntin'." With that, he strode away.

The resigned droop of his shoulders hit Rose hard, and tears stung the backs of her eyes. His attitude toward her wasn't exactly rude, but it was impersonal. Painfully impersonal. She couldn't decide whether to cry or scream.

Robert, who'd followed at a more leisurely pace with Shining Star, caught up to her. "Where'd Nate go?"

"Hunting."

"Must'a heard that gobbler." His tone remained nonchalant, as if nothing was amiss, but he flicked a glance up at the clouding sky. "Let's find a dry spot to spend the night. Looks like we could be in for some snow."

Star smiled at Rose and moved behind her to lift the cradleboard from her back. She propped the sleeping baby against a tree trunk. "Jenee oui-saw."

"Yes. She's been very oui-saw." Returning Star's smile, Rose again noticed how much the Indian girl reminded her of her youngest sister, Lily. How she wished the two of them could sit down and have a relaxed conversation over a cup of tea, the way she and Lily so often had done in their cozy kitchen. But Star's English was almost nonexistent, except for a few words she rarely used, so that was not to be. A deep sigh came from inside.

She could tell Robert wanted to question her about Nate, but she had no answers. Avoiding his inquisitive look, she blurted the first thing that came to her mind. "I shall look for dry firewood under the trees."

After that, Rose did whatever she could to stay occupied. While on her knees gathering needles for their beds later, she reached up in a fir branch to swipe away a cobweb. As she did, she saw Robert and his lady sitting together on a shared robe before the fire, his arm wrapped around Star as they snuggled within the confines of the other robe.

Looking closer, she saw that he was reading a scripture and then translating it. Star would listen intently, now and then asking a question. With the young maiden's sweet nature and her willingness to learn about the Lord, she and Robert would have no problem finding a place to build their nest. All one had to do was look at them to know they were God's choice for each other. Or were they? Nothing seemed clear anymore.

Off in the distance, the sharp report of a gunshot echoed through the trees.

Nate must have gotten his turkey. He'd be back any minute. Rose crawled out from under the tree and brushed needles from her hair as her heartbeat picked up.

Rose, Rose. . .my Rose of Sharon. Aching inside, Nate knew he'd only been fooling himself. No matter what she might say now, once they reached a town, she'd see what a rough cob he truly was. *Lord, help me to accept that she's way outta my reach. Help me to let her go, like a real gentleman.*

Releasing a pent-up breath, he reloaded his weapon. A snowflake landed on the musket barrel, followed by another on his hand. He looked up at the leaden sky as more flakes swirled around him. He'd better get back to camp before the storm let loose. Picking up the turkey he'd shot, he glanced around in the quickly fading light. From about a quarter mile away, the unmistakable glow from a campfire was like a beacon drawing him home.

About to head toward it, he detected a staccato of familiar padding sounds coming his way from farther up the trail. . .moccasined feet! The Senecas! All eight of them! They came to a sudden halt mere yards from where he stood.

Crouching low, Nate couldn't tell if the Indians had seen him. But what he saw made his heart stop. One of the trackers pointed wordlessly toward Bob's campfire. It had to be the same trackers who had been dogging them for a week.

Still panting from their run, the Indians poured powder into the flashpans of their muskets, preparing for an attack.

Confident that they didn't know he was there, Nate pulled the plug from his own powder horn and loaded his musket, knowing the sounds he made would only blend with theirs. Then he took careful aim at the one who appeared to be the leader.

He pulled the first trigger, then the second. The flash from the explosion blinded him momentarily, but he heard the man grunt, then groan. He'd hit his target.

Now he was one.

The first rifle fired at his flash.

He dodged to the side.

Whooping and yelling, the war party emptied their weapons. Musket balls whizzed past him, thudding into the ground.

Lord, let Bob hear all this and be warned. He crashed through the brush in a different direction, hoping to draw the Indians away from the camp. The women needed time to hide.

From the corner of his eye, Nate saw the fire's glow suddenly disappear. His friend had understood. He'd surely send the women to safety.

Father God, don't let 'em get Rose and the baby. Protect them!

Lacking a second to reload, he dropped his musket to free his hands and pulled out his hatchet and hunting knife as he sprinted on.

Half the Indians followed after him, splitting off from the group.

Knowing the rest of the Indians were headed for Rose and the others, Nate swerved in that direction.

A flash and an explosion echoed from camp.

A yell of pain pierced the air.

Bob had hit his mark, but he might not have time to reload before the Indians were on him.

The runners weren't far behind. Nate knew from the sound of their feet that they'd reach the camp about the same time he did. And even with two of them down, six still remained.

Too many for him and Bob.

Lord, hide the women so they won't find them. Only You can help them.

"I'm comin', Bob," he shouted into the growing darkness.

A flash and crack split the air, followed by another yelp.

"Got one more," Bob yelled back.

Guided by the spark of light from his friend's rifle, Nate charged into the small clearing just as the remaining Indians got there.

"Over here," Bob hollered, and Nate rushed to his side.

Holding his empty musket like a club, Bob stepped around to cover Nate's back with his.

The braves knew they had the upper hand. They circled and taunted, their fiendish voices mocking as they jabbed their muskets toward Nate and Bob in sport, then danced back. Finally one of them tired of the game and swung in earnest.

Bob blocked the blow with his rifle, while another wielded his at Nate.

He fended it off with his hatchet, but the musket barrel sliced across his thumb. He almost dropped the weapon. Behind him he heard the sound of steel meeting steel.

One of the Indians swung from Nate's other side with the butt end of his musket. Nate put up his knife arm to block it. Pain shot up to his shoulder. A few more well-placed blows and he'd go down. If only he hadn't discarded his musket back there. Rose—

"Lord," he bellowed, fending off a vicious jab, "take care of the women!"

"God be with them!" Bob hollered.

Two braves swung their muskets at Nate. He blocked a head blow. The other caught him behind the legs, taking him down. He had to get up.

A musket shot rang out.

A Seneca brave slammed heavily into Nate then slid to the ground beside him. Pushing the man off, he scrambled to his feet.

As the other braves turned toward the threat, one more shot found its mark. Another of them grabbed his belly and sank to his knees.

Two more reports from smaller weapons caught one in the throat. The other shot missed either of two braves who'd dropped into a crouch.

In one swift motion, Nate brought his hatchet down against one Indian's neck as Bob flipped his musket butt first and took a mighty swing at the last one's head.

Stillness filled the air.

The two friends glanced at one another in the near dark. All the enemy were down. But how? Who had fired those shots?

At that moment, longhunters Reynolds and Stuart emerged into the open. "Howdy, boys," Reynolds said nonchalantly. "Thought mebbe you could use some comp'ny."

Nate stared in shock, his mouth gaping.

"Better check an' see iffin' any of them redskins is playin' possum," Stuart suggested. "Wouldn't want no surprises, would ya?"

"No, we sure wouldn't." Recovering his senses, Nate uncovered the smoking ashes with his foot until he found some live embers. Then, grabbing long sticks off a pile, he jabbed them into the coals to set them afire for use as makeshift torches. "I counted eight of 'em when they stopped on the road."

The hunters and Bob reloaded their muskets.

After a head count of the war party's dead, they found that only one had escaped into the wilderness. Nate looked around for the women but couldn't spot them. "Wherever you women are, stay put," he yelled, then he turned to Bob. "You better stay here, just in case." Then he and the longhunters took the torches and started after the runaway's tracks.

"There's no way he's gonna be a threat." Nate rubbed a knot on his arm. "Look at that trail of blood he left behind."

Reynolds gave a sober nod. "Yeah. He'll bleed out soon enough." The threesome headed back to the camp as the light flurry turned into a steady snowfall.

Chapter 39

As he and the other men returned to the camp, Nate saw that Bob had dragged the corpses into the brush and had a blazing fire going. The women had also come out of hiding. Rounding a drooping fir tree, he could feel the warmth emanating from the flames. But it was the sight of Rose that really chased away winter's chill.

She turned around, and her blue eyes locked with his.

Nate felt his knees go rubbery. She'd come so close to being taken or killed. But God had sent the longhunters to save her. To save them all. His eyes smarted as he went to her.

She opened her arms to him. Wrapping her in his embrace, he drew her close, kissing her hair, her upturned face, never wanting to let her go.

Suddenly he swept a frantic glance around. "Where's Jenny?"

Rose reached up and cupped his face in her hands. "Right over there, propped against that boulder." She tipped her head in that direction.

Tugging her along with him, he strode over and picked up the cradleboard, holding it between them.

Jenny Ann grinned at him around a piece of slobbery jerked meat clutched in her fist, and Nate bent his head and kissed the baby's plump, rosy cheek. "God heard our prayers, little angel," he whispered hoarsely.

"He saved us all."

With a tremulous smile, Rose touched his face. "So He did. The Lord surely cares for His own." A slight frown drew her brows together, and she took a step back. "By the by, where's that turkey you went after? It would appear God sent us some company for supper."

Nate laughed and pulled her close again. "He sure did."

The enticing aroma of roast fowl permeated the air as Rose snuggled close to Nate. With Jenny on his lap, the man had yet to stop grinning, and the pair were a sight to behold. The little one gnawed on a bit of a wing he'd sliced off for her as everyone waited for the gobbler to cook through.

Across the fire, lovebirds Robert and Shining Star sat with their heads together, whispering back and forth in their own little world.

Mr. Reynolds turned the spit, his eager eyes willing the bird to finish so they could all delve into its juicy meat.

"Wish we had somethin' besides the bird to offer you boys," Nate said, watching him. "What made you turn back, anyway?"

Stuart shrugged a burly shoulder. "Luck. Pure luck. We just pulled off the trail so's we could unload the horses b'fore the storm cut loose." He peered up at the lightly flaking sky. "Thought fer sure it'd be snowin' a lot harder by now. Seems it's slowin' down."

"Anyway," Reynolds cut in, "we heared them Injuns a'runnin' up the trail an' knowed they was the ones ya tole us about." He caught a dripping from the turkey and licked his finger.

His partner nodded. "Who else'd be runnin', 'ceptin' if they was chasin' somethin' or bein' chased. So we pulled the animals down below the trail an' drew our muskets an' waited." He patted his brace of pistols. "Them redskins stopped when they seen our tracks, mutterin' amongst themselves whilst they caught their breath."

"Yeah." Reynolds smirked. "One kept pointin' our way. But they decided to keep goin'. Figger they was fixin' to come back after us once they took care of y'all."

Stuart's gaze centered on Rose. "Couldn't let them savages get at you purty little ladies."

As Nate stiffened beside her, Rose pressed her hand over his to make sure he remained calm.

"That wasn't luck, friends." Robert looked from one hunter to the other. "Even before we cried out to the Lord, He had help comin'. Ain't God good?"

Shining Star tugged at his sleeve.

"Oh yes." He smiled at Rose. "Star wants you to know she's gonna learn English as fast as she can. She wanted to tell you before not to be afraid, that ever'thing would be all right. She said. . ." The fire reflected against moisture in his eyes as he drew a ragged breath. "She knows He's her God, too, now, because He speaks her language, not just English." He lowered his dark eyes to Star and winked. "The Lord told my bride not to fear. Ain't that somethin'?"

The sight of the couple blurred behind tears of her own as Rose realized the full meaning of Robert's words. His bride. . . Nothing could prevent him from taking her to be his true wife now.

"Well, congratulations!" Obviously understanding his friend's comment, as well, Nate whacked his thigh with his palm.

The two longhunters exchanged uncomfortable glances. Stuart cleared his throat and stood up. "Me an' Reynolds better go unload our animals whilst that gobbler finishes up. Mebbe we can come up with somethin' to add to the meal, if'n you folks don't mind us stayin' the night."

A muscle worked in Nate's jaw as he set Jenny on the robe beside him.

"Of course we don't mind," Rose blurted before Nate could come up with an excuse for them to leave. "I can probably find some fairly dry needles for beds under that big tree yonder." She pointed to one a sufficient distance away.

"Why, thankee, ma'am." Tipping his cap, Stuart nodded to his pal and the two started back to the trail to collect their packhorses.

Once they were out of sight, Rose turned to Nate. "There's something you need to get straight, Nate Kinyon." She hiked her brows to emphasize the point as she looked deep into his eyes. "You were doing some real backtracking this afternoon. But if you think I'm going to release you from your marriage proposal, you can just forget it. I happen to be in love with you, and I'm holding you—"

His lips collided with hers, effectively silencing her with a breath-stopping kiss. She melted into it, wanting it to last forever.

But they'd forgotten about Robert. Across the fire from them, their chaperone gave a meaningful "harrumph."

Eventually Nate broke away from Rose and chuckled at his pal. "Quit worryin'. Soon as we get to a preacher-man, Rose and me are gonna marry up. Right and proper." He met her gaze, a mischievous glint in his eye. "Yessir, right and proper."

Those precious words rendered her momentarily speechless.

With Jenny snuggled inside the cradleboard on her lap, Rose watched the muscles in Nate's back stretching and tensing as he and Robert paddled downriver on the Potomac, dodging chunks of ice. After two days they would reach Nate's and Robert's childhood settlement, Conococheague, a name she still had problems pronouncing.

She flicked a despondent look at the masculine attire Nate had acquired for her at the horse trader's trading post in exchange for his hatchet. Though worn and oversized, the garments were better than her nightgown, to be sure, but Rose cringed at the thought of having to meet Nate's mother and his brother's family with men's clothing cinched about her waist.

She'd had the last laugh, however, when she'd presented herself in the frayed and stained outfit that swallowed any hint of her feminine figure. "If my proper English neighbors could see me now," she mused with a wry grimace.

Surprisingly, Nate's expression turned worshipful. "You've never looked more beautiful to me."

Emotion swelled within her at those tender words. How could she not love him? Unable to reach him now, since Shining Star occupied the bench ahead of her, Rose flipped the cradleboard around and planted a kiss on the baby's cheek instead. Jenny giggled and mashed into Rose with a sloppy kiss from her little wet mouth. It made Rose's heart contract. The darling wouldn't have many more chances to return her kisses once she was relinquished to her grandparents next spring. Rose refused to expose the child to any more winter weather.

Glancing again over the top of the cradleboard toward Nate, Rose noticed Shining Star's rigid posture. The Indian girl had been deadly silent since Robert had announced they'd be docking soon. Recalling how fearful she had been herself of going into a strange and unknown foreign world, she leaned forward and tapped Star's shoulder, motioning for her to turn around on the seat.

When the girl complied, her dark, doelike eyes held a wary look.

Rose placed a palm over Star's tightly clasped hands and smiled. "Not afraid. God is with us."

Shining Star pursed her lips together, and a tiny smile trembled forth as she gazed upward. "Not afraid."

"We're comin' in," Nate hollered over his shoulder. "Conococheague's dead ahead."

As Star stiffened, her eyes flaring wider, Rose gave the girl's clenched fists an encouraging squeeze. Then she pointed at Star and then herself. "You, me, together. Not afraid."

The Indian maiden smiled as she clutched Rose's free hand between both of hers and leaned forward. "You, me, Nate, my Bob."

Rose grinned. Shining Star and *her* Bob, and Rose with *her* Nate. Very soon now, she and Nate Kinyon would become husband and wife. Her heart nearly burst with joy.

⌒⌒

Riding beside Rose on horses borrowed from the blacksmith, Nate

305

chuckled to himself thinking of the surprise his family would have when he arrived with an almost-bride and a baby. He tightened his arm around wide-eyed Jenny, noting how her sweet smile drew attention from passersby. His gaze drifted to Rose, his love, wearing the tattered and smudged maroon cloak over her frontier attire and looking more beautiful to him than any woman he'd ever seen.

Nevertheless, she hadn't relaxed the tight set of her mouth as they neared his family's home on the muddy road. Nothing he'd told her about his kind, loving mother or his spry sister-in-law allayed her fears.

"We turn here." Reining his mount onto the less-traveled path through the woods, he looked over his shoulder at equally tense Shining Star, riding alongside Bob, and gave her a reassuring nod. "We're almost there."

"Wonderful." A flat smile accompanied Rose's comment.

There had to be a way to perk her up. He tipped his head. "Bob's place is just up the road."

Staring toward an upcoming clearing, she gave an aloof nod.

"Looks like Jonah cleared more land," Nate commented as they reached the edge of the still-bare trees. "He plants wheat and corn mostly, and some flax for spinnin'. Course, it's all plowed under now. Looks lots better come spring. He's got a couple half-growed boys to help out."

"How nice."

Nate could barely hear her soft answer. He saw her focus on the large cabin ahead with smoke curling up from its twin chimneys. No one was in sight, but two spotted dogs crawled from beneath the front steps and started barking, announcing their arrival.

"Halloo the house!" Nate hollered, adding to the ruckus.

Immediately the cabin door swung open and a pair of young redheaded boys ran out. James, the gawky twelve-year-old, gave a loud hoot. "It's Uncle Nate! An' Bob Bloom!"

Evan, his ten-year-old sibling, gawked, stretching his mass of freckles. "An' they brung women!"

That brought broad-shouldered Jonah into view. He emerged

carrying three-year-old Gracie, his golden-haired daughter. The last time Nate had seen her, she was a mere babe. And on Jonah's heels came his slim, reddish-blond wife, Margaret, along with their mother, who had aged noticeably in his absence. "Nate, my dear boy," she murmured, the care lines in her face softening with her smile. "High time you got back." She drew her shawl close about her thin form as she hurried toward him. Then her gaze landed on the cradleboard in front of him. "You got a babe, Nate? And I ain't even met yer wife!"

Nate lowered Jenny down to her. "This is Jenny Ann, Ma. An' she ain't my baby. Leastwise, not yet." He swung down and wrapped his mother and the baby in a big hug. "I'm sure glad to be home." He meant every word.

Stepping back from her, he turned to Rose, who hadn't attempted to dismount. He reached up and helped his reluctant love down then wrapped a protecting arm around her. "Ma, Jonah, Maggie, this here's Rose."

"How do you do," she managed as the rest of the family crowded close.

"Well, come inside outta the cold," Jonah said. "You all must be hungry." He looked up at Bob. "Why're you still sittin' up there? You come, too."

Bob shook his head. "I think mebbe me an' Shining Star oughta head down to my place." He slid a glance to her.

"Nonsense," Margaret cut in, her green eyes twinkling. "There ain't nothin' but mice an' spiders at that ol' place of yers. Come in an' warm up."

Bringing Rose with him, Nate reached over to Margaret and gave her a grateful hug. Unlike so many of their neighbors, his family had always made Bob welcome despite his Indian blood.

Margaret eased out of his embrace and arched her golden brows at Bob. "'Sides, if you don't come in, we won't know how many of Nate's tall tales to believe."

Everyone laughed as she yanked Nate's scruffy beard. It was then he realized how much he'd missed the gal's quick tongue. He switched his attention to Bob and watched him help his lady to the ground.

Leading the way to the house, Jonah nodded to his sons. "James an' Evan, go see to the horses. An' rub 'em down good."

"Yes, Pa."

Ma, still holding Jenny, sidled over to Bob and tugged his shoulder till he bent his head for a peck on his cheek. "Well, now. I see you got yourself a woman, too. Purty li'l thing she is." She gave Shining Star a welcoming smile.

He drew Star close to his side. "This is my sweet bride."

"Seems you boys've been real busy." She turned to eye Nate and Rose. "I reckon you up an' married, too, an' without so much as lettin' yer ma know."

"That's not how it is, Ma. Rose is my betrothed. We—"

Her mouth gaped. "Oh." She glanced lovingly at wide-eyed Jenny then placed a sympathetic hand on Rose's shoulder. "Sorry about yer loss. You got a fine lookin' babe here." She made a silly face at Jenny Ann and earned a gap-toothed grin.

Despite the fact that Ma was mistaken in her assumption, her sympathetic gesture must have done the trick. Nate felt Rose relax against him as they walked up the porch steps.

Bob followed a step behind. "You don't know the half of it. Once we get our gals in out of the cold, *I'll* tell you all about it."

"Now that's what I like," Margaret gushed. "An eager tattler."

⌒

Nate stood with his brother and Bob at the potbellied stove, watching James and Evan, in their Sunday breeches, lighting every candle in every holly-decorated sconce in the simple church. Two days after arriving home, he and Bob were marrying their sweethearts. Two days that had lasted forever.

Fragrant pine boughs with trailing red ribbons adorned the ends of the dark, wooden pews. Breathing deeply of the evergreen scent, Nate couldn't help grinning. "Sure was nice of folks to decorate the church for our weddin'."

Jonah chuckled. "It's for tomorrow's Christmas Eve service."

"Well, I'm gettin' my Christmas present early."

"Sure hope Shining Star likes it." Bob let out a nervous breath. "Everything's so new to her. But we both wanted a proper church ceremony to give our marriage credence in the eyes of our neighbors an' to say our vows before God."

Nodding, Jonah gave Bob's shoulder a squeeze. "Even so, it's best we're just havin' the minister an' the family. That timid bride of yers would'a had a hard time with a passel of strangers gawkin' at her."

"Aye. An' with Rose an' Nate stayin' with us till spring, she'll have time for Rose to teach her the white way of doin' things. Mebbe my ma would've felt more welcome if she'd had somebody like Rose helpin' her."

Nate's heart swelled with the realization that others knew how special Rose was. He was the luckiest man alive. This was his wedding day, and his bride would be walking up the aisle to him any minute now. . .if those fussy women ever got here.

Jonah's brow furrowed. "I just can't figger out why a educated lady like Rose would wanna hook up with a rough-an'-tumble rover like my brother."

Nate was about to say something in his own defense when he heard the wagon roll up to the church. He quickly rubbed a smudge from his buckled shoe on the back of his other knee-length stocking.

"They're here!" James hollered at the top of his lungs.

Starting forward, Nate felt his brawny brother's hand staying him. "No you don't. I'll go help the women. You two go stand up front. You ain't allowed to see yer brides till they come traipsin' up the aisle."

Nate swapped a wry glance with Bob as Jonah and his carrottops hurried outside.

It seemed to take forever for the door to open again. But soon enough, it swung wide, and Jonah's dark-haired younger sons, Norman and Nathan, burst in with the exuberance possessed only by seven- and five-year-olds. Both were in their Sunday best, rumpled from play. "We're here!"

Little white-haired Pastor Reynolds, bespectacled and attired in somber black, followed the boys. He shook a bony finger at them. "You boys need to settle down and be quiet. Sit over there." He nodded to Nate and Bob as he joined them down front.

The waiting was getting to Nate. He swiped his damp palms down the fancy maroon frock coat he'd borrowed from his brother then grinned at Bob, who wore a gold-trimmed brown outfit he'd left at home and looked as anxious as Nate felt. "Sure are a couple'a dandies, ain't we?"

Bob, in a cravat of ruffles up to his chin, grunted and kept staring at the door.

Finally it opened again, admitting Ma and Margaret in their finery, carrying Jenny and three-year-old Gracie. Reaching the front pew, Ma handed the baby to Maggie then ambled up to Nate and Bob. She fussed with their frilly cravats and tugged down the backs of their frock coats. "There." She stood back and looked them both up and down. "You'll do." Turning around, she spotted James in the back of the room. "Tell the gals they can come in now. Then you an' Evan come sit with us."

Hand in hand with Shining Star, Rose stepped in, looking like a princess in a frilly lavender frock of Margaret's. A garland of holly wove through her upswept hair, while wisps of soft ringlets around her face added an exquisite fragile quality to her delicate features. Nate could hardly draw breath at her incredible beauty.

Beside her, Shining Star looked equally stunning in another of Margaret's dresses, this one in ivory taffeta with ecru lace, a combination that accented her tanned skin. A wreath of holly adorned her glossy black hair that hung straight to her waist.

Nate heard Bob's sharp intake of breath at the sight of his beloved, and he wondered how he and Bob could have gotten so lucky. *Thank You, Lord.*

But his brother was right. How could someone like Rose want to marry him? Was she coming to him merely out of gratitude? He had to know. Ignoring her solemn expression as she drew nearer, he shook his head. "Reverend, would you be kind enough to excuse us a minute?"

Grabbing Rose's hand, he all but dragged her to the back of the church, leaving behind a chorus of gasps. There he turned to her, positioning himself as a shield to hide her confusion from the family. He took her by the shoulders and looked deep into her eyes. "I'm givin' you one last chance to back out, Rose. You're much too fine a lady for a backwoods fella like me. You don't have to go through with this weddin'. I'll still take you anywhere you want to go, get you an' your sisters set up however you—"

She put a finger to his lips and stared up at him a moment. "Could it be that you're the one who's getting cold feet?"

He stood his ground. "Your last chance. Once we're married, that's it. I ain't ever lettin' you go."

"I'll hold you to that, my loose-footed frontiersman. I told you I love you, Nate Kinyon, and I do. More than I can ever express. So let's go get married."

A huge grin spread across his face. He hauled her into his arms and gave her the kind of kiss he'd wanted so long to give her.

"Nate. Nate." Jonah tapped his shoulder. "Don't you know nothin'? The kiss comes after, not before."

Nate gazed down at his Rose. "Yeah. After, too."

"And every day after that," Rose whispered, her eyes on him alone. "Every day after that."

Epilogue

Drinking in the fragile beauty of spring, Rose walked up the knoll that soon would be theirs. Nate trotted ahead with giggly Jenny Ann on his shoulders. Watching after them, Rose noticed that the snow was gone from all but the highest hills, and the meadows overflowed with wildflowers in a rainbow of hues.

"Come on, slowpoke." Nate motioned her forward. "Let's eat in the kitchen."

Smiling to herself, she grasped the food basket tighter and hurried to catch up. Today was finally warm enough to have a picnic. . .on the very spot where Nate would build their home. Robert had so wanted them to live nearby he'd deeded half his father's farm to Nate.

"Our kitchen'll have milled boards." Nate swung the toddler to the ground. "An' as many windows as you want. We'll paint the place any color you fancy."

Rose reveled in the joy in his eyes. Her husband had insisted on spending the savings his mother had socked away for him to build her a *proper* house, as he called it. "I'm partial to yellow, I think, with black shutters and a front porch. Yellow will always remind me of Jenny Ann after she goes to live with her grandparents." At the thought, some of her joy faded.

Nate tugged her close and kissed her cheek. "Today, sweetheart, Jenny's ours. And today me and our little angel are hungry. Ain't that right, firefly?"

The little curly-top looked up from where she squatted to pull at a violet.

"Lunch it is, then." Rose lowered the basket to the ground. "Where exactly did you say the kitchen would be?"

Before he answered, Nate spied their two friends coming up the road in the farm wagon and waved at them with both arms. "Here come Bob an' Star. Do we have enough to share with them?"

Rose laughed. "By all means. They shall be our first guests in our new home. Help me spread the cloth, sweetheart."

While Robert parked his wagon in front of the barn and started across the meadow with Shining Star, Rose got out the platter of fried chicken and the loaf of fresh-baked bread and set it on the tablecloth with the not-so-welcome help of Jenny Ann.

"You two are just in time." Nate gestured toward the food. "As Rose said, our first guests."

Happy and relaxed even after a trip to the settlement, Star smiled at Rose. With a toss of her long hair, she pulled a bunch of colorful ribbons from the pocket of her sage chambray skirt. "Ribbons. For you and me and Jenny."

"Wonderful." Appreciating the thoughtful gift as much as Star's advancement in learning English, she patted the spot beside her. "Sit down. I want to hear about your day."

Once everyone was busy eating, Nate turned to Bob. "Any word in town about what the French are up to these days? Now that the rivers are thawed good, we should be hearin' somethin'."

"Aye." Robert wiped his mouth on his napkin. "Remember that Washington fella what was headed to Logstown an' Venanga with them letters? You know, from Governor Dinwiddie, askin' the Frenchies to leave? Well, hear tell he managed to escape by the skin of his teeth—an' we know how that feels. Folks along the seaboard have made him a big hero. The governor's sendin' him up to Frederick County on the Virginia side of the Delaware to raise a militia. An' he sent Bill Trent, Washington's tracker, farther south to Augusta County to raise another one."

Noticing Nate's keen interest in the news made Rose uneasy, but she kept quiet, waiting to hear what he had to say.

"Augusta County. Ain't that down where the Shenandoah splits off? Sounds like the governor's finally takin' things serious."

"That ain't all." Robert smirked. "He sent letters to every other governor, lettin' 'em know his plans, an' letters to all the tribes to take up the hatchet against the French."

"Good." Nate gave a thoughtful nod. "Insist they take one side or the other, not desert us like the Shawnees did."

"Frederick County ain't but ten miles away, across the river. What say we go give them boys a hand?"

The thing Rose feared most Bob had put into words. She turned troubled eyes to Nate.

He pulled her into a hug. "It's all right, honey-pie. I ain't goin' nowheres till we have the house all built, the crops planted, an' a garden in, just like we talked about. An' not till after we see your sisters an'—" His gaze shifted to Jenny, sitting in the middle of the tablecloth, chewing on a crust of bread in her little yellow dress.

Rose knew what he'd left unsaid. *And till we take Jenny up north to her relatives.*

"Right." Bob cut a glance to Star. "The war ain't goin' away anytime soon. We can always join up later. Oh. Speakin' of Rose's sisters, I brung back letters. The post rider come through last week."

Letters! Rose could hardly wait for Robert to pull them out of his linsey-woolsey shirt.

"This one's for you, Nate." Robert handed the first to him. "An' Rose, these're for you."

She quickly scanned the outside to see who they were from. Two were from England! She hadn't heard from her father since she'd left Bath. The others were from her sisters. "Would you excuse me for a few minutes?" Without waiting for an answer, she strolled away from her friends and walked down the hill. She knew she'd cry and didn't want them to see her tears.

She opened her father's first, and her eyes swam at the greeting penned in his familiar hand: *Dearly beloved daughter*. Blinking to clear her vision, she breathed with relief as she read of arrangements he'd made with his debtors to pay off the remainder of his debt.

Do not worry. . Your brothers and I are working hard to become
solvent again. Then every pence will go toward retrieving my
darling girls. I will not rest until I see each of you happily situated
once more.

His second missive brought even more hope:

I have sought out a solicitor who was able to retrieve thirty of the
fifty brooches Lord Ridgeway absconded with. Once I sell them,
I should have funds enough to send for you girls within the year,
the good Lord willing. . . .

Rose hugged the stationery to her breast. Perhaps she'd done the right thing for Papa and the family after all. She herself would not return to England, but hopefully Mariah and Lily would be able to go home.

Next she unfolded Lily's letter:

Dearest Rose,
     I must send my deepest congratulations on your marriage.
It filled my heart with joy to hear that you are happy and have
a life of your own with a loving husband. That is my dream, as
well, as I suppose it is for most girls. Perhaps someday I will find
similar happiness.
     I miss you so much, Rose. I long for your visit this spring. I
know I shall love your Nate. After all, how could I not love the
brave hunter who has made my dear sister so happy? We shall

have so much to talk about. I shall count the days until I can hug
you to my heart. Until then, do take care, and keep me in your
prayers, as I keep you always in mine. . . .

Rose's heart crimped. Sweet, priceless Lily. How grand it would be to
show off big, handsome Nate, the husband she never would have had she
stayed in England.

With a happy sigh, she unfolded Mariah's missive:

Dear Rose,

I was glad to hear from you. I assumed I would have
wonderful news to relate by now, that Colin and I had pledged
our love for one another. I know he cares for me as I do him, but
alas, we get only the smallest snatches of time together, a mere
moment here and there.

If Papa ever forwards money as he promised me, I shall buy
back my papers and room with another family nearby. Then
Colin will be able to visit me without the watchful eye of his
mother. I am sure he will propose then. Of course, an elopement
would be ever so romantic, do you not agree?

Mariah, Mariah. Rose shook her head. It was imperative to get to the
girl soon and have a serious talk with her, if it wasn't already too late. She
read on:

Speaking of romantic, I could hardly believe that you, the ever-so-
serious older sister, actually got married. You and not me. Who
would ever believe that?

Rose rolled her eyes. Would that girl ever grow up? As disturbing as
it had been to see Mariah sold to a plantation owner, at least she'd been
placed in the home of a virtuous matron. Rose shot a prayer of thanks
heavenward. When she and Nate reached the plantation, she'd thank the
woman profusely.

"Rose! Rose!"

Glancing up from Mariah's closing words, she saw Nate hurrying toward her with Jenny riding high in the crook of his arm. He sported a grin from ear to ear while tears streamed down his face.

"What is it?" Alarm clutched Rose's stomach. Nate never cried.

"You're not gonna believe this." He held out a letter in his free hand. "It's from Jenny's grandparents. Seems old Mr. Wright got caught in a blizzard an' got frostbite. His lungs ain't so good now. He an' the missus had to move in with their son, who's already got a bunch of young'uns, an' the wife's with child. Mr. Wright says they're not able to take in another mouth to feed. He says if we're willin', they'd be pleased to have papers drawed up so's we can keep Jenny. Can you believe it? Jenny's ours. Ours!"

It was too good to be true. "Let me see that letter." Snatching it from his fingers, Rose scanned the words. Tears of joy sprang to her eyes, and she grabbed her two loves in a big hug, smothering them with kisses.

Finally able to gain control enough to speak, she dried her face on her apron. "This has to be the crowning moment of my life. To think I get you *and* Jenny. God is marvelous!" She held up all the letters. "And everyone in my family is doing fine—except maybe Mariah. Gorgeous, willful Mariah."

"Don't worry about her." Nate wrapped Rose in his free arm and kissed the top of her head. "We'll be goin' to see her soon enough. An' if God can make everything turn out this good for us, I'm sure He can whip that sister of yours into shape, too."

Rose looked up into the hazel eyes she so loved and laughed. "Quite right. Our God can do anything." Taking Jenny Ann out of Nate's arm, she twirled the little girl around, making her giggle. Then, getting misty-eyed again, she gazed up at her beloved, stalwart husband. "God has given me more happiness than I ever dreamed possible. No one can ask for more than that." Raising to tiptoe, she planted a kiss on his lips, just knowing it would bring out that mischievous smile of his.

She could never get enough of that.

Sally Laity has successfully written several novels, including a coauthored series for Tyndale, three Barbour novellas, and six Heartsongs romance novels. Her favorite thing these days is counseling new authors via the Internet. Sally always loved to write, and after her four children were grown, she took college writing courses and attended Christian writing conferences. She has written both historical and contemporary romances and considers it a joy to know that the Lord can touch other hearts through her stories. She makes her home in Bakersfield, California, with her husband and enjoys being a grandma.

Dianna Crawford is a California native. She has been published since the early 1990s and writes full-time. Her first inspirational novel was the premier of a six-book series for Tyndale that she coauthored with Sally Laity. Dianna is married and has four daughters and seven grandkids.